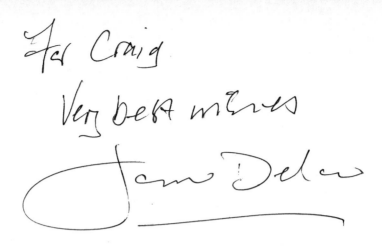

"Writing is an expedition into madness; a quest for a peculiar Utopia."

Virgil Hare

LEEPUS
DIZZY

Jamie Delano

First publication

LEPUS BOOKS

2014

ISBN: 978-0-9572535-4-4

LEPUS BOOKS

lepusbooks.co.uk

1

BludKlash coming on.

At one end of the dripping underpass—four silent BurkaBabes with horror dogs on chains. A cohort of HateBoyz at the other looking for frontation.

Caught out in the killzone. Heed the need to fade.

One veiled sister giggles weird—slips leash from playful puppy. The dog fast and loose. Bouncing muscle. Snot festoons. A shrunk-down snorting bull.

Sidestep swift. Veronica into shadow.

The dog snuffles and bustles past on the scent of HateBoy groin. Nut-clamped human dogchew howls. BurkaBabes ululate—let go another mutt. Nervous bruvvas flicker machetes backlit by sick moonlight.

Wall-slide snot-slick tile. Ooze towards the glimmer.

Shrieks and bellowed battle-cries reverb in the dark. The electric thrill of violence flashes razor stripes.

Out! Scramble the garbage-avalanche stairwell up into the stink smoke of NoGo.

∞

Night rain in the rookeries. A street of dead-car tortoises—carapaces rusting.

Step steady down the centre-line. Imagine a destination.

Cross-legged on a cardboard prayer mat beneath a naked tree—a ragman. Damp dreadlocks brightly beaded. Placard hung round scrawny neck—crooked grey-skin finger underlining its scrawled message.

Step closer. Read.

Kik me for a wunna. Kil me dedd for ten.

A barricade of worn-out white goods defends a cul-de-sac of maisonettes. Trashcan brazier smouldering. Yard guard in sandbagged shelter. He looks up from handheld porno—picks up a pistol crossbow.

Eyes front. Maintain casual momentum.

∞

Footbridge over railway.

Zigzag up ramp. Blood pumping. Midway across—a rush.

Weird fingers hooking diamond-mesh of rusty no-jump cage.

Look down.

Track-veins gleam in deep red cutting. Motion-quake trips palpitation. Disturbs vision. Excites bowel. Iron sings and whistles wet. A midnight SafeTran punches through. Shrieks—dives into howling tunnel.

Look up.

A mile away—haphazard geometry of dark buildings piled behind the Fence. Floodlit razor-wire spike-collar encircling anxious civic throat. SafeCity—a municipal reservation. Strivas toiling reassured. Predatory poors at bay.

Catch a breath. Taste sour electricity—a blueness on the tongue.

Sway dizzy.

Dizzy.

Dizzy.

∞

Freemart on washland outside River Gate.

A squabble of late-home privs jams the priority channel. Flash-highs dissipating. Clammy hands thrust passfones. Curfew-waiver timeout soon—they need to get checked in.

Thrill shills hiss the revellers—pass out scratchcards. Casino suckabags of freeroll chips. Cocktail tokens. Whore maps. Burga vouchers. All kinds of brightly coloured shit to suck up unspent playkrip—encourage repeat business.

Alongside—the loser lane.

GateGoons shove daywork shufflas into scantraps. Swipe tags. Feel them up with sniffer wands. Run random biometrics—stash rejects in the cage. Make the deportation quota. Snag a tasty bonus.

Pick an exit route.

Hesitate uncertain—another rush squirms sick. Tightens perineum. Assaults hypothalamus.

Hallucination bubbles pop pop pop. Heartbeat paradiddles.

Surrender to distraction.

Veer into market aisles.

∞

A complexity of subprime commerce. Tables. Blankets. Barrows. A spilled cornucopia of crap.

Tarp-caves stuffed with dead tek. Blind TVs. Cable tangles. Multifarious media. A million old fones.

A musty suffocation of jumbled pissy clothes.

Bent cutlery. Cracked crocks. Stopped clocks.

A sprawl of car parts.

Battered bikes.

A wall of batteries.

The sickly smell of streetmeat—gut-rot foodcarts steaming. A sweaty tattoo tent.

The musk of mildewed books.

Keep moving. Nothing to see there.

∞

A constellation of LEDs dapples a battle booth—blood-spray patterned curtains obscuring smack and grunt. A fiva gets you fifty if you beat the monsta down.

Erbwitch squats in the entrance of a plastic-patchwork bender—peers up through cataract curtains. Need heart pills? Love powders? No-pain potion? Stiff-dick lotion? Any kind of poison to settle up your scores? Got all those things and more here to ease those old-man sores.

Fuck tents flank an oozing alley.

Kid shitting in puddled shadow.

Temptation in a candlelit vinyl boudoir. She smiles—uncovers tattooed breasts.

Turn away. Move on.

Temptation pouts—hip-sways and rolls down pants.

Move on now.

Temptation shows off swinging cock and hairy balls.

Too late. Shadow swooping.

Black-tooth scab-lip snarl. Spittle fleck. Bubble eyes and grease-spike hair.

Low-held blade gleams: Gimme!

Act compliant. Slip hand into deep coat-pocket.

Expectant desperado extends palm—thinks it might be Christmas.

Bring out PocketPyro. Thumb-spark fuse and toss.

A butane-fire halo—oiled hair flaring. The desperado yelps and flaps. Flame contagion ignites fuck tents.

Leave now. Get lost.

Tread quick on shadow heels. Out-pace incandescence.

Walk.

Walk.

Walk.

Walk mapless into madness. Misery. Despair.

∞

Dawn.

The sun heaves up behind Craphills—blears through a chink in filthy cloud and emits a stale gust of light.

Another phony new-day promise.

Shitgulls launch up screaming yellow. The sky filled with off-white wheeling. A refreshing squall of guano.

Walk on.

Rotcarpet softens underfoot concrete.

Hawk. Taste brass. Spit.

Creep of surveillance prickling nape.

Not law. Gulls would mob an overseer. Blind beady eye with blood and feather. Mashup dizzy rotors with splintered hollow bones.

It's skavvas squinting from their burrows in the screes and scarps of waste. They're sniffing threat potential—assaying scrap value.

Could be they got a verminator out to check his snares—out to snag a battla to keep and savage-up. He'll run it in the playpens—make himself good gold.

Could be they got a peedofuk looking for some tight. Or just some stupid lost meat wandering bad ground. Something to jump out on. Something to drag down. Shoddy shit to be recycled for a snap of krakkle.

Duck through scrub out of skavva sight. Follow stream. Cross bombed-out NuHope zone.

Step surer here on known ground. Things starting to make sense.

∞

Stencilled sign on terrace gable: WORLD'S END CAFÉ 400 yards.

Looking good. Maintain course for imminent safe touchdown.

Downhill glide past burned-out gallows-dodger barracks.

Across an allotment jungle—old girl foraging veg.

Give her a friendly wave.

Just sixty or so fluttered heartbeats now to breakfast chillpill. Caffy. Smokes. Recovery womb at Mother Mellow's. Warm oblivious downtime. Wake with consciousness rebooted—faculties restored. A cognitive renaissance.

But the world pitches. The world yaws. Progress wobbles—stalls.

Pull up! Pull up!

Dead dog in puddle. Oilslick iridescence swirling.

Closer.

Pull up!

Pratfall splashdown. The lap and slap of tiny waves. A bubbling of breath.

The forager applauds the hapless idiot.

Staccato handclaps fade ironic into black.

◊◊◊◊◊

2

'**G**ood night then, is it?'

'Caffy?' Leepus ignores Mike's question—waves to the inscrutable dark flesh-mountain behind the bar. Mother Mellow fills fat sails—billows into motion.

'Yeah.' Mike tosses gauntlets onto cup-ringed table—unzips greasy leather breastplate. 'Eggs'n'rashas too. With a double side of fungo. And a gristle burga—heavy on the ketchup.'

The leaky espresso machine hisses steam. A bulbous shadow moves in the mist.

Mike scrapes out a chair and sits—shakes a smoke deft from the wrapper slid across by Leepus. 'Two hours through the rain. Half a dozen checkpoint face-offs with arsey militia cunts. I need a full fuckin' breakfast.'

'Two minutes,' Mother Mellow wheezes clattering plate into microwave.

Leepus sparks Mike's weedstick. 'Have to buy it yourself, mate. Do my bastard stack.'

'Fuckin' mug.' Mike inhales—coughs harsh. 'That explains the filthy backyard weedsticks and general air of dejection. So what about the stab-wound eyes? And the fuckin' corpse-stink clothes?'

'Dizzy, I think. Maybe krakkle. Maybe a bastard cocktail.'

'Old habits still not dead, then?'

'Spiked,' Leepus says tight-lipped.

Mother Mellow delivers Mike's breakfast—lumbers back to the bar.

Mike shovels in a lurid forkful. Yolk drips. 'Then you're a double cunt, aren't you? For going into shit town unprotected. And getting head-raped and fucked over.'

'Spontaneous operation, mate. Get a ping on that doorstep organ-loan bastard—one who forecloses on Tattooed Sally's eldest's kidney when Sal loses her gig at the KashBak hospice and falls down on her payments?'

Mike saws a rasha with gusto. Leepus lunges—scoops smokes clear of slopped caffy ruination. 'Fool fancies his chances in Sick Dick's Big Fat Sunday live game,' he continues. 'Feel the urge to buy in too. Kick his parasitic arse and win old Sal some compo.'

'Only a twat plays Sick Dick's solo.'

'No choice. Backup's fucking AWOL.'

Mike masticates a gristle-wad—swallows. 'Personal shit to take care of.'

Leepus wonders—decides not to ask. 'Anyway,' he says, 'fish is an open book. I've got him down verbatim well before the dizzy hits.'

Mike bread-mops surplus ketchup.

'So—' Leepus smoke signalling for attention. 'Hand sixty-nine. Prick's got a neck-pulse telling he's good pre-flop, but likely not that good. We get a bunch of chips in. Flop hits him. Hits me harder. All-in shove. Snap call. Nice—except the idiot sucks out. Badbeat on the river, Mike. Nothing fucking worse.'

'Yeah there is.' Mike extracts a trapped connective-tissue strand from between pearly canine and bicuspid.

It looks like meaty dental floss Leepus observes idly.

Mike's long-lashed stare is green-eyed and unflinching.

'What?' challenges Leepus. Window light picks up the old fragscar question-mark curled around Mike's cheekbone. Unfortunate disfigurement or curious enhancement he wonders—not for the first time. 'What's worse than a river badbeat?'

Deadpan Mike finger-rolls freed floss—flicks and says, 'Having to listen to some sad cunt replay his bad card-karma blow by arse-ache blow, when you don't have a clue what he's whining about due to not

8

giving a soft shit about poka.'

'Sorry,' says Leepus. 'Want to hear what happens next?'

'Dunno. Will it make me laugh?'

'Maybe the part where the horror-dog chomps HateBoy bollocks?'

'Ho ho.'

'And the rascal whose ugly head I set on fire so he burns down half a market?'

Mike frowns. 'How?'

'He just goes flapping and screaming off crazy through some fuck tents.'

'No. How'd you torch the silly cunt's head?'

'PocketPyro.'

'You successfully deploy a novelty weapon?   Now I am fuckin' impressed.'

'Thanks.'

'Impressed you don't get charcoaled in a blowback—those things are ten years past their use-by.'

'You never mention that.'

'You don't buy them if I do. Never dream you'll find the balls to spark one.'

'Dizzy makes me reckless.'

'Yeah—that's what I recall.'

Leepus leans forward and narrows his eyes—drops the butt of his smoked-out weedstick into the dregs of Mike's caffy. It sizzles and dies sodden. 'You done?' he asks her cold.

Mike smiles sweet. 'Sorry—it's only 'cause I care.'

'I mean are you done eating?'

Mike shrugs.

'Because you might want to wipe off the ketchup lipstick,' Leepus says and stands. 'It's just a bit unsettling. Makes you look like a mad fucking sex-clown.'

Mother Mellow's playing roulette on a fone.

Leepus crosses the desolate bar. 'Bit slow in here today.'

'Right.' Mother Mellow eyerolls the redundant comment. 'Punters clock your sick mate's ride outside—lose their appetites.'

Leepus watches Mike fixing her face in stab-knife mirror-steel. 'Yeah,' he says. 'Mad cow's a liability but I just can't shake her off. No clue why she's turned up here this morning.'

Mother Mellow sniffs. 'I give her a shout when I find you dizzy-daft outside—face down in rotten-dog juice.'

'Only yourself to blame, then.'

'Don't mention it. You're welcome.'

'Okay. What's the damage?'

'Rescue. Resuss. Vomit cleanup and disinfection. Womb time with sedation. Weedsticks, food, lost trade—even at mate's rate that's two-fifty.'

Leepus shrugs—grabs the fone from Mother Mellow and fingerslides chips onto random numbers. He passes it back with virtual wheel already spinning—says, 'That hits, you're covered with gratuity on top.'

Leepus leaves Mother Mellow staring and follows Mike outside. Hoarse exultations wheeze through the old café-door clattering shut behind them.

'What the fuck?' Mike cocks her head. 'You picking up reads on fones now?'

Leepus winks—folds into the armoured sidecar. 'Shot in the fucking dark, mate. Even idiots sometimes get lucky.'

◊◊◊◊◊

3

Leepus up on the roof of his high tower looking out. Lichen continents creep tectonic over the parapet concrete. His fingertips trace their coastlines. There's a time when he can name them and the nations that comprise them. But geography is unstable now—globally rebranded. He can barely recognise Inglund.

A sudden ragged clatter. Imperfectly combusted biodiesel gusting skyward.

Jackdaws lift from treetops—call raucous disapproval riding twitchy on the wind.

Mike coaxes the stuttering engine into throaty eloquence. Lurches the massive bike and sidecar around the compound turning-circle. Blares out through the briar-tangled anti-vermin fence.

The portcullis rattling down automatic.

Fumes persist as the noise recedes down the rutted tarmac lane. Booms through the scabby coagulation of rural habitations locally known as Shithole. Fades over Hanging Hill.

Jackdaws plane weightless back into position above twiggy filigree—extend hooked-claw landing gear to touchdown dark on brittle perches.

Effortless precision.

Air dank—autumnal. Leepus sucks up a restorative lungful.

A ride in Mike's combo is never relaxing. Trace dizzy eddying through cortex. Exhaust stink. Intolerable savage vibration. Five miles more and he's plucking his own damn eyes out.

Whining for mercy is futile. Hardboiled Mike's soft spot for her hand-built pride and joy is borderline maternal—complaint is bound to be perceived as extraordinary bad manners.

Mike does not appreciate bad manners. Bad manners demand payback. For strangers—a short sharp shock of physical retribution. But for a transgressor she decides ought to know better—the remorseless application of protracted mental torture.

Leepus' masochistic tendency is marginal at best. He judges it best to bite his tongue—adopt an aspect of cheerful endurance.

Something invisible stirring the air. A damp chill pushed up the valley. The pressure wave provokes the wind turbine—its blades turning in elegant motion. Alternators whir. Amps trickle. Batteries effervesce minutely.

Leepus shivers—grasps cold steel rungs. Climbs the ladder down into the re-purposed old water tower. Pistons hiss hydraulic—the heavy hatch-lid lowering slowly closed above his head.

The tank room quietly cavernous—close to hypothermic.

Leepus opens the stove. A hint of dull red in the ashes. He stuffs its empty belly and increases carburetion—watches glimmer glare to inferno.

Heat penetrates his heavy greatcoat—irradiates grateful bones. Leepus stares—mulls the odds on the water warming sufficient for a survivable shower before he crashes.

In the meantime—food.

Leftover broth lingering in the cold safe. He fetches it—sets it to warm on hot cast-iron and then stumbles to the cracked-leather sofa to kill time rolling a smoke.

∞

'What's this?'

'Huh?' Leepus parts gluey eyelids.

The tank room air is cool again. There's an aftertaste of cremation—the rank memory of smoke. A diminutive figure looms over him plump in layered coats—stares down accusative with scorched cooking pan inverted. 'Waste of top bleedin' food, that,' says Doll. 'Think our Duane risks 'is arse poachin' GreenField veels for you to

12

burn to ashes when there's babes starvin' down in the 'ole?'

'Sorry.' Leepus rubs eyes. Swings legs from the sofa. Winces at imminent bladder rupture. 'Moral compass on the blink.'

Doll's lip-ring twitching disdainful.

Leepus tries to stand. Tries again and succeeds. 'So this is a nice surprise,' he says with curious eyebrow arching.

'I always come on a Wednesday. Wednesday's my day, ennit?'

'It's Tuesday, Doll.'

'No it ain't.'

'You sure?' Leepus hobbles to the bathroom. 'It's Monday when I nod.'

' 'Ave to take your word for that—but I wouldn't be surprised. Obvious you've been at it.'

'At it?' Leepus standing over the toilet—anticipating relief.

'Badness. Getting off on dirty shit again.'

Pan-clatter in kitchen sink. Tap-water splashing. Leepus swaying grateful—his spring rising sympathetic.

' 'Ave a squint in the mirror,' nags Doll. 'Eyes like constipated cats' arseholes.'

Leepus gushes heedless.

'An' close that bleedin' door.' Doll's words eroded. 'There's 'orses that piss quieter.'

∞

'I make you eggs.' Doll nodding toward kitchen table.

'Cool.' Leepus sits—waits.

'I'd get stuck in or they will be.'

'Spoon? Fork?'

Doll huffs and jangles in a drawer. Hands over a random utensil. Holds on as he accepts it.

Leepus tugs. 'Thanks,' he says belated.

'No problem.' Doll bundles away—slams open the dumbwaiter stacked with logs. 'Hope it bleedin' chokes you,' she says enfolding an awkward armful.

Leepus munches impassive. A peripheral flicker on the monitor high-mounted on the wall. The remote on the dresser. He reaches it over—pans the rooftop *camera obscura*.

Red kites rising spooked from a hillside gorse-clump beyond the lane.

Leepus tilts up—zooms.

Blue overseer beacon blinking in a gyre of carrion birds.

'Fukkit.' Leepus spits out a crunched eggshell fragment—switches to infrared.

A green-laser godfinger incising the screen. It's pointing down cold and steady—accusing a suspect gorse-clump.

Leepus thinks about it—opts for procrastination. He abandons his dirty plate on the table—follows a trail of bark scabs into the tank-room dense with smog.

Doll squats under the cloudbase. She's feeding a log to a feeble smoulder—nurturing an appetite for fire in a reluctant cold-iron belly.

Leepus coughs. 'Fukksake, girl.'

'Some twat only leaves the woodshed door wide-open, dunnit? So the rain's pissin' in for days.' Doll clangs the stove door shut—stands and smears back a lank forelock with sooty finger. 'And less of the bleedin' 'girl'. I'm forty-three year-old, mate. Got three granbabs back indoors.'

'And I could be your dad.'

'Bollocks.'

Leepus on the sofa rolling up a smoke. 'Don't judge a book by its cover, Doll. I'm functionally dead inside.'

'Our Em's first boy, Ryda. He likes to look at books.'

'Beat the kid within an inch of his life and throw them on the fire.'

'What's wrong with books?'

Leepus shrugs—fires-up his weedstick.

'I'm thinking maybe you've got a few old ones knocking around,' says Doll unbuttoning one coat-layer. 'That the lad could have a lend of?'

'Thinking?'

'Something I hear.' Doll's eye probing. 'That there's a time when you're to do with them. You know. Before. Back then.'

Leepus obscure behind his smokescreen. 'Forget it, Doll,' he says. 'Then gets wiped in the dizzy years. Now there's only now.'

Dolls sniffs disgruntled. 'Alright, whatever you say. No 'arm asking, is there? Our Ryda's a pretty goodun. Not like his fuckin' dad.'

'Pleased to hear it. Your Em slips up badly there.'

'Can't blame the girl for gettin' took in by mental Jago. She fancies him for a right bold bastard—sly enough to jump the fence on those fanatics that raise him and 'ave it away with a chunk of their treasure. Who knows years later he'll flashback all mad fuckin' godly again—whip our poor Em naked up the yards for turnin' his 'ead with her 'fanny magic'?'

'Prick's no trouble now, though?'

'Still skulking up the woods for all I know. Whatever Mike tells 'im on her 'nature walk' sorts his nasty shit out.'

'Mike knows how to make a point.'

Doll smiles appreciation studying the stove. 'Fire's caught.'

'Yeah,' says Leepus. 'I might be warm in another hour.'

'Reckon I'm done for today then,' says Doll hovering expectant.

'Sit for a bit.' Leepus offers the weedstick.

'Okay.' Doll takes it—props her arse on the arm of the sofa. 'But last time I have a smoke with you I go off without getting paid. Don't think you can tink me twice.'

'Treat me as a bank.'

'Yeah.' Doll inflates her bosom. She holds—scans the hazy concrete chamber and snorts smoke-jets down her nose. 'Must be nice to be a solid gold bastard snug up 'ere in his castle. I'm surprised you're not

15

more cheerful.'

'Me too.'

Doll cocks her head—delves and scratches an armpit. 'I could do you a nice shag if you fancy it? Only an extra fifty?'

'I don't.'

'Let a girl down gentle why don't you?'

'Not personal,' says Leepus moving to his strongbox. 'There's a time you don't have to offer twice. These days I just don't.'

'What—not ever?'

'Can't be arsed.'

'Fair enough.' Doll buttons up—waits.

Leepus counts out a stack and hands it over.

'See you next Tuesday then,' says Doll riffling chips as she drifts for the lift.

'Don't you say your day is Wednesday?' asks Leepus without thinking.

'Gotcha!' Doll smirking—the concertina-gate rattling shut. 'The old ones are still the best, mate,' she says disappearing beneath floor-level.

◊◊◊◊◊

4

'Name?'

'Leepus.'

'Leepus what?'

'Just Leepus.'

'D. O. B.?'

'Uncertain. Data rinsed. Reduction minus a few decades—give or take.'

'Stakeholder registration?'

'Disinvested.'

'Entitlement?'

'Expired.'

'Means of support?'

'I play cards.'

'Whose colours?'

'Strictly freelance.'

'Scrutinised by OurFuture on any prior occasion?'

'What? The College not omniscient, lad?'

The prefect noncom stiffens—says, 'Respond in Inglish only.' The cohort behind him shifts leery—students hefting weapons.

Leepus reads adolescent gestures. Eye-flick in shadow of helmet visor. Stabvest breastplate thumb-hooked—forefinger pointing at voltwhip. The prefect feeling horny. The illiterate twat wants to jolt him.

Leepus opts to muck—stoops and loses a couple of inches.

The prefect leans in with his headcam saying, 'Detail your last forty-eight hours.'

'Asleep.' Leepus coughs.

'For a full two days?'

'Been feeling a bit rough.'

'Rough?'

'Bringing up blood and stuff.' Leepus hacks ragged—spits out a whirling phlegm bolas. The prefect eyes it dangling from the twisted metalwork of the portcullis. Leepus picks up his thread—says, 'Erbwitch down in the village sorts me out with some magic powder. Puts me into a fucking coma.'

The prefect inching back then saying, 'Any activity out here you observe? Maybe you hear a vehicle? Some other kind of commotion?'

Leepus shakes his head—leans on a concrete doorpost.

'You reside here alone?' The prefect craning—scanning the ivy-veined tower.'

'Yeah—except for the bats in the lift shaft.'

'Wildlife harbours disease.'

Leepus shrugs—summons another expectorant spasm. 'Can we carry this on inside?' he wheezes. 'Damp air's killing my chest.'

The prefect's nostrils flattening reflexive. 'Preliminary investigation concluded,' he says. 'But scrutiny is ongoing.'

Leepus watches the students remount their armoured TacTruk. The vehicle snarls. Steel screams as it guns free of the mangled portcullis—turns and bellows off down the lane in a rattle of pulverised tarmac.

Leepus thinks about climbing the hill. He decides to give it ten minutes—rides up to the tank room instead for a smoke. When he gets there his fone is ringing. He finds it in the pocket of his greatcoat hidden in the wardrobe by mischievous Doll—answers it,

'Wrong number.'

'Cunts gone?' Mike's voice phasing through static.

'Heartbeats off the premises. Don't know about the drone.'

'Cloudbase is low but I can't see it.'

'You coming in?'

'Best not. Meet me.'

'Where?'

'Woods.'

'Fuck's sake. It's dark in twenty minutes.'

The fonescreen flashes Call Ended.

Leepus shrugs into his greatcoat and heads for the lift. He diverts to the armoury locker—pockets liquid capsaicin ampoules and a couple of poppers for good measure. Feral dog-packs hunt in the forest. The brutes like to run down humans—occasionally eat them.

∞

Leepus out on the hill. He noses through the plastic screens around the crime scene. A gorse clump felled at ground level—cleared vegetation heaped. Exposed turf glistens black and greasy. Bad-meat molecules taint his tongue.

A plodbot swivels on its tripod logging data. Leepus winds in his neck—spits and clumps up the hill.

Daylight dissolved in drizzle. The forest dark in the valley—a neighbourhood wilderness. Leepus descends gloomy—picks a random route through dripping trees to the derelict Cabin Café car park.

A straggle of buddleia erupting through ancient asphalt. Fronds drip around crouching Leepus. Eroded lettering suggests his space is reserved – in a long-lost quaintly sentimental era – for the convenience of the disabled.

Leepus checking out the café ruins. Red glow—a breeze fanning embers in tumbledown shadows.

Leepus infiltrates the collapsed-wall logjam—acquires a new

perspective. Mike's bulk dark against dying fire. He hisses a soft greeting—moves closer. Mike unresponsive. Head slumped—chin on chest. Mike asleep on watch.

Leepus is amused. He sneaks up behind—delivers a toe-prod to Mike's kidneys.

Mike topples.

'Fuck!' says Leepus jumping back as Mike's body impacts the fireplace—sends sparks mosquito-dancing brief above dark sizzle.

Leepus' heart's a panicked hare trapped inside his ribcage. Sudden branches rattle. He turns to find buddleia looming—tumbleweeding from shadow.

'Ah!' Leepus dives—scrabbles through damp leaf-litter in search of an improvised weapon.

'Easy.' Mike's voice from foliage. 'Sorry if I spook you, mate. Don't lose your fuckin' arse.'

'Pissoff,' says Leepus down on hands and knees. 'Shit's not even funny.'

'Right.' Mike shrugs off her camo cape and stoops—rolls the stumpwood avatar from the fireplace and recovers her scorched leather. 'I follow you in from the tree-line—you don't have a fuckin' clue. Mine to shag at will, mate.'

Mike scattering kindling on embers—raising tentative fire.

A mouldering banquette in a ruined log-wall corner. Leepus brushes off debris and sits down sullen. 'Fucking paranoiac,' he says. 'You could just come to the tower.'

Mike arse up head down—lighting twin smokes from nascent flame. 'Don't think so, mate,' she says standing and moves to join Leepus on slimy vinyl. 'Sweaty College pride'n'joyboys squirting all over the gaff? I might do something silly.'

They smoke. Leepus waits till Mike opens her mouth to ask—then says, 'I pick up the drone but get distracted by Doll looking to top up her wages. By the time she's safely out the door the hill's already captured. I decide to mind my own business.'

'Overseer finds something murky?'

'Must do. Tags it for ground patrol.'

'You see what it is?'

'Not really. They have a squint and screen the site.'

'That's when I roll up. I'm scoping from Fox Covert.'

'Bodydump is my best guess. Grass is all black and nasty.'

'They haul it out in five plastic bags. One little wanker pukes.' Mike lights a smoke. Leepus takes it from her. Mike lights another—continues, 'And then they have a sniff around—decide to canvass suspect towers?'

'I'm halfway down to let them in and they've rammed the damn portcullis. No call for that shit, is there?'

'Classic force projection, mate. Cunts see a castle they have to crack it. My advice—rebuild stronger. Include a few IEDs.'

'Pretty sure pink-misting the Prefecture's finest counts as a capital crime. But it's probably fun at the time.'

'So—they chat you up a bit. Any intel on the dead meat?'

'Head Boy's pumping testo. Officer material—wants to make an impression. So I fold under minimal pressure, throw a bit of a coughing fit and put the fear of diseases in him.'

Mike frowns. 'Obvious this corpse is tracked—and well-enough connected to warrant search and rescue. Not what you need on your doorstep.'

'My sentiment exactly.'

'Right.' Mike stands—zips leather. 'I'd give it some serious thought, mate.'

'We can chew it over indoors,' says Leepus kicking humus to smother the fire. 'Maybe make some calls.'

'Another time, mate. Running late.'

'Not out here to visit then?'

'Nah.' Mike looks off into darkness. 'Just sliding through when I see the fuss.'

'What's up, Mike?'

'Stuff going on.'

'Stuff?'

'This and that. Nothing special.'

'Later then,' says Leepus too old and wise to press.

'Yeah,' Mike says fading. 'Mind how you fuckin' go.'

◊◊◊◊◊

5

A mile beyond Shithole—the river.   A valley-side scrub jungle intervening.

The scorched stumps of watchtowers felled by fire—climbing weeds drag down rusty chain-link strung between them.

Twin rows of sooty concrete hut-pads with grass infringing.   Their geometry disordered by a charred sprawl of fallen frames. Charcoaled wood decaying—velvet black mosaic eroding into mulch.

Leepus salutes the fortitude of the righteously assertive tactical-default commando that kicks off the first debt-slave rebellion—picks up the crumbled asphalt of Repayment Pathway #1. He pauses for a moment—appreciates the ambient dereliction.   Then he strolls on down through the trashed infrastructure of the DebtShrink Honest Labour Park.   Marches out past the exploded gatehouse.   Stops where road meets water.

Lamppost tops chalky with bird-shit track the submerged roadway across the flow.   Cormorants silhouetted on them—black flags hanging static above turbulent green.

The road re-emerging on the far bank vague through murk. Skeletons of drowned trees.   The spire of the submarine church.

The river rising year on year—widening into mere. Wetlands oozing closer.   Fish and fowl encroaching.

Leepus on the stonepath above waterside scrub-willow.   Rats scuttle for cover in root clumps.   Coots racket sudden—foot-slap alarmed across water.   A red-eared terrapin slips from a log.

Terrapins, thinks Leepus.   Since when do they live in Inglund?

A wall of vegetation defends a blackwater oxbow. Leepus negotiates a maze of weed-cloaked junk—arrives at a greasy wooden wharf. The rotten hulk of Bodja's houseboat floating a cable-length offshore.

A faded sign nailed to an alder: RING IF I NO U – FUKKOFF FAST IF I DONT!

Leepus picks up the hammer provided—beats the corroded cast-iron chunk chain-hung from its miniature gallows. Steely tintinnabulation cuts the swampy air.

Leepus gives it a couple of minutes—rings again. Bodja doesn't show.

A two-stroke motor echoing in stillness. An outboard on the river—puttering closer. Bodja nosing his skiff into the oxbow. His attention on the houseboat. Leepus lights up. Smoke catches Bodja's eye. He alters course and kills the motor—broadsides the skiff to the wharf. 'Leepus?' he says blinking frog-like. 'What up? Got trouble, man?'

'Trouble?' Leepus raises an eyebrow. 'You'll need to be more specific.'

'Mike's not with you, is she?' asks Bodja peering wary.

'No.'

'Okay.' Bodja relaxes minutely—hands the skiff's painter up to Leepus. 'Don't see you down here for a while. Think maybe something's occurring.'

'Do you, mate?' Leepus loops the wet rope around a bollard. 'So what are you up to when I ring?'

'Just a bit of fishing.' Bodja clambers onto the wharf.

'No good?' Leepus sniffing—scenting only unwashed Bodja.

'Into a fuckin' monster. Catfish I reckon. Have to let it take my line or it sinks the skiff and eats me.'

'Obviously not picky then, those catfish?'

Bodja frowns—scratches manky beard with ragged nails. Dark residue in cuticles. Crusty tideline between fingers.

Leepus follows Bodja's gaze to the listing houseboat. 'Old wreck's still afloat then—or is it the mud-bank keeping her up?'

24

'Couple of sprung planks to caulk when we get some working weather. Bilge needs pumping now and then—but I generally keep my arse dry, if it's any of your business.'

'Okay—just banta.' Leepus shrugs. 'No need to get the hump.'

'All right for you coming down here to take the piss.' Bodja sniffs disgruntled—musters a half-hearted comeback. 'Leepus Tower still fuckin' standing, is it? Bet you haven't got round to rigging that lightning conductor yet.'

'Slipped my mind.'

'You'll be sorry when you hear a bang one night and wake up carbonised.'

'Maybe you can sort it when you're over to fix the portcullis.'

'What's wrong with the portcullis?'

'Traffic accident. Kids in a fucking halftrack.'

'Welding job, is it?'

'I'd say so.'

'When do you want it doing?'

'Soon as you like.'

'Got jobs outstanding on the boat. And I'll have to service the jenny.'

'Come over tomorrow.'

'Need a few chips up front—welding rods and fuel. Say fifty?'

Leepus measures off a short stack. 'Should be seventy-five there. Get a handful of weedsticks too—improve your fucking mood, mate.'

'Cheers.' Bodja trousers the chips—steps down into the skiff and rewinds the outboard pull-cord.

'Okay, mate.' Leepus shrugs wry as the motor revs high—settles to a steady splutter. 'I'll be on my way, then. Better things to waste a day doing than bandying fine words with you.'

∞

Leepus trudges back up the hill through the pissing rain. 'Fuck Bodja,' he mutters under his dripping hatbrim. Bastard's too far up

25

his own arse to offer hospitality on board—Leepus is soaked to the fucking bone now. But that's probably best in the long run—an hour in that festering houseboat's a proposition that likely proves fatal.

Even bathed in sunshine - an event not recalled by many - Shithole is not classically picturesque.

A few streets of abandoned artisan-cottage holiday homes repossessed by Blud of Inglund squatters in the aftermath of the Reduction.

Two-dozen sound old council houses strung sullen along Windy Edge preserving inbred village-bloodlines.

The enclave of unfinished StrivaHomz caged in rusty scaffolds. Flapping blue-plastic roofing. Plank bridges strung precarious across mud and flooded trenches. A few families of co-operative self-builders huddled despondent in un-glazed kitchen-diners awaiting better weather.

Behind a dark conspiracy of yew on a stonewalled barrow of ancestral bones at the ancient heart of the village: the Peasants' Party Palace—formerly St Peters. It's a shrine to godless pleasure now. Sexually energetic locals gather there on arbitrary shindig-days to indulge in joyous affirmation of community cohesion. Devotional intoxicants are imbibed—bonkers music relished.

And at the corner of High Street and Knacker's Lane overlooking the trash-filled duckpond: the Queen's Head on a Spike. His hat sheds water cold down Leepus' neck as he clocks the gory caricature of royal decapitation swinging over the door of the pub.

The past jumping out on Leepus—some arty anarchistic gal taut-arsed on a ladder. She hangs her rebel masterpiece—turns and flushes proud. Ribald Poors Militia lads raise sloppy glasses cheering.

It's one of those fleeting moments—a wildly optimistic recognition of a glorious but ultimately futile spasm of social-levelling with violence. Leepus buys the artist a drink—entices her to bed to revel in the slaughter.

Or maybe he just wants to. It's sometimes hard to tell with dizzy what really happens and what doesn't.

Leepus ducks into the snug. A dim fire flickers a faint welcome from the hearth. There's a comforting fug of weedsmoke marred by a pissy bouquet of wet dog. John Fox and Bob the Butcher turn from the bar to check him. Dribbling Dave's curled up poorly on the floor—Bob's dog lapping happy at pooled vomit.

The bar untended—Big Bethan in the corner passing slack time with video poka. The landlady looks from gambling machine to Leepus. 'Fuck me,' she squawks in greeting. 'Look what the rain flushes out.'

'Alright, Leepus?' Bob nods sly and lifts his empty jar. 'You're just in fuckin' time.'

'Thanks.' Leepus nods back. 'Mine's a caffy, mate.'

'Walked into that one, Bob,' John Fox says and chugs off his ale. 'Old Leepus ain't no fish.'

'Up himself is what he is,' Bob the Butcher says sour. 'Fuckin' caffy's liquid gold. What's wrong with regular bevvi?'

'Devil's piss,' says Leepus pulling up a stool. 'Look what years of drinking it does to you.'

Bethan gathers empty jars—ladles ale from a barrel and glances shrewd at Leepus. 'I'll be needing to see someone's gold on the bar before I put beans in the grinder.'

Leepus pulls out his chipstack. He measures a squat column on the sticky counter—sighs and tips it over.

'Nice one, mate.' Bob the Butcher is relieved.

'Pleasure,' says Leepus. 'Just don't blame me when you find yourself in the shitta one fine morning squirting out your liver.'

'That can't really happen, can it?' John Fox looking queasy.

Leepus shrugs. 'Just saying. Chance is yours to take.'

'Here,' says Bethan. 'I do my best, but the beans seem kind of furry.'

'Thanks,' says Leepus. 'As long as it's got some jangle. Get a jar in for yourself while you're at it. And Dave too—when he's feeling better.'

'Much going on up your ends then?' Bob shifts heavy on his barstool—adjusts the overhang of arsecheeks.

Leepus shrugs. 'Time passes, mate—thanks for asking. Any fun to be had down here?'

'Squad of fuckin' snotface studs roll through yesterday. Aggy round the yards a bit—try to scare-up background rabblegabble on "the dirty disease-bag grizzle scrote who lives up in that scabby tower".'

'Daft Danny tells 'em you're alright, though.' John Fox chiming in. 'Just as long as we throw you a juicy priv virgin now and then.'

'Yeah? They piss themselves at that, I bet,' says Leepus.

'Nah—but poor old Danny-boy fuckin' does when the top stud gets into him with a voltwhip.'

'Ouch,' says Leepus passing more chips to Bethan. 'Bottle of grog there for the lad when he stops twitching. Tell the dope I'm proud.'

'What do they want then, up at yours?' Bob not letting it go.

'Mystery.' Leepus gulps the last of his foul caffy. 'Anyone got any special problems?'

Big Bethan shakes her head. 'If they 'ave then they're not saying. I 'ear every bastard's troubles. Makes me right depressed.'

'Other strangers about?'

'Pack of tinkish scuttlas doorsteppin' looted bits and bobs.' Bob the Butcher spits disgusted. 'Slippy little shits. Blink and they rob the eyeballs out your head while you ain't looking.'

'Steady, Bob.' Leepus cocks his head. 'There's a clause in the Articles on ethnic slurs. Says they're out of order.'

'Fukkoff!' Bob's jowl wobbles. 'No way that applies to fuckin' tinkish scrotes. That'd just be mental.'

'Yeah.' Foxy sneers. 'Anyhow, this one mucky little tart—can't be more than twelve—says she'll toss me off for twenny.'

Big Bethan aghast. 'You never.'

'Course not.' Foxy smirks. 'Like I'm going to pay you twenny for a hand shandy, says I—when the barmaid up the Queen's only wants ten for a gobble.'

Big Bethan not amused. Her straight arm jutting across the bar—bursting Foxy's nose. 'Landlady, you cheeky sod,' she says. 'An' I'd want at least a nundred.'

Leepus sidesteps as Foxy topples facedown onto flagstone. The dog barks surprise—sniffs and lunges eager after nose blood.

Bob the Butcher mirthful—struggling for breath.

'Later.' Leepus winks at Big Bethan. 'Thanks for the entertainment.'

'Don't be a stranger.' Big Bethan winks back. 'Always glad to put on a show—for a minted old griz like you.'

Leepus is halfway out the door when a flicker catches his eye—the poka machine flashing alluring. He ducks back and feeds it chips—waits to see how the virtual cards fall.

Deuce. Another. Ace. Ace. Ace.

Full house—that's nice, thinks Leepus.

Tinny electronic trumpets fanfare his good fortune. Leepus whips his hat off—holds it at the ready. The machine pukes a copious rattle.

His hat brimful—overflowing.

Big Bethan's face a picture.

◊◊◊◊◊

6

Leepus up on the tower roof checking his dish connection. There's a tourney kicking off in twenty and he can't get a signal. The situation is fucking frustrating.

Even when accessible the net is largely unravelled. A mastermind with dementia. A degraded virtual catacombs where simples hang out talking shit and acting trashy—then leave a mess of carelessly abandoned data for the maid. Tireless robot formulae mine the grubby residue—glean prejudicial intel and target threat-reduction.

A veiled backdoor is risky but an occupational hazard. Liquidity is an essential hedge against turbulence. And a legit bankroll greases stealth incursion of municipal jurisdictions. Lucky the online card rooms are full of fish with kripChip. Leepus wins it from them.

But his balance is currently depleted—a deposit overdue.

So now the spydaGlyda's dropped his thread. And there's rain on the filthy wind.

And Bodja's smoking quaddie bouncing reckless over South Commons. Towing a loaded trailer.

A loaded trailer off road? The bastard's fucking puddled.

∞

The quaddie parked up down in the tower compound. Bodja dismounted and breathing heavy.

'Thanks for coming,' Leepus greets his grey-faced pal. 'Take a wrong turning, do you?'

'What?' Bodja doesn't get it.

31

'I know the lane's no PayWay but it's easier than the heath. Surprised you don't throw a half-shaft.'

'Right.' Bodja heading inside. 'Posse of bloodthirsty tinkish trotting chariots round the green. Think it's best I work around them.'

'Tinkish?' Leepus tuts. 'Don't call them that to their face, mate. They get cross if you hurt their feelings.'

'Bastards don't have feelings.'

The lift ascending. Leepus holding his breath. Bodja less than fragrant.

So—' Leepus leads out into the tank room. 'These rovers got a point to make, or just expressing their exuberant culture?'

'Dunno.' Bodja plucks at his beard. 'But they're smashing windows with slingshots and dragging Bob the Butcher's poor old dog along behind them all mashed up on a rope.'

'That's not very nice.'

'Maybe you could give Mike a shout?' says Bodja fumbling to ignite a weedstick.

'Too soon for a raise like that, mate. Mike's a weapon of last resort.' Leepus turns on the monitor—pans the *camera obscura*. 'And anyway, she's off doing good elsewhere.'

'So what are you going to do?'

Leepus zooms on smoke rising thick from somewhere near the sty-field on the forest side of Shithole. A trio of rover chariots slaloming a field of panicked pork. Slaughter on the run.

'Do?' Leepus shrugs—turns from screen to Bodja. 'I'm going to put the kettle on while you start on fixing the portcullis. Mind my own fucking business. Hope it all blows over.'

'What if they come up here?'

'Not sure.' Leepus thinks about it for a moment. 'I suppose we might get our heads cut off if you haven't finished welding.'

Bodja swallowing his Adam's apple. 'That ain't funny, man.'

'Right.' Leepus prompts Bodja into the lift. 'Surprised you think I'm joking.'

32

∞

Leepus lights a burner under the kettle. Then he sparks a contemplative weedstick—mulls the potential for problematic synergy of recent random complications.

Sky-burial on hillside. Overseer in airspace. Student scrutineers up arse. Rovers on a rampage. Fucking Mike gone walkabout. Bodja vibing dodgy.

Some kind of game afoot but Leepus doesn't see it. He needs to sharpen up.

Water boiling steady now—clouds threatening kitchen rain. Leepus takes down his glass teapot. Dumps in a couple of spoonfuls of Mother Mellow's VitaliTea. Inundates the pungent herb-mix and adds a kicker-wrap of patent Thinking Powder for a bonus synaptic de-coke.

Leepus gives it a couple of minutes—studies the murky convection of entheogenic infusion. Then he pours it into his best china cup. Gulps down a snake of bitter liquid.

Catalytic squirm in stomach. Warm peristalsis creeping gut. Nervous system energised—dull visuals resolving and the aural world enhanced. Distant dropped pins clattering like girders.

Bodja's rattling jenny dying down in the compound.

Leepus checks the monitor. Sweating piebald ponies trotting chariots up the lane. Wild rovers with their blood up—pork-heads raised on spears.

Leepus re-lights his weedstick—modulates his rush. Then he cloaks himself in his greatcoat—breathes deep and summons the lift.

Batteries low. Winch motor groaning slow. Leepus waits impatient—considers his armoury locker.

Escalation's a risky play in this position. Best to deploy revitalised intuition. Read tells. Catch bluffs. Make moves and earn respect. Worst case—cash-in even. No harm in pinging Mike though. Leepus ducks back for his fone.

Grog bottles lined on the tank-room bar catch his flicking eye. He snags a sociable afterthought—slips it into a deep coat-pocket.

33

The compound gate framed by the tower doorway. Leepus looks out from shadow.

Arc-welder cabled to silent jenny. Open toolbox on gravel. Straightened spars of angle iron propped upright against the quaddie. Trailer tarp discarded careless in a heap.

The portcullis mackled up by Bodja in a hurry.

Three wild rovers in chariots halted at the gate.

Bodja's location not apparent.

The charioteers remain mounted. They're statuesque in leather breeches—sheepskin jerkins over naked skin the colour of cured ham. Random crow-feather adornment. Black braids wound with silver. Facial tat and scarification patterns typical western upland nomadic.

Brasses jangle—the charioteers twitching traces. They're settling their lathered ponies as they reconnoitre the tower.

One fit lad stoops. He comes up with a severed pork-head finger-hooked by nose ring—whirls and hurls like a hammer thrower. The meaty missile arches high across the fence. It impacts heavy in front of the tower doorway—grins up at Leepus stepping out. He bends and grabs it by an ear sauntering up to the cosmetic portcullis. 'Appreciate the thought, boys,' he says as he edges out. 'But I'm still a bit full from breakfast.'

Blood dribbles cold up Leepus' sleeve as he hoists the bristled delicacy in the direction of Head Hurler. The rover scowls offended.

He's not the only one disconcerted.

Wet pink equine nostrils flare. Brown eyes roll—flash white. The pork-spooked pony snorts and bolts—lurches its chariot into motion. Leepus watches the runaway contraption pitching reckless over the tussocks. He shrugs apologetic—anticipates retribution.

But the rover lads are tickled pink by Head Hurler's spontaneous excursion: one white-knuckled hand clinging tight to chariot frame—the other clawing frantic to recover trailing traces. His enthusiastic comrades cheer on the risky caper with heads thrown back and cackling raucous. Crowing stormcocks wild as wind.

'Sly ol' stunt yow's pullen there,' says one rover youth approving. 'Fair fooken play t'yow, Chief.'

'Thanks—but credit where credit's due,' says Leepus. 'It's this old hog what does it. Payback for cutting its head off.'

'Chopped snortas juss a warna, Chief. Be fambly bonces as gets tekken off t'morra.'

'Fambly?'

'Yow's clannurs, mun. They shitturs in thur dirt 'oles dyn by trees b'low.' A thumb-jerk in the direction of Shithole. The charioteer rests his case.

His companion still unspeaking. He's distracted—miming vigorous masturbation. Leepus follows his gaze to see the scorned Head Hurler now returning—flogging his pony abashed up the hill.

'C'mon, don't take the piss.' Leepus shrugs rebuttal. 'Just because those simples are neighbours—doesn't mean we're fucking related.'

'Shitturs braggup yow fer Chief.' The charioteer's not buying it—pushing out a bet. 'They bastids does us evul—ow yow reckun t'fix it?'

'Grog might take the sting off,' says Leepus producing hopeful bottle.

'Thass fair manners, Chief—but grog dunt buy nah gurlee.'

'I don't want to buy nah gurlee.' Leepus pops the cork.

'Gi'us'er fooken back, then. Wi' a big bitta gol' fer compo.'

'Right.' Leepus takes a swallow of grog—picks the bones from the rover's demand and takes another swallow. 'I'll need some time to look around. See if I can't find her.'

'Sound.' The charioteer leans down and takes the bottle—drains it halfway down before Wanker grabs it from him. 'Lang as er's still suckin' air an lookin' pretty.'

'What happens if she's not?'

'Reckun Queenie'll say on that. Mos'like er'll want yow's fambly bollox chopped. An' all they gurlees dopted.'

Leepus dwells—takes his time about it.

Head Hurler back on-scene now wresting the bottle from smirking Wanker. He's not happy to find it empty—flings it spinning past Leepus' head and springs down onto the turf.

Leepus reads a deep desire for retribution etched in his facial rictus.

'Yow mekken us oot contish, yow sly fooken griz,' says Head Hurler stepping up shifty. 'Nah yow fooken fight us.'

Leepus reads the other rover faces for potential intervention—deduces this unlikely. 'Okay, matey. I'll have a go with you,' he bluffs. 'But watch out for my dirty magic.'

Head Hurler scowls—pulls his dagger. 'Fooken magic thissun!'

'Easy cuzz.' The charioteer signals caution. 'Jussa bitta bareknuck, neh? Yow kin beat he but dunt dedd he. Chief thur sez he's sound fer dealin'.'

Head Hurler spits—then wipes his mouth and says, 'Kay, us settles fer snowt an' lugs.'

Leepus reads the first slash coming. He twitches his head and evades it—skips swift round the nervous pony.

Head Hurler vaults the chariot saying, 'Fooken jibba. Stay yow groun' an fight us.'

Leepus' footwork isn't too fancy. He's quickly outmanoeuvred—backed against a piebald flank and breathing the reek of pony sweat as Head Hurler dances round him.

Head Hurler weaving in. Leepus looks past the hypnotic curlicues described by the dagger point. He slips hand into pocket—palms an amp of capsaicin. He waits for Head Hurler's eye-tell—twists away a nanosecond in advance of his lethal thrust.

It's not the pony's day. It whinnies shrill with knees folding—the rover's long dagger-blade jammed deep between its heaving ribs. Head Hurler tugs but he can't free it from spasmed muscle.

Leepus takes advantage—slaps amp to enemy forehead and feels it shatter nicely.

Head Hurler blinking rapid—mucous membranes blazing. He lets go of the dagger—staggers back with hands clapped to eyes and collapses caterwauling.

The stabbed pony going down too now—deranged by pain and commotion. Pink lung-spume flecks the grass. Its hooves thrashing frantic—galloping over phantom turf with death a short nose behind.

Head Hurler is suddenly silent—prone with arms flung wide. An oily spring of bloody fluid wells from a hoof-shaped cranial crater.

Leepus assesses his opponent's wound is likely fatal. So does a baffled Wanker.

The other charioteer's more proactive. He swings down grim with cradled spear—stoops over the knackered pony. A few whispered words in a flicking ear. A gentle heart-thrust delivered.

Leepus maintains a respectful silence—waits for the pony to stop twitching. Eventually he announces, 'I'll count that as a win then.'

'Fook.' The charioteer turns to Leepus—shakes his head impressed. 'Yow bollox solid fooken gol' a fooken cert.'

'Ax cont ow he fooken duzzat,' says Wanker finding his tongue. 'Smek us lad dyn on't dirt—mekken he wail an bawl all babbish? Tin't natrul. Thass wha' fooken us sez.'

'His dagger. My magic slap.' Cocky Leepus raises his hand. 'Want to check it out?'

Bad mistake, thinks Leepus just too late to take it back. The rover chivalric tradition prescribes absolute confrontation of any perceived challenge.

'Yuss,' says Wanker coming at him. 'An' us bonce dunt get nag-kicked neethuh—case yow wishun it duzz.'

Leepus in retreat. He's forgetful of the dead pony—falls backward over its carcass and sprawls in a slime of heart blood. He looks up at Wanker grinning cold down his levelled spear-shaft.

Leepus averts his gaze.

A flash. A sound in the periphery of his awareness.

He looks again. Wanker kneeling on the sod now—he's looking down disappointed. His torso in tatters and flayed red-raw. His shattered ribs imploded. A steaming stream of lifeblood floods his finger-dam.

Two ponies bolting—empty chariots on their tails.

The surviving rover clutches his spear a bit uncertain—stares at a tail of gun-smoke wisping from a nearby hawthorn thicket.

'I'm thinking drop it now, mate,' Leepus suggests helpful. 'Or likely yow gets dedded too.'

'Fook,' the pallid rover says.

Then Mike's ducking out of the hawthorn holding her sawn-off on him.

'Fook,' the rover says again—tosses down his weapon.

'Good lad.' Mike steps up. 'On the fuckin' ground, now. Facedown. Hands on fuckin' head.'

The rover spits then does it.

Mike moves brisk—nuzzles rover earlobe with sawn-off muzzle and plants firm knees in rover kidneys. A cable-tie looped round rover wrists and then yanked tight.

Leepus on his feet now. He's just a tad unsteady. Mike stands too—narrows her eyes and waits.

'Not my fault,' says Leepus. 'I only come out to have a chat but it all gets out of hand.'

Mike grunts noncommittal—hauls the disabled rover across blood-slick turf by his hair and props him against the dead pony.

'It's the grog that turns it ugly,' says Leepus. He's divining Wanker's entrails not foreseeing any upside.

'Tinkish wild lads running riot and you fill the twats with grog?' Mike's disgust is plain. 'Common fuckin' knowledge they can't handle grown-up liquor.'

'Common fucking ignorance,' Leepus says defensive. 'I try to rise above that kind of negative stereotyping, mate. Grease the wheels of diplomacy with a little bit of respect. Maybe buy an edge.'

'And so now two grog-mashed stereotypes are dead in your fuckin' yard, you pompous arse.'

'Not to mention an innocent pony.'

'We don't need a war at the moment.'

Leepus lights a weedstick—drags and passes it to Mike.

Mike looks over into the compound. 'That Bodja's fuckin' quaddie?'

Leepus nods.

'How come he's not out here with you?'

'Off on his toes when he sees them coming, I suppose. Probably still going.'

'Twat's not to be relied on.'

'Rovers sporting down in Shithole. Then they follow him up here. Plus I wind him up a bit. No wonder the idiot spooks.'

'Yeah. I come up past the green in the bloody aftermath. More useless pant-pissers down there, all moping around outside the Queen's reviewing the engagement. No chance of an objective debriefing, but I kick a couple of peasant arses and catch the drift.'

'Rover girl goes missing? Shithole on the spot?'

'Five tinkish kids come through on the sell the other day. Only four get back to the campground. Clan wants the missing girl back safe in its tender bosom. Chariot lads blow in to reinforce their claim— spree it up terrorising village idiots, dragging fuckin' dogs about and sticking porks.'

'Who comes up with this old bollocks about me being some kind of fucking headman—sends these rover boys straight to my door?'

'No time to ask. I'm playing catch-up, aren't I?' Mike frowns, stares down at the dead Head Hurler.

'Yeah—you cut it pretty fine. I'm just about drawing dead.'

Mike crouching now—peering into Hurler's head-dent. 'What you get for living in a castle, I suppose—being a winna and having opinions. Poke your nose in peoples' business often enough they start to think you care.'

'Still well out of fucking order.'

Mike picks a tiny glass-shard from the forehead of Head Hurler. She examines it on her fingertip—looks up at Leepus suspicious. 'So what the fuck is this, Chief?'

Leepus shrugs. 'Capsaicin amp. Works like magic, mate. Lucky I have a few handy.'

'Another fuckin' silly-arsed novelty weapon?'

'I prefer 'sub-lethal self-defence aid'.'

'Not this fuckin' time, it isn't.'

'It's an improvised response to aggression. Not my fault the pony kicks off.'

'Fair enough,' Mike says weary. 'But you're going to regret not wearing fuckin' gloves at least, the next time you scratch your bollocks.'

A sudden skylark trilling. Trilling again—louder. But muffled under sheepskin.

Mike rifles the captive's jerkin. She finds the fone and checks the screen—asks, 'Who's Queenie?' The rover just looks glum.

'Give it here, mate,' Leepus intervenes. 'Best if I have a word.'

Leepus takes the fone—and then a breath before he keys it. He listens—responds, 'No, sorry missus, this is Leepus speaking. Young Brock's sitting this one out for now. Maybe I can help.'

Leepus listens. Queenie's dialect's impenetrable but clearly she's not pleased. 'Here's an idea,' he interrupts. 'I'll talk—you sit quiet and mind your manners.'

Leepus holds the fone arm's-length—waits till it stops shrieking. Then he puts it back to his ear and says, 'Two of your lads here bite off more than they can chew and fail to stay alive. That's a matter of regret to me—but you can argue they have it coming. Brock'll bring them home for their burying in a bit—as long as we can reach some kind of mutual respect-based understanding.'

Another interruption—this time a shade less shrill.

'I don't know what happens to your gurlee, missus—but I'll do my best to find out. Turns out someone round here harms the child they'll have to answer for it. Word of blud on that.'

Leepus listens—responds, 'Leepus, missus. I already tell you. Ask old Dadda Reynard with the Red Runners up on Sky Moor. He'll vouch my name's a goodun.'

'There—never as bad as you think, lad.' Mike hauls the rover to his feet. 'Least you get to go home with your head on.'

'Thass summut t'luk forrud at,' Brock says kind of hollow. 'Rekkun ol' Queenie fooken skins us raw, tho', when 'er fooken sharps us.'

Mike struggles to look sympathetic.

'Okay. Deal,' says Leepus to Queenie. 'First we call it all square on today's bit of a commotion. Then I give up your lost young 'un and/or the guilty party, or suitable compensation, before the next full moon—or you "blayzup alla conten parish an' mekken fooken shitturs inta burga fer t'feedup fooken war-dags." Is that what we agree on?'

Queenie's voice in Leepus' ear. Mike waiting for his nod before she cuts Brock free.

'Sound,' says Leepus into the fone. 'Fair play to you then, missus. And I'm sorry for your trouble.'

∞

The strayed ponies whistled in and calm now. A lonely rover loads two chariots like hearses. 'Us'll sen' sum cuzz fer't dedded nag'n'wheelie, nah Chief?' he calls over to Leepus with Mike in the compound.

'Nah.' Leepus shakes his head. 'Spoils of battle, lad. Pony goes for eating. You can buy the chariot back later. That's the usual custom.'

'Shot boy's rig there is mine too by fightin' rights,' chips in Mike. 'But I'm all fuckin' heart today.'

'Kay. Fair fooken play t'yow, killagurl.' The rover spits friendly over his shoulder—tongue-clicks his mournful ponies an instruction to plod off. 'Us'll ketch yow sum fooken t'morra.'

Leepus takes the weedstick Mike offers. A sudden finger tremor. Mike deadpan—lighting it for him. 'So, how long till the next full moon, mate?' she asks as the chariots disappear over the hillcrest.

'No idea.' Leepus winks. 'You're the one with the menstrual cycle.'

'That's irrelevant, you fuckin' halfwit.' Mike ejects shells from the sawn-off. 'I'm a woman, not a werewolf.'

Leepus leaves it at that.

'It's only eighteen days,' says Bodja's muffled voice. 'Even if you trust the bastards to wait.'

Leepus looks at Mike—smiles wry. Mike shakes her head disgusted.

Bodja creeps out from under the trailer tarp and stands up shaky. 'They come mobbed up we get slaughtered, don't we?' A tremor in his voice. 'What're we going to do, man?'

Mike sniffs the air—looks curious at Leepus. 'You don't just drop one, do you mate? Smells like some cunt shits their knickers.'

'Not guilty.' Leepus grins.

'Funny.' Surly Bodja blinking pale. 'Easy to be a hard-arse, ennit— standing up behind a fukkoff shotgun?'

'Standing up's the important part.' Mike stomps off to the tower.

Leepus watches the clouds race and doesn't comment.

'Sorry, Leepus,' says downcast Bodja. 'Have a bit of a wobble, there. Reckon I let you down, man. Give us a chance to make it right?'

Leepus reads twitchy Bodja—considers old times passed. 'All right, mate—settle down. It's not the end of the world.'

'Thanks, brer.' Bodja's relief is almost childlike. 'I'll make it up, I promise.'

'Yeah.' Leepus turning away disappointed. 'So just fix-up the damn portcullis, pronto. Rig that fucking lightning conductor and sort my tek so I can get into a game tonight—and we forget it ever happens.'

'Stick and a bracer and I'm on it.' Bodja rallies—gets coolered by a second thought. 'Uh, that goes for Mike too, does it?'

'Hard to say.' Leepus inside tower the doorway now—he's not looking back at Bodja. 'Probably wouldn't bet it all. You know what fucking Mike's like.'

◊◊◊◊◊

7

'Want me to hang around?' Mike says and twitches the throttle. The engine blares—settles to a ragged bass rumble.

Leepus clambers from the sidecar. 'Not if you've got a better offer.'

'Right.' Mike kicks into gear. 'I might be busy for a while. Try to stay out of trouble.'

Leepus waves a careless hand as Mike putts off down through unlit village byways. She turns south at the parish boundary—picks up High Road from Robber's Roundabout and moves out of earshot into the night.

Leepus waits while the local yard dogs quieten. An alley flanked by roofless stonewalled workshops—he steps into its dank exhalation. A short squelch over mud-sunk cobbles. A reeking midden skirted. A flight of greasy steps to climb up a dripping ferny bankside.

Mike's got a right to her secrets. No reason for Leepus to be arsey.

A landing in the flight of steps. Leepus turns off onto a concrete terrace. Wan light oozes through a threadbare blanket hung as a curtain—reveals a window cut in the corrugated wall of a rusty shipping container.

Leepus clangs his toe on hollow metal. The blanket-curtain darkens. Leepus kicks again. This time he does it harder. Something furtive inside. 'Don't worry about tidying up, chap,' he says. 'Just get the damn door open.'

'Leepus?' John Fox's voice is a little strangled.

'Fukksake.' Leepus waits.

'Who's with you?'

'No one.'

A rattle of bolts. Dry steel hinges squealing. A gust of fetid smoky air. John Fox peers out into the night backlit by dim stove-glow.

Leepus steps in past him—locates the lamp and relights it while his host secures the door. 'What's up?' he says then. 'Think it's rovers, do you?'

'Why would it be rovers?' John Fox shifts non-specific garbage from chair and table. 'Sit down. I get me bits an' skin one up.'

'No need.' Leepus sits—pulls out ready-made weedsticks and passes one of them over.

'Nice one.' John Fox's hand is shaking as he leans down for a light. His nose is still swollen clownish.

'Clear another chair and sit down, chap. We need to have a chat.'

'Do we?' John Fox follows Leepus' instruction. 'What's it all about, then?'

Leepus takes a toke—and then another as he scans John Fox's lair. Walls collaged with gynaecological glamour. Faded centrefolds gaping pink—gloss paper damply rippled. Mattress heaped with a fusty bedclothes-tangle. Rusty foodcans stacked on a counter. A pan of something noisome simmering on the stovetop. 'Have a guess,' he says exhaling.

'Fucking tinkish, ennit?'

'What about them?'

'Catch us with our dicks out.'

Leepus raising an eyebrow. 'How d'you mean?'

'It isn't me, man.'

'It isn't you that what?'

'Drops you in it. You know—tells that crew of savage raggles you're the man to talk to.'

'About the child, you mean?'

'Child?'

'The one you slag off in the Queen's the other day. The 'mucky little

44

tart' those rovers say's gone missing.'

John Fox swallows. 'No way. I never. Don't put that shit on me.'

'Never what, John?' Leepus staring hard.

'Never nothing.' A foxy tongue-tip licks thin lips. 'Never touch it, do I? Never fucking hurt it. Never do fukkall.'

'Need to get her back, John—or we're all in fucking trouble.'

John Fox cornered—trapped in his chair. He finger-combs thin hair from flaky forehead. 'Fucking straight up, Leepus man. It's not me that fucking does her.'

Leepus picks up tells—sniffs bullshit. 'I'm reading a different story.'

'No. I tell you in the pub what happens. Tinkish skank's well up for it but I ain't buying am I? Nothing else to say.'

'You're sweating, John.'

'The weed, man—it's got a dirty edge.'

'Yeah? Feels sweet enough to me. Something on your conscience?'

'No.' John Fox struggles to make eye contact. 'I don't do nothing to her. It ain't fair to say I do.'

Leepus looks straight back. 'But you think about it, don't you? Juicy little wild girl drops into your clammy hands—you think of stuff to do.'

John Fox looks away—gnaws lip with ochre tooth.

Leepus lights another weedstick—hands it over. 'So tell me how it goes, John—start to finish, eh? Best to clear the air.'

John Fox sudden on his feet eyes sparkling wet in lamplight. 'Fukkoff! Leave me the fuck alone! You got no right to pressure me the fuck like fuckin' this.'

'Pressure?' Leepus looks up cool. 'I'm only asking, chap. Mike's the one does pressure.'

John Fox sits down heavy. 'Cunt,' he says defeated.

Leepus deadpan—waiting.

'It's sometime in the morning when it lets off fuckin' raining. That's good—I need to split some firewood. So I've only done a couple of logs when old Ma Apples kicks off squawkin' how she's letting the bastard dog out. And there's tinkish scuttlas gobbin' curse-rhymes right back at her. I look over and see half-a-dozen of the little shites working up the lane—pushing their fucking leather-craft, magic stones, dodgy 'lectrics, all that tinkish crap. But there's not a lot of fat to suck up our end, is there? Better pickings down Sunnyside—so they all swarm off through the backs.'

'But not the girl.'

'She looks up from the end of the alley—checks me standing there an' decides I'm worth a punt.'

'No one else out and about? Nothing out of place?'

'I hear a motor up on Top Lane but I don't pay it no attention.'

'What kind of motor?'

'Just a motor. Little diesel—or two-stroke, maybe. Nothing very hefty.'

'The girl, then—how does she look to you?'

'Red hair. Blue eyes. Big bone earrings. Tasty enough, I s'pose— once you hose the crud off.'

'That'll make her squeal.'

'Yeah.' John Fox licking lips.

'She'll be all wet and wriggling bare-naked.'

'A sight to remember, I reckon.' John Fox narrows eyes. 'Shame it never happens.'

'What does?'

'Not much. She shows me the stuff she's flogging.'

'Nothing tempts you?'

John Fox sucking his weedstick. Leepus lets the question hang.

'Maybe the slash-pic's worth a bid. 3D tinkish knife-gals 'ard fuckin' at it.'

'Gets you going, does it?'

'It might do—if she don't ask fifty for it.'

'So how does it go from there?'

'I never hurt 'er.'

'You already say that.'

'She's wearing this tight shammi-leather shirt thing—squashes up her titties.'

'How old do you say she is?'

'They're only little.'

'Succulent though, I bet?'

'Yeah—that's the word'

'And she senses your attraction—offers you a tug?'

'Yeah,' John Fox says a little hoarse—weedstick trembling between forked fingers. 'Long as I pay her ask on the 3D pic.'

'Bollocks!' Leepus juts his neck—slaps the weedstick out of Foxy's hand and backs him against the wall. 'I'm not having this old tosh.'

'No—no okay.' John Fox regrouping. 'I get a bit confused there.'

'So?' Leepus pushes again.

'So I tell the bitch I'll give her an extra twenny if she lets us have a look.'

'And?'

'She says she will—"but keep yow fooken hands off".'

'So you get your eyeful, do you?'

'Sly cunt undoes a couple of buttons—says I have to show her "fooken gol', mun," if I want a proper see.'

'Smart kid.'

'Dirty tinkish little tease. Fuckin' asking for it.'

'For what?'

John Fox shrugs.

'Come on—let's hear the worst.'

'I have a lunge at it, don't I? Grab a fat little handful.'

'But she doesn't take it easy?'

'Fights like a sack full of cats.'

'Gets you well worked up, I bet. You probably shoot your load.'

'I wish.' John Fox scowling dark. 'Skank back-kicks me in the fuckin' nuts so hard I near puke me fuckin' ring up. By the time I get me breath back she's legging it off up Top Lane like a hare with a dog up its arse.'

Leepus lights himself a weedstick—maintains a chilly silence.

'Fuckin' say something then.' John Fox on the hook. 'I ain't spinning, honest. I tell you it isn't me that does her. You fuckin' b'lieve me, don't you?'

'Yeah.' Leepus sniffs. 'I believe you—you worthless drip of cock rot.'

'That's a bit strong, mate.' John Fox representing umbrage.

'I'm not your mate.'

'No?' John Fox is disconcerted.

'No. I don't have mates who disrespect the Articles—and sex around with kids.'

'Ain't a kid, is it? It's a fuckin' tinkish prossi.'

'That kind of shithead attitude's no longer acceptable in Shithole.'

'What? You're fuckin' joking, ain't you? Anything goes in Shithole.'

'Not the sexual exploitation of vulnerable children just out to earn a crust and avoid a beating.' Leepus stubs out his weedstick. 'So I reckon you're fucking banned, John.'

'Banned?' John Fox's face leeching colour.

'Two days to get your shit together and sling your dirty hook.'

'Fukkoff! You can't ban me. I live here fifteen year.'

'We can have a court if you want one—but then the rovers get to have their say on the issue too.'

'But—'

48

'Two days.'

'But I don't even fuckin' do her.'

Leepus on his feet now buttoning his coat. 'That's why you get two days.'

'No—come on. Please, man. Where am I going to go?'

'Somewhere I can't see you—if you've got any fucking sense.' Leepus moves to the threshold and opens the door—breathes in a lungful of clean night air.

'Fukkoff!' John Fox croaks. 'You ain't got power over me. We're all levelled here in Shithole.'

'Two days,' calls Leepus starting down the steps. 'I'll send Mike to wave you off.'

∞

Leepus plodding up Top Lane—the lost rover child running ahead of him ghostly through the dark. Bitch. Tart. Slag. Prossi. Gurlee. If he can't do any more for her he'll at least find out her fucking name.

Some will say he's too harsh on mucky Foxy. There's plenty in Shithole capable of worse. And it's not like the kid's one of theirs. But others will say 'good riddance' to the reckless dodgy fucker. Taking liberties with little tinkish gals is fair enough. But not on fucking home ground—so everyone pays the blud.

For a moment there Leepus thinks he's got the guilty bastard bang to rights—and now it's just damage limitation. The poor kid's body recovered and cleaned up. A respectful repatriation. Shithole sheds a few crocodile tears—gives up John Fox to rover justice. They haggle over compo. Then everyone moves on.

Nothing to be proud of—but then there rarely is.

It should be so fucking easy—but John Fox just isn't sly enough to be double-bluffing. He's just a minor monsta running sordid interference—not the girl's end-user.

Leepus needs more information.

A door slams in the last dark terraced-cottage before pavement turns to muddy path and sets off across rough heath. A dark figure swinging a leg over a pushbike saddle. A wobble into motion.

'Oh!' A squeaky groan of brakes—forward progress obstructed by a sudden-looming Leepus. Sorry,' the voice continues, 'I really should look where I'm going.'

'No harm done,' says Leepus. 'That you there is it, Prof?'

'It is. A good evening to you, Leepus.'

'Thanks. You too. It's been a little while. How're things with you, friend?'

'Oh, as well as can be expected.' The man's white hair reflecting glimmered moonlight. 'Or perhaps 'not quite as well' would be more precise—at the risk of appearing pedantic.'

'A minor crime—but one easily misconstrued by the ignorant and self-righteous. Be careful who you confess to.'

The Prof puzzled for a moment—his caterpillar eyebrows hunching pale. 'Ah. I see,' he says and chuckles shy. 'No news of the poor rover child, yet? I hope I'm not under suspicion.'

'You're a long way down my list, Prof.' Leepus skips a beat. 'But you don't happen to see her the other day? Word is she's up this way.'

'I don't. I'm at the Academy, I'm afraid—as is my daily custom.'

'Good. Pleased to hear that.' Leepus gropes after small talk. 'Demand for education reasonably buoyant?'

'We have six of our local youth enrolled. Most turn up most days—if only for our excellent free breakfast.'

'I applaud your dedication.'

'I fear the effort is largely symbolic—our light of knowledge all but overwhelmed by the barbarous dark.'

'Oh well—every little helps,' says Leepus ready to disengage now. 'But I'm keeping you from your pleasure.'

'Yes. An insalubrious excursion. I am forced to repair to the Queen's Head on a Spike in a desperate search for illumination.'

'Careful, Prof. Too much hooch enlightenment is likely to send you blind.'

'Unfortunately I have no choice.' The Prof sets his pedals for departure. 'Student essays need reviewing, my theorem should be progressed—but here I am benighted by defective photovoltaics.'

'A good enough excuse for a sly drink or two, I reckon.' Leepus winks. 'But why not give old Bodja a shout? He's the man to fix up your tek.'

'So I thought when I employed him. And normally his work is good. But I can't afford too many repairs that don't even last two days.'

'No. I suppose you can't.' Leepus thinks about it. 'Two days?'

'Barely that.' The Prof pushes off. 'I pay him yesterday morning, content that efficiency is restored. This afternoon the system relapses.'

'Right. You take care then, Prof.' Leepus watches the portly cyclist accelerate precarious downhill into the gloom. 'I'll have a word with Bodja when I see him.'

∞

Leepus up on the heath path—he's heading home to the tower. Starry constellations swirl around his head. Strange how the skies are only ever free of cloud at night now—while long days are oppressed by greyness. The caprice of a deranged climate? Meteorological tyranny? If there's a better explanation Leepus hasn't heard it.

The hillcrest black and ragged against stellar maelstrom. His tower behind a gorsey shoulder sheltered by murmurous trees.

A redoubt. A sanctuary from mayhem. A reassuring bunker. A last-ditch defence of precarious sanity. A monument to pragmatic paranoia. There's a time – perhaps in another life – when Leepus scorns the vanity of self-reliance that fuels the tower's fortification. These days he's a lot less sniffy about the effort.

The heath path curving down. Leepus orbits the tower—searches pockets for portcullis controller. Hopefully Bodja does a better job on the gate than he does on the Prof's photovoltaics.

'Bodja, Bodja, Bodja.' Leepus shakes his head. 'I hope you don't let yourself down, mate.'

A strange vibration passing above. The thrum of a stooping wing? Leepus stiffens—listens. Another rapid whirring movement—Leepus swivels his head to track it. A startled bird? Not likely in the darkness. He cups his ears and scans three-sixty—locates a humming oscillation.

Leepus peers—sees a shadow flitting bat-like against the distant galactic spatter.

Adrenalin drips—catalyses a nervous reaction. Leepus slips on his OwlEyes—modifies his vision. A flare of infrared laser jitterbugging the tower compound. It's a MappaSnappa hoverflying—rapid-shifting its perspective between multiple trig-points.

'Fuck,' breathes Leepus. He fumbles a tight-folded CoolCape from his coat survival-pocket. ThermaFoil rustles as he spreads it—creeps under its protection. This type of high-end observation is significantly disconcerting.

Leepus suspects the survey drone dragnets local comms too—decides to relocate his fone to screened stealth-pocket. Better safe than—

Fuck—the fone vibrating against his palm. Leepus nearly drops it.

It's the King of Clubs who's calling.

'Hey.' Leepus whispers discreet hoping his BaBBle is updated.'

'Whattup, brer?' The King's bass voice booms alarming.

'Head down at the moment, mate. Got a bit of a situation.'

'Whassat?' the King bellows back. 'Fokkin speak up, griz.'

'Never mind,' hisses Leepus. 'Just cut to the chase mate, will you?'

'Game.' The King takes the hint. 'High rollers. Shuffling up in an hour. Empty chair if you want to sit in. Chance of a decent payday.'

Leepus thinks about it for a moment—says, 'Tempted. Could use a bit of diversion. But I'm going to need a ride.'

'You'd better bring Mike too, brer. If you fokkin have to.'

'Mike's got another game going.'

'Kay. Lesta's there in twenty. But it costs you five fokkin points.'

'Three. And that's a rob.'

'Deal.'

'Tell Lesta not the tower. Pick me up at the KashBak crew-bus pull-in on the PayWay. If I'm not there, don't wait.'

∞

Leepus makes it undercover of the forest tree-line and checks back for the MappaSnappa. If it's on him it's not apparent. He stows the CoolCape and moves off through the wood—tries not to think about hungry dog packs.

But his personal security is threatened—the tower surveyed for possible penetration by a serious covert power.

But which fucking power—and why?

OurFuture the obvious suspects—the students promise scrutiny after the bodydump encounter. But this kind of sophisticated tek's not usually available off-the-shelf to local clients.

The Prefecture might request specialised assistance—but glacial bureaucracy makes its prompt deployment unlikely. Unless somehow he's pushed a red button.

Or maybe it's an aggrieved independent—some misery-vulture resentful of regulation and having a go at adjusting their losses.

Like the mercenary contractor whose Hiring Heroes gig goes tits-up when its celebrity-shill host gets snagged and bagged by local insurgent hostage-takers.

Or the Opportunity Enabler doped and sold downriver for signing up simple village boys and girls as 'apprentice hospitality workers'—otherwise known as sex slaves.

Maybe it's fucking godly fanatics pissed off their missionaries always crawl home from Shithole tarred and feathered?

The autocratic agrico that annexes Shithole commons—then finds its RoboRancha command and control entertainingly deranged by artful hackers?

The gangmaster whose renegade serfs claim asylum in the village?

Or even just some vindictive shoal of busted sharks looking to restore lost pride and a crippled bankroll.

There's certainly no shortage of kosha grudgees who'd be glad of a pop at Leepus. It's some kind of read on the fucking 'why' that he could do with to narrow it down.

∞

At the far side of forest now. Leepus ignores the sign caricaturing the likelihood of random anti-trespass munitions and steps out onto the PayWay clearstrip. He angles down the embankment—follows the roadside electrified fence along to the safety gate.

Camera-shy Leepus stands with collar up and head down under hatbrim. He pocket-fishes a cloned KashBak workforce keystick. Checks east and west along the empty PayWay. Buzzes the gate-lock open and climbs down the steps to the bus stop.

It's hard to imagine six lanes of filthy traffic once rush here twenty-four/seven. Intercity travel is now accessible only to privs—and poors-rate casual labourers bussed about by conscientious JobsProvs to cover eighteen-hour shifts and think themselves fucking lucky.

Leepus waits five minutes before the first vehicle whines down the road. It's a SafeTeam cruiser westbound—its scarlet beacons strobing hi-vis banditry deterrence.

Leepus keeps his head down. The cruiser slows but rolls on past.

Another fifteen minutes and it's raining. It's nearly midnight already—where the fuck is Lesta? Leepus pulls out his fone. He's still waving it around in search of a signal when the limo slithers kerbside in a whistle of turbine steam.

Lesta cracks his window—and a gold-tooth grin. 'Leepus, my brer. Long time no gabba, griz.'

'Right.' Leepus reaching to open the door. 'Let me get in out of the rain and we'll catch up while you dri—ah!'

Leepus looks up at the limo. He's sitting on his arse now—arm numb from wrist to shoulder.

Lesta squints down sly. 'Shit. Sorry, brer. I forget to flip off the NoJak.'

54

'Forget?' Leepus gets back awkward to his feet—his arm tingling but still useless.

'Distracted thinking how you mug me for a fokkin ingot with that chilli-eating prop bet—when I'm too krakkled to know any better.'

'You get sucked in by the odds, mate. Can't hold it against me for ever.'

'Nah.' Lesta winks. 'Evens now, I reckon.'

'So I'm safe to fucking get in?'

'Pick a door,' says Lesta. 'Inna back like a fokkin priv winna—or ridin' shotgun with the help.'

Leepus gets in the front. 'I don't mind sitting with you, mate—long as the loser doesn't rub off.'

'Loser?' Lesta shakes his head—checks the mirror and sets the limo rolling. 'An' here's me smooth-ridin' easy street,' he says five seconds later as the needle nudges ninety, 'while you wait mopeful at the fokkin bus stop in the rain.'

◊◊◊◊◊

8

Two hours into the game. Leepus on the balcony sitting out a couple of hands. It's time to enjoy a weedstick. The King of Clubs doesn't tolerate indoors smoking—he's got some kind of bonkers notion it's not healthy.

A commotion—the palace parkland suddenly floodlit. A pack of snarling warhounds contesting below on the jousting lists. A trespassing fox dismembered. The King's homegames are strictly invitation only.

The King's a major economic engine. Gambling chips are common currency for commerce in free Inglund. The King's card rooms are always busy—his cash games keep the money moving hand to hand. A modest rake from every pot adds up to considerable power.

The King's the master of his manor—loyal retainers manage operations from his palace.

But the King's a player too. It's his habit to socialise—mix up disparate movers and shakers at his regular poka round table. He likes to study them under high-stakes pressure—manipulate their alliances and exacerbate enmity. Any weakness he perceives is targeted for exploitation.

Leepus is dealt in from time to time to play loose cannon—unsettle equilibrium and provoke revealing behaviour. He separates winnas from losers.

The King gets solid intel from the deal and Leepus what he can win—plus the added value of the King's ongoing recognition of Shithole's territorial independence.

That's the customary set up. Tonight is a bit off script.

Six seats at the table. No player histories offered.

The King in seat one. He's a little tense—playing unusually tight. Not much banta or needle.

Seat two is Leepus aka 'Griz'. Currently it's empty.

Seat three's introduced as 'Jax'. A mercenary demeanour. Ferrety little fucker the colour of baked desert. Only goes with premium hands—bets out big and smashes resistance.

'The Numbers' takes seat four. A gaunt indoor complexion with grubby stubble-shadow—he's some sort of College infocrat and he plays like an accountant.

A fat man overloads seat six. He styles himself 'Big Bobby'. A GreenField lapel-pin leaks a little background. Bob's a local agrico exec—tonight's chosen chip-donator.

Seat five's a mystery. She presents herself as 'Sally'. But 'Sally' doesn't suit her. Leepus prefers 'Chilly'.

Chilly's accent isn't local. Neither is her dress sense. A lean body seductively sexless in a crisp black fashion jumpsuit. Cropped white hair. Pale eyes. And tiny little earlobes. A Citadel insider. She plays like a fucking razor.

And she seems to be picking on Leepus.

∞

A buffet inside the door. Leepus snags a couple of raw-fish snacks and a napkin. He eats one heading back to his seat—wraps and pockets the other.

Leepus sits and play continues.

A dozen or so hands go by—the chipstack skyline changing. Leepus takes Jax to a showdown—routs him on the river. Chilly deflates Big Bobby. The King nibbles away at The Numbers.

Leepus engages Chilly. Chilly parries—raises back. Leepus tries to read her but her face is a fucking mirror. He calls just to see what she's holding. Chilly's hands are long-legged spiders as she gathers his chips and stacks them.

Leepus is going to have to work harder.

Chilly bets out. Everyone folds but Leepus. He studies Chilly steady—catches a tiny eyelash tremor. A tell? Significant of strength—or weakness?

Leepus shoves. Chilly folds. Leepus starts to feel better. He studies Chilly harder.

∞

An hour more and Leepus is a little richer but no wiser. Jax and The Numbers are busted out. They're talking badbeats with Big Bobby at the bar now. The King's not really up or down. His heart and soul not in it.

Now Chilly's coming on strong. Leepus is almost rattled—every time their eyes meet she sucks up more information. Or at least that's what it feels like. The woman's not just a reader she's a fucking mental rapist.

With her perfect teeth and manicured talons—her tight-lipped calculation and hostile pheromone emanation. Chilly's definitely a player. And her game is interrogation.

Leepus cocks an eye at the King.

Sorry, says the King in body language. It's not that I want to screw you—but they put me under pressure.

The King's not ordinarily susceptible to pressure. Chilly's influence super-heavy. Leepus needs to get out from under. Sooner rather than later.

'Raise.' Leepus blank-staring Chilly.

Chilly's smile is microscopic. She calls. The King gets out of the way.

The flop leaves Leepus gutshot. He dwells—then bets out big.

Chilly's re-raise is even bigger.

All-in or muck then—Leepus looking for her tell.

Chilly's eyelash trembles. A pink tongue-tip moistens her lip. Leepus reaches for chips. He's just about to push them in when Chilly breaks her silence—launches tactical small talk. 'Soo, Griz.' Her voice wheedling girlish—almost doll-like. 'I'm a little concerned as to the whereabouts of Marcus. Can you share any information?'

Fuck. Leepus is nudged off-balance. A data-burst of suppressed recollections. An unsettling mental landslip.

Marcus.

A baby cosy at a milky breast provoking curious envy.

A young lad asleep in bed across a darkened childhood bedroom. Another reading late by torchlight.

A fit blond schoolboy winner on a pointless winter sports-field.

A soldier in a uniform—with medals.

Global trouble brewing. Chickens flocking home to roost. A die-hard man-of-action debates ugly futures with a cynic.

Two men with shared expectation of catastrophic convergence—one enacting a survival plan and the other sneering.

And then it all goes dizzy.

Leepus blinks his head clear—looks at Chilly. She knows he's got a read on her. She's trying to spook him off his hand.

Or maybe keep him on it.

'Marcus who?' says Leepus deadpan.

'Oh please.' Chilly smiles—an eerie kind of coquettish. 'It's just a simple question.'

'Okay.' Leepus is sure she's bluffing now. 'I'm all-in. If you win you can ask me another.'

'Call.' Chilly's smile's a white-enamel trap. She turns over her pat hand.

'Nice.' Leepus a fish on Chilly's hook now. She sets him up with a phony tell and he fucking buys it.

Only four cards in the deck to evade tricky conversation—and then only in the short term. Chilly's obviously a pro—guaranteed she's always reloading.

All eyes on the board. And—

Okay—the turn card hits. Leepus goes ahead.

The river doesn't help Chilly. Everyone takes it in.

'Someone shoot the goddamn dealer,' Chilly mutters icy. It's not apparent that she's joking.

'Nice move,' says Leepus conciliatory. 'I'm outplayed there on Fourth Street—thinking I catch you at it.'

'Right. Ninety-three percent I stay ahead.' Chilly smiles hard and slides back her chair. 'Can't say I'm happy to see you suck out.'

'Oh well. That's poka, ma'am.' Leepus winks and gathers chips. 'Even idiots sometimes get lucky.'

∞

Dawn—soft grey and coolly humid. Deer grazing in-between sparse palace-parkland trees. Their heads go up. Ears flick. And then they're bolting.

The complex bass of multiple airborne rotors. Rooks abandoning treetops.

Leepus on the garden terrace by an ornamental fishpond. Carp submarines ripple the surface. He drags a last gasp from his weedstick—flicks the roach mischievous into the water.

A coppery swirl of fins. Fat lips slurping. A bucket-mouth gapes and gurgles—re-submerges. The water momentarily untroubled—and then the roach pops up again. Leepus is mildly regretful of his prank. He turns away—watches Chilly's quadrocopter land on the lawn below.

Chilly lawnside on gravel apron. She's wearing a scarlet cape now—an incongruous flash of primary colour in the muted palette of early morning. She's talking to the King. Two praetorians with automatic weapons scan the hazy tree-line.

Downdraft picks up damp leaves and whirls them. Chilly's a black flagpole—her cape a wind-cracked banner.

Jax stepping up to Leepus' elbow. A whiff of sweat and grog. 'She takes it well, considering.'

'Considering what?' says Leepus.

'Warrior of the Republic—raised from birth to win, man.'

'Not everything goes to plan.'

61

'I'm you I worry about payback.'

Heavy motors throttling up to an arrhythmic crescendo—Chilly's transportation ascending. It turns away dark over palace—dissolves in morning murk.

'Appreciate the heads-up,' says Leepus as the decibels diminish. 'Any other insight to offer?'

'Careless talk costs lives, man.' But I'm happy to quote on a personal-security upgrade—if you want to insure for peace of mind.'

'I'm covered for close protection.'

'You must be referring to Mike.'

Leepus watches the King climb the steps from lawn to terrace. 'Mike?' He frowns. 'Mike who? Is he a friend of fucking Marcus?'

Jax shrugs. 'Just offering,' he says and turns away. 'Mike's good. But sometimes even the best of us get distracted and drop a bollock.'

'Okay. That's that,' says the King of Clubs to Leepus. 'Come and have some breakfast.'

'I'd rather have an explanation.'

'I know.' The King's uncomfortable—he follows Jax inside.

Leepus stands his ground. 'So what's it all about then?'

The King looks back from the threshold. 'No clue, brer. Her people just call and say she wants to play—and make sure Leepus is at the table.'

'People?'

'Sorry.' The King shrugs—circumscribes the palace with a flutter of his hand. 'Got a lot to lose here.'

'Fair enough,' says Leepus. 'Stuff your breakfast up your arse. Tell Lesta I'm in the limo.'

The King of Clubs lets Leepus get to the top of the terrace steps—calls, 'You could have a chat with The Numbers—if you don't mind sharing your ride.'

Leepus grunts noncommittal and walks on down. 'So I'll bank your winnings for you,' the King's voice booms from behind. 'And just so there's no bad feeling we'll forget the fokkin commission.'

∞

'Who's first?' asks Lesta over his shoulder.

The Numbers looks at Leepus beside him in the limo backseat—says, 'I've got an early meeting.'

'Fine by me.' Leepus shrugs. 'No need to delay College business.'

'Thank you.' The Numbers relaxes into padded leather. 'But I'm not acknowledging the job description.'

A wordless slow-rolling minute as the limo crunches gravel. The palace perimeter-berm topped with a high concrete slabwall. They hiss into an access tunnel. Blast gates open automatic. Lesta gives it a bit of steam—squirts them up the exit ramp directly onto the PayWay.

Intermittent car-trains roll the early-morning road—stakeholders trapped in auto-transit between high-security Heritage Hamlet and municipal duty-station.

The limo's turbine howls—cleaves traffic. Lesta stitching the car-trains with high-velocity vapour. Commuter composure fraying.

'So—they say if you can't spot the fish in the first ten minutes it must be you.'

'Yes,' The Numbers replies to Leepus. 'Someone should tell Big Bobby.'

'Big Bobby not a serious player there, I reckon.'

'Just dealt in to fatten the pot.'

A weight-based joke? Leepus checks The Numbers' face for sign of intended humour—finds his hypothesis unsupported. 'How do you read killa Jax, then?' he follows up.

'Not to be relied on. A brute force at the table—confrontation best avoided. But definitely a player.'

'Dangerous?'

'I'd say the probability is high—if he senses weakness.'

'That leaves you. And Republic Chilly.'

'You mean Republic Sally.'

'Whatever. I seem to catch her eye.'

'Yes. But don't be flattered. Sally's more harmer than charmer.'

'Romance not recommended?'

'How high's your threshold for pain?'

Leepus looks out the limo window. The fenced PayWay flanked by the ruined sprawl of NoGo. Intermittent anti-bandit towers. Traffic slowing for East Gate safety plaza. 'But if you were thinking about sending flowers,' he wonders aloud, 'what address would you put on the label?'

'Easy to see how you get in trouble', says The Numbers tapping fone-keys. He shows the screen to Leepus.

Leepus memorises the information. 'I don't look for it,' he says. 'It just gets dumped on my doorstep.'

'Maybe you should move your doorstep.'

'Horse already bolted.'

The Numbers raising an eyebrow. 'Good instinct. You might want to follow that thought.'

Leepus takes the hint. The limo rolls non-stop past gate congestion and into the priority tunnel. Leepus keeps his head down as camera-flash probes tinted windows. When he looks up they're in SafeCity. The streets here calm and ordered—strivas strolling around. They seem relaxed and healthy—contentedly imprisoned.

Leepus feels claustrophobic. 'So, this dead meat on my hillside is AWOL from some kind of incarceration?'

'A logical first assumption,' says The Numbers. 'But maybe it goes further.'

'Fugitive tagged with a tracker. Someone does them harm. Drone runs down the remains—calls in the 'fects to have a look. Seems pretty ABC to me. You're saying there's a twist?'

The Numbers doesn't deny it.

'So who owns the runner?'

'Who do you think?'

'Okay,' says Leepus. 'Republic property goes missing—Chilly's the skip-tracer. Absconder recovered in my manor. Obvious she needs to look at me—make sure I'm not part of the story.'

'An atypical happy ending.'

'No harm hoping, is there?'

'Problem is too many heads, chap,' says The Numbers. 'None of them the escaper's.'

'Heads?'

'Three.'

'What about bodies?'

'The same number—but explosively dismembered, then partially consumed by vermin.'

'Who are they?'

'Not a hundred percent on that—but it seems likely they're colleagues of Chilly's.'

'This tag on the absconder—implant or a bracelet?'

A ghost of a smile from The Numbers. 'Originally a bracelet. Implanted when they find it—deep inside a dead rectum.'

'Absconder with a sense of humour.'

'And a considerable degree of anger.'

'So who is this irate joker?'

'And more to the point, where are they?'

'Main gate, or round the corner?' asks Lesta from the front.

Leepus looks out at the College guardhouse—student prefects strutting their stuff.

'Round the corner,' says The Numbers. 'Reporting for duty with heavy stubble just reminds the upstarts that you're ageing.'

'So, a useful chat,' says Leepus. 'But I'm not seeing your percentage.'

'Administration arrogance can sometimes get a bit irksome.

Muddying the Republic's water aids the relief of tension.'

The limo at the kerb now—door sliding open. A pleasing melange of male-grooming aromas wafting nostalgic from a barbershop doorway.

'I'll leave it with you,' The Numbers says easing from the vehicle. 'Feel free to keep me updated via the King. But on the off-chance it all goes shit-shaped you're on your own.'

The Numbers gone now. Leepus considers his position—rubs stubbled chin with fishy fingers. He feels a little jaded.

Fishy? Leepus recalls the snack stashed in his pocket. He takes it out and leans down—stuffs a sliver of slimy salmon deep into the floor-level air vent. And then does the same with his fone.

Fuck Lesta and his NoJak stunt—with luck the bastard loses his mind before he tracks down the source of the stink.

'Straight back to rural squalor is it, brer?' says Lesta without turning round. 'Or d'you wanna tool around a bit—goggle the wonder of privilisation?'

Leepus doesn't answer.

'Just say the word,' Lesta presses. 'I'm always up for a spree, griz.'

The driver puzzled by continuing silence—he turns to look for an explanation. His puzzlement increases when he finds the backseat abandoned.

◊◊◊◊◊

9

Leepus at large in the heart of SafeCity. It's a spur of the moment decision—if he doesn't have a plan to follow it can't get pre-empted.

But spontaneity has its downside. Hitting an unlucky pop-up checkpoint gets him automatic rendition as a hostile infiltrator. Leepus needs to keep his head down until he can pick up a sterile passfone.

Municipal casinos along the river. The faded architectural splendour of rust-streaked concrete and grimed glass. Hives of anxious players peering into screenglo. They're grinding away in the money mines doing their digital duty—deploying tired algorithms to fund the Bank of Inglund.

Every stakeholder must contribute their full measure of blood or sweat. The hard-pressed Republic milks its cash cows hard. Dominions that miss dividend targets get aggressively disinvested—rolled back into catastrophe.

Inglund's municipalities under the gun. Productivity must be marshalled—industry encouraged. The College handles inspiration. The Prefecture does chastisement. Students torment the indigent and nip the heels of flagging strivas. Rough justice discourages disaffection—stiffens the resistance of timid souls unsettled by Liberty's distant howling.

A galley slave secure aboard a municipal ironclad—or a buccaneer freebooter adrift on uncharted deeps? Even if he has a choice Leepus opts for the Jolly Roger.

Emporia of imported goods surrounding an uptown plaza. Privs ebb and flow at leisure shedding surplus kripChip. They're all dressed up bright and pretty. Leepus in shabby greatcoat and mashed trilby with buzzard feather. He looks a bit out of place here. Liveried doormen check him wary.

A row of rickshaws on a rank. Lean youths in skintight leotards wait restlessly in harness. They massage massive muscled thighs—rub knotted calves with cramp oil.

Hiring a ride off meter could be a twennystripa—but Leepus is playing loose today and he doesn't feel like walking. He checks for busybodies and nobbles the first runner. A yellow fleck tapped into an outstretched palm from a shaker of tiny nuggets. An eyebrow cocked in wordless enquiry. The youth licks his lips—has a shifty shufti and nods Leepus into his rickshaw. 'Buys yuh half an hour, griz,' he says easing them into motion.

'Trot south, brer,' says Leepus. 'Preferably on roads less-travelled.'

∞

Leepus sitting back in the rickshaw absorbing urban atmospherics.

The runner's pavement foot-slap. Hard-tyre rumble. Creak of harness.

An avenue of scabby plane trees. Veg stalls line its centre—a parliament of market traders barking ration tariffs. Shops and services flanking.

The bloody breath of a butchery. PayPork guarding its entrance—checking wealthy carnivores one by one through a turnstile.

Not enough krip for red meat? EelDeel is taking delivery of a fresh slick squirming tank-full.

And BugBites NutriValu is alive with the chirrup of crickets.

But it's the smell of fruit that's making Leepus salivate. Fresh pineapple and banana. Some bold gambler's ship's come in from a place where the sun still shines.

A sudden change of direction. Prefects on patrol. The runner sees them before Leepus—swerves into cobbled narrows.

A left. A right. Another left. Gloomy storefronts flicking past. Occasional pedestrians about their modest business.

A bicycle repair shop.

An umbrella seller.

An erect red-neon penis flashing above a labial doorway. SexSerfs posed like half-dressed mannequins behind a dripping steamy window.

A Licensed Justice Broker.

A Benni's Blood Vat franchise: *Deposits Wanted. Top Rates Paid. Mandatory Disease Check.*

A Little Strivas Work School.

The warm doughy gust from a baker's.

DroneDoc diagnosis booth outside AffordaFarma.

A KashBak assessor's on a corner. The rickshaw turns it.

And a cleared bombsite that's now a kids' playpark. Sheer cliffs of brick surround it—loosestrife sprouting ragged purple from crumbled pointing. Remnants of painted plaster. Picture-frame ghosts. The memory of a chimney breast—tiers of dead fireplaces sucking heat from phantom rooms.

An OurFuture propaganda mural dominates the playspace: big sun rising bright and proud over green and pleasant Inglund. NOTHING TO FEAR, its slogan comforts, IF YOU KEEP YOUR BEHAVIOUR ABOVE SUSPICION.

A tangled swing hanging lopsided. A rusty climbing frame. Empty handcuffs dangle over bloodstained safety matting.

A rainstorm dusk descending. Lightning X-rays buildings—thunder shakes them. Leepus deep under cover of the rickshaw canopy. He looks out at a rolling cityscape crosshatched bleak by sleet.

A sudden desire for a blanket. Soft. White. Knitted. Scented with reassurance. Leepus closes his eyes. Now he's a baby blithe under pram hood. A naive new-arrival nestled in the moment—with absolutely no idea where the fuck he is or where he's going.

Foot-slap rhythm slowing. Stopped now. Leepus opens his eyes.

On the concrete shore of the flooded quarter—a skein of rhythmic honking geese wedging low over a wide grey lagoon. Rooftop reefs. Groynes of chimneys. A penthouse archipelago. Squalls writhing—

whipping up wavelets. Everything watercoloured.

The rickshaw runner bent and panting hands on hips. 'Thass as south as it gets, griz,' he says squinting up at Leepus. 'I's'll need another bitta yella to run yuh west or eastside.'

'That's all right,' says Leepus climbing out. 'I need to stretch my legs, mate.'

∞

Leepus picks an ad hoc route around the lagoon between abandoned waterfront buildings. Glass crunches jagged under sodden trodden weeds. Collapsed brickwork. Fallen girders. Snarls of rusty cable.

Pigeons clatter inside the hollowed shell of a flooded warehouse.

An acrobatic squirrel scampers a sagging highwire—yellow cat's-eyes watching from an overturned plastic barrel.

Mudlarks on the shoreline sift cold black ooze for treasure.

Lightning flickers in the depths of massive dark cloud-lanterns.

Twenty squelching minutes under a thunderous barrage. Leepus flailed by hailstone shrapnel—his greatcoat drenched and hat bedraggled.

An inlet—estuarine. Lagoon overflowing the old canal. A bridge offers welcome shelter—ivy curtain trailing from its ancient low brick arch. Leepus ducks beneath it. Squats on his heels on the gritty towpath. Pulls out a weedstick and lights it.

Antique iron on the bridgework corners. Horizontal notches carved by patient straining ropes. Centuries of stoic horses hauling laden boats and butties. An artery of commerce once—and then of recreation. Choked by silt and trash now—narrowboats long sunk. A derelict linear wilderness of covert navigation. A green lane sneaking in amongst the eastside tenements. Back access to Leepus' urban safe-house.

The weedstick warms his mind if not his body. Leepus takes the strain again—plods on down timeless towpath.

Emerald and sapphire: kingfisher iridescence pathfinding the overarch of trees. Leepus follows into gloom.

The spoor of fox and deer. Human footprints too—some bare and others booted. Fellow discreet travellers keep the towpath nettles trodden.

A thoughtless mile.

And now another bridge ahead—brick buildings ranged around it.

A lock to pass by first. Old oak gate jammed shut—path blocked by balance beam. There's a ghostmark scratched on its heavy timber—an iconic eyeball tipping the wink to surreptitious overwatch.

Infiltration's a dangerous game. Players look out for each other. Leepus ducks and covers his face—fades into path-side foliage and picks up a detour ratrun.

Rusty fence with bent steel-paling—a swag of orange plastic flags the gap. Leepus squeezes through it—comes out on embankment above area workhouse.

A knotted-cable mountain inside a high-walled yard. Half-starved indigents in lean-tos strip off casings. Skeletons clothed in sweat-streaked coal-dust stoke a furnace. A crucible of molten copper—volcanic incandescence. Leepus feels its heat. Tired now and chilled he's tempted to bask—take a moment to catch his breath.

But now there's a siren whooping. A heavy engine growling. Brake-squeal on the bridge then. Shouted orders. Slamming doors. Boots clumping down abutment steps—doubling along the towpath. Radio squawk and weapon rattle.

Leepus on the move again considerably excited. A bit of slither and slide. A heavy-breathing scramble along the shadowed workhouse wall-side. A drainage culvert under the road. He crouches and duck-walks through it. Smears oozing stalactites of algae. Snags spiderwebs with stubble.

Wet ground between tenements and canal here—Leepus splashes across it. He lopes into the mouth of a cobbled alley—checks back for hue and cry.

No eager prefects on his arse—and better still no dogs. Leepus pushes on. Side-stitch under his ribs and an irritating knee-throb. There's a lookout balloon in the murky mid-distance tethered over the eastside perimeter fence. He takes his bearing from it—zigzags a grid of alleys.

And finally he's there.

A mossy-walled enclosure of dense dark holly and laurel. A rusty wrought-iron gate jammed open. A peeling sign beyond it.

"THE RIVER"

RETIRED GAMBLING-LADIES' REFUGE

Leepus walks on leaf mould over gravel. It's a dreary redbrick gothic townhouse with boarded windows. A porch shadows its plate-steel front door. He steps up and prods at the keypad—buzzes himself inside.

The first three floors are abandoned. Stale draughts roll dust-balls through them. Redundant paper drifts. Leepus climbs the stair.

There's a camera on each landing. And Lucifer at the summit.

Leepus stopped just short of the top by deep purple eyes and yellow teeth—a panted gust of meat breath. Man and beast on a level. Lucifer all a-quiver. Leepus leery. 'Come on then,' calls offstage Jasmine. 'He won't bite the hand that feeds him.'

'I'm more worried about the throat.'

'Good boy.' Jasmine whistles dry. 'Let the scaredy-cat by.'

The dog looks disappointed—turns and pads the hall. Leepus follows—ducks his head round the doorjamb of Jasmine's boudoir. 'Alright, gal?' he asks.

Jasmine abed under mounded blankets and wrapped in shawls—in a red woollen hat with a bobble on it. A shisha pipe still smouldering on the bedside table. 'All the worse for seeing you, babe,' she says waving him in. 'So where are my bloody flowers?'

'You don't like flowers.'

'Still would be a nice gesture. Considering it's my birthday.'

'Every day's your birthday, you fucking shameless freeloader.'

'Ten years go by since you lose that bet. It's time you stop crying about it.' Jasmine beckons—presents plump cheek for kissing.

'Who knows you'll drag it out so long.' Leepus' lip-brushes powdery

72

skin. 'Terminal cancer my arsehole.'

'Be careful what you wish for,' says Jasmine smiling sweet. 'And always ask for a second opinion.'

'Point taken.' Leepus straightening too fast—his vision speckled and face-blood draining. 'So—chance of a bite and a reviver?'

'There's grog and a selection of herbals—but you'll have to run down to the corner for something you can chew on.' Jasmine frowns. 'I'd have a wash and brush-up first though—unless piss-pickled walking dead man is really the look you're after.'

∞

Jasmine sitting up in bed tucking into a nice eel curry—Leepus on a chair beside her. They're watching 'Beat the Hangman' on interactive SafeCity Cable. Nine condemned felons in a sandpit wearing only blindfolds and tattooed numbers. They're all gripping melee weapons. The last of them still standing wins a slot on 'Run Krim, Run!'

'So pick me a winner,' says Jasmine.

'Fukkoff,' says Leepus with his mouth full. 'How low do you think I go?' He pauses to chew and swallow. 'Besides, I'm a mug when it comes to sports bets.'

'Okay. Bad taste. I'll turn it off.'

Jasmine does it. They finish their curries in silence.

Then Jasmine says, 'You do your best to stay on solid ground. But sometimes it gets so overwhelmingly insane it just sucks you down.'

I know.' Leepus pours Jasmine a shot of grog. 'But happy birthday anyway. Here's to a better tomorrow.'

'Thanks.' Jasmine knocks it back. 'I'm only sixty-nine, you know. But I feel like fucking ninety.'

They sit another little while in silent contemplation.

'Confession,' says Leepus. 'I'm shit at dates. I've no idea it's your birthday.'

'Don't feel bad, babe,' says Jasmine winking. 'As far as I know it isn't.'

'Bravo,' says Leepus. 'Fish in a fucking barrel.'

'Don't be arsey.' Jasmine pouts. 'It's only a bit of flirting.'

'I'm feeling kind of fragile.'

'Oh?'

'Playing at Sick Dick's. I neglect to pay attention and wake up lost and dizzy. Head still in a bit of a whirl now.'

'Neglect?'

'Yes.'

'Idiot. And Mike must be asleep.'

'It's Mike's night off.

'Night off to do what?'

Unclear. She doesn't say and I'm too shy to ask.'

'She off again tonight?'

Leepus nods.

'So?' Jasmine frowns. 'You worried? Want me to run her down?'

'It's not top of my list.'

Jasmine waits.

Leepus lights a weedstick—inhales rich smoke then coughs and says, 'Mike's a minor mystery. It's fucking Chilly that spooks me.'

'Chilly?'

'A player for the Republic. Turns out she wants to take me on, leverages the King to make it happen.'

'Oh? How does that go?'

'I get lucky.'

'But?'

'She's got some kind of deep read on me. Gets the needle into a sore spot—digs up old stuff I've forgotten.'

'How old?'

'Fucking prehistoric, gal. Antediluvian.'

'Really?' Jasmine frowns doubtful. 'I run you half a dozen times and never find a footprint. Maybe you leak a tell, and she grabs a spot to bluff it?'

'Feels more like she's exploiting partial intel.'

'So what's this prodigy's endgame?'

'Unconfirmed—but rumour has it there's a person of interest fugitive from a scene of significant carnage.'

'Rumour?'

'Carnage is actual, within a stone's throw of the tower—POI a steer from a sympathetic College player.'

'How sympathetic?'

'Remains to be seen—but I don't read him as malicious. And he gives me a marker on Chilly.'

'Any other players?'

'A military contractor at the table—odds-on he's got some kind of stake in the metagame.'

'Domestic distractions? Excepting this local carnage everything's calm in Shithole?'

'A regular Arcadia—if you overlook a young rover girl abducted from the parish, and her clan counting down the hours to an orgy of blud and compo. And Mike off somewhere half the time playing fucking solo.'

'So—' A twinkle in Jasmine's eye. 'Enough to keep your old mind active.'

'All grist to my tireless mental mill, gal,' Leepus says and yawns. 'But extra insight's always welcome if you feel like putting a shoulder to the wheel.'

'Fetch my jar of working mixture and reload the fucking shisha.' Jasmine leans down and gropes under the bed—hauls out her antique dashboard with cobwebs trailing. 'You'll need to give me a precise timeline, and more focus on the detail. Then you can haul your arse off to bed and leave me to diddle my data.'

∞

Leepus with his head down in hypnagogic limbo. Random imagery

75

entertains him.

Driving in an old SUV with some children and their mother. Rioters break from a burning building—run through teargas. A tattooed girl in a tiger mask cornered against their vehicle—cop batons beating her down. Wipers smear her blood on the windshield as he steers for the moral high ground.

Rain. A sodden urban sports-field. Tyre-churned turf. Earthworks beside a fresh-dug pit bookended by broken goalposts. A tipper-truck backs up to it grunting filthy diesel. Hydraulics whine. The dump-bed inclines. Tangled corpses cling—then slither out through the swinging tailgate. He's supposed to meet the children here but he's late and he can't find them.

He's tramping a grass ridgeway overlooking urban sprawl. Opaque sky—invisible ghost-jets howling around it. Fire-flowers vaporise buildings. Black smoke pillars rise and topple leeward. A mockery of magpies flees a ragged timpani echo. He counts seven of them chuckling—kiting ruffled black and white. Three for the little lost girl. Four more for the boy.

Now the serious rain's set in and it isn't stopping. Floodwater rinsing the world clean—flushing it all away. The money and the houses. The books. The cars. The churches and the flags. The bloated corpses of the drowned. The rafts of fighting rats. Nothing left worth clinging onto—he surrenders to the maelstrom. It squirts him into the whirlpool. Sucks him to the bottom. Holds him down asleep ten years spun deep in the dizzy dark.

◊◊◊◊◊

10

Leepus wakes in bed and it's still raining. Eaves-drips sprinkle past his window. Gutter downpipes gurgle. The dirty glimmer seeping in suggests it's already morning. He burrows under his pillow.

A creaking stair-tread stirs him some time later. A bony finger pokes his shoulder. He opens a vaguely hopeful eye but the day is no less gloomy.

'Brew here for you, mista.' The voice singsong—male but girlish. 'Milady says you need to rise and shine now—and then you should look at your messages while I help her complete her toilet.'

'Who the fuck is Milady?' says Leepus sitting up grumpy.

'My dear respected client, of course.' The boy is heavily muscled— wears crisp white shorts held up by red braces over a skintight matelot vest. A tidy little nurse's cap screens precisely planted cornrows. His hands are skinned in latex. 'I am Angel O'Mercy— Milady Jasmine's personal carer.'

'Very nice.' Leepus declines the offered handshake. 'Tough fucking job you've got there mate, but I s'pose some twat needs to do it.'

'Do enjoy your brew, sir.' Angel smiles tight—then exits.

∞

Cold eel-curry's not an ideal breakfast—a tumbler of grog required to help it down. Leepus enjoys volatile fishy repetitions as he types his dead-letter login and opens a message from Mike: *Deep shit and you're well in it. Limo trashed. Lesta kneecapped. K of C not happy. Enough of this bastard radio silence—time you come up with a plan.*

Leepus mulling the information. A damp gust of soap and

toothpaste—Jasmine rolling up behind him in her Angel-powered wheelchair. She's saying, 'Looks like your girl's still on the job at least part-time, then.'

'Just as well—Milady,' says Leepus sniffy. 'Budget won't stretch to multiple carers.'

'Don't be such a tight arse,' Jasmine says as Angel parks her bedside. 'A sick old girl's got a perfect right to a fit young chap to plump her pillows now and then and cheer her up. It comes under fucking subsistence.'

Leepus grunts—waits while Angel scoops Jasmine from wheelchair to mattress and tucks her in. Then he waits some minutes more as Angel stands by impassive. 'Run along now, there's a love,' Jasmine eventually prompts. 'The nasty griz won't hurt me.'

'I'm supposed to give you your pedicure.' Angel hovers persistent. 'Deviation from the contracted care-plan is liable to attract demerits.'

'Fukksake, mate.' Leepus fishes out a tenna—offers it to Angel. 'There's a slot shop round the corner. If you really need to push your luck, fukkoff and do it there.'

Angel gestures refusal. 'Sorry, mista. Gambling on company time's an instadismissa—plus mandatory tenstripa.'

'Take Lucifer out to do his business.' Jasmine pats a hard round buttock. 'You can trim my toenails later, dear—when we're all snuggled up on our own.'

Angel milks it—sighs. 'If you insist, Milady,' he says and glances disdainful at Leepus.

Leepus shakes his head wordless as the boy finally makes himself scarce.

'I know he's a silly arse and a bit possessive,' says Jasmine. 'But he's got lovely warm strong hands.'

'Oh well.' Leepus sparks a weedstick—raises smoke. 'That'll be a comfort then, when they're clenched round your fucking throat.'

'Sweet of you to be jealous, babe—but the way I wake up feeling some days that might be considered a blessing.'

Leepus considers extending the repartee with a reference to

78

KashBak—declines harshness in favour of smoke inhalation and waits for Jasmine to update his worldview.

'So,' she says in her own sweet time. 'I look up 'Chilly' for you.'

'The ID-string The Numbers gives me turns out kosha?'

'She's superficially invisible—but deft forensic archaeology uncovers persistent traces in the deep security strata.'

'Republic player, then. We already know that.'

'Patience—there's more.' Jasmine leans back into her pillows and shuts her eyes as if scrolling data on closed eyelids. 'She's Cohort Commander INTL-XTRK, Honor-Trublood—given name Atalanta.'

'Let's stick with 'Chilly', shall we?'

'Age thirty-four. No genealogical record, but she's inducted as a high-aptitude cadet from an early Republic foundling program—so likely orphaned by execution. Girl does good in the Legions—catches a promotion thermal. Her last five active-duty tours she's coordinating elite glean-teams way down south in the Tropic of Hate. Always seems to stay hands-on though. Must like to get up close and sweaty with those fanatic planners of evil—hacking into their neural networks, filleting out mycelial conspiracy and interdicting bio-bombers. Her performance rating's 'superlative' at a recent competence assessment.'

'She can't be that fucking good. The Republic doesn't waste interrogation adepts on the waterlogged minds of old Inglund.'

'She's getting a bit senior—maybe jumps before she's nudged. Opts for status work—finds something in the deepfreeze with un-exploited value that she can milk for a heritage citation.'

'So Chilly finesses her own assignment?' Leepus sits on the bed and lights a smoke.

'It's still conjecture.'

'I don't read her as straw in the wind. Clear she's got an axe to grind. Any detail on her mission?'

Jasmine appropriates the weedstick. 'Your initial hypothesis checks out. She's having a second look at detainee AZ002384/1020-ABSCON. No personal history accessible but it's an early number. AZ is one of the northern offshore black sites. The suffix is recent—confirms the POI is a runner.'

'This 'AZ'—an absconder before or after Chilly takes an interest?'

'No precise information—percentage call says after.'

'And why am I on her radar?'

'No clue there either. Sorry babe. Perhaps she picks up something from the studs who secure the bodydump. I'm guessing they get facial vid—maybe capture a rheumy iris?'

'Yeah, but you say yourself I don't leave any footprints. All my historic data's rinsed.'

'It is from Dominion records, but the Republic's memory is longer. There could be a smear of digital DNA lingering in some obscure cached archive-fragment I can't get at.'

'So I guess I need to talk to Chilly. Any backdoor I can use to surprise her?'

'Unwise. She's working out of the Citadel. Lion's dens and so on. I can give you her internal mailbox.'

'Cool.'

'But if you're asking for an assignation I'd pick a virtual venue. Signs are Chilly's worked up bit of a lather about you. If you give her premature facetime she might struggle to control her passion.'

'The shit with Lesta and the King's limo?'

'Obvious she drops snatchas on your fone. And then there's the stuff with The Numbers.'

'What happens to The Numbers?'

'The College is all a-rattle—seems some hapless chap gets rudely snagged from his barber's chair mid-shave. His head falls out of a clear blue sky an hour later, cracks the drill-square concrete, seriously dents the composure of young prefects on parade.'

'Ouch. Chilly playing Republic hardball. No talking out of school, kids.'

'And that's about all I have, babe.' Jasmine pats Leepus' hand. 'Maybe I glean a bit extra if I know what old bones she digs up to spook you?'

Leepus disdains her bait. 'What about this sly bastard 'Jax'?'

'Mercenary—like you say, babe. Major Arturo Ajax. He heads Discrete Force Projection. They're scalphunt contractors, giving gainful employment to blood-happy ex-ComplianceCorp killas— doing wet work, exemplary reprisals, renditions and special logistics.'

'Right.' Leepus walks to the window—stares out at steady rain.

'I'm sensing you're not happy, babe,' says Jasmine.

'It's all a bit wide-angle.' Leepus turns back frowning. 'I prefer the world in a smaller frame.'

'I know,' says Jasmine. 'It's hard for us old-schoolers when someone stirs the pot. We think we've made the jump okay from then to fucking now, nailed the lid down on what's lost—but it's all still festering away there, buried deep inside.'

'Steady girl, you're showing your soft centre.' Leepus swoops over Jasmine—surprises her lips with a kiss. 'It's tempting but I'm not buying. What's gone is gone—and I say gone for good. The past is where the dead live and tomorrow never comes. Now is where shit happens. Let's just try to keep it fun.'

'Okay. Whatever you say.' Jasmine's not sure how to take him. 'But maybe grog for breakfast's not the ideal choice, babe. You get a bit weird when you're pissed.'

∞

Leepus in the cellar now picking random tools from the safe. The front door above buzzing open. Angel creaking up the stair—Lucifer scrabbling ahead.

Fresh passfone reassuringly charged with a stack of kripChip. A half-spoon of extra nuggets. A mini blowpipe and wallet of darts. A tube of weapons-grade LaxBoms. Leepus loads greatcoat pockets. Then picks up a stylish ebony StunStik—stands brooding distracted in the half-light swinging it by its pommel.

Angel. Angel is a problem. Jasmine's let the boy get too deep inside her bunker. Her neediness is understandable. But also fucking

81

reckless.

'Pre-empt the risky fucker fuckin' pronto.' Mike's voice in Leepus' head. 'Disappear the caring cunt's arse.'

Leepus recognises Mike's pragmatic wisdom. But chopping off Jasmine's 'lovely warm strong hands' seems a little bit harsh—and probably counter-productive. Jasmine's likely to get touchy—bitter and twisted even. Maybe she's even so pissed off she decides to do some damage. Like giving him up to Chilly. In the cold light of day she's sorry but by then it's way too late—Mike's already padding up the stairs to cut off her fucking head.

Leepus doesn't like that dismal destination. He derails his runaway paranoia—young Angel gets a letoff.

∞

There's long-term empathy between Leepus and Jasmine. It begins among the ruins. The last bloody wave of the Reduction finally on the ebb. Both of them left standing. Sort of.

Jasmine's an insider in early days of the College. She wants to rebuild dear old Inglund—thinks intel-led rough justice is the best way to beat the crazies. She's sadly deluded in hindsight. Her good intentions subverted. Inevitable really—but Jasmine's no more to blame than any other freaked-out survivor. No one's thinking all that straight in the shock of aftermath.

Once Jasmine's in she's in. But analysis is stressful. She plays poka for relaxation—comes up hard against Leepus one fine evening at Sick Dick's. Intrigue sparks across the card table. Passion flares in bed.

Leepus has some dark internal corners of his own—weird dues he needs to pay. He tweaks his moral balance working pro bono loss-adjustment—wrangling improvised justice for random crime-predated poors denied affordable cop-cover. Mike chips in the muscle. It's a kind of mutual rehab. Mike confused by blood-soaked years of dirty warfare. Leepus deranged by dizzy.

Jasmine comes on board to handle intel. She's happy to be included—gets off dipping the database to do undercover good. But nothing lasts forever. Student zealots sniff a rat. A Loyalty Tribunal discharges her with case unproven but her College days are over.

And the blemish on her record evaporates her pension.

Leepus acknowledges some duty of care—although it's only fair to say that grog's a significant factor in Jasmine's downfall too. And the poka. And the fact she's no spring chicken—and the kids of OurFuture are shoving.

Jasmine hangs onto some College library backdoor keys. She still freelances knowledge to Leepus—but the job doesn't bring in near enough to sustain the style to which she's accustomed.

But Jasmine's not the sort to let bad luck get her down. Not when the cards run ugly. Not when her legs stop working. Not when she stops wanting Leepus and he stops wanting her. Jasmine's too proud for charity but she's not eager for KashBak either.

So Jasmine ponders her options—decides on a sly little wager. She takes her time with the setup. A grog diet. Cosmetics eschewed. A pharma bill on expenses. The stoic demeanour of a brave lonely soul afflicted by cruel disease. Jasmine doesn't exactly spell it out—but Leepus is easily led to believe that the poor old girl expects to cash-out sooner rather than later.

One night she cooks him a 'last supper'. Fond reminiscence. Some blinked-back tears. A bottle of Yellow Scorpion grog and a bushel of sandbag weed. And then Jasmine gets the cards out and shuffles up. 'Best out of three heads-up, then?' she offers matter-of-fact.

'Why not?' agrees Leepus bleary. 'What's the pot?'

'You lose, you pay my way until I snuff.' Jasmine lays it out straight.

Leepus dwells a minute—does the maths and shrugs. 'Okay, but what if I win?'

'I trot off to KashBak. You rake whatever I make.'

'Fair enough, gal.' Leepus winks. 'Every little helps.'

But of course he doesn't win. And Jasmine doesn't die. She costs him a fucking fortune laying around in her sickbed forever.

'Sly cunt stacks the fuckin' deck for fuckin' sure,' Mike says later when she stops laughing. 'And you're a soft twat to let her.'

Leepus can't deny the charge but he likes to think he's big enough to see the funny side.

Leepus on the move now down a greasy backstreet. He's feeling dappa with his StunStik tip-tapping sharp in the murk.

It's time to depart SafeCity. A clean passfone is normally enough for the gateGoons to nod him out. But Leepus assumes his ugly mug is now uploaded and tagged for capture—courtesy of Chilly. Just his luck today he picks a trap with working I-Ball.

It's not a good spot to gamble. The stakes are high and Chilly's in position eager for action. Dangling his tender biometrics under her nose is asking to get them snapped off.

Leepus opts to go underground. He taps his way down Justice Street—cuts a dash across Gallows Place. Then he saunters up the Avenue of Light and fones through the Strivas' Peace Park turnstile.

Five minutes nodding at priv joggers among tired trees and despondent flowers—then Leepus exits onto Endeavour Way and hops aboard a trolley. He rides it out to the ragged fringe and disembarks at Hope Market—climbs mud steps down the embankment into a shady depression. A SafeTran moaning past above. Ragged indigents clumped below on the puddled waste-ground.

Leepus swims through shoals of would-be workfish. Imploring fingers pluck his sleeve. Hungry eyes appeal. Leepus keeps his head down. He's not recruiting serfs today—and he doesn't need a cheap kidney.

A food hall hidden under dripping railway arches. Leepus pushing in. Low light—a fug of sweat and broth-steam. Condensation slicks cold black concrete. Intermittent wall-screens loop a bland tutorial: a stern young Motivator reminding the hope-limited of the option of liquidation—while a big old clock with a jerky hand counts down their value.

Leepus at the counter now. A sulky girl with lardy skin scurries to attend him. He buys a brace of KuppaCheers—tips large and gets rewarded with a tight-lipped toothless smile.

He needs a navvi with the Knowledge to taxi him out safe through the tubes. This service seriously clandestine. Providers risk death with pain. But there's bound to be some young dodja here hungry to hook him up. Leepus just needs to run up a flag. He sips from one soggy paper cup—sets the other to cool inviting beside him on the Formica.

The big old clock-hand jerking. Leepus bets he gets a bite before it ticks round one more minute. He counts off twenty-three seconds— then a scrawny kid with a weepy eye shifts over and picks up the cup.

◊◊◊◊◊

11

'Juss eight good bitsa yella, griz.' The navvi dangles balance scales.

Leepus lifts his nugget shaker—hesitates and asks, 'Bubblesuit and rebreather included?'

'Yuss.'

Leepus taps flakes into the pan until the balance levels. 'Nice,' he says and looks up sharp. 'I'm expecting to pay more.'

The navvi misses a beat. 'Dodja sez yurra gen'rus tippa,' he recovers with a wink.

'Okay,' says Leepus shrugging. 'Got to respect a man with gamble.'

∞

An old pump-house over-crept by dark-green ivy—Leepus inside it with the navvi and his monkeys. The monkeys get Leepus bubblesuited. He stows his top clothes and kit in the DriBag—clips it to his belt.

The navvi looks like a baggy seal. He flaps a rubber flipper. The monkeys scurry—slide back the heavy tube cap. Subterranean water gurgles throaty.

The navvi hooks Leepus onto a guide-leash—says, 'Don't go gettin' claustro. You start up flappin' an' squawkin' I's'll fukkn drown you certain. Fukkn 'fects got ears down there that trip off 'cussion charges.'

'Relax,' says Leepus. 'I'm easy money. You float us through on a nice clean route I'm bobbing along happy behind you.'

The navvi says no more. He pulls down the hood of his rebreather—

waddles over to the tube-hole and descends rungs of rusty rebar. Leepus slips on OwlEyes and adjusts his own rebreather. He waits for the navvi to tug on the leash and then follows him below.

The monkeys slide the cap shut.

∞

Leepus up to his waist in tube slime—clammy rubber water-pressured skintight to his legs. Some might find this sensation pleasing. Leepus doesn't.

OwlEyes are only marginally effective in total darkness. Bioluminescence silvers the navvi's wake. A faint green sheen of algae blooms on tunnel tiles. Leepus reaches out a gloved hand—smears a dark ghostmark in the shimmer. And then another at the first corner. He's not planning on needing to find his way back alone but bad things sometimes happen.

Ten minutes crouching and wading—his knees already aching and Leepus is starting to sweat. Facemask dripping condensation. Throat rasping—a taste of recycled foulness. He wonders if it's halitosis or marsh-gas leaking in.

More corners. A sudden plunge into deeper water. A thrilling squirm between thigh and wall. Leepus thinks of albino eels—how big and pale they might grow here.

A dark buoy in the swirl there: the navvi's head above water sucking under a low arch. Leepus paddles against the flow. A gloved hand breaks the surface and clamps squid-like over his skull—submerges him in the urgent surge of a lightless torrent.

A few moments of helpless terror without sense of up or down. Leepus thrashes to the surface—finds bottom and stumbles wheezy up the slope of a concrete beach. Its surface is strangely spongy.

A glare of magnified natural light from a narrow grille above. A tideline of rotten flotsam. Leepus idly identifies drowned cats and rats and dogs. And then he looks for his guide.

The navvi's not in sight. Leepus tugs slack leash. Ignoring his read is reckless—the cheap ticket is obviously shwonki and now the bastard's cut him loose. He tugs some more—and faster. Feels the weight of solid resistance.

One last haul. The navvi breaching whale-like—wallowing up onto the carrion beach. Leepus is both relieved and aggravated. The navvi's mush is blurred by mask-steam but it looks like he's laughing his arse off.

Another five minutes of mazy wading. Leepus follows the leash. He's getting a bit tired now.

Then a roar of plunging water—a second rebar ladder to climb through a vertical cascade. The navvi ahead breaks the force of the flow or Leepus probably doesn't make it.

A mouth of crumbling concrete. Daylight beyond it. The navvi squirms through the gap and Leepus follows—corroded steel-bar tooth-stumps snarl the slack of his clumsy suit.

Leepus is blinded by daylight. He pulls off the hood of his rebreather and stows the OwlEyes. Veined green umbrellas of gunnera overhang a shallow stream. Mangled shopping trolleys choke it. They scramble. Leepus is all but exhausted now. His knees are weak and his heart erratic—skin rubbed raw by sweaty rubber.

An acre of black ooze sprouting thickets of scrub willow. Rusted truck-hulks mired to their axles. Leepus slithers and stumbles in the relentless wake of the navvi.

A startled heron croaks and beats up heavy through the rain.

A concrete wall at shoulder height—scuffed plastic fender along it. Leepus is reminded of a boat dock. The navvi vaults up spry—sits with both legs swinging. 'So this is as far as I go, griz,' he says. 'Jump up here an' de-bubble.'

Leepus tries but he can't do it.

'Fukksake.' The navvi stands—hauls Leepus up on the leash. 'Useless fukkn crip,' he says. 'Orta go fer fukkn KashBak.'

'So I'm guessing you've given up on the tip then,' says Leepus sprawled at the feet of the navvi—the 'dock' now revealed as the loading bay of an old Jumbo's ShopDeeLite. A derelict square-mile of melted siding and scorched breezeblock. Incinerated homeware spilled from aisles of toppled racking. Commercial desolation re-greened by abundant thickets of hogweed.

'No diss, griz,' says the navvi shifting position. 'Time passes an' I's

89

not easy out late in NoGo.'

Leepus rolls down his bubblesuit—stands skinny in his skivvies. Cool drizzle soothes his sweat rash. The navvi unzips the DriBag— shakes out Leepus' clothes.

Leepus has his trousers on but only one foot booted when he clocks the overseer. The navvi's looking guilty—scrabbling kit together.

Leepus says, 'So how much am I worth, prick?' palming the mini blowpipe from his pocket.

'Sorry, griz. Not personal,' says the navvi set to go. 'A letoff cred is hard to resist when yurr doin' big-risk bizzniz.'

'Only myself to blame, I s'pose. It's not like I don't see it coming.' Leepus grabs a lungful of air and loads the blowpipe. 'But you're the treacherous low arsehole who spits on the Code of the Lawless.'

The navvi taking off now—Leepus lifts the pipe to his lips and huffs disgusted. His target squelches on through the ooze. The barb lodged unnoticed in the back of his neck is tufted with fluorescent yellow. Yellow, muses Leepus—that's a 'Kreepa'. Give it fifteen minutes and the rat-bastard's brain is bubbled. Hard to navigate the tubes when you're fighting the screaming horrors. Leepus isn't betting big on the scrote ever getting to play his letoff.

∞

Boots laced and greatcoat flapping now—Leepus loping through the ruins. No doubt Chilly's snatchas are hanging handy. He needs to dodge the overseer before it puts them on him. He's halfway down a sooty aisle of melted flatscreens when the fucker loses patience. Lets go a couple of parachute-stunnas. Double-smacks him into blackness.

∞

Leepus wakes in a world without sound. He's got a bad headache and a nosebleed. Three all-action paramils pose over him statuesque. Contractors—kitted out natty in surplus Republic Camo/Mk3-urban. Armoured gloves grip ugly weapons. Laser-dots spot his chest.

Leepus tries to be polite—but maybe his greeting translates flippant because one of them stamps on his hand. Another's mouth is moving—probably issuing curt instructions. But Leepus' ears are not working yet and his lip-reading skills are deficient. The speaker sneers and lowers his weapon—leans down and grips Leepus' windpipe in clenched fist. Leepus gags—shares the goon's disgusted POV of his own swollen and distended tongue reflected in heavy-duty mirror goggles as the bastard hauls him erect. And then the third of the unfriendly fuckers completes his sensory deprivation. Rolls a tight black rubberised transit-cocoon down from his head to his ankles.

So now he's a prick in a condom.

He waddles squeaky from the scene of capture. Gun-muzzle rib-jabs guide him. Leepus finds the situation mildly creepy. He suspects a taste for sick S&M is a common feature of rendition-tech profiles.

Five minutes of silent shuffling suffocation. A pregnant stationary moment before a sensation of sudden commotion. Multiple percussions pummel Leepus' solar plexus. He sways uncertain—then the hot slap of a major shockwave knocks him on his arse.

The cocoon a bit too snug now. Heat-shrunk fabric wraps his face. Leepus flexes and gnaws in breathless confinement. Eventually the tightened latex splits and gives birth to his grateful head. He emerges into a dreary damp dusk enlivened by violent action.

A wilderness of car park spreading in front of the derelict mall. A blown-up ShuvTruk blazing cheery.

One contractor sprawled prone—his heavy-duty mirror goggles punched through by a crossbow bolt. A viscous dribble of eye blood.

A human torch in the mid-ground dancing on the spot. Frantic flapping arms implying an urgent desire for flight. Leepus detects faint screaming beyond his deafness. He guesses its shrill origin is in the throat of this hapless chap.

The third paramil is a lively sprinter—but the horror-dog pack jumping at his arse still seems likely to have him for dinner.

And then there's the overseer: an eye lit flickering green—it's locked in a wireframe pyramid projected by ground-based lasers. It tries evasive manoeuvres but it's baffled by the dazzle. Its gyros get the wobbles.

A giant stained-white Jumbo sculpture astride the car park entrance. Fading lettering on its flank invites infantilised consumers to 'DIG DEEP AND BUY BIG FOR INGLUND'. The overseer swooping low now—Leepus tracks its swift descent to elephantine destruction.

His hearing getting better by the minute.

The snuffle and growl of dogs somewhere worrying a carcass.

Belch of igniting fuel. Shriek of heat-tortured steel.

A shrill of ululation.

Leepus vulnerable in cocoon bondage. He exercises knees and midriff—strains up to a seated position.

Vague black figures in shifting robes moving eerie through drifting oil-smoke—BurkaBabes approaching. Some of them swing choke chains. Others carry crossbows.

A crescent of graceful shadow-girls focused on helpless Leepus. The ones with crossbows point them at him. Another fishes out a flask from mysterious folds of clothing—pours liquid onto wadded rag. Dark eyes glint through a veil-slit as the slight figure stoops toward him. Leepus tries to grab a read but there's no information leaking.

'Thanks,' says Leepus as a gloved hand cups his nape. 'I'm not going to be dog food, am I?'

'Shush!' the woman hisses and smothers his face.

A sweet oily fragrance pervades. Leepus doesn't struggle long. The tranquillity of oblivion is a surprisingly welcome relief.

◊◊◊◊◊

12

The giggle and squeal of small children.

Sparrow chittachatta.

Light rain-patter on plastic.

A woman singing.

Leepus snug in a nest of pillows. He doesn't want to open his eyes but he supposes that he ought to.

A small room—bare-walled and painted white. A washstand in one corner. Light from an open balcony. A planter of trailing flowers.

Leepus turns back the sheet—looks down mildly disconcerted to find his body naked. He scopes around for his clothes—no sign. He may as well take the opportunity for a bit of a wash and brush-up.

Standing reveals that his bladder's full and there isn't a pot to piss in. Only one solution. Leepus feels a bit uncouth as he empties into the basin—but at least he has the nous first to check that it's plumbed to a drain. And there's more than enough water in the jug to flush before he washes.

There's soap and a towel—a battery shaver too. Leepus sponges the grime off and mows his stubble.

∞

Leepus on the balcony now. He's clean and towel-kilted—feeling fairly chippa. He looks out on a hanging garden: a gravelled courtyard bounded by four-storey buildings. Plants cascading from windows. Creepers climbing. A pond with bright fish and a tiny fountain. Small children playing peaceful under a crooked silver birch. Rowdy sparrows echoing about beneath polycarbonate roofing.

A knock disturbs his observation. Leepus steps back into the room and tries the door. He's surprised to find it not locked. A veiled BurkaBabe on the threshold—she hands him his clothes neatly folded. It looks as if they've been laundered.

'Thanks,' says Leepus. 'Good of you to bother.'

'Had to be done.' The woman shrugs. 'Aunty needs to look at you and man-stink makes her queasy. Get that nasty old bod covered up and downstairs in five minutes.'

∞

Leepus cross-legged on the floor in front of a cushioned dais—a tiny figure in gaudy silks squatting on it froglike. Aunty's face is dog-chewed leather with bright gold-piercings. Leepus is not supposed to know this—but the tubby eunuch who shows him in leaves a chink when he fixes his blindfold.

An aromatic fug of incense—and also caffy. The eunuch holds a copper tray with a solitary cup balanced on it. Leepus is disappointed. Aunty drains it in one mouthful—gargles noisy and spits on the floor. The eunuch whips a cloth from his sash and stoops to wipe the mess up.

'Leepus is it?' croaks Aunty. 'The man who likes to gamble?'

Leepus assumes the question is rhetorical—waits for Aunty to follow up.

'So you're not as slick as your reputation,' the old lady duly says.

'Everyone has their off-days.'

Aunty cackles. 'Senility is a killer, foolish man. Lucky for you my sistas are there to give you succour.'

'Not that I'm ungrateful, but I don't remember calling for full-on lethal intervention.'

'Klash is always coming, brotha. Those oppressors owe us blud. You're just a pop-up opportunity to offset violence with mercy.'

'Blud?' says Leepus curious. 'What kicks that off, then?'

Aunty claps her hands. The eunuch pours more caffy. Two cups this

94

time—Leepus guesses he's making a good impression.

Aunty says, 'NoGo is a high-risk environment for children. All types of beasts with bad appetites think it's their ancestral hunting around. The Sistas of the Veil maintain domains where kids can some get some playtime.'

Leepus sips. The bean is a fine one and well roasted. It's hard to resist the temptation to swallow—but Aunty gargles and spits again and he's wary of giving offence. He waits for the eunuch to swoop in with his cloth—then responds to a mischievous impulse and follows the old woman's suit.

The eunuch rises mournful wiping spatter from his face. Aunty sniggers—says, 'What? There's something wrong with my caffy—or you don't like my poor eunuch?'

'Just respecting local custom,' says Leepus. 'What's a eunuch?'

'Foolish man. Caffy is angelic on my taste buds but a savage in my bowel. There's no need for you to waste it.' Aunty pauses—wags a finger. 'And eunuchs are just mucky boys who get caught out once too often peeping at ladies they're not supposed to.'

'Ouch,' says Leepus. 'Busted. No disrespect intended, but forbidden fruit is tasty.'

Aunty giggles coy. 'Quite the sly old charmer, aren't you? Take the blindfold off then, and get a proper eyeful.'

Leepus does it—risks a wink.

'Steady, lad,' warns Aunty. 'You've got me enough of a flutter that I might just call your bluff.'

'All-in shove guaranteed,' says Leepus. 'Be careful what you wish for.'

'Oo-er,' Aunty whoops—slaps a scrawny thigh. 'Don't make me laugh, you foolish man, I'm likely to wet my cushions. Once upon a time I might give you a go—but I'm too wise, and you're too old now, to make it worth the struggle.'

Leepus is a bit offended by Aunty's defamation—but not desperate to disprove it. 'So, these provocative paramils,' he says by way of distraction. 'What outrageous liberty do they take, then?'

'Failure to respect a checkpoint is their first serious offence.' Aunty's lip curls disgusted. 'And then reckless endangerment and vehicular assault—namely ploughing through a walking-bus taking toddlers to feed the ducks.'

'There are fatalities, I imagine.'

'Two sweet little chaps get squashed to death,' says Aunty quietly. 'And then the Big Sista who tries to stop the vehicle leaving the scene. Poor girl's leg-bone is poking out through her thigh, the other kiddies tell me, when the oppressors strip her naked. She's strong though—still breathing even after the beasts are done with their voltwhips. So they chain her up to the truk's riot-shovel and drive her to death through the hogweed.'

'I'm sorry to hear that, Aunty.' Leepus is sincere. 'Hard to argue those savage shits don't deserve a dose of rough justice.'

'Not justice—revenge. All expressions of barbarity are iniquitous and shameful. But then we're the useless old grizzlas who let our opportunity slip away—so we can't go crying crocodile tears now we find things getting bloody.'

'Let?' Leepus is not sure of Aunty's meaning. 'You're saying shit doesn't just happen?'

'Come on, griz. Don't try and duck the blame. The Reduction's a god-given opportunity to imagine a new civilisation and all we manage to come up with is more dog-eat-dog.'

'Right. I'll have to think about that,' says Leepus. The conversation's tacking weird—he needs to grab the tiller. 'But I'd argue with 'god-given'.'

'Really, brotha?' says Aunty baffled. 'It's just a figure of speech.'

'Sistas of the Veil? The modest costume? Being nice to feral orphans? It's not that I'm trying to pick a fight, but you have to admit the semiotics is just a little bit godly, and that cult shit makes me queasy.'

'Ah.' Aunty chuckles wry. 'Ease your mind on that, griz. One thing BurkaBabes are not is any kind of holy. Religions are just sly protocols of oppression. Scared old beards dream them up back in prehistoric days to keep us weak, flawed females humble and compliant. Sistas of the Veil exist to subvert that abusive worldview. Our fashion sense is ironic, brotha. BurkaBabes cover up in black battledress because it makes them weird and scary. And weird and scary is a useful look when you're trying to hold ground in NoGo.'

'Yeah,' says Leepus. 'Those girls are definitely scary. And just a little bit sexy—although it's probably wrong to say it.'

'Not wrong,' says Aunty smiling dry. 'But maybe wiser not to.'

∞

A quadrangle confined by tall brick-buildings with barred windows. It's some kind of institution once—maybe an asylum.

There's a silent congregation of BurkaBabes ranked around a pyre of blazing floorboards—Aunty watching solemn from the padded seat of a tricked-out golf cart. Leepus stands beside her. One of his cheeks is seared by firelight. Cool-night drizzle soothes the other.

A flurry of wind brings the tang of grease smoke. Flames shift— reveal a shrivelling darkness at the heart of the funerary fire.

And then the sudden flare of collapsing charcoaled timbers. Embers erupting—a vortex of incandescence rising clear of inferno. The accompanying shrill of mass ululation gives Leepus the collywobbles. He shivers—stands swaying for a strange minute of dissolving comprehension. Next thing he knows he's out of his head and flying over NoGo in a sparky flock of firebirds.

∞

A little girl with a gap-tooth smile brings Leepus breakfast in his chamber. Fresh bread spread with honey. It's a big improvement on eel curry—although he's not so sure about the beverage which gives off a whiff of manure.

'Thanks,' he says to the waiting girl. 'You can run along, now.'

'No I can't.' The child folds her arms. 'Aunty says not to leave you alone till you take your potion.'

'Potion?' says Leepus. 'I'm not even sick.'

'You are last night.' The little girl sniggers. 'You spew up all over Aunty. An' then try an' jump in the fire.'

'Bollocks,' says Leepus affronted.

'Don't be rude.' The girl frowning stern. 'Check your eyebrows if you don't b'lieve me. They're all crispy like burnt grass.'

Leepus is embarrassed to find this true.

The child juts her dimpled chin. 'Toldya,' she says. 'Now you 'ave to say sorry.'

'Sorry,' says Leepus. 'Will you go away now?'

'Say please.'

'Please.'

The girl stares Leepus down—says, 'You still 'ave to drink your potion. So 'old your nose and 'urry up—I 'aven't got all day, griz.'

Leepus knows when he's beaten. He knocks back the whole noxious glassful. The stuff tastes worse than it smells.

'Well done.' The girl smiling sweet and stepping back. 'But I think you're s'posed to sip it. P'raps I forget to say.'

'Right,' says Leepus. 'So what happens if—?' And then the potion hits him.

The girl is already scampering out the door as Leepus lunges for the basin. The brat is likely half-a-mile away by the time he's finished throwing up his heart and set off in quest of a shitta.

∞

Leepus in the watchtower catching up with Aunty. They look out over high brick-walls topped with rusty electrified-fencing. Swamp beyond—reed beds surrounding the Sistas' stronghold squatting on a low island. Turns out it's an abandoned women's prison ironically reclaimed. A narrow plank-causeway spans the gap between gatehouse and tribulation.

Leepus is still a bit breathless. The watchtower stairs are steep—but Aunty scuttles up ahead of him embarrassingly spry.

'An hour sitting there, you say?' Aunty stifles a chuckle. 'I hope you don't block our plumbing.'

'I'm thinking I'll die in that khazi,' says Leepus. 'Getting poisoned isn't funny.'

'It is the way those sistas tell it. You hobbling around moaning all pale and sweaty with a sheet clutched round your middle, and your skinny mowka clenched so tight you'd struggle to pass a needle.'

'Yeah,' says Leepus sulky. 'Those 'Babes should be grateful I make the effort.'

A rattle of rain on the watchtower windows. Wind ripples reed-beds. A smoky smudge in the far-distance rising over murky NoGo ruins. Big old nautical binoculars on a rotary pedestal—Aunty swivels them to bear. 'HateBoy ground,' she murmurs. 'Looks like they're having a bonfire.'

Leepus is only half-listening but inspired to fish for a weedstick. 'So what's the crack with this kid and her poisoned chalice? Some kind of twisted payback for letting myself down last night?'

Aunty regards him steady and shakes her head. 'We worry about your state of mind, griz. Attempting spontaneous self-immolation is not usually an act of the mentally stable. A healing sista looks you over—says you need a thorough purging.'

'Appreciate the concern,' says Leepus lighting up. 'But if I'm you I'm worrying more about my own precarious situation.'

'Oh?' Aunty sniffs. 'Do you think we're all so foolish too then, to habitually corrode our brains with toxic psychotropics?'

Horses for courses, Aunty,' says Leepus. 'Anyway, a bit of healthy paranoia might be just what the doctor orders. Executing paramils, not to mention trashing Republic overseers, is guaranteed to provoke harsh reprisal. The prospect of all you kind ladies laying about dead and dismembered in the smoking ruins of your stronghold is not one I much relish.'

'Bless you for caring, griz,' says Aunty. 'But that's not going to happen.'

'It seems like bad taste to offer odds but I'm definitely tempted.'

Aunty shrugs. 'Feel free, brotha,' she says. 'I'm happy to take a bet—but it's only fair that you're aware I've had practice sucking eggs.'

'You don't think they'll come after you? I'm surprised they haven't already.'

'The ambush is a dangerous play, I'll give you that, but the risk is calculated—and our planners always hedge. First, the beasts we kill are contractors—just expendable munitions in the inventory of the Oppressor.'

'Their corpses are undeniable evidence of offences against the Republic. Forensics will point the finger. Reprisal is automatic.'

Aunty disregards the interruption—says, 'Second. Friendly skavvas get tipped to the kill-site first—and they've got access to backdoor KashBak. By the time the killas get off the ground, the carcasses of that rendition team are already recovered and recycled.'

'What about the weapons? They look like Republic military spec, and that kind of high-end hardware comes with onboard FindMe.'

'Of course it does.' Aunty smirks. 'But HateBoyz are tired of getting their bottoms smacked by sistas. They think shiny automatic weapons are all they need to stop being losers. They're too busy indulging their gun-lust to worry about keeping safe. Which maybe explains the bonfire.'

'Pretty dirty move there, Aunty.' Leepus raises an admiring eyebrow. 'Some might even go so far as to call it sick.'

'They might, brotha,' the old lady comes back. 'But the same goes for tactical rape. If HateBoyz want to play no-limit the Sistas are going to bust them.'

'Okay,' says Leepus. 'Your rules of war are up to you but there's still one fly in your ointment.'

'Yes. Unlikely as it seems, griz, you're obviously an object of desire for someone of influence and power.'

'It's always reassuring to feel wanted.'

'We could monetise the liability, I suppose. Cash you in. Earn a little indulgence.'

'It's an option.' Leepus takes a moment to light another weedstick. 'But one not without its downside. I have numerous associates capable of inflicting serious vengeance.'

'Ah.' Aunty smiles. 'You're talking about Mike.'

Leepus sucks in weedsmoke.

'Three messages from that name, so far,' Aunty continues a little smug. 'Their tone is increasingly impatient. The latest suggests you have less than four hours to 'get your worthless arse to Ma M's for extraction, or you're on your fuckin' own, mate'.'

'Shit,' says Leepus, 'you're reading my fone? You're not supposed to be able to do that.'

'Foolish man.' Aunty wags a finger. 'Your BaBBle would baffle most, I'm sure—but the Sistas have encryption techs equal to the challenge.'

'I think you should give it back now.'

'Of course, brotha.' Aunty fishes under her silks. 'But don't fret, we already let Mike know you're safe and sound here under the Veil.'

'Nice,' says Leepus. 'That'll cheer her up.'

'I wonder,' Aunty says and taps at the fone.

Aunty scrolls and chuckles.

'Gimme,' says Leepus curt. He takes the fone from her tiny hand— reads: *So what's the fuckin ransom? And don't be fuckin greedy bitches—or you can just kill the silly cunt.*

'So what do I tell her?' asks Leepus.

'Tell her ladies who call other ladies bitches are skating on thin ice.' Aunty turns for the watchtower steps. 'Add that she should sweat it out at Mother Mellow's while she waits for further contact. And that I strongly recommend she passes the time rehearsing a sincere apology for her reckless use of disrespectful language.'

◊◊◊◊◊

13

'So what just happens there?' asks Mother Mellow as Mike muscles into the bar.

'Grog,' says Mike. 'And make it fuckin' snappy.'

'Only asking.' Mother Mellow pouts and serves her. 'No need for rudeness, is there?'

Mike mouthwashes theatrical—swallows hard.

'Good outcome,' says Leepus pulling up a stool. 'Thanks for making it happen.'

'Fukkoff,' Mike says to Leepus—and then demands 'Another grog,' from Mother Mellow.

Mother Mellow pours—says, 'I don't get it. Way you front those 'Babes out there I'm sure there's carnage coming.'

'Leave it,' says Leepus to Mother Mellow.

'Kay,' says Mother Mellow. 'I just don't expect to see Mike down on her knees all sheepish while some dog-girl's grabbing vid.'

Mike clumping out the door. It slams. Shattered glass cascades.

'Fukksake,' says Mother Mellow. 'I'm only asking, aren't I?'

'Mike's a pro,' says Leepus turning to follow her out. 'She knows how to take a bullet.'

Leepus finds Mike outside the World's End mounted on the combo. She's winding up the throttle—blaring clouds of diesel smoke across the desolate car park. 'Get in,' she mouths over the racket as he hesitates by the sidecar.

Leepus does it. The whiplash of violent acceleration nearly snaps his head off.

∞

'Caffy is it, griz?' says Big Bethan in the Queen's Head on a Spike.

'I'll risk a grog,' says Leepus pulling up a stool. 'Long as the label's kosha.'

'Mike not feeling sociable? I hear her bike outside.'

'Just running a quick errand.'

Bethan shrugs—positions a crate and climbs up on it to reach down a top-shelf bottle.

'Thass right,' Bob the Butcher slurs from down the bar. 'Only the best for the big fuckin' chief.'

'One for that fuckwit, too,' says Leepus. 'It might just finish the sly mope off.'

Bob waits until his fat hand is round the shot glass—says, 'Hard to be fuckin' chippa, ennit, stuck drinkin' alone in this dismal tomb?'

Leepus sparks a weedstick. 'Something on your mind, Bob?'

'Foxy never does no 'arm. You got no call to ban him.'

'Sez you. Way I read him he has it coming.'

'This is s'posed to be a freetown, with Articles what says ev'ry cunt's s'posed to be tret straight, an' get 'is fuckin' fair shout an' all.'

'Foxy's bang to rights for risky behaviour. Arsewipe decides not to plead.'

'Maybe he's frit of Mike. Or getting dragged to death by fuckin' tinkish—like they do to my old dog.'

'Maybe he should be.'

'Fukkoff! You know the soft prick's not so dark he tops that tinkish tart.'

'Not this time.' Leepus signals Bethan for a second shot—shakes his head when she cocks the bottle in Bob's direction. 'But someone fucking is.'

'Poor little thing.' Bethan scowls. 'Not 'er fault she's born a rover.

104

Whatever rotten shitbag 'urts her needs 'is nuts squashed with a brick. You know who it is yet, griz?'

'I'm narrowing my focus.'

Bob the Butcher sneers. 'Better get a shift on, Chief. Those raggle bastards don't get their blud they're gunna burn us down. Savage fuckin' scrotes.'

Yeah,' says Leepus chilly. 'But don't you worry, Bob. All else fails, I just pick some random drunk fat-sack out of the hat and fit the mouthy bastard up.'

'What?' Bob gulps. His lardy white face wobbles. 'You fuckin' wouldn't—would you?'

'Call me 'Chief' again and see.' Leepus stubs out his weedstick—terminates the conversation in favour of video poka.

∞

An hour on the gamble doing badly and then the pub door shudders open. 'Finally,' says Leepus. 'Clear for me get on home now, is it?'

'You'd want to be feeling lucky, mate,' Mike says over his shoulder. 'So the way that robot's robbing you I'd say give it a miss for a while.'

'Overseer?'

'Nah—nothing that fuckin' clever.' Mike appropriates the weedstick lodged on the poka machine. 'Just a brace of clowns in rubbish camo scoping the gaff from a half-arsed obs nest in the heather.'

'Shit,' says Leepus as his last chip fails to win.

'Yeah.' Mike blows smoke. 'Want to tell me who the fucks are, mate?'

'Contractors, most likely,' says Leepus. 'Doing darkwork for Chilly.'

'Who the fuck is Chilly?'

'Let's get a drink and sit down, Mike,' says Leepus suddenly weary. 'Couple of twists and turns in the road since you drop me off at Foxy's.'

∞

'So,' says Leepus outside the pub an hour later, 'what am I supposed to do all day—just wander about in the pissing rain?'

'Up to you, mate,' Mike says tart. 'I'm busy for a while. And anyway, it's nightwork.'

'You'll ping me?'

Mike nods and fires up the combo.

∞

Leepus plods the church path past the garden fields. Makka cutting kale. Pretty Joli with her skirts tucked up unblocking a flooded ditch. Kids with slingshots after pigeons. And here's Red Rosa calling over the gate with a gift of carrots.

'Thanks,' says Leepus, 'but I'm off for a stroll. Leave them with Doll for us, missus. She can bring them next time she's up.'

The path turns down along the GreenField fence. A quarter-mile long bug-house—extractors vent the pungent stink of concentrated crickets. And then a giant veel-shed lowing plaintive—pink scum from the kill-plant dribbling into a vat. A RoboGuard blinks alert and tracks him from its tower. Agricos don't get so fat by feeding thieving poors.

Leepus is reminded of Big Bobby. The GreenField boss is the only one at the King of Club's shwonki poka table who's playing without a subtext—at least according to The Numbers. And The Numbers is fucking dead now. That leaves Chilly and Jax still in it. It's clear Chilly's the prime mover with the mercenary under contract—who also appears to have some private action on the side. Leepus is going to have to improve his read on Major Ajax.

∞

'Major Cunt,' Mike says in the pub when Leepus fills her in on the players. 'That's what everyone calls him back in Camp fuckin' Ashcan days. His killas don't hit their bodycount quota, one in ten gets striped. There's this virgin has the wobbles once on his first compound extermination. Ajax sticks his popgun in the soft shit's fuckin' shell-like. Makes the twat cut the bastard heads off half a dozen praying orphans.'

'He's got a lot of respect for you,' Leepus says to wind her up.

'Unfinished business,' Mike says then. 'Major Cunt should to watch his step.'

106

'Business?' queries Leepus.

Mike finishes her drink—wipes her mouth with the back of a hand. 'Yeah. His cohort gets tired of being flogged from arsehole to breakfast time. Leggies have a bit of whip round—rent some friendly fire. Fuck's luck fuckin' there, though. Ajax gets rotated out of Ashcan before I can take the shot.'

'Nice,' says Leepus. 'And now here the prick turns up on Chilly's ticket.'

'I'd ask myself why this sly twitch isn't tasking the job in-house. Citadel's got praetorians to represent its interests—and killa's like them are way too handy to get done over by a bunch of cult fuckin' backstreet bandits.'

'The way I read it she's moonlighting this operation, or at least finessing protocol.'

'Why would she want to do that, mate? What's her game objective? Where do you fit in?'

'Dunno.' Leepus yawns. 'The Numbers says it starts with that bodydump commotion, and a detainee gone AWOL. Jasmine has a bit of a shufti, pretty much backs that up. Other than that I'm no fucking wiser. The last few days are not exactly conducive to calm deduction.'

Mike gives Leepus a hard stare then. 'Right,' she says. 'That's the problem. The fuckin' Republic's up your arse and you're a headless chicken. It's time to come up with a plan, man.'

'Easy to say,' says Leepus pushing back, 'when I'm working still half-dizzy. And I've only got random cover.'

'Well boo-fuckin'-hoo,' Mike says raring up. 'I tell you I've got shit to do so don't go playing risky. Next time I look up it's full-tilt uproar with fuckin' corpses. And there you've only got yourself banged up in some freak-girls' fuckin' dungeon. In future hire-in some other silly cunt to eat shit to pay your ransom.'

'It's not me who calls the Sistas 'bitches' and impugns their integrity,' says Leepus standing too. 'Apologising is the right thing to do and I respect the fact you do it. But it isn't a fucking ransom, so the fault isn't fucking mine.'

Mike's green eyes are radioactive. Leepus feels their heat. For a moment there he's worried—but Mike dials it down saying, 'How am I supposed to know these BurkaBabes are straight players? One of those fuckin' black-robe's comes flappin' at you out in the sandlands you slot 'em before they explode.'

'Okay,' Leepus says relieved. 'Sit down and have another drink, mate—and then you can tell me your troubles.'

'Prick,' says Mike with the hint of a smile. 'That's none of your fuckin' business. Just sort your own messed-up shit out. And then deal with the fuckin' rovers.'

∞

A cold prickle on Leepus' neck now. Someone watching as he leaves the GreenField fence behind him—crosses the stile and forks for the river. An overseer above the cloudbase? A pair of Jax' rented eyeballs? Itinerant footpads lurking?

Leepus slips out the StunStik and extends it telescopic—doubles down behind the hedge and diverts to the old railway cutting. He stops and takes cover behind a clumped elder—stays down for a good five minutes. He's just getting around to moving on when a startled pheasant breaks from the hedgerow back by the stile.

Leepus holds his breath as clattering wing-beats diminish. A figure climbing the stile now—dark fatigues hanging from a scrawny frame thatched with a white flash of hair. Carbine slung on stooped shoulder. Binoculars in hand.

A twinge of recognition but Leepus can't summon a context.

The binoculars go up and scan around one-eighty. Leepus in his elder bush at the periphery of the sweep—the watcher holds his gaze there for what feels like half an hour. Leepus is sure he's detected. He plots evasive manoeuvres. But just before he makes his move the stalker gives it up. Lowers his bins and turns away—climbs back over the stile.

Leepus holds his position. The stalker doesn't reappear. But that doesn't mean the bastard's not still out there somewhere watching.

The railway cutting is steep-sided and darkly choked with briars—but there's a deer-path tunnelled through it. Leepus is a good bit bigger than a muntjac—so a half-mile bent double and scratched by thorns is not all that appealing. But while his StunStik is certainly stylish it's not what he wants to be holding in a heads-up situation.

Ten minutes duck-walking through the narrow briar tunnel—Leepus needs a sit-down and a weedstick. He waddles on two minutes more. Just in time there's a badger sett at the foot of a big old ash. Exposed-root fingers with arthritic knuckles grasping a burrowed red-earth bank. Dry spoil scattered across a clearing rain-proofed by low bramble. A cosy spot for a private moment. Leepus shuffles in.

Burning weed and badger musk—a soporific mixture. The hypnotic random plop and pop of raindrops on high leaves—but no precipitation at ground-level. It's not long before he's relaxed enough to let his mind out for a wander.

∞

A different time. A different world. A different cavern of vegetation.

An endless droning summer. Two careless boys at large in the park— they're playing 'kill or capture'. One of them grows bored with the game—the chase no longer thrills him. He ditches his younger playmate on an idle whim of mischief.

A rough hedge of dog-rose and hawthorn. A secret space beneath it between dry leaf-mould and dense prickles. Tattered magazines there promise lurid Male Adventure.

An hour lost in a strange musty world of brutal men and tortured women. The dark excitement of harsh word and sordid picture.

But enemies invade their game while the elder boy's distracted. He's derelict in his duty—neglects to respond to the call to arms until the battle's over.

Not that the younger boy gives up easy.

It's getting on for dark by the time his brother finds him alone at the drinking fountain - lip split, eye swollen shut, knuckles battered bloody - silently washing the dog shit out of his shock of wild blond hair.

∞

It's the message tone of his fone that curtails Leepus' reverie. He fishes it from his greatcoat pocket—reads: *Tower cleared of clowns now, mate—but not by fuckin me. Just blood traces in the heather. Mystery player a handy cutthroat. Mind you stay awake.*

That doesn't take long, thinks Leepus—then realises it's dark. Early afternoon when he sits down—he's been on the nod at least three hours. It's lucky he's not eaten by badgers.

But at least he feels a bit sharper. The residual dizzy metabolised and full mental competence restored? Leepus likes to think so.

∞

His OwlEyes get him through the briar tunnel with only minor lacerations. The track-bed emerges from the cutting. Leepus follows the ballast causeway across the marsh as far as the derelict signal box where the Goose Man once resides—before that griz meets his sticky end out wildfowling alone on the mudflats one drunk and moonless night.

Steps here climb down the embankment. Bodja's secret bog-path starts at the bottom—concrete sleeper stepping-stones laid an inch underwater. Leepus uses his StunStik to probe the safe way across. He's wary of 'doing a Goose Man'.

There's a dim light showing in Bodja's for'ard cabin porthole but Leepus struggles to get his attention. The hefty chunk of cast-iron that usually serves as a bell is missing along with its chain and his shouts all go unanswered. Several improvised missiles splash-down short before a rusty shackle finds its mark and shatters the wheelhouse window. Leepus waits for Bodja's response. It comes in the form of a crossbow bolt unzipping the air past his head.

∞

'Mind where you tread,' warns Bodja steadying skiff against houseboat thwart. 'There's a soft-patch in the gunnel.'

Leepus climbs aboard grumpy—says, 'There's another one in your fucking head, chap. Lucky you don't have my eye out.'

Bodja pushes past him into the wheelhouse. 'I tell you I'm sorry, don't I?' he says. 'But putting some bastard's window in when they're laid up fuckin' groggy counts as asking for it.'

Bodja has a point. Leepus lets it go—says, 'So I'll settle for a brew—as long as you boil the water at least ten minutes.'

110

∞

Bodja's cabin is not capacious. A plank table with bench seats—
filthy vinyl cushion covers pitted with foam-rubber ulcers. The light
lunar—a single LED on a wire shaded with spider silk. A tumble of
disembowelled tek-shells pillaged for handy spares. Toppled stacks
of arcane media. Mildewed boxes of damp paper. A shelf of antique
bottles. And a galley with a spirit stove beyond a peeling plywood
bulkhead. With a hammock and a piss pot.

Leepus sits across from Bodja trying to breathe shallow. Even dense
with weedsmoke the air is redolent of polecat.

'So,' Bodja says, 'I'm up at the tower a couple of times but I don't see
you.'

'That's because I'm not there, mate,' says Leepus idly wondering if
it's possible to drink his brew without his lips actually touching the
mug.

'Off gambling again, are you—hi-rollin' with the winnas?'

'You know me,' says Leepus.

'Yeah—all these years I fuckin' should do.'

'So what's happening up at the tower? Finish sorting the portcullis,
do you?'

'Sound as a pound now,' says Bodja. 'Whatever the fuck that means.'

'That's good.' Leepus sparks a fresh weedstick. 'I like to feel secure.'

'I do that lightning conductor too, mate. And service the turbine
while I'm at it—new alternator brushes.'

'Very conscientious.'

'I owe you a favour, I reckon, after I brick it with those tinkish.'

'Water under the bridge, mate.'

'Really?' says Bodja hopeful.

Leepus sucks up smoke. He watches Bodja silent for a moment—
then says, 'But talking of repair jobs, I bump into the Prof the other
evening. He has a bit of a grumble about his bolloxed photovoltaics.'

'Ah,' says Bodja looking shifty. 'I change out a couple of fuses for him.

111

But I only have fifteen-amps in my box and they should be twenty-fives. Mean to drop back up there.'

'Easy to get distracted.'

'Must be they blow out again. I'll sort it in the morning.'

'I have a word with John Fox, before I see the Prof.'

'Yeah—Bob the Butcher says.'

'I hear a whisper the grubby scrote might have a fiddle with that gurlee—think maybe he gets carried away.'

'You think he's got it in him.'

'Everyone's got it in him.'

Bodja thinks about that.

Leepus lights another weedstick—picks up with, 'Easy to see how it happens. A passing opportunity coincides with a savage impulse. Next thing you know the beast is out and the rest's all blood and squealing.'

'Fukksake.' Bodja swallows. 'That's too dark for me.'

'Sorry,' says Leepus. 'It's a dark thing that gets done, mate.'

'But you still let Foxy slide.'

'The rover kid sees it coming and has it away on her toes. Foxy's beast's a bit too sluggish for the chase.'

'Those tinkish don't fuckin' know that.'

'No, mate.' Leepus grinds out his weedstick on Bodja's table. 'But I do—and I'm never going to be happy watching some sacrificial mug panting along behind a trotting pony with his guts tied to its tail while I know the real sick shit's sitting tight.'

'Fuckin' savage fucks,' says Bodja looking queasy. 'You wouldn't let them do that, would you? Even to someone that's guilty?'

'I'd argue the toss,' says Leepus. 'But I might not have a choice.'

Bodja on his feet now. He blunders up into the wheelhouse and heaves a cable over the side.

∞

'Seasick?' Leepus asks sly as Bodja wobbles back.

'Weed's a bit heavy on top of parsnip grog. Or maybe my crayfish are dodgy.'

'I should leave you to sleep it off.'

'Up to you, mate,' says Bodja. 'But it's nice to have a visit from a pal—brings back memories, y'know?'

'That's a good thing, is it?'

Bodja ignores the question. 'Good times are hard to come by, but you and me have more than a few.'

Leepus slow-rolls another weedstick—says, 'Yeah, I suppose we do.'

'Like that big winter-flood year when the boat nearly washes away. You getting all the lads from the Queen's to help us work the ropes. Everyone stupid drunk and falling about in the mud. Rotten Eric nearly drowning. And no-one even notices the silly fucker's AWOL till those rafters bring him back upriver two days later and still pissed.'

'Rotten Eric,' says Leepus. 'Doesn't he move somewhere high-ground?'

Yeah.' Bodja looking solemn. 'He claims squats on an old derry farmhouse out on Sky Moor by the road. But it's too late to help his swamp-lung. They say he starts coughing lumpy blood up—and his kids pack him off to KashBak.'

'Oh well,' says Leepus. 'At least he has fun while he can.'

'Looking out for each other—that's what it's all about, man. Those that can help those that can't.'

'Or at least that's how it should be.'

'Like you're a winna playing cards but you've got no idea how to fix things. So you need me to keep your tower maintained and I—'

'Right,' Leepus interrupts a little curt. 'I think I get the point, mate.'

'Sorry,' says Bodja hangdog. 'I'm rattling on again.'

'Yes, mate,' says Leepus. 'But don't feel bad about it. Least I can do is lend half-an-ear if there's something you need to get off your chest.'

'Thanks mate. I know that,' says Bodja combing grimy fingers through manky hair. 'So what about these fuckin' tinkish? How does Shithole pay the blud?'

'I'll work something out,' says Leepus, 'when I find out what really happens.'

'You're saying it's not Foxy. You looking anywhere else?'

'Last sighting's up on Top Lane. Foxy says he hears a motor.'

'Oh?' Bodja says flat. 'When's that then?'

'Day you're up at the Prof's, mate. I don't suppose you see her legging past?'

'No,' says Bodja quickly. 'But then I wouldn't, would I? Not when I'm working inside.'

'You don't see anyone later? Which way do you go when you leave?'

'I go over the commons—and then down to the bridge and along the stonepath.'

'You're on the quaddie then?'

'Yeah.' Bodja frowning. 'And now I come to think of it, there's a big old yawl laid up out there by the sunken church. I remember I think they might be fuckin' pirates—but when I nick back later for a shufti the bastards've upped and away.'

'Pirates?' Leepus raises an eyebrow.

'Yeah,' says Bodja. 'I s'pose I should probably say something, but I never make the connection. Shit, man—what if that little girl's on board and I miss a chance to save her?'

'She's lucky if she is,' says Leepus. 'At least if it's slavers they don't kill her.'

'Do you think the tinkish buy it if you tell them that's what happens? Does it get Shithole off the hook?'

'Definitely an option,' says Leepus getting up. 'I'll keep it my playbook in case I don't scare up the truth.'

∞

Midnight now or thereabouts—Leepus all but home. But he's having

114

a squint through his OwlEyes from the shelter of a gorse bush. Just in case of lurking cutthroats.

The screens are gone from the bodydump site and so is the prefects' plodbot. The tower looks secure—and the portcullis seems to be working fine when he blips it with the remote. So Bodja's not lying about that.

Twenty minutes bleary watching and nothing moving but a fox. And now a walking tree? 'Fuck.' Leepus blinks. Struggles upright. Acknowledges an urgent need to get his knackered arse indoors and spend the rest of his life in bed.

◊◊◊◊◊

14

Thin cloud and a breeze from the south—the landscape leopard-spotted by wan fluctuating sunlight. Leepus is up on the tower roof having a breath and a weedstick. It may be just an effect of the weather but he feels mildly optimistic.

A hiatus in the game with Chilly. It's two days now since he wakes up refreshed and decides its time he shows some backbone. He's expecting she'll snap-call or re-raise him. Curiously nothing happens—his challenge to a rematch is churlishly ignored. Hesitation usually signifies weakness—but the wrong assumption in his position is likely to prove expensive. Leepus needs better information before he pushes harder. Late last night he calls Jasmine. She says give her three or four hours and she'll sniff around a bit.

∞

Daylight that casts visible shadow is a phenomenon not often observed in Inglund. Her natives are creatures of the gloaming—unadapted to the sun. Leepus retreats inside to his dashboard afflicted by prickly heat.

There's a message in his dead-letter box—a prompt response from Jasmine. It says: *No facts, but rumour has it the lovely Atalanta catches a cold. Diplomatic incumbents resentful of her heavy-handed tactics re the College. They complain she treats the 'well-ordered dominion of Inglund' as if it's an insurgent hot-zone, abuses her impunity and undermines their mission. The Citadel puts the brakes on. Word is she's restricted to working passive intel—no more hands-on mischief without Administration sign-off.*

Leepus lights another weedstick and ponders the ramifications.

∞

'No fokkin chance!' says the King of Clubs when Leepus fones to tap him. 'Why would I stick my dick in and risk getting it snapped off?'

'For the love of the game,' says Leepus. 'And because you don't like being a fish.'

'Leepus—don't you fokkin play me!' The King's tone is decidedly frosty.

Leepus gauges the thickness of the ice on which he's skating—says, 'Coming from the sly bastard who sets me up that's almost fucking funny. I'm you I'm grateful for the opportunity to make amends.'

The King of Clubs dwells for a full tense minute. Then he says, 'You've got some fokkin bollox, griz. I'd worry some chancer doesn't chop 'em—weigh 'em in for the fokkin KashBak.'

'So you'll do it,' says Leepus.

'Pick a venue—as long as it's not here. I've got contacts in the College I can nudge to pass a wispa.'

'You do hear The Numbers loses his head?'

The King doesn't deign to answer.

'Sick Dick's then. Tomorrow night. Make it sound as if I'm spooked—running bad and playing worse.'

'Kay,' says the King. 'But that's as far as I go.'

'Not quite,' says Leepus on a roll. 'I'll need a ride to get there too. Send Lesta with the limo.'

The King intakes a sharp breath. 'You're taking the fokkin piss now, griz. Lesta's fokkin busy.'

'Busy doing what?'

'Laying around neckin' laudanum an' tryna grow a new kneecap. Doesn't Mike fokkin tell you?'

'Ah,' says Leepus. 'Now that you remind me, maybe it rings a bell. Lesta gets unlucky there—tell the poor bastard I owe him a drink when I see him. Meantime I'll make do with the new man. I'm guessing you replace the limo?'

118

'No, griz—that's out of your fokkin pocket. You've got just about enough left banked with me now to buy Lesta his drink and a nice bunch of flowers.'

∞

'What's this, then?' asks Leepus as Doll puts his plate down on the table.

'Tatas with onion gravy. What's it bleedin' look like?'

'I'm looking forward to carrots.'

'Oh?' Doll looks away.

'Red Rosa says she'll drop some off for you to carry up here.'

'Yeah, well you tell me you don't like carrots, griz—say they give you rotten wind.'

'That's parsnips, Doll. Carrots are my favourite.'

'My mistake—next time I remember.'

'Right.' Leepus spoons his gravy. 'Bit fucking sly though, isn't it—taxing my carrots for a bottle? I'll have to dock your wages.'

Doll flushes. 'Fair enough,' she says tight. 'But I don't 'ave 'em for no grog.'

Leepus crunches a half-cooked tata—says, 'Go on then, I'll buy it.'

'It's the babby, ennit? She keeps breaking out all scurfy—an' Ryda always 'as the squits, kid could shit through the eye of a needle. Erbwitch says we need to feed 'em more fresh veg.'

'Plenty of plots on the garden fields. Someone'll find you a spade.'

'Yeah, an' there's only about a nundred kids in our house to look after all bleedin' day—not to mention doing for you an' cleaning the 'Cademy an' the pub. I'm just a lazy slag, I s'pose—I could easy fit in a bit of diggin', 'stead of sleepin' three hours a night.'

'I reckon two should be plenty,' says Leepus deadpan.

'Then you're just a rotten bastard,' Doll says close to tearful. 'A clueless stuck-up shitbag.'

Leepus pushes his plate away. He let's Doll get halfway out of the door—says, 'Gotcha! I don't even like fucking carrots.'

119

∞

Leepus out in the tower compound waiting for his limo—Doll huffing home down the lane. Even a bonus fifty in her payday chipstack doesn't serve to make amends.

Four hours of stony silence. It's only a bit of a wind-up. Leepus doesn't intend a ruction. It's just a shame he forgets Doll once tells him about the time when she's a scared little girl watching her mam get dragged screeching out of their house to be tied-up naked to a lamppost and branded 'skiva'.

At least Leepus hopes he forgets. He'd really have to be a callous prick to use that kind of privileged insight just to get the needle in and win a friendly hand of banta.

∞

The King of Clubs is another one who enjoys a bit of a sly wind-up. The new limo turns up an hour late—and it isn't a fucking limo.

It's a van that looks like it spends fifty years losing demolition derbies—and the krakklehead in the driving seat stinks like a man dead ten years longer. They're already a mile inside NoGo before Leepus catches on to the fact that the loon's sporadic chicken-clucks are conversational gambits.

∞

Sick Dick's is the card room of choice for players who think they're contenders. Less than one out of ten might be right—the rest of them are shark-bait.

Anything goes at Sick Dick's—except violence and cheating. A heavy roster of watchful thugs ensures that any scrote who ignores the rules is at risk of a sound punishment beating. But the world is full of chancers and bloodshed is not uncommon.

'Only a twat plays Sick Dick's solo,' Mike says of his last unhappy excursion. She's probably right about that—but Leepus has a contrary desire to prove he can carry a play without her. He's not exactly wet behind the ears. And brute force is not always the answer. He still pings her to remind her he's alive though—but so far she doesn't comment.

There's a time when Sick Dick's is a library—if the inscription on the lintel of the damp-greened granite portico can be taken at face value. Another redundant institution. Books all borrowed and not returned—the carpentered shelves that once contain them long since firewood. The only reading done here now is of players' poka faces.

Leepus tells the driver to wait and disembarks the van. The krakklehead just bobs his head and drives off clucking.

A queue of hopeful punters straggles the steps for pat-downs. This formality strictly for mugs—it doesn't apply to Leepus. He strolls past them up to the revolving doors manned by Shitehouse Franko— tips that stout fella twenny and gets to keep his StunStik. Then he climbs the staircase to the gallery for a squint down at the action.

Leepus circles the chipped marble balustrade beneath the leaky cupola—weedsmoke and sour sweat-stink seething under its dome. Its stucco green and decaying. Stalactites of bird shit. A desiccated bat-corpse in an array of security cameras.

Twenty active tables down below him in the pit. A hundred-and-fifty or so players wrangling cash games. None of them is Chilly.

But one is that fucking organ-loan runner—the bastard who sucks out on Leepus the night he comes over dizzy. And the scrote's nursing a nice stack of chips. The arsehole needs a lesson—and Tattooed Sally still needs her compo. Leepus might as well be doing something useful while he waits for his date.

'Buy a lucky suksuk, winna,' says the bust of a forgotten literary hero from a nearby shadowed plinth. Leepus double-takes. An obscure swish of fabric—then a pretty little prossi slithers out lithe and pouts red lips.

'Suksuk?' the tart insists. 'Or fukfuk's only four-duzzn.'

'Pass,' says Leepus. 'I only buy sexplay from grown-ups.'

The prossi is affronted—says, 'It's kosha,' and hikes up a tight satin shorts-leg—exposes the five-year bond tag tattooed on a pert buttock. 'I'm stabled here sixmonth now.'

Leepus has no desire to prolong the conversation. He shakes his head and turns away—trots back down the stairs. He idly wonders as he goes which way he'd bet on the harlot's gender.

121

∞

The table is six-handed and the loan runner's cleaning up. Leepus speed-reads his opponents while he settles in and stacks his chips.

A cold-eyed goon with a top-knot and knuckle-bone earrings. A battle boss fresh from the playpen—with the smell of blood still in his nose and a bundle of chips to burn. He's probably raising loose.

A paleface with twitchy nostrils like a rabbit and a slick of hairline sweat—a grubby bandage over his ear with an ooze of blood. A loser with an unpaid debt—he needs to be a winna tonight or tomorrow he plays one-handed.

A gaunt old gal with a graveyard cough. Nice clothes—modest life-savings neatly arranged in front of her on the felt. She's playing like she means it. No way she grows her stack enough to buy a sawbones and kosha parts though. But at least she gets off on the thrill of the gamble.

The grinder seated to his left is in it for his kids. He's happy to play percentages—win them food and shoes. Maybe one day he even hits a monster in position and plays it sly enough to get paid—buys them into a skillmill and future serfdom. Most likely that never happens if he doesn't up his game. But everyone's free to dream.

The loan-runner clocks Leepus as soon as he sits down—licks his lips and riffles a chipstack with plump fingers ringed with gold. His bald scalp is reminiscent of a mushroom past its prime. There's dandruff in his eyebrows and blackheads on his nose.

'All right then, you fucking leech?' asks Leepus declaring war. The scrote doesn't acknowledge the prod—just slides a hand up under the skirt of the hostess topping up his grog and whispers something that makes her giggle.

Leepus lights a weedstick. Concentrates his smoke.

A couple of hands later and the hostess is putting down a tumbler at Leepus' elbow. 'On the 'ouse f'luck there, mista,' she says syrupy with catarrh.

Leepus' hand darts. He pinches her earlobe between finger and thumb—pulls her head down close enough to whisper his own endearment. 'I think you're a little bit naughty, Giggles—and if

Franko tastes your shwonki grog he likely spanks you till you're dizzy.'

The hostess jerks free—grabs up the tumbler saying, 'All cool, griz—nah need f'nah fuss here, mon.' She shifts away with twitchy eyes—shuftis across the table in search of reassurance.

The Leech refusing contact—studying his cards.

∞

Fifty or so hands later and Leepus is pretty chippa. With his target read and understood he's just about in position now to set up for the kill.

The dealer's a slim boy with the hands of a girl whose name-tag says he's Abul. He sprays out hole cards deft to the players.

Top-knot raises under the gun. Paleface calls. Dead Lady will see a flop too. Grinder mucks without thinking about it.

The Leech's eyes flick to two o'clock—he's going to try and steal it. The last three times he makes that move Leepus lets him take the pot. This time he comes back over the top and triples the sly prick's raise.

Too rich for the other three. They all get out of the way.

The pressure's all on The Leech now. He dwells. Leepus tots up tells.

A chip twirl from The Leech says he's caught bluffing with poor cards. A double-blink then—he thinks Leepus is bluffing back at him and maybe a shove will take him off it.

Leepus nudges chipstacks around to suggest that outcome is unlikely.

The Leech reads this as a phony tell—flat-calls Leepus' bet in the hope of catching.

The dealer spreads the flop on the board. All paint—that's probably not good for The Leech.

The Leech counting out a bet nonetheless. A twitchy vein at his temple. A fingertip taking his neck-pulse. He flicks a sly look at Leepus—then pushes a big raise across the line.

Leepus sitting with a pair and a solid chance of improving—it's obvious he calls it.

The turn card gives Leepus the nuts. He holds his fire for a minute—bets enough to get decent value.

But it must be the turn hits The Leech nicely too because here he comes back with the re-raise.

Better and better. Now Leepus just has to decide whether he shoves here or waits for the river. He considers for a couple of minutes—chews his lip and checks his hole cards over and over. The Leech is certain he's got him—gets impatient and calls the clock.

Leepus savours the countdown close to zero. He's just about to push it all in when The Leech shifts his weight a bit edgy and flickers his gaze off stage.

A heavy presence behind Leepus' shoulder. Another sly fuck with his hood up moving to shade the dealer.

'Okay—time to fuckin' go now,' says a voice in Leepus' ear. 'Muck the hand and get up slow, brer.'

'Fukksake,' says Leepus groping for his StunStik. 'I'm sitting pretty here.'

Something coldly metallic pressed under Leepus' ear now. He looks up to see the dealer's throat lassoed with a cheese-wire. And then Shitehouse Franko yelps sudden—cartwheels down from the gallery and egg-splats on the floor.

'Leave it!' says the voice. 'Or it's gunna be a wipeout.'

Leepus looks at the dealer. The mope's face is throbbing purple and he's pissing in his codpiece. There's random pistoleers neutralising startled floormen—and three shotguns up on the gallery covering the pit. He gives up on the StunStik.

There's a world somewhere where Leepus just says 'Fukkit' and plays out the hand—but in this one he counts seven heartbeats and then tosses his cards face-up. The last thing he sees as the hood comes down is the fat pot left heaped on the table—The Leech just sitting there sucking wind and goggling his sick fucking windfall.

∞

Leepus spends the first thirty minutes of the journey coughing up a lung. The snatchas exit Sick Dick's under cover of choke smoke. By the time he's paying attention they're smooth-rolling down some PayWay already well out of town.

The high whine of the full-tilt turbine is drilling his weak tooth. Leepus wants the hood off—but his body's strapped to a gurney and his arms immobilised. 'So what's it all about, lads?' he asks muffled. He supposes he's not riding alone.

'No clue, griz,' a voice says bored. 'Ask the fuckin' client.'

Contractor's then—but Leepus already knows that. 'Okay,' he says to keep the conversation going. 'When do I get the chance?'

'When we fuckin' get there,' says a different voice this time.

'How long'll that take, killa?'

Voice number-one laughs gruff. 'Amazed we're not halfway back already, way this mental cunt's squirtin' steam.'

'That's the thing,' says Leepus. 'I'm feeling a bit queasy here. Wouldn't look good, would it, if I drown in a hood full of sick? You might not get your bounty.'

His captors think about it—then one of them whips Leepus' hood off while the other winds the gurney up till his torso is halfway upright. It looks like the straps are staying on though. But at least he can see out the window.

They're in the back of what looks like an armoured ambo. Two hefty killas perched on jump-seats with weapons handy—Leepus tries matching voices to blank faces. 'So how about we smoke up my weedsticks?' he prompts after a couple of stony minutes. 'Play a few hands to pass the time?'

'I don't mind takin' your krip, griz,' says the face that Leepus tags as 'number one' in the voice of 'number two'. 'But those sly shotguns tax your sticks to blow on their ride home.'

'Whatever—there's no burnin' in the vehicle,' the other killa says. 'I'm 'llergic to that crap. An' I can't be arsed with fuckin' poka.'

'Fair enough,' says Leepus peering out through an armour-glass porthole. 'I'm deep enough in the hole today—best if I stop digging. Anyway, that malevolent floodlit concrete fortress out there across the causeway can only be the Citadel—so I'm guessing I'm snug in a Republic dungeon before we can shuffle up.'

'Sorry for your trouble, griz,' killa number one says insincere. 'But that's what happens to cocky badmen.'

∞

Leepus wakes up in absolute dark still strapped down to the gurney. No way to know how long it is since the medics slide him from the ambo and shoot him up.

He remembers a long corridor behind a service-deck blast door—a neon centreline flashing above as they trundle him along it.

And orderlies in pale-green fatigues—'Sanitation' signed in warning yellow across their shoulders. They're peeling off rubber gauntlets—having a bit of banta by a beverage dispenser. Their white gumboots are splashed with blood.

That's when the anaesthetic coldness creeping Leepus' veins finally reaches his brain.

∞

A warm draught on him now though—he's clammy in his skivvies. The creak and tick of ducting piping in stale cooking-smells and a fragmentary soundscape.

A faintly intermittent buzzing: an electric insect trapped in a jar.

A jangly fragment of The Republic Prevails: someone's patriotic ringtone.

A distant lost female whimper.

Footsteps and casual laughter.

Leepus concentrates on calming his breathing—wonders how much they'll hurt him.

∞

Hours pass—maybe it's even days before harsh light stutters and then blares away the darkness. Leepus is still blinking blinded when his cubicle door bumps open and a service cart noses in. It's pushed by a shuffling former malcontent wearing a hobbled clownsuit— 'Now I Get It' stencilled bold on its front above a smiley face and a barcode.

An awkward minute without eye-contact—and then a white-coated adolescent in spots and wire-frame specs bustles in and joins them. *Quarantine Tech C-Grade: Codee, A.* says the tab on her breast pocket.

The technician blinks at a handheld—says, 'Hygiene pack, one.'

Clownsuit fumbles in the service cart—comes up with a foil-wrapped package and loads it onto a tray.

'Ration, one.'

Clownsuit finds a carton—adds it to the tray.

'Shock watch.'

Clownsuit hands over a heavy plasticised bracelet. The technician snaps it around Leepus' wrist.

'So what does the 'A' stand for?' asks Leepus friendly as Codee unclasps his restraints.

Codee taps her handheld—sends a sharp jolt up Leepus' arm. 'Speak only in response to a question,' she says as Leepus sits up scowling. 'You have three minutes to consume your nutrition. Five more to strip and proceed across the hall and enter the shower stall. Ensure you deploy the hygiene aids provided. An audible tone will instruct you when to pass through the gate to Interrogation. Any delay or deviation will be punished.'

Clownsuit blunders the trolley back out of the cubicle then. 'I'm starting the clock now,' says the technician and follows him out.

Leepus picks up his ration carton and reads its label: *Compliant-Inmate Privilege - basic/GrAVee-hot/1 unit.* He's not exactly appetised—but it seems likely that a stamina boost is something he's soon glad of. He pops out a flaccid rubber teat and sucks down warm sweet grease.

∞

Ten minutes later and Leepus is on schedule—sterilised by a douche of scalding disinfectant and scraped dry by high-pressure air blades. A buzzer sounds. He steps naked from the shower stall—follows arrows painted on cold floor-tiles along a concrete corridor to its end. A sliding door snaps open. He steps through it—feels rapid upward acceleration.

The lift car's at rest a tension-building thirty seconds before its doors re-open. Leepus takes a deep breath—counts to five and steps out shaky.

Chilly eyes him from a sofa. 'Nothing sadder, is there,' she says, 'than a scrawny old man with no clothes on?'

Deep-pile carpet and ambient lighting. Plush seating. Vid-art in a wide-screen frame: low sun tinting windswept prairie-grasses pink—cloud castles building above a backdrop of dark mountains. A bar arrayed with fancy bottles. A bedroom through an interior door—a big bed with a scarlet duvet and a bathroom beyond in an alcove. A floor-to-ceiling plate-glass window—rain-swept floodlit 'copter-pad outside below on the rooftop. It's not the setting Leepus anticipates for this encounter.

Chilly shakes her head slow and wafts her wine glass. 'At least have the common decency to cover your shrivelled penis.'

Leepus glances down. 'Nothing shrivelled about it,' he says, 'I'm just classically proportioned.'

'Whatever.' Chilly picks up a fone from the caffy table between them. 'It's appearance is not appealing.'

Leepus shrugs.

'Moron,' snarls Chilly into the fone. 'Get his garments up here directly, or get set to ship out for the sandlands.'

Chilly studies Leepus a bit longer. She takes a sip of wine. A drip falls on the tight white fabric of her vest—spots the domed slope of her breast with livid purple. She purses her lips—buttons up her black tunic. Her crossed legs are resplendent in scarlet jodhpurs and high-laced boots. 'Help yourself to a beverage,' she says. 'I would invite you to sit—but I do not want your nasty ball-sweat on my leather.'

She's pissed, thinks Leepus as he pours himself a shot of some kind of vintage grog. He weighs a wine bottle—finds it empty and weighs another. 'Top up?' he asks and steps across to Chilly.

'Sure.' She raises her glass with eyes averted.

A rumble from the lift. Its door pings open. Leepus' clothes folded on its floor—his possessions in a tray beside them. 'Just the garments,' says Chilly sharp. 'Any move I don't approve and I shock your fuckin' shit out.'

'Fair enough,' says Leepus. 'We don't want to ruin the carpet.'

∞

Leepus dressed and seated now with grog in hand—Chilly peering at him through a veil of amused disdain. 'Leepus. Lee-puss.' She dangles the word from her tongue before she drops it. 'So why do they call you that?'

'It's my name.'

'Is it?' says Chilly. 'I wonder. It sounds a little made up.'

'Coming from someone called Atalanta Honor-Trublood?'

A barely perceptible tightening of an eyebrow shows Chilly's impressed by his research. 'Difference is I know mine's a random generation. Not that I'm embarrassed. The Republic is my family—it can call me what it likes.'

'Right,' says Leepus. 'But you'll always be 'Chilly' to me.'

'Virgil.'

'What?' Leepus frowns—a muffled scuffling from a locked room somewhere lost inside his head.

'If we're giving each other pet names I like Virgil for you.'

'I don't get it.'

'You've got a tell says different.'

'No, really. Straight up—I've no idea even what this fucking game is. There I am just minding my own small business day-to-day—next thing there's body-parts on my doorstep and a swarm of vested interests crawling up my arse, shooting peoples' kneecaps off and chucking heads about. You want to help me pick the bones out?'

'What I want is Marcus.'

'That's what you say at the King's. And I say I don't know anyone called Marcus.'

'But you do.'

Leepus pours them another drink—says, 'Any chance of a weedstick?'

Chilly ignores the question. 'So let's go back,' she says. 'To a time before the Reduction—when Marcus is a soldier and Virgil makes up stories.'

'Stories about what?'

'Details are unavailable—no copies have yet been recovered.'

Leepus feeling vaguely queasy—he gulps down a swallow of grog.

'But gleaning eroded literary databases does reveal sketchy information about a series of trashy 'Leepus' fictions featuring an eponymous hipster gumshoe and written by a hack named Virgil Hare.'

Leepus stares hard at his grog glass absorbing this information. 'Absolute fucking bollocks,' he says after due consideration.

'Of course you can't admit it without undermining your whole existence. Or maybe you actually have gotten lost inside some kind of ruined imagination, come to believe your own deranged story? That would be kinda sad. What deep personal tragedy, do you think, could inspire such pathetic self-delusion?'

'And more to the fucking point, why would you fucking care?'

'I don't, Virgil—or only in so far is it pertains to the whereabouts of your younger brother Marcus.'

Leepus dwells on that. Chilly lets him—swirls her wine around the bowl of her glass as she counts his heartbeats. Rain rattles against the big window. 'Okay,' he says when he settles down, 'ignoring that fucking obvious bluff—'

'Never mind the DNA match,' Chilly string bets.

'Let's focus on why the fuck you want some absconding black-site detainee so badly you're prepared to splatter your pristine record with shit and blow up a sparkling career.'

Chilly raises an eyebrow. 'You think that's what I'm doing?'

'Playing off reservation? Getting into bed with a shwonki fuck like

Ajax—a mad dog who splashes so much blood around he pisses off your bosses and gets your autonomy circumscribed, so now you're confined to quarters?'

Chilly chuckles—it sounds like she's gargling blood.

Leepus frowns. 'I say something funny?'

'If you ever find me in bed with a freak like Ajax you can shoot me. The same goes for playing poka in some filthy badlands plague-pit. Why would I risk a fatal disease when I can just have you snatched and brought here to torment in comfort?'

'Comfort is good. Torment is counter-productive.'

'Not the way I do it.' Chilly twitches wine-dark lips. 'But there are subtler forms of coercion.'

'I sense a bet on the horizon.'

'All you have to do is give up Marcus.'

'That's not in my power.'

'If it's not then it soon will be. A couple of decades buried in detention—then he gets a chance to run. His escort duped and slaughtered, left as an offering on your stoop—it's obvious he'll look for help from his big brother. Where else does he have to go?'

'They say blood is thicker than water. If it's true I have a brother, why would I betray him?'

'Because, Virgil, if you don't I'll cause every last living person Leepus gives a fuck for to suffer a prolonged and excruciating death. And then I'll bury you alive in a pit with their ruined bodies.'

Chilly's eyes are diamonds. He doesn't think she's bluffing—but Leepus can't just give it up without an inch of needle. 'Too much passion, Atalanta. A pro like you doesn't run so hot unless the deal is personal. You want to share a secret?'

Chilly doesn't. But her nostrils flare minutely as she stares him down and says, 'Jasmine first, I think. Then Mike. Doll next, and all her mongrel grandkids. And maybe a gas strike on that fuckin' mess of peasant shanties you call Shithole is the cherry.'

'I'll need a while to dwell on that,' says Leepus getting up. In the meantime, call me a cab.'

'Let's say ten days, shall we? If Marcus isn't to hand by then your life-story comes unravelled.'

'Steady, Atalanta.' Leepus shrugs on his coat. 'Chances are I'm beat here—but overplay this 'Virgil' bollocks and I might just say 'Fukkit' and shove. Then anything can happen.'

Chilly smiles thin and drains her glass as the lift-door pings open behind him.

◊◊◊◊◊

15

For a couple of days after he gets home Leepus feels like he's walking on bog moss.

Setting up a heads-up with Chilly is always going to be risky—but probably worth it in the long-run to find out what she's holding. He's expecting to get pushed around but he thinks she'll play it straighter—give him some kind of clue to her tactical thinking. But there's nothing straight about Chilly. Getting a clear read on her is like trying to knit with eels. Now Leepus feels a bit seasick.

And that's probably just how she wants him.

Having him snatched and spooked by the threat of harsh interrogation is pretty ABC. Leepus anticipates a degree more discomfort from his gambit than it turns out is forthcoming. But the private apartment location and creepy naked humiliation? Coming on half-cut—challenging his worldview and undermining his self-image? And then letting him glimpse a weak-spot? He definitely reads that—but is she bluffing to suck him in? Chilly's play is weirdly erratic for a pro. It's hard for Leepus to figure out whether that's strategic or if she's tilted.

∞

'Well that's poka,' says Jasmine when Leepus calls to update her. 'Sly vix outplays you there, babe—gets right inside your head. And there's quite a lot at risk, personally speaking—so if you can't get good information from this fucking dominatrix, maybe you should pick on a weaker sister.'

'Wait for this shady absconder to make a move?'

'I'm thinking have a pop at Major Arturo. You say he's got chips

133

invested. Why not squeeze him—see what he's willing to give away to protect his interest?'

'I'd need some kind of lever.'

'The College doesn't like him. He spoils a major play once—something they're running on the Citadel, back when things are harum-scarum and the game's still up for the grabbing.'

'What kind of play is that?'

'Sorry, babe—details beyond reach. But the upshot is Ajax's Discrete Force Projection outfit gets fat on twenty years of preferential Republic contracts. Including special-prisoner transportation.'

'Sounds like a decent payday.'

'And a probable cause for involvement.'

'Somewhere to start, I suppose. I'll let you know how it goes.'

'Do that,' says Jasmine and pauses. 'So, any update on this bit of rover nasty business?'

'Coming to a head. But hard to see a good outcome.'

'Oh well,' says Jasmine sympathetic. 'I'm sure you'll do your best.'

'Thanks, gal.' Leepus is on the verge of hanging up then but he doesn't.

Jasmine doesn't either. She says, 'You know I'm always here for you, babe, if there's something you need a hand with? The world is weird and ugly these days. Easy to get confused sometimes, lose track of who we are and what we're doing.'

'Yeah,' says Leepus. 'But onward and fucking upward, eh? And don't look back at the wreckage.'

∞

Leepus at his dashboard contemplating deadlines. He feels a bit under pressure. At the moment it's a toss-up whether it's Chilly who wipes out Shithole first or fucking Queenie. Either way the world wobbles on. No one loses too much sleep over the casual erasure of a gaggle of poors and their soggy parish. Not that there's much prospect of a long-term future whatever. Ten more years of rising damp and the village is drowned ground—Leepus' tower left standing alone on a craggy headland. Maybe he should get Bodja to rig a beacon on the roof. Turn it into a fucking lighthouse. With a few cannon to ward off pirates.

Pirates on the river when the rover girl goes missing. Bodja clutching at straws there. A bit of wishful thinking. He's feeling it all going bad.

Leepus prefers it if things are different but they're not.

Old Bodja puts in a lot of work on the tower. Maintenance and modifications—innovative installations to enhance his old mate's lifestyle. And all for grog and weed handouts and an occasional scrap of affection. Bodja is annoying—but entertaining too. His loyalty is canine. Leepus is content for him to string along—as long as he doesn't shit indoors or start killing livestock.

The *camera obscura* is one of Bodja's tower upgrades. Military optics scavenged from an overseer downed by militia hackers and covertly mounted atop a flagpole. A couple of days of electric knitting and Bob's your uncle. Three-sixty HD surveillance from the comfort of Leepus' armchair. Two bottles of Blind Man grog and a jar of sticky buds—a couple of hours of boring banta and Bodja trots off happy. It's likely useful skills like that soon get harder to come by. And also more expensive.

But the Articles are binding. There's no case to be made for exceptions. Leepus will have to just grin and bear it.

A nostalgic impulse has him turning on the system for a quick review of the local prospect. He probes hillside gorse for camouflaged stalkers—zooms on likely movement.

A stag chewing bracken with flies round its head. Its antlers shedding velvet.

He pans across to the lane.

A flash of red through the hedge. It's young Mags—Wonky Tom's pretty little gal from up on Windy Edge. It looks like she's out after berries with a likely lad in tow. Brown hands undo fastenings— reach to weigh ripe swelling. Pursed lips savour hard dark fruit.

Leepus moving swiftly on—Mags left to her juicy pleasure.

Johnny Sawdust and his boys there down at the forest edge. An old beech laid low on the ground. They're at its corpse with smoky chainsaws—butchering it into logs. Heavy horses standing by in chain-haul harness breathing steady. They're loading up on oxygen—anticipating the dead-weight of lumber.

Over to Kwezi's terraced garden. His lad out running the crows off. A plastic feed-sack poncho. Snot-ropes trailing. With his skinny legs booted with clumped clay the kid's a figure proportioned cartoonish.

A grid of yards with washing drying.

Hopping Alice propped against her outhouse wall tightening her leg straps.

Smoke from Jordy's brick kiln.

Glasshouses stuffed with green behind chainlink and barbed wire. Dogs the size of bullocks pad the compound. Dredd Gary content in a plastic chair under his caravan-patio awning. He's kicking back with his old clay pipe—quality controlling.

A rowdy ball game on the kids' ground.

And a commotion behind the pub—two brawny boys in blindfolds stripped to the waist and swinging cudgels. Bob the Butcher taking bets from an enthusiastic posse of hopelessly drunk sports fans.

The random pass over Shithole leaves Leepus surprisingly sentimental. As a model for living lawless the place is far from flawless. The ramshackle settlement subsists under precarious self-regulation—its fuckwitted venal communards squabbling raucous from cradle to KashBak. But he'd rather their chaotic lives to look down on from his high tower than some dreary congregation of diligents bunkered up in a Heritage Hamlet.

Leepus 'downs periscope' and heads to his medicine chest—picks out a selection of ingredients beneficial to cognition enhancement. He needs an angle on killa Jax to improve Shithole's chance of survival and he doesn't have time to lie around waiting for inspiration.

∞

The resort to frontal-lobe stimulation is premature as it turns out. His idea-broth is hardly at a simmer when Leepus' fone interrupts. 'Can't talk now,' he says abrupt. 'Try again tomorrow.'

'You don't need to bleedin' talk, griz,' says Big Bethan a bit breathless. 'Just get Mike over here and pronto, or he says they shoot our eyes out. I already shout 'er but she ain't hearin'.'

'Whoa,' says Leepus confused. 'Who says fucking what?' But Bethan is disconnected—and she doesn't answer his callback.

Leepus lights a weedstick and returns to the *camera obscura*. Now there's a black armoured six-wheeler on the corner across from the pub. A gun parapet on top—and 'DFP' stencilled on its doors in a shield with wings of fire. Leepus finishes his weedstick—considers the situation. Then he pings an SOS to Mike and puts his coat on—lights another smoke to enjoy on his way down to the pub.

∞

It's raining steady as Leepus passes the duckpond. No residents abroad. He turns up his collar and pulls down his hatbrim—angles across the road on course for the door of the Queen's. A heavy machine-gun slides around its parapet rail to track him.

'Pub's closed today,' says a harsh amplified voice. 'Keep on shufflin' by, griz.'

'Not to me, mate,' Leepus calls with a casual wave. 'I'm here to buy the Major a drink from Mike.'

'Wait!' The command is metallic.

Leepus does that—takes the opportunity to light another weedstick.

'Kay,' says the voice after a minute. 'Step inside. Hands in full view. Be prepared to submit to search.'

'No problem,' calls Leepus loud and clear as he pushes at the door. 'But warn them not be too rough, or it's likely I go bang.'

∞

A killa in each corner with automatic weapons. A log-pile of regular drinkers hogtied on the floor: Bob the Butcher its foundation—Big Bethan draped on top.

'What kind of fuckin' bang?' Jax at a table by the fire staring cold at Leepus. 'Saying you're wearing a vest?'

Leepus shrugs noncommittal.

137

'Open your fuckin' coat.'

Leepus shakes his head.

'It's a bluff.'

'Shoot me and see.'

'I'll shoot a hostage. Pick one.'

'Go ahead.' Leepus shows his portcullis remote. 'That'll make something happen.'

Jax frowns and thinks about it.

'On you, mate.' Leepus reaching for a chair—the killas shifting twitchy. 'Call me if you think you're ahead. Or fold and negotiate.'

'Kay.' Jax with a shit-eating smirk. 'It doesn't have to be carnage—long as I get Mike.'

'I'm surprised she's not here already,' says Leepus sitting down. 'Your name comes up only yesterday in casual conversation. The prospect of a reunion excites a rush of blood-lust—takes me an hour to talk her down.'

'My name comes up?' Jax representing vague intrigue—but he really wants to know.

'Just reminiscences about Camp Ashcan days. I say 'your name', but the object of Mike's brutal desire is referred to as 'Major Cunt'. Perhaps I'm jumping to conclusions.'

A stifled guffaw from a killa in the corner. The muscles of Jax' jaw bulging—combined with his sandy complexion and rodent eyes this makes him look like a rabid hamster. Leepus does a better job of concealing his own amusement. 'So,' he says, 'seeing as how Mike wants your head on a pole, why would you come looking?'

'Let's just call it a question of honour.'

'You'll have to paint me a picture.'

'Two of my employees are MIA. Only one killa in this dog-fuck parish with the motive and skills to disappear them.'

'Motive?'

'My lads are tasked with observation. Someone local runs

interference for a fugitive from justice. The suspicion is that's you. Last I hear it's Mike who's tasked with your protection.'

'I'm you I have a word with Chilly, mate. Get yourself updated.'

'Who the fuck is Chilly?'

'You probably have to call her "Commander Honor-Trublood, ma'am". But I enjoy more intimate terms since the other evening. But I'm thinking you know that, since it's your dogs of brute force and ignorance who trash Sick Dick's and drag me off for a cosy chat in a Citadel basement.'

No contradiction in Jax' demeanour. Leepus blows thin smoke. 'Upshot, me and Chilly have a deal now, so you can pull your weasel dick out.'

'Deal?'

'Confidentiality clause. I'm not supposed to disclose details.'

'You're an idiot if you trust her.'

'First rule of poka, Arturo—even idiots sometimes get lucky.'

Jax assessing his position. Leepus has time to chain another weedstick before his opponent shrugs and says, 'Thing is, I could do with finding some luck, man. This twist has fuckin' jinxed me. Need to get some rep back.'

'I'm interpreting 'rep' as 'absconder'.'

'Right. My boy's are twats to lose the bastard. This high-octane XTRK girlie blows in from overseas all fired-up on some veiled mission. She needs this old loser disinterred and delivered for close inspection. DFP has the contract for Citadel detainee transfer. Nothing in the paperwork to say it's not routine.'

'But somehow the job blows up.'

'Transport vehicle goes dark about an hour north of here on the PayWay. Turns up burned out in an old quarry a couple of miles away, with the driver oven-roasted. Prisoner is tagged, of course, but it takes them two days to put up overseers and come up with a location. Random prefects out on patrol get tasked as first responders.'

'And find the shambles on my doorstep.'

'Unidentified hired-guns all blown to burga. This fuckin' psycho perpetrator free to run amok.'

'The College's involvement is peripheral then—sucked in via the 'fects? That's how The Numbers grabs a seat at the table?'

'Yeah. And this security princess—what're you calling her, Chilly?— isn't happy about them trespassing, decides to secure her jurisdiction.'

'You do the blood work for her?'

'Just basic pick-up and deliver. The shit with the head is her play.'

'Crippling the limo driver?'

'You're supposed to be in the vehicle, the mope won't say why you're not.'

'Could be the poor fuck doesn't know.'

'That's the conclusion we come to.'

'So Chilly knows I'm in SafeCity, posts a tempting bounty and gets lucky with my navvi.'

'Those snatchas are alpha killas, griz. Beats me how you get those fuckin' tribals to take them on.'

'They do that all by themselves, mate. I'm just happy to grab a passing chance to make myself scarce.'

'Nice for you. I look a useless cunt though.'

'And now Chilly doesn't trust you—suspects you're playing shwonki.'

A flicker in Jax' eye there confirming that he is. But he's not about to travel that road with Leepus. 'Let's just say it's good for future business—if I make good on the outstanding task and hand Chilly this fuckin' runner.'

'Why would you think I'd help?'

'Because, bottom line, you and me are Inglunders, griz, and that sick twitch fuckin' isn't. And whatever she tells you get for handing in this scrote, you know the deal is never kosha—because she's playing for the Republic and you don't even count.'

140

'Intrigued you think of us as kin, mate—you being a shameless collaborator, sucking your daily blood-krip from the Republic's nasty arsehole. Puts your sincerity under question.'

Jax shrugs, spreads hands palms up—says, 'Your enemy's enemy is your friend, griz. Together we can both be winnas.'

'Is that what you say to the College?' says Leepus fishing. 'Back there in the day—before you fuck them over?'

Neck flush. A suspended exhalation. Something bitter swallowed. A hit—Major Cunt unsettled. 'No clue what you're talking about,' he says and moistens dry lips.

'Just something I hear,' says Leepus easy. 'Probably nothing in it.'

'Half a bar of gold then, as a token of good faith?'

'Plus everyone in here stays alive—and Mike gets out from under the gun on this missing snooper bullshit.'

A turd on the table in front of Jax—its bouquet flaring his nostrils. He thinks about it for a minute. And then he swallows—extends his hand. 'This runner in my custody before Chilly gets a look-in and we can call it even.'

Leepus shakes. The hand feels like a dead man's.

'Strong fuckin' play you make there, griz,' says Jax pushing back his chair. 'Make sure you fuckin' follow through now, or you're going to die hurt—'

A flash then and a glittering blizzard—the geometry of the bar assuming a weird perspective. Everything flickers dark and silent. When Leepus blinks up from the floor Jax is in the fireplace and there's a gnarly truk-tyre jammed in the window.

Another microsecond or two. Now one killa's down and twitching—his face eroded to the bone by explosive dermabrasion. But the other three are pros and they're still lively. Two of them crunch shattered glass moving to defend from the window. The other alternates his weapon-aim between the collapsed hostage-pile and Leepus.

Jax clambers up from the hearth. He isn't very happy.

'Bus is a total loss, boss,' says a killa from the window.

'No available targets,' adds the other.

'Deal's off,' says Jax to Leepus—wipes a blood-dribble from his chin.

Leepus doesn't comment.

'Kill every fuckin' cunt in here,' Jax snarls then to the third killa. 'And shoot anything that moves outside while I sort out extraction.'

A coincidence of action.

The appointed executioner raising his weapon—sidestepping to cover the hostage pile and position the bar as a backstop.

Leepus sucking in a breath. Then he's rolling and pulling his tube of LaxBoms from his pocket—thumbing off a full-load salvo.

Mike stepping out of the shittas with her sawn-off. The executioner's head exploding.

Skull-shrapnel. Blood and brains. A green roil of emetic vapour. Multiple gorges rising—high-pressure vomit projecting. Bowels convulsing—sphincters jetting.

Leepus glimpses Mike's retreat as he hurls himself for the door. He gets as far as the gutter before he collapses to huddle foetal in the glow of the blazing tactical vehicle. His guts are pythons fighting. He's holding on to continence but maybe not for much longer.

Silence inside the pub—and then two more shotgun percussions.

A minute or so later—Leepus still rhythmically dry-heaving when Mike barges out through the door. She's got a wet roller-towel wrapped round her face—and Jax' collar gripped in her clenched fist as she drags him down the steps. 'Fuckin' classic, mate,' she says muffled muscling past—Jax slithering behind her trailing a slick of foul body-fluids. Leepus doesn't fail to detect the heavy irony in her tone.

Mike hauls her filthy burden on to the edge of the duckpond—heaves it into the muddy water. 'Drown if you want, you fuckin' disease,' she says unwrapping her head. 'But climb out of there without permission and I stamp your fuckin' face in.'

∞

An hour later back at the tower. Leepus steps from the shower—

142

finds Doll with hand over nose. She's craning his filthy clothes into a bucket with a stick held in the other.

'Sorry,' says Leepus reaching for a towel.

Doll exits with bucket held arm's-length. 'Can't believe you don't strip off outside, man,' she calls back over her shoulder. 'Just basic 'ygeine, ennit?'

'I'm thinking I can make it,' says Leepus. 'Turns out I'm marginally over-optimistic.'

'I oughta rub your face in it,' Doll says fading. 'Whole place is a bio'azard.'

'Mike's the one to blame.' Leepus heading for the tank-room stove now to take the chill off. 'Those killas are eating out of my hand until she goes fucking nuclear and detonates their transport.'

'Coming from the twat who fire's off a tube of LaxBoms?' Mike growls from ambush in the kitchen. 'What do I fuckin' tell you about arseing about with novelty weapons?'

'I'm trying to forestall a bloodbath,' says Leepus changing direction. 'Who knows you pop up out of the shitta?'

'No choice once the war's on, is there?' says Mike with a brew at the table. 'And just to be fuckin' clear, it's not me that bangs the TacTruk.'

Leepus frowns—leans to reach weedsticks down from the shelf above her as he waits for elucidation.

'Fukksake.' Mike winces. 'Sort that fuckin' towel out. So far I keep my breakfast down, but your grizzled swinging bollocks at close range'd gag a maggot.'

Leepus' greatcoat on the drainer. It looks like Doll's sponged it down. He hangs it from his shoulders—sits down and lights his weedstick. 'So, the mystery player lays another lethal turd on our doorstep?'

'Right. But whoever the foxy fucker is, it's Major Cunt's chickens he's killing.'

'Any witness statements?'

'Most of the pointless turds go to ground. But that kid from the bread shop up Knacker's Lane says he sees this "white-hair griz" shift out from Shag Alley behind the Queen's with "somethin' as looks like a drainpipe on 'is shoulder what lobs a rokkit at that gun truk". Kid has more brains than most round here, gets his head down before the flash.'

'Got to be this white-hair griz is Ajax' absconder. He's working off a serious grudge with a campaign of attrition.'

'And he's doing it fuckin' stylish.'

'Slitting throats and disappearing corpses is one thing—but deploying military munitions in a residential district is recklessly antisocial.'

Mike shrugs. 'It's only fuckin' Shithole. And it's a precision strike with a specialised weapon—other than the leggie in the TacTruk it's only broken glass.'

'And lethal mayhem sparked.'

'Only adversaries die. And the hostages get off with a bit of a fright if you don't chip in with your LaxBoms.'

'It seems like the best move at the time.'

'Tell that to Bob the Butcher when you see him. He's tied up at the bottom of the stack when they all lose their arses.'

Leepus pictures the scene and giggles childish. Mike acquires his infection. 'Human fuckin' shit-wells,' she says when she catches her breath. 'Bar's an open sewer. And then when they're all grovelling about bare-arse in the yard, trying to wash off in the pissing rain— every fucker out there goggling, trying not to laugh. Some cunt'd better have vid, mate.'

'All very well you heartless bastards 'avin' bleedin' 'sterics,' Doll says coming in stern. 'You ain't the soddin' mug whose job it is to clean that pub out, are you?'

Mike and Leepus belly-laugh then—at least until Doll slaps them.

'So,' Leepus asks Mike, 'what do you do with Ajax?'

'Kick his arse to the lockup and stuff him in the hole. Some of 'em want to hang the prick. I say I'll do it later.'

'Admirable restraint. Alive improves his value. What about the cleanup?'

'TacTruk's still towable with horses. Firemen mobilised. They're supposed to load up the dead fucks, then drag it down to Goose Marsh and lose it in the sink mud.'

'What about its FindMe?'

'I send a kid to the PayWay bridge to toss it into a passing wagon.'

'It's all good then, mate,' says Leepus. 'Doll can make us all a brew while I fill you in on my chat with Chilly—then we'll have a wander down for a shufti at Arturo.

'Suits me,' says Mike. 'Just put some fuckin' clothes on.'

∞

'Hang me?' says Ajax from the dank depths of the village dungeon. 'That's bollocks. Harming a Republic affiliate guarantees your arsewipe township gets reduced to a smoking crater with burned meat-scraps.'

'We know that,' says Leepus peering down through the grille.

'But it's not us who has the say,' Mike adds dangling her noose. 'And the rest of the idiots out here don't think quite so strategic.'

'So fuckin' spell it out to them.' Ajax' voice with a bit of a wobble.

'I do, mate,' says Leepus. 'But they're seeing it as a blud thing.'

'Could be a lot worse though, killa.' Mike hawks juicy and spits in the pit. 'I'm all for letting them gut you first, but Leepus here is a soft old twat—puts in few words in your favour. Lucky for you he doesn't know all the sick shit you pull in the service.'

Noises from below that could be stifled sobbing.

'Best for you if we do it sooner rather than later, I reckon,' says Leepus into the darkness. 'Cruel to keep you waiting down there, terrified and hopeless in that rat hole, soaked in shit and pond slime, trying not to blub.'

'Just keep your chin up for an hour while they finish off the scaffold.' Mike lighting up a weedstick—grinning in the match flare. 'Then it's just a few seconds rapid-breathing in the hood, a short sharp drop and a bit of kicking.'

'Fukksake, man,' moans Ajax. 'This doesn't have to happen. Why not let me walk? Word of honour there's no comeback.'

'Word of bollocks,' says Mike vindictive. 'Say please, you spineless turd.'

'Please. And I make you rich.'

'I'm rich enough already,' says Leepus. 'Maybe Mike's for sale.'

'Nah.' Mike blows a perfect smoke ring. 'I'm a spiritual cunt. Gold doesn't make me happy.'

Silence for a minute—then Ajax' shitty hand clawing up from shadow. 'Fuck you,' he snarls. Fuckin' fuck it all and fuck your fuckin' arses. Just fuckin' hang me high enough so I can piss in your fuckin' faces.'

'Yeah, that's the spirit, killa,' says Mike. 'No one lives for ever. Take it like a soldier.'

Leepus takes Mike's half-burned weedstick from her—smokes silent until it's finished. 'Then again,' he says pinching it out between thumb and finger—a flurry of brief sparks falling. 'There is one thing might get you off the hook—but it's not likely you can deliver.'

'Try me.'

'You'd still need to stump up a hefty ransom. Plus make good on the pot I have to leave on the table when your snatchas lift me from Sick Dick's.'

'Yes?'

'And take some punishment running the gauntlet.'

'Fuckin' spit it out, man.'

'I want Chilly's head on a plate. Figuratively speaking.'

'Done,' says Ajax. It sounds like he thinks it's his birthday.

'Hang about.' Mike sticks her oar in. 'Can't just take the sly shit on his word.'

'Course not, mate,' says Leepus. 'So if Major Cunt tries to play shwonki, the Citadel gets uploaded vid of the negotiations we have in

146

the bar just now, before it all turns to shooting. Chilly won't like the deal he makes to cut her out. Maybe there'll be punitive interrogation, trial for treason and a lethal injection—but more likely he just gets a hooded 'copter ride and dropped into the briny.'

∞

'He's obviously bunkered up in the forest,' Leepus says to Mike on the tower roof when the fun with Ajax is over. Big clouds tumbling over the horizon—a rolling tide of night.

'With a handy stash of munitions.'

'Which says he's playing familiar ground.'

'He must be a long time gone, then?' Mike's lips dribbling thoughtful smoke. 'If we don't fuckin' know him.'

'Maybe we do,' says Leepus. 'It's easy to forget things.'

Mike catches a tell in his tone—flicks a sideways glance. 'Something you're not sharing here mate, is there?'

'I could ask the same of you.'

Mike sucks her teeth. A flight of crows tumbling above ahead of the rain. 'Better if you don't.'

'I'll show you mine if you show me yours.'

'Some things are fuckin' private.'

'So it's a sex thing?' Leepus says fishing the green pools of her eyes. 'Some shag's got you on a string, dividing your attention?'

'Don't,' Mike says cold then.

'Don't what?'

'Don't try to read me. Not ever. Save your hoodoo for the mugs. What I want you to know I'll tell you.'

Leepus looks away—says, 'Sorry. Don't mean to be possessive.'

'Twat,' says Mike and heads for the hatch. 'It's not a fuckin' sex thing.'

'I really need you to stay handy, mate—get a muzzle on this mystery killa.'

147

'Fair enough.' Mike clatters down the ladder. 'So call me when you find him—or *vice* fuckin' *versa.*'

∞

Leepus stays on the roof in the rain until Mike's combo is out of earshot. The sky is dark and the landscape darker. He stares at the charcoal scribble of forest trees along the horizon. There's something out there staring back. Something that he can't quite see—or maybe doesn't want to.

Fuck Chilly and her mind games. Fuck paranoia. Fuck doubt. Fuck dizzy.

Leepus goes inside and puts the tower into lock-down. He barely makes it into bed before a potion from his medicine chest does the same thing to his head.

◊◊◊◊◊

16

Leepus dreams he's tormented by banshees—wakes up sudden in a muck sweat. An eerie luminescence infiltrating his bed-space skylight. A resonant hum in the tower's concrete. And outside the banshees howl on. 'Fuck,' he moans as he sits up in bed—frost-flowers creeping his skin. A screama is all he's short of.

Nine hundred and ninety-nine days out of a thousand it's a sou'wester that blows over Inglund. Lukewarm ocean scooped up and relocated to saturate the rolling hills and top-up flooded hollows—a near-constant inundation. Then once in a while it turns around—slices back down all arctic.

Leepus shivers into multiple layers—goads the stove to the point of meltdown. He's still waiting for the kettle to thaw when there's a clatter and thud from the roof above and a sudden cessation of humming. 'That'll be the turbine down then,' he mutters sullen.

The kettle on the gas-ring creaks and hisses—Leepus in dubious hope of a brew. He smokes a weedstick considering options. A retreat to bed with a stack of quilts is tempting. But that won't get his power back before the batteries are exhausted. And there are serious deadlines looming. The damage doesn't fix itself—it needs hands-on intervention.

∞

'Unlucky, mate,' says Bodja when he finally picks up his fone. 'Likely a frozen goose takes it out, way this bastard's blowing.'

'So I need you to get it sorted.'

'That's what I'm here for, ennit? On it as soon as the screama's gone through.'

'Not good enough,' says Leepus. 'I want it done today.'

'Fukksake.' Bodja isn't happy. 'I'm all iced-in down here. Pressure on the hull. I'm worried the old girl pops a plank. And anyway, this wind could carve your face off. You'll have to fuckin' wait, mate.'

'Sorry for your trouble,' says Leepus frosty, 'but I'm not asking, am I? Be here inside two hours.'

∞

Leepus gets busy in an online card room while Bodja works on the roof. He plays high stakes—wins big. But it doesn't make him happy.

A cold blast from the open hatch says Bodja's coming down the ladder. Leepus abandons his dashboard and moves to the tank room to meet him. Bodja is a polar bear stiff in a suit of ice armour. His beard is whitened hoary and his goggles crazed with rime. He tries to speak but it's just a stutter.

'Job's good then, is it?' asks Leepus.

Bodja nods—fumbles at topcoat fastenings with stiffened bloodless fingers.

'Right,' says Leepus. 'Get that shit off in the kitchen. I don't want your melt soaking my rugs. Put the kettle on while you're out there.'

Bodja bundles out. His demeanour suggests he's disgruntled. Leepus warms his arse at the stove and burns a stick. He's halfway down a second before Bodja shudders back with slopping mugs. 'Fukksake.' Leepus moves to take them off him. 'Be a bit fucking careful.'

Bodja sits by the stove and shivers.

Leepus passes him a last gasp of weedstick. 'Bit parky up there, I bet.'

'I think I fuh-freeze my cock off.'

'Oh well,' says Leepus staring steady, 'that's probably a good thing.'

'Yeah?' Bodja scowls. 'Why the fuck is that?'

'You tell me,' says Leepus.

'I've no idea what you're talking about. Fuckin' obvious you're on one. You treat me like shit from the off today—and your face says summut spiky crawls up your arse in the night and fuckin' dies there. You need to see the erbwitch, mate. Get yourself a cheer-up potion.'

'Nice if it's that straightforward. But it's multiple tribulations impacting my fucking colon—solid arse-ache constipation.'

'Unlucky.' Bodja winks. 'But why not look on the bright side, mate—at least it's left off raining.'

It's an old joke and Leepus ignores it. 'Human carrion scattered about. Mystery killa roaming the heather. Some twisted Republic amazon messing around in my head. A bloodbath in the pub. Never mind the pack of wild rovers threatening a wipeout because some scrofulous cunt on a testo binge disappears their 'gurlee'—and some sorry scrote who wants to call me 'mate' rubbing salt in by lying about it.'

'Oh?' Bodja swallows hard. 'So what the fuck does that mean?'

'It means,' says Leepus leaning in, 'that you've stepped beyond the pale, chap.'

Bodja's a pinned snake squirming. He chews words silent for a minute before he spits a few out. 'Right enough it's a tricky spot—but you can fix it, can't you?'

'Oh, I can pay the rovers' blud price and rustle up some compo. But that's not going to resurrect that little girl now, is it?'

Bodja stares—then says, 'Resurrect? What's that?'

'Don't play the moron, Bodja. Okay, the damage is done. Your play went bad and now you're fucked. I'm sorry this is how it ends but at least have the balls to admit it.'

'Ends?' Bodja sits stunned. Fear in his eyes—interior turmoil. But something else as well. A glimmer of hurt and anger. 'Okay, I'm bang to rights for being sly—but you and me go back, man. I deserve some fuckin' leeway.'

'Sorry. That's not how I read it.'

'Yeah?' Bodja clamping down now. 'So how's that you cold fuckin' prick?'

Leepus leans back and lights a weedstick—blows a smoke-stream in frigid air. 'Okay,' he says, 'if that's the way you want it. But feel free to jump in any time. I'd still rather hear it from you.'

Bodja on the edge of his seat staring at the floor. He gulps once like a fish—then blows a silent bubble.

Leepus takes in a smoky lungful—leads off into the darkness. 'It's not like you plan it, is it? I know you're not that sick. Maybe it starts in your sleep. A touch of the old grog horrors. Some sort of twisted nightmare—a spasm of sweaty passion, and you wake up a bit weird and wired? And you don't even know it but the badness is sparked in your head—a few sick cells coagulating into a cancer of ill-intent.'

Bodja shivers. Leepus continues: 'So you take the quaddie up to the village to sort out the Prof's photovoltaics. Normally the job's a doddle but today you can't really be arsed. You just want to get paid and be gone.'

Bodja nods. 'The Prof does my fuckin' noggin in with all his poncy gabble. The clever books that bastard reads—still can't repair his own tek though, can he?'

'Right. You're entitled to feel resentful. So you're chugging off up Top Lane on your quaddie—just as gurlee's away on her twinkle-toes frit by leery old Foxy.'

'I don't know that, do I?' says Bodja. 'She comes over the wall right in front of me. For a moment I think she's a deer, give it a swerve and ditch it. When I climb out she's sat on her arse in a puddle with a tyre track up her leg. I get her on her feet alright but she can't hardly hobble. I tell her to sit tight and I'll fetch her pals. But she starts up bawlin' then, 'cause her bag of swag is all mashed up in the mud and spoiled. And if she "guzzome wi'out goods or gol' the biggun gi'us a dedd battuh". She says I have to pay her compo for her losses. I'm thinking about that when she just moans and falls down sparko. I get worried maybe I kill the poor kid, and what's that going to cost? And then it's pissing rain down. So I gather up her bits and bobs, hold her in front of me on the quaddie and wobble on down to the mooring. Maybe not the sharpest move but that's the way I play it.'

'Slippery slope,' says Leepus. 'All downhill to the bottom.'

'Depends on your point of view, I s'pose. Granted it gets messy.'

'Yeah,' says Leepus staring. 'So there you are bunkered up in your lair with a helpless gurlee. Probably you don't mean to do it, when you uncover some skin to clean her up, and give her a first-aid snifta.'

'Do it?' Bodja frowning.

'But it's strange for a lonely old hermit to have a warm young body handy, all sweet and a bit grog-fuddled, with not a lot of clothes on. He's bound to get a bit excited, wonder how far he can push it.'

Bodja sitting upright hands on knees. He sucks wind—starts breathing hard and faster.

'Maybe gurlee seems almost willing, to start with. She's probably still a bit floaty. Perhaps she thinks she's dreaming. But then she gets a full whiff of Bodja, feels the scrape of horny hands, starts up shouting and fighting. But she's not strong enough to stop you.'

Bodja's fingers flexing—his wide eyes stare disgusted. No comment is forthcoming. Leepus lights a smoke and carries on. 'It doesn't take that long. The kid has her share of abuse in the past. It's what she expects from men. I don't suppose she cries any tears about it, at least none she's letting you see. Most likely she just curses and gozzes in your face. Or starts laughing, takes the piss at your poor performance, mocks your weedy cock. And then she puts the squeeze on—says if you don't give her a fat ol' sack of gol' she dobs you to her clannurs. And then it'll be a blud thing. So even if you cough up triple they still tie you to a tree and skin you. And then use sticks to poke your eyes out.'

'No.' A croak from Bodja.

'So you're scared and ashamed, and angry. Your head is full of roaring. Next thing you know you've got a hand round her throat and the other one's punching her lights out. And when you're done she's all limp and broken.'

'Stop it,' murmurs Bodja. 'Please. This isn't fuckin' fair, man.'

'That's what she says, is it? You dirty rotten bastard.'

Bodja's reply is a strangled gurgle.

'You think about what you do then, staring at her lying there all wide-eyed and accusing. You probably puke before you bundle her up in a greasy tarp with her bag of crappy swag. Then you drag her up to the wheelhouse. It's hard because you can't stop shaking. You don't remember doing it but you get her into the skiff—putter off to some quiet murky lagoon and leave her to play with the catfish. You get back dazed and confused—and there I am all bright and chippa on your doorstep.'

Bodja on his feet now shaking his ragged head.

'I see her blood on your hands, man. But I don't know what it is then. No wonder you go all wobbly when the chariot lads roll up at the tower. And then you slink home and start to worry. You dump her in a hurry—maybe she bobs up, and now she's still floating around. So you grab something handy and heavy and go back to finish the job. And that's why there's no chunk of old iron hanging by the wharf to hammer on when I plod up for a chat. And you're so grogged up and hair-trigger you try to nail me with your crossbow.'

'Bastard.' Bodja glaring dark. 'Fuckin' know-all cunt. All these years I'm proud I'm your mate, having a lark and helping you out. Now you put this dirty black shit on me?'

'You put it on yourself.'

'No.' A gleam of a tear in Bodja's eye.

'Crying about it won't put it right. You'll just have to face the music.'

'Just like that?'

'Yep.'

'Written off by the Big Chief in his tower?'

'If that's how you want to see it.'

'Right enough.' Bodja takes a breath. 'Serves me fuckin' right then for mistaking you for a pal.'

'If you run it'll be the rovers,' says Leepus suppressing the shake in his voice. 'Best if you wait for Mike.'

Bodja's in the kitchen then grabbing up his togs. The clatter of the lift gate. A slow whine of descent. And then the sound of the quaddie-motor hunted down the hill—ripped to shreds in the teeth of the screama.

A low growl in Leepus' gut now. He stands and walks dark to the bathroom—punches through its door.

∞

'Well, it could be a whole lot worse, babe,' says Jasmine on the fone. 'At least now you can deal with Queenie.'

'There's always a silver lining,' Leepus mutters under a mound of quilts.

'And you come out ahead against Ajax.'

'Just plastered in blood and shit.'

'Not yours though.'

'No. Well—'

'You didn't?' Jasmine chokes on a snigger. 'Now that'd be a sight worth seeing.'

'Fukkoff.' Leepus sticks his head out and lights a weedstick.

'So,' says Jasmine switching topic, 'our fugitive's here to play, then— and he's not too shy about raising.'

'You say it as if it's a good thing.'

'Got to admire a man of action.'

'You sound like fucking Mike.'

'And you sound a little bit peevish. The two of you still out of synch?'

'Might just be me, gal,' says Leepus. 'That touch of dizzy giving me the wobbles—but since this escapee grabs a seat and starts moving chips Mike's all distracted and touchy.'

Jasmine sniffs. 'Well, babe,' she says wary, 'at the risk of stoking paranoia, she does have previous with Arturo—maybe she's got some history with this mystery player too?'

'Some sort of dodgy killa threesome?'

'Just a thought,' says Jasmine. 'I don't mind having a look.'

'Goes against the grain,' says Leepus glum. 'But fukkit.'

'Kay. Meantime you're working on moving on Chilly?'

'Absolutely,' says Leepus diving back undercover. 'Engine of creativity, gal. Tactical options endless.'

155

Leepus in bed in the dark cold-sweating. He's overdone the thinking potion and woken up snarled in confusion.

Moonglow refracted by snow through the frosted skylight. An icicle of condensation dangling over his head. He breathes a pallid mushroom-cloud into the still cold air.

And outside the banshees howl on.

∞

It must be he sleeps again then—because the next time his eyes blink open the icicle is gone and there's a cold damp patch on his pillow.

And the hot acid tang of the overcooked stove. The sour fug of wet laundry dried to the point of scorching. And a rhythmic hiss and rumble from the tank room that sounds like snoring.

Leepus' first thought is it must be Bodja—the sorry fuck creeping back in the dead of night to plead. Or Mike—maybe overcome by a nocturnal impulse to weaken and confide. It's unlikely to be Doll— unless she's had another barney at home and stormed out in high dudgeon. And none of them is daft enough to be out after dark in a screama.

But the tower is a fortress. Who the fuck else could get in?

Leepus cloaks himself in a quilt and finds his fone. He pings Mike for urgent assistance—listens. No message tone from the tank room. Snoring unabated. He recovers his blowpipe from his coat—loads it with a magenta-tufted 'ragdoll' dart and stashes it in the sleeve of his thermals. Then he grabs his StunStik for good measure.

∞

The stove glowing cherry-red—the tank room tinted hellish. A snoring foetal figure steaming on the sofa. In vintage battledress. White hair blushed by incandescence. Head nestled snug on one crooked arm. The other one trailing—long fingers tickling the trigger guard of the carbine on the floor.

Leepus slips his blowpipe out and powers up the StunStik. And then he reconsiders. Maybe it's a bit more clever to just bunker up in the panic room and wait for Mike to sort it out. He likes that plan—

starts to back off. And then fucks it up by coughing. The sound is a trapped bird flapping around the concrete chamber. Before it finds a resting place the figure is thrashing awake. Rolling from the sofa. Grabbing up the weapon.

Leepus exhales a wild dart—sedates a sofa cushion.

'Wait!' croaks the white-haired man on his knees as Leepus lunges with the StunStik.

Contact. Pop and crackle. A sudden convulsive rigour. The carbine spasmodically discarded—clattering over the floor.

Leepus maintains a wary distance as he circles his prone opponent. A reflex shudder of respiration—the jolt of volts doesn't kill him. The dart recovered from the cushion and reloaded. Leepus wets lips. Gathers breath. Leans in point-blank over his target. Perforates a twitchy buttock.

The home invader satisfactorily 'ragdolled'. Leepus exits to scare up shackles.

◊◊◊◊◊

17

'So speak to me, you sly bastard,' says Leepus from the sofa—the white-haired griz now chained awkward to a wooden chair dragged in from the kitchen. 'I've still got volts in the StunStik.'

'Don't know where to start, bud,' his guest says with a mild Republic accent. His face is a wintry stubble-field—haggard furrows smoothed by snow with eyes sunk deep in piss-holes.

'Kick off with your name, and how you manage to infiltrate my impregnable fucking fortress,' says Leepus lighting a smoke.

'Short tag is SlashTenTwenty.' The captive squinting wry. 'I come up the tunnel and in through the priest hole. How else am I going to do it?'

'What fucking tunnel? What fucking priest hole?'

'The tunnel to the stone-pit bunker from the hidden trapdoor in the lift-well.' The prisoner shaking his ragged head. 'You're saying you never find it? How many years do you squat here?'

Leepus momentarily nonplussed. 'Squat?' he defends. 'This tower is mine forever.'

'But you don't know about the tunnel? So what about the bullion vault—surely you sniff my gold out?'

'What I know and what I don't is none of your fucking business. You're the scrote tied to the chair, Slash, and I'm the man asking questions.'

'So you are.' The captive winks. 'Ask away then. But keep it nice and friendly if you're after mining intel. I've broken a dozen pro-scrutineers with intransigence in my time, left them weeping and suicidal.'

'Fair enough,' says Leepus. 'Tell me why you're here.'

'Because the wind is solid ice out there and I want to stay alive.'

'Never mind the weather. You've been haunting this parish over a week now. What's the attraction in Shithole?'

'Not a lot that I've seen so far. But you're the one who lives here.'

'Right. That's why it pisses me off when some random cutthroat litters my yard with mangled corpses, disappears a brace of stalkers, and then has the fucking brass bollocks to bang a paramil TacTruk outside my local.'

'Just delivering an overdue fright to a backstabbing weasel.'

'The offender being Ajax?'

'Sorry if you're pals.'

Leepus ignores the suggestion—exhales a gust of smoke and says, 'So how does he betray you?'

The smoke cloud drifts around and past the captive's grizzled head—provokes a fit of coughing. A minute or so's violent hacking later and Slash is a sick shade of purple. Leepus is concerned enough to fetch a shot of grog. He holds it handy for sipping. That seems to do the trick—but when SlashTenTwenty raises his head there's a snail of bloody mucous slithering down his chin. He cranes to smear it on his shoulder as Leepus returns to the sofa saying, 'Nasty cough you've got there, mate. You need some lung pills from the erbwitch.'

'That's what you get from decades sixed in Republic cold-storage,' SlashTenTwenty croaks. 'So how about giving the smokes a rest before you set off a terminal spasm?'

Leepus thinks about that. 'Okay,' he says. 'Abstinence is a challenge—but as long as your story keeps making sense I'll keep making the effort.'

'Top man,' says Slash. 'Feels like we're almost friends now. Want to share your name?'

'Leepus,' says Leepus reaching for a weedstick. 'Now fucking entertain me.'

160

'Really?' Slash cocks his head. 'Kind of rings a bell somewhere. Any chance we have prior contact?'

'Seems unlikely.' Leepus fidgets with the unlit weedstick.

'Only here you are living it large in the stronghold I once sweat blood to build to see me through the apocalypse and enjoy a ripe old age in comfort. Feels like perhaps I should know you.'

Leepus frowns a warning and flicks his lighter.

'Easy, killa,' Slash says and winks. 'I'm only clearing my throat here.'

'You come through the Reduction, griz, you must be my generation. Where are you enjoying your life when it all goes tits-up?'

'Somewhere hot, weird and nasty. Fighting for civilisation.'

'Winning at that, or losing?'

'Just about breaking even, before the fireball. Then tactical support gets patchy. Takes a while to get my leggies back to their birth-land—what with the unreliable transport situation, and half the world either wailing and praying or eating their children.'

'The aurora are something to see, though. The Seven Veils of God lighting up the sky for weeks—pretty fucking trippy. Hardly surprising all those simple souls get overwhelmed by the glory.'

'Right.' Slash coughs. 'My lads celebrate their homecoming shovelling corpses into fire-pits and putting up Exit Haven's for the ones who cop for the rotters.

'Yeah—viral double-tap. Not a lot of laughs that year. You lose anyone close?'

'Thankfully I'm solo then. I think maybe an estranged brother, and he had a wife and some kids, but there's no way to be certain. So how about you, griz?'

'None,' Leepus says short. 'Not that I remember. But I've got a chunk of missing time. And then there's a spell of confusion.'

'But somehow you stagger through, find my castle to bunker up in.'

'Everyone needs a place to call home. Tower's abandoned when I find it. No one turns up to evict me.'

'I'm busy in the aftermath—fighting the warlords and crazies, trying

161

to set an example.'

'Imposing martial law and order. Securing the money and guns.'

'Not everyone finds their own fortress. Weak citizens need protection to survive the instincts of the fittest. The wonks in the College do their best to lay down a few basic rules—but there's way too many dogs in the fight, they might as well juggle water.'

'Lucky the Republic has a blueprint—and well-armed Compliance Advisers.'

'Resistance is futile, it's been said. Best pull up a chair and tuck in. I'm a freelance by now on a Citadel rolling-contract. '

'Looking out for Merrie Inglund in your downtime?'

'The Republic's not as indomitable as it tries to make believe. Its armour's a bit rusty, rivets under pressure, corroded by disaffection. Sometimes internal stresses and strains can be worked for local advantage.'

'You play that kind of dirty poka much?'

Slash smiles weak. 'I flirt with the game a little.'

'High stakes?'

'I've got a wife and child over there in the Homeland by now. I don't want to bet my whole bankroll.'

'But poka can get messy.'

'It's certainly not a team game.'

'I'm sensing a move going bad.'

'I'm nicely embedded and playing a stack of College money, in position to push the button on a darkco trying to finance an executive beheading. Not really any of our business, except they're screwing with the numbers to put Inglund into the hole. Plan to force a fire sale, snap up exploitation rights and suck off all our fat.'

'Push a button on them how?'

'A compact little demo-bang in a hotel lift-car, when the bagmen are in-country sizing up the pot.'

'Ah,' says Leepus diving in. 'And Major Arturo fucking Ajax jumps ship to the asset strippers, and your sly squib gets pissed on?'

'Good read, as far as it goes.' SlashTenTwenty pauses to cough. 'Ajax tweaks the timing—so a beloved Hero of the Republic gets publicly pink-misted instead.'

'Cue outrage and savage reprisal?'

'The Hero's heir to the power. But now it goes to a rival faction. The Citadel culls the College—conspirators grabbed up by praetorians for punitive interrogation. Most of them fail to survive.'

'You're made of sterner stuff?'

'Some fortunate misinformation leads them to believe I know a lot more than I'm telling. XTRK gleaners work me a couple of years before they get bored and tomb me. I grow old on my own in a cold steel box in a dark corner of a black site on a windswept offshore rock.'

'Grim,' says Leepus. 'And now here you are, free at last, but all knackered, bitter and twisted.'

'Whereas you haven't changed at all.' The captive lifts his wintry face then—looks out at Leepus through its piss-holes. 'All that water under the bridge and you're still just a snide shallow smart-arse who thinks he's clever.'

The tone of voice makes Leepus queasy. 'Still?' he queries. 'What the fuck does that mean?' And then he's reaching out—forestalling a potential answer with a deft sharp prod of the StunStik. Shocked Slash shudders rigid and topples unconscious.

∞

'Busy, mate,' Mike says to Leepus in the kitchen a few hours later. 'And it's too fuckin' cold to travel. I come as soon as it's melting.'

'What's it like on the road now?'

'Nothing moving. Half a dozen ponies on the moor froze and dead on their feet. Shame to waste good meat. Someone should go up and get 'em before the crows do.'

Leepus hands Mike a brew. She cradles it in blueish hands—inhales soothing steam. 'Sorry it's a goose chase,' he says. 'Turns out my novelty weapons and low cunning surpass your expectations.'

'Even idiots sometimes get lucky.'

'And there I am all warm inside thinking you'll be impressed by my self-reliance.'

'Twat.' Mike snorts and splashes brew. 'This killa turns seriously hostile and you wake up fuckin' headless. But the shit about a secret tunnel—telling me that's kosha?'

'Comes up in a cubby-hole under the lift-well. I go down and have a shufti. Trapdoor under thirty years of crud and some rubber matting.'

'Fuckin' Bodja needs a slap. What kind of half-arsed janitor misses that one?'

'Fucking Bodja is right,' says Leepus with a mouth twist. 'Turns out that old boy's been playing a bit shwonki. You might need to pay him a visit.'

'Yeah?' Mike says with a sigh. 'What's the silly arse been up to?'

'Turns out it's him does the rover gurlee.'

'Shit.' Mike frowns. 'That's a shock. He's always been a bit fuckin' sly but I never flag him as a raper. You get him to cough for it, do you?'

'Fucker doesn't exactly confess and grovel for forgiveness. It's a pretty simple read though.'

'Fair enough.' Mike cracks her knuckles. 'When do you want me to do it?'

'Need to work out the politics—how to play it best with the rovers. Maybe put some eyes on him in the meantime? Make sure the scrote doesn't freak and leg it.'

'I'll have a word with Doll's eldest grandkid, Ryda. He's a crafty lad.'

'Good,' says Leepus brisk. 'I'll ping you later, mate.'

'Hang about.' Mike drains her mug. 'I need some fuckin' breakfast first. And what are we going to do about this cunt you've got banged up?'

'Leave him a while.' Leepus lights the gas under a crusty gruel-pan. 'And then I'll have another word—dig out a bit more of his story.'

'Sure you can handle that, mate?' Mike raises a wry eyebrow. 'This old lad's had practice escaping, and he's likely to be a good bit livelier once he's thawed and rested. That's if he's even still in there. For all you know the place is riddled with fuckin' priest-holes.'

'Even if it is he won't get far in shackles.'

'I s'pose you give him a good searching?'

'One carbine, a fighting knife, a stiletto in his boot—a couple of minibombs in his pocket, and a wire-saw bracelet.'

'A lock-pick could fit up his arsehole.'

'Hands shackled in the front. But I suppose he might do some contortionist bollocks and grab it with his teeth.'

'Just saying, mate.' Mike shrugs as Leepus passes her a spoon and the seething gruel-pan. 'Killa knows his work, and his armoury's comprehensive.'

'Yeah—he says something about a bunker in the old stonepits, at the end of this fucking tunnel. You ought to check that out and secure it.'

Mike grunts—concentrates on relocating hot slop from pan to stomach. Eventually the spoon scrapes metal. She uses her cuff to wipe her mouth—then says, 'I'm not quite feeling this. This joker's got the moves to slaughter his escort, and inside knowledge of the tower—so it's not just chance he runs here. And what about this blud thing with Ajax?'

'The sooner you fuck off, mate, the sooner I can ask him.'

'Don't you tell me once you win this gaff from some fish in a game of poka?' Mike is undeflected. 'Way back in the fuckin' dim-distant, when I'm just a sweet little giggla?'

'Sounds plausible enough.'

'I bet you fuckin' cheat him. And now he wants it back.' Mike frowns. 'But then why not just chop you there and then—or chuck you out to freeze in the screama—before he settles in by the fire and puts his feet up? What's the fucker really after? You certain you don't know him?'

'A lot of years go whirling by while he's incarcerated,' Leepus explains gnomic. 'Stuff that's true when he gets tombed probably

165

isn't now. He's lost and alone in the future. He needs someone he can trust to put him in the picture. Maybe he senses I'm that person.'

'Right,' says Mike flashing pearlies. 'So who are you going to deal him to—Major Cunt, or fuckin' Chilly?'

∞

A bowl sliding across the panic-room floor. SlashTenTwenty reaching in chains—picking it up and peering. 'What's this?' he asks turning his nose up.

'Gruel,' says Leepus from the threshold. 'Always good to start the day with a hearty breakfast.'

'I get better on the rock.'

'I'd eat it while it's hot, mate.'

'How about loosening my restraint, then? A spoon'd be handy too.'

'Handy to scoop out my fucking eyeballs. Old killas can't be trusted.'

'Enough of this damn bullshit game,' SlashTenTwenty growls. 'You may be a freeloading deviant twerp begging for comeuppance, but I'm hardly gonna exact lethal retribution on my long-lost big brother.'

'That might be more reassuring,' says Leepus after a pause for reflection, 'if that's who I am, Slash.'

'Marcus.'

'What?'

'You heard.'

Leepus turns his back then—drifts off to fetch a spoon.

'You look a bit on the pale side, bud,' the captive says accepting the utensil.

'We all have shit to deal with. Some of us manage it better than others.'

SlashTenTwenty spoons gruel in silence. His shackles make this tricky. Leepus watches through narrowed eyes and smokes a weedstick. Lucky the smoke drifts into the tank room away from his invalid captive.

166

'Fair enough, bud,' Slash says when he finishes eating, 'No harm in you role-playing 'Leepus', I guess, if that's what gets you through. Picking scabs and waving shrouds is probably not productive. It's obvious we're both past our prime, with unreliable recall, so maybe it's simpler to start over.'

'Thanks, Marcus.' Leepus nods. 'Appreciate you seeing it my way, brer. I'll fetch the key for the shackles.'

∞

Leepus at the parapet watching the landscape defrosting—the clean white crackle of vegetation softened grey-green by dank mizzle. Buzzards over the heather scouting for carrion left by the screama. He sways a little staring up to watch them wheeling. Everything in dizzy motion. For a moment he feels like he's falling into the endless sky.

'Good view.' His guest a sudden anchor behind him. 'At least you can see it coming.'

'You never see it coming,' says Leepus. 'That's how it fucking gets you.'

Marcus blinks and scans the horizon. 'You forget how big the world is, shut up in a six-by-eight box.'

'Smaller than it once was, in terms of most peoples' outlook. And more of it's fucking water.'

'Bound to see some changes if you live as long as we do.'

'Yeah,' says Leepus. 'You couldn't call it boring.'

'Just quieter without all the people.'

'Once the blood lust settles down, and the godlies have slaughtered each other.'

'The College gets a lid on the chaos eventually, I guess, with a bit of support from the Republic.'

'Not really, thank fuck,' says Leepus turning for the ladder. 'Three or four municipalities keep the timid and feeble-minded fenced in safe and their noses to the grindstone. NoGo is full-tilt freedom—life there is rowdy and brutal. But the rest of us bumpkins are left alone to make it up as we go along—as long as we keep our heads down and don't frighten the strivas.'

'A paradise for free-thinking gamblers and outlaws?' Marcus follows him down. 'Jolly pirates lallygagging in libertarian enclaves?'

'Paradise is a bit of stretch. It's a struggle for the poor and simple. The peasants are still downtrodden. Lots of factions pushing and shoving. Big dogs gathering packs, trying to take advantage. Occasional outbreaks of savage violence—but generally we manage to work things out with a bit of political poka.'

'So I'm guessing you're a useful player—some kind of a local hero.'

'Everyone loses now and then, but generally I'm lucky.'

'And it helps if you're rich to start with.'

'Enough about me,' says Leepus in the tank room. 'Why don't you sit yourself down, mate? Tell me how your story goes between disinterment and my fucking sofa.'

'How about some refreshment first—cup of whatever that warm piss is that you call brew, bud?'

'Doll gets it from the erbwitch—some dried weeds that grow in the forest. Tea and caffy are luxuries now, reserved for special occasions.'

'Doll?' Marcus raising a bushy white eyebrow. 'I'm thinking I detect a conscientious female touch about the bathroom—despite the fist-hole in the door. She the romantic interest?'

'Not likely, mate.' Leepus smiles as he fills the kettle. 'I just pay her to come in and suppress diseases. My romantic interest gets subsumed in a past reckless passion for dizzy.'

'Dizzy?' Marcus sniffs. 'Some kind of twisted dope, bud?'

'A useful self-medication. Helps you see the funny side—takes the fucking sting out. Best not to use it too long though, or your synapses go a bit haywire.'

'Right.' Marcus takes the kettle—a wobble in Leepus' hand. 'A lot of good things get lost, I guess. I can see why you'd want to forget them.'

'Makes you wonder sometimes how you stay alive when you try your hardest not to. And nowadays they call you griz if you manage to live past fifty and stay out of fucking KashBak. Sometimes it doesn't seem quite right to be still going strong, mate.'

'Cursed with a gene for survival. It's natural to feel guilty when you have to leave people behind—but that's the way the cards fall.'

'Yeah. Sorry,' says Leepus. 'Don't usually get all hangdog. I must be missing my weedsticks.'

'Come on,' says Marcus leading back to the tank room. 'Forget about the weedsticks—the last blood-drenched instalment of my misadventures'll cheer you up.' He takes a couple of silent steps. 'So what the hell is KashBak?' he mutters as Leepus follows.

∞

'First clue I get something's going on, confinement techs snag me from my box and wheel me over to HealthCon. That's usually a one-way ride. I get a little bit anxious—but the medics give me a calm-down shot and shove me through the DroneDoc. Seems nothing I've got is infectious, so they code me fit to travel and fit me with a bracelet. Ten minutes later I'm all tarted up in transit diapers and a crisp new paper-jumpsuit. Then they tuck me up snug in a padded crate and haul me down to the ferry.'

'With no idea where you're going?'

'"Don't know. Don't care," is all I get from the pretty nurse who clamps the lid down. So I make the most of the sedative to grab a bit of beauty sleep and see what's changed in the morning.'

'You don't know Ajax is the contractor handling your delivery to Chilly?'

'I get a whiff of Ajax when I wake up. But where the hell is Chilly?'

'It's not a place, it's a person—INTL-XTRK Cohort Commander Atalanta Honor-Trublood.'

Marcus shrugs and shakes his head. 'Pretty sure I'd remember the name.'

'They say her career is stellar but she's barely grown up. She'd need to have been a precocious brat to have any professional status during your early incarceration. But something piques her

169

retrospective interest. Signs are it's a spec investigation—maybe extra curricula even.'

'Surprising level of insight, bud,' says Marcus cocking his head. 'You must have handy sources.'

'You need to pay attention if you want to be a winna.'

'So, you playing cards with this bad girl?'

'Never mind Chilly,' says Leepus. 'Let's hear about Arturo. How does it go waking up?'

'Right.' Marcus sighs. 'It's a bit of a shock if I'm honest. There I am rocking gently along all warm and cosy in my dreamboat. Then there's some pitching and tossing and shouting—next I know I'm over the side and submerged in deep dark water. I kick and claw for the surface, open my eyes and I'm screaming like a man on fire in a burning ocean.'

'Clue there in the use of 'like'?'

'I just have time, as the first hurt-squirt wears off, to figure out that I'm out of my crate in the back of an ambo—before one of three dark-visored bastards hits me with the second. This time I'm outside and sprawled on gravel when the pain stops. There's a full moon above some treetops. "Griz muss be a fuckin' werewolf," says a joker shooting vid. "Way the mad cunt's howlin'." And then the cab door opens and the driver's bailing, scrambling after cover. A killa lifts his carbine—shoots the runner's foot off. They drag him back to the ambo by his hair and toss him in the back. You can hear him moan and whimper even with the door shut.'

'Must be a bit distressing, mate,' Leepus says as Marcus breaks for a spasm of coughing. 'How are you reading the situation?'

'Obvious the driver's not copied in on the operation, and doesn't see a good personal outcome. The rest doesn't make a lot of sense, until the lead killa gets a call. He listens, then tells the vid guy the ID's good and to "haul the fuckin' wolfman over here so the Boss can have a word." The connection's not great, and I'm still hurting, but the face that matches the voice I hear belongs to my old brother-in-arms, Arturo-the-Arsehole Ajax.'

'A lot of years gone by—you must have plenty to catch up on?'

'Long story short, he says he's surprised to find out I'm even still alive when the Citadel orders me dug up and brought in for special interrogation. He's in an awkward spot now, and he's going to have to disappear me—unless I've got anything stashed away he can use to ensure his continuing status as a high-value Republic asset. In which case he's happy to fix it for me to live the rest of my life in anonymity and moderate comfort on a faraway tropical island.'

'Obvious he thinks you do or you're dead already.'

'If the fool has a hint of sense in his head he tells those killas go ahead and slot me there and then. But he's always just a greedy coward who thinks he's a player.'

'So you tell him you've got treasure buried, and you'll bring the kill-team to the tower—so they can secure any smoking guns and get him out from under before they sink you in some swamp?'

'He thinks I'm as simple as he is.'

'Twat has it fucking coming. Let's hear how you take down the killas.'

Marcus smiles weak. 'At this point that's not a given. I'm still a long way behind, bud, and needing to get lucky. But it's likely I'm holding live cards, at least, with a fighting chance of improvement. So I make out I'm hazy about the tower's precise location, but I'll know it when I see it, they just need to get us near.'

'And they buy that? I don't think I'm that trusting.'

'I come on a bit feeble and weepy. Worn-out scared old griz schooled by generations of black-site compliance technicians. They're not seeing any threat. They turn off the ambo's FindMe and cut off my bracelet—one of them stashes it in a stealth pocket for later remote disposal. And then we drive on south.'

'And park up in the old quarry.'

'I tell them the tower's likely controlled by hostiles, but I reckon I can walk them in safe across the fields before the sun's up. The top hand says okay—they'll torch the ambo and arrange extraction via the PayWay. The mug in the back's not happy with the plan, though, starts banging on the sides and wailing—pleads for them to let him out and how he'll keep his mouth shut. Top hand tells him it's a

171

shame but that's not going to happen. "Need one to hang for the gang, brer," he says. "And you're the cunt elected." Then he drops a bangstik in the gas tank, and we leave the mug behind there all hot and bothered and shrieking.'

'You bring them down the hill to the hollow and on to the forest?'

'Decades since I scout that ground but it feels like I know where I'm going—except there's a marsh and a lake I'm not expecting.'

'It never stops fucking raining. Lot of kids these days getting born with duck feet.'

'Right.' Marcus frowns uncertain. 'Anyhow, off we splash with a song in our hearts along the valley to the tree line. It takes me an hour to find the stonepit in the dark, because it's all grown over with briars. Sun's just about up behind the fog by the time we've cut through and uncovered the bunker. I'm thinking by now it's certain to be compromised and looted, or someone resets the keypad—or maybe I misremember the number. But the bolts snap back first pop. It takes a bit of heaving and cursing to get the blast door open. I get sent in first, in case it's wired to bang. First impressions are reassuring. As far as I remember everything's how I leave it—just covered up with spiderwebs and about six inches of bat shit.'

'Everything being what?'

'Survival kit and munitions.'

'And something to surprise these killas?'

'Yeah.' Marcus grins a little bit cold. 'I tell them there's a chip crammed with juicy intel locked up in a strongbox—along with a couple of pounds of gleaming treasure. The information cheers them up and they give me a minute to find it, or else they start back in with the hurt-squirts.'

'Bet you're lying about the treasure,' says Leepus grinning back.

'No, bud.' Marcus winks. 'But the intel chip is pure bullshit.'

'Go on,' says Leepus hooked now.

'I tell them, drag it out and dust the crap off, and I'll give them the combination. "You do it," says the top hand sly. "I'm not in the mood for surprises." I try to look disappointed at being outsmarted—take my time about getting it open. Chumps stand well back for a minute once the lid's up. Then I get a gratuitous squirt of hurt, and they start counting out ingots. The pain's a bit distracting. I'm only just through the blast door and round the corner when the timer clicks down to zero, detonates the little chop-charge I build into the lid of the strongbox.'

'That must make your ears ring.'

'Lucky the blast is contained by the bunker. Same with most of the meat-chunks. Just the top hand's ugly head blows out—whacks on the turf of the pit-side, rolls back down to rest at my feet looking up sort of puzzled.'

'Sounds like a tidy job, mate,' Leepus says approving. 'So how come you gather all that carrion up and haul it half-a-mile across the hill to dump it on my doorstep? Why not just leave it sealed up out of harm's way in the bunker instead of making gratuitous mischief?'

'Squeamish.' Marcus grins. 'Bunker's stocked with handy kit—don't want to be knee-deep in rats and rotting corpses every time I drop back to re-up.'

'Plus you want to make a point and vent your spleen.'

Marcus looks blank.

'Tracker bracelet kicked up a dead arsehole must be intended to send a strong message. Dirty work like that takes thought and effort, a degree of pent-up aggression.'

'I did that?' Marcus shakes his head. 'Not exactly professional— must be I'm lost in a red-mist moment, having a bit of a howl, bud.'

'Oh well,' says Leepus. 'You probably earn the right.'

'All a bit hazy there now I try to recall details. I guess then I grab some essentials and close up the bunker—because I wake up nested snug in a hollow oak-stump deep inside the forest, with a couple of gore-soaked ration-packs and a random selection of weapons. No way of knowing how long I sleep, but the footprints I leave gathering bracken for bedding are at least seventy-two hours old, now.'

'By which time the prefects have picked up the pieces and kicked my door in.'

'Right. I pass a couple more days refining my woodland bivvy and getting my breath back. Next time I check on the tower there's a shaggy old lad with a quad-bike working on the gate.'

'Bodja.'

'Handy with a welder but not good on observation.'

'The least of his character flaws.'

'I'm not the only one watching.'

'The stalkers in the heather.'

'I keep my eye on them a couple more days waiting for something to happen—then your tame killa turns up on his combo, makes them in a blink of an eye and blows back down to the village. I follow him down to the pub and find the two of you outside talking. Sign round your neck says King of the Dump—so I dog you for a couple of kliks, thinking maybe we'll have a confab.'

'But I see you on my arse and lose you at the railway cutting.'

'Sort of.' Marcus smiles. 'Obvious you're spooked—I can't be bothered chasing you down and fighting for your attention. So I figure I'll hang around back at the tower. Maybe do a good deed while I'm waiting, to keep from getting bored and win a bit of favour.'

'Sudden death for the stalkers.'

'Sudden death for one of them. The other gets to buy a couple extra minutes pleading—says I'm messing with the wrong man's mission, Ajax is a psycho who's gonna hunt me down and eat my balls for pissing up his leg. I tell him good and I can't wait—and then I cut his head off.'

'What I say about pent-up aggression.'

'Just enjoying the novelty of free will and self-expression. It's good to make things happen.'

'As long as you're not the hopeless mope trying to make the best of his ragged hand when some maniac with a chip on his shoulder blows the fucking game up.'

'Quit crying. Your killa's always waiting in the wings to bail you out.'

Leepus broods silent for a minute.

'So, your move now I think, bud?' says Marcus with a weird kind of glint in his eye. 'I've just stirred the pot a bit. It's up to you to fish the meat out.'

The rattle and drone of the ascending lift provides a useful distraction. Marcus shifts uneasy in his chair and looks around suspicious. Leepus smirks at his discomfort. 'Relax,' he says after a moment, 'it's only old Doll come to boil up some veg. I haven't cashed you in yet, mate.'

∞

'Sparrers mainly,' says Doll later in response to Leepus' raised eyebrow, 'an' a couple of starlin's for flavour. Screama freezes 'em out of the eaves. I stew 'em up to treat the kids but they moan about the fevvers. Think I'll bring the leavings for you to enjoy with your special guest sooner than bleedin' waste 'em.'

'Hardly a fatted calf,' says Leepus sniffing bubbling bone-broth. 'How do you know I'm entertaining?'

'Mike says. She stops off for a word with Ryda.'

'So what's happening down in the hole?' asks Leepus making conversation. 'Any news I should be abreast of?'

'Halfsharp Sean's a dead 'un. Only goes and falls asleep all grogged up in the out'ouse. His missus finds 'im in the morning when she's after slopping out. Mope's froze rigid on the shitta halfway through his business. Gives her a right dose of the 'orrors.'

'What's the situation with the pub?'

'Bethan calls in some favours, gets the windows boarded up. I sweep up the broke glass and sluice the floor down. Still whiffs a bit when the fire gets 'ot, an' I don't get all the blood out, so your feet kind of stick to the carpet.'

'Everyone's happy enough though?'

'You're bleedin' jokin', ain't you? Mercenaries warring up the High Street. Icebergs on the river. A cock monster stalkin' the parish— that poor tinkish lass still not laid to rest, an' her savage bredren coming down on us any bleedin' day now. Bob the Butcher says it's your fault.'

'Maybe it is,' says Leepus. 'Remind me to give you chips when you go. Put a stack behind the bar. Tell Bethan good grog on me for everyone—excepting Bob the-fucking-Butcher. And let it slip the rover thing's sorted, see if that cheers the whiny mopes up.'

'Is it?' Doll flicks a glance.

'Yeah,' says Leepus deflecting. 'Just need to haggle the gory details.'

'Good.' Doll ladles out boiled sparrows. 'Go and wake up your brother then, an' I'll get this on the table.'

'What?' Leepus glares not moving. 'Who tells you the fucker's my brother.'

'No one,' says Doll a bit taken aback. 'But it's plain enough that griz an' you pop out of the same bleedin' fanny—just he's a good bit younger and nicer lookin', ennit?'

'Bollocks,' says Leepus tight-lipped as he heads out the door. 'You need some fucking specs, mate.'

◊◊◊◊◊

18

'Bless you, Doll, for that delicious meal.' Marcus leans back replete. 'It's been a long time since I enjoyed home cooking.'

'Kind of you to say so, lad,' says Doll giving Leepus a look. 'I'll get the kettle on for a brew then.'

'Lovely.' Marcus winks. 'If there's no hope of anything stronger.'

'I might find a nip of grog.' Doll looks for Leepus' approval.

'Why not?' Leepus shrugs expansive. 'But not the Yellow Scorpion. That's reserved for celebrations.'

The men share a silent minute of mutual regard while Doll fetches a cobwebby bottle—pours them brim-full shots.

'A toast,' declares Marcus raising his glass. 'To freedom and friends, and hearth and home.'

'And family, too, while we're at it,' Doll chips in with a clink.

'Yeah.' Leepus knocks his shot back. Marcus follows suit—and then has a fit of coughing. Doll sets about refilling. 'Not for me.' Leepus stands. 'I'd love to stay and loll about getting all sentimental, but I've got a mountain of shit to shovel.'

'Shame.' Marcus sinks his refill. 'I'm in the mood to party.'

'Me too,' Doll says and giggles.

'Knock yourselves out,' says Leepus leaving. 'Just don't do the whole fucking bottle.'

∞

Leepus walking the ridge above the river-valley trying to divine a signal. He's got a weedstick cupped in one hand—fone outstretched

177

in the other. Must be the screama wipes out the cell-blimp. Or komSecs kill his hookup. He'll give it a shot from the Witches Graveyard—or else it's a drag back down into Shithole to scare up runners.

And then the fucking rain starts. Leepus is bedraggled long before he reaches the Tooth Stone. Its lee is a rabbit toilet—but if he huddles low enough it just about keeps the wet off. And at least his fone shows bars now. Got to hand it to those old megalith builders—they know how to put up shit that lasts and engineer a hot spot.

Leepus makes a tent of his coat and rolls himself a dry weedstick. He smokes it peeping out as the cloud comes down around him. And then he rolls another. 'Fukkit,' he mutters when he tires of the gloomy outlook. 'Cards are in the air, now. Might as well fucking play them.'

∞

'You're takin' the fokkin piss,' rumbles the King of Clubs through the ether. 'You've used up all your favours, brer. And I'm not seeing a house percentage.'

'Forget the rake, you cheap bean-counter. This game only pays in the long-run. I play it right and the College wins big, and you grab a fat chunk of the glory.'

'What if you get unlucky?'

'Never known to happen,' says Leepus. 'But just in case the world burns down, or I die at the fucking table, I'll put up a hefty chest of treasure you can hold as a deposit.'

'Hefty?'

'You'd struggle to lift it alone.'

The King of Clubs thinks about it. Leepus doesn't push him. There's a big black dog in the circle of stones now. It's walking widdershins. Head down and grey tongue lolling. Leepus isn't superstitious but it looks a little bit eerie.

'So when do you want to sit down?'

The hound pricks its ears and looks over. Leepus doesn't answer—shrinks back into his coat.

'Fokksake, griz—I'm not talkin' to my fokkin self, here.'

Leepus concentrates on keeping calm as the beast pads up to the Tooth Stone. Sniffs. Cocks leg. Lets go a squirt of urine into the chink between collar and hatbrim. 'Fukkoff, mutt,' he hisses.

'What?' The King's not amused. 'This conversation's over.'

'Wait.' The hound lopes off on its stony orbit. Leepus watches the murk dissolve it. 'No offence intended, mate. I think I'm having a mythic moment.'

'You're off your fokkin trolley.'

'Maybe. You think getting pissed on by a spirit dog is good luck or fucking bad?'

'Last fokkin chance, brer,' says the King. It sounds as if he means it. 'When do you want to do this?'

'Two days,' says Leepus wafting his coat to vent acrid piss fumes. 'I need a table in a private room with virtual face-to-face, an ambiance of mutual respect, and omnipresent security to represent some balance of power.'

'That's it?'

'Maybe a selection of tasty snacks? And a car to fetch me? But not that mad scrote you send last time—he does my fucking head in.'

'The Roosta?' The King chuckles sly. 'Fokkin diamond, that one. Funniest old boy on the payroll, griz—long as you speak chicken.'

'Cluck off,' says Leepus. 'Now you're just being childish.'

∞

'I've been better, babe, if I'm honest,' says Jasmine a few minutes later. 'Bit of a disappointment in the intimate care department. Young Angel lets me down.'

'That's a surprise,' says Leepus without feeling. 'Fucker looks chippa enough, though. Must be his heart isn't in it.'

'What his heart's in isn't the problem.'

'Okay,' says Leepus wary. 'We don't need to get into specifics.'

'Tell that to my poor Lucifer.'

'What?' Leepus pauses to spark a weedstick. 'That sounds a bit unhygienic, gal—not to mention risky.'

'Dog-bowl dosed with eZee. I roll in and there they are, full-tilt in matching muzzles.'

'Sorry, gal,' says Leepus choking off a giggle. 'Must be a nasty shock.'

'I suffer emotional devastation.'

'I'm imagining some payback.'

'Right. Figure I'll make it poetic. I'm waiting while the sick little bastard showers—a hundred mils of eZee handy in a blunt hypo. I get most of it into an arsecheek. Boy squawks and then goes into loving meltdown. I give Lucifer a whistle. Tell him this time it's his turn—and forget about the muzzles.'

'No,' says Leepus after due consideration.

'No what?'

'No I'm not buying that old nonsense. It's a fucking wind-up.'

'Bollocks,' says Jasmine. 'You think I've got it in me to make up sick shit like that?'

'Granted it is a bit twisted—even for a veteran degenerate dark artist, like you.'

'Want to go again?'

'Shit, gal—I don't have time to fuck around here.'

'Just one word. Truth or lie. This time your decision is final.'

The rain has shifted direction. Leepus hunkers back inside his coat to weigh the odds. If he says she's bluffing and calls it right Jasmine is going to be arsey. Less inclined to be helpful—if not downright obstructive. But if he says her story's kosha and it's not she wins this hand of wind-up. And winning makes Jasmine happy and productive. 'Truth,' he says in a voice contorted by the tang of dog piss.

'Wrong.' Jasmine chortles. 'Another bad read from the so-called poka legend. Angel's right here with me now, giving me a cheeky foot-rub.'

'Nice one,' says Leepus. 'I must be under the weather.'

'Baffles me sometimes, babe, how a hopeless fish like you ever comes out ahead.'

'Not many players at your level, gal. That's why you're still on the payroll.'

'Oooh, yes. More please. You know how to reach my sweet spot.'

'I have a lot of practise, don't I? Some things are hard to forget.'

'Hah! Gotcha again,' says Jasmine. 'I'm not talking to you, babe.'

'Fukksake.' Leepus is suddenly impatient. 'Get shot of that fucking gigolo and lay off the grog for an hour—then maybe I call you back.'

'Easy, tiger,' says Jasmine. 'I'm only bored and playing around. So I'm guessing your foul temper's a clue this game is properly on now. Something you need me to do?'

'Yes,' Leepus says as the rain drums on. 'If it's not too much fucking trouble.'

'Speak up,' says Jasmine. 'Where the hell are you calling from? Sounds like you're in the shower.'

'I'm in the Witches Graveyard squatting under the Tooth Stone. I try to commune with animal spirits but all I get is pissed on.'

'Witches Graveyard? Some kind of club for grubby old grizzas, is it? Mind you don't catch something nasty.'

'Shut up,' says Leepus, 'and fucking listen.'

'Best you get right to the point, babe,' says Jasmine a bit breathless. 'Young Angel's working hard here. I can't hang on much longer.'

'I need you to bell Mother Mellow to sort me out with a bunker and hook up a ghostFone. I don't want to know the location. Mike's handling logistics, work out the detail with her.'

'Don't you say Mike's under suspicion?'

'You turn up something shwonki?'

'Not a thing, so far.'

'Good. This play crashes and burns without her.'

'So I'm guessing you lay hands on the mystery player, and now you're going to deal him to Chilly? Got a name I can add to my data?

It might shine a light in the shadows.'

'No.'

'Okay.' Jasmine sounds doubtful but doesn't pursue it. 'And you're dealing with the rovers?'

'Getting there.'

'How does it go for Bodja?'

'I'm thinking Viking funeral. Call me a soft old twat if you have to, but I feel like I owe him a gesture. Scrote loves that rotten hulk of his like a fucking wife. Maybe I give him a chance to finally cast off on his cruise-of-a-lifetime downriver. Coffin ship sinks inside ten minutes on open water and Bodja knows it. But he also knows it's his only chance to make a half-dignified exit trailing a few tattered scraps of honour.'

'I'm blinking back the tears, babe.'

'So Bodja's loaded to the gunnels with high-explosive ballast. And Mike's on hand with her deer gun. Rovers witnessing from nearby high ground. We let him get out onto open water, feel the sea-breeze in his hair—and then Mike turns the poor fuck's lights out and detonates his ballast. Cue a pyrotechnic spectacle of justice— jubilant rover catharsis. And then it's just smoke on the water and driftwood.'

Leepus waits but Jasmine doesn't comment. 'So what do you think?' he prompts.

'I think it must really mess up your head, babe, playing Sheriff of Shithole. I'm sorry for your trouble.'

∞

Another ten minutes and the deluge dissipates to drizzle. Leepus creaks to his feet—totters off around the stones in a torment of cramped muscles. He lights another weedstick—inhales vaporised dog-micturition. His throat is feeling sore now. He's had enough of talking so he taps out a message to Chilly.

Okay, I fold. You can stand down the forces of genocide and get set to extract value. Fugitive to hand now. Watch this space for venue updates and be prepared to play at immediate notice.

Leepus finishes his weedstick as the mist rolls back from the valley. Shithole down below him leaking homely chimney smoke. A minor lump in his throat. Maybe its just the tainted weed—but Leepus feels a deep-seated need play his cards right. There's a tremor in his finger as he sends his second message.

Over your fright yet, Arturo? Got a man here who thinks he knows you. Situation a bit fast-moving—all previous deals superseded. Chilly's circling the table on the scent of some rotten old secrets. Feel the need to re-buy? Just come up with my weight in gold to be in with a chance of an invitation.

Leepus walks the ridge back to the tower. The turf is vivid green and soft beneath his feet. He enjoys the way it seems to put a bit of a spring in his step.

∞

Doll in the kitchen at the sink—she's rinsing out empty bottles. Leepus raises an eyebrow. 'Likes 'is grog, does that ol' lad,' says Doll with a gleam of defiance. 'Seems rude not to keep it comin'.'

'Three whole fucking bottles? Hard to imagine he's still breathing.'

'I do my best to keep up with 'im, to be soshabul an' spare 'is liver.'

'That involve a degree of gossip?'

'Not s'much 'bout you, mate, if thass what you're gettin' at. We chat a bit about kids an' stuff—the things you can miss when they're growin' up if you're too busy to pay proper 'tenshun. Makes 'im come over all teary.'

'Tugs at your heartstrings, does he?'

'Can't say I mind if 'e does, griz. It's a change to be talked to nice.'

'Fair enough,' says Leepus shucking off his coat. 'Just don't go getting too attached, scrote's off on his travels later.'

'Not for a good few hours, I reckon,' says Doll looking suddenly queasy. 'But what the fuck are you up to? You whiff like rotten nappies.'

'Over-familiar hellhound. Clothes'll need a rinse out. I'll go through and get them off while you start running my shower.'

''Kay,' Doll says and fumbles her sleeves up. 'But I'm bookin' a nextra hour. And I'd do it by the fire, mate—'less you want to risk that stink makin' party-boy puke in your bed.'

'Fukksake, Doll,' says Leepus. 'You put the drunk bastard in my room? What the hell's wrong with the sofa?'

'He pukes on that already. Comes over poorly all of a sudden while we're 'avin' a knees-up, ennit?'

Leepus shakes his head wordless. Doll wobbles off to the shower.

∞

Doll's bundled in her coat and sat waiting when Leepus returns in his dressing gown. His skin is sore from hard abrasion but he still smells distinctly doggy. Or perhaps it's his imagination. 'What do you reckon?' he says inviting olfactory inspection.

Doll sniffs and leans back sharpish. 'Not 'xactly roses—but then you never are.'

'Filthy brute,' says Leepus. You ever get up there to the Witches Graveyard, mate? See something that gives you a fright?'

Doll thinks for a moment swaying. 'Can't say I do, griz, she says attempting a bleary wink. ''Least, not since I'm a ninnocent young lass gone out shrooming with Foot-Long Frank. Just the memory of that awful thing makes my eyes bleedin' water.'

'Sounds like I get off light, then,' says Leepus scrabbling for a weedstick. He lights it sitting down with Doll—smokes it while she looks on unspeaking. 'What's the matter?' he says then. 'Stringing out the overtime—or incapable of locomotion?'

'Cheeky old scrote,' says Doll blundering upright unsteady. 'I can 'old me grog, mate. Drink you into a coma.'

'Off you fucking trot, then. I've got stuff to see to.'

'S'payday, ennit?' Doll stares him down.

'Parasite,' says Leepus. 'Follow me to the strongbox.'

'There.' Leepus counts chips into Doll's cupped hand. 'That's your wages up to date—though by rights you've drunk them already. And here's an extra couple of hundred to leave at the Queen's like I tell you.'

'Right you are.' Doll tucks loot into pocket—stands there shuffling awkward.

'Now what?'

'Well—' Doll chews her lip. 'I do little bit extra, ennit, in the 'ospitality department.'

'And I already say I don't dock you for the grog.'

'I know, but—' A hint of flushing about Doll's neckline. 'Marcus is a sweet ol' lad. An 'e's locked up and lonely such a long time I reckon 'e needs a cuddle.'

'Fukksake.' Leepus shakes his head. 'Whether the sly fuck does or whether he doesn't, it's not my business, is it?'

'No,' Doll says extending her hand, ' 'cept, when I tell 'im I've got about a thousan' mouths to feed, 'e says you won't begrudge coughin' up to see me right, because you owe 'im bigtime.'

'I might have a different opinion.'

'Even if you do, griz, it'd be a gen'rus gesture.'

'How much, you shameless baggage?' says Leepus with teeth gritted.

'I tell 'im the goin' rate's a nundred—so seventy 'cause I like 'im.'

'Fifty's all you ever ask me for.' Leepus measures another chipstack.

'Yeah,' says Doll securing her prize and turning swift for the exit. 'But that's only 'cause it's bleedin' plain as day a dizzy-shagged ol' griz like you 'asn't got a long go in 'im.'

Leepus struggles to get his tongue round a suitable comeback. Doll's gone while he's still thinking.

∞

It's halfway through the morning before Mike condescends to putt up. Leepus isn't happy. He doesn't sleep well on the rug by the fire and he's already been up a couple of hours before he pings her at sunrise. 'The job is fucking full-time, mate, for as long as the game is running. I need to know you're paying attention.'

'Coming from you?' Mike sniffs. 'I'm not the one running around like

185

a cat on fire with my drug-fucked head up my arsehole. Lot of ways this thing goes bad if you don't have shit covered.'

'Saying I don't know what I'm doing?'

Mike shrugs. 'Just one bad read in a dodgy spot and we're all fuckin' hurting.'

'I don't make bad reads.'

'Yeah you fuckin' do, mate.'

'Bollocks,' says Leepus. 'Name one.'

'Bodja.'

'What?' Leepus stares. 'How the fuck is that, then?'

'He doesn't do that tinkish kid.'

'How the fuck would you know?'

'Doll's lad, Ryda, tells me. I give him a spyglass to help with the obs job on Bodja. He sees the old boy take his skiff out on the river and head across to Rat Island.'

'Probably just going fishing.'

'Ryda says there's a bender on the island, hidden in amongst the alder—and there's a "slinki what comes out wivvout 'er shirt on, ennit?—to 'elp 'im tie 'is boat up?".'

'Shit.' Leepus shakes his head. 'This is kosha, is it? It's definitely our gurlee?'

'Unless your man's on a sex spree.'

'Bodja. Fuck. Why doesn't the halfwit just come out with the truth and ask for help when I front him?'

'You tell me,' says Mike a bit sly. 'Maybe he thinks he shouldn't need to.'

'Whatever,' says Leepus. 'This vix wants her arse slapped. Likely she's running a game here to milk the simples.'

'Bottom line, mate,' Mike says, 'You get it arse-backwards on Bodja, and now I'm supposed to have your back while you get stuck into the Republic?'

'That's right.'

'I worry you're sucked in too deep here. What if you're still fuckin' dizzy?'

'I'm not,' says Leepus. 'Trust me.'

Mike stares at him and taps her foot for what seems at least a minute. 'Okay,' she says then. 'Run down your fuckin' tactics, griz— convince me you're still a winna.'

∞

'And there I am all nice and relaxed thinking we have an understanding,' says Marcus a bit disgruntled as Mike tightens his restraint.

Leepus says: 'It's probably for the best, mate. If you stay here any longer there's going to be friction.'

'Sorry about the thing with Doll if that's the problem. Any red-blooded lad is tempted. The grog erodes my resistance.'

'It's nothing to do with Doll. But you're a fucking shit-magnet and this is where I live, man.'

'So turn me loose with a weapon or two and I'll find some neutral ground to fight on.'

'Sorry,' says Leepus lighting up. 'There's no payday for me in that option.'

'Bastard,' says Marcus. 'You've already got it all.'

'Yeah, including you. And Chilly wants to take you from me but I don't know why. And that's a bit fucking irksome.'

'Chilly?' Marcus coughs. 'I'll deal with her after Ajax.'

'That's the spirit, killa,' says Mike hauling her prisoner upright. 'But I've got first refusal when it comes to chopping Major Cunt.'

'Hah,' says Marcus. 'I forget that's what they call him. But you'd better be quick on the draw, lad, I'm not passing up any shots.'

'Fair enough,' Mike says frosty. 'But call me fuckin' 'lad' again and the fuckin' discussion's redundant.'

'What?' Marcus frowns as Mike swoops and slings him over her

187

shoulder.

Leepus sucks smoke and grins. 'Nice one, mate,' he says exhaling. 'Not optimal to offend the lady whose hands your life's in.'

Marcus tries to answer but he's too busy coughing and turning purple.

∞

Leepus kicks back and lets the dust settle. Then he mixes up a medicinal cocktail—a tincture of rare mushrooms and hand-picked herbals. He's tempted to neck it there and then but he needs to review his agenda. He pings Ajax—gives him an early appointment at the King of Clubs' palace tomorrow. Chilly's slot is a little later. He'll let them have a sniff of Marcus and wing it as he sees how the cards fall.

But what about fucking Bodja? Leepus jumps to the wrong conclusion there and now the dope's all arsey over being painted a black-hearted villain. At least the fact the girl's alive means they won't have to top him—as long as he comes to his senses and gives her up. But it's an added complication to the dodgy business with Marcus. The last thing Leepus needs right now is additional guilt to carry. Bodja's sense of betrayal will have to fester on a bit while he finesses Ajax and Chilly.

Leepus retires early to bed with a weedstick and his cocktail. He lies snug in contemplative intoxication as the sky darkens beyond his roof-light—drifts finally soothed into grateful sleep by the lingering scent of groggy passion.

◊◊◊◊◊

19

'So,' says Leepus to Ajax as the King of Clubs' cashier tots up his buy-in. 'Basically it's an auction now, between you and your Republic client.'

'I already bid pretty big,' says Ajax nodding goodbye to a trolley of ingots.

Leepus shrugs dismissive—says, 'That's just bunce to grease to the wheels, mate. The King already bins it.'

'And you're thinking Chilly goes better? I'm you I don't get too greedy. Your XTRK sweetheart's bankroll might not be as fat as you're betting. I tell you how she's playing offline, and the Citadel's not happy?'

'But she's playing and that's what matters. And you know I enjoy a gamble.'

'Yeah.' The throb of rotors rattling rococo mirrors on stucco. Ajax shifts uneasy—scans the palace atrium as armed retainers hustle. 'But a bird snug in your hand, man—when Chilly might blow up? Put me in the middle here and everyone gets paid.'

'Rule one,' says Leepus strolling towards the light. 'Never make a deal on the run with a clown in a uniform sweating nuggets. I say we all have a sit-down and talk it through with the man of the moment.'

'Fucker.' Ajax at Leepus' elbow on the threshold. Chilly marching up the wide steps at the heart of a praetorian phalanx. 'You put me in a spot here. She doesn't know I'm in it.'

'Oh well.' Leepus winks. 'Just wing it. Try your best to stay alive. Find a chance and take it.'

Praetorians and retainers in a doorway stand-off. The King of Clubs looming over. 'Sorry,' he booms diplomatic. 'No fokkin indoors weapons. Health and safety issue. You leggies grab some freeroll chips, hit the hospitality tables. Relax and let the Commander here enjoy my personal protection.'

'Under my close supervision,' says Ajax hustling accreditation.

Chilly looks him up and down and then does the same to Leepus. Her escort hasn't moved yet. 'Okay,' she snaps. 'Praetorians dismissed. Gamble if you want to, but remember your honour code. No being a sore loser, smashing tacky shit up and stomping tribals. And don't get busted cheating, or I flog you down to bloody bones for being an obvious asshole.'

The King of Clubs steers Chilly to the staircase. Leepus and Ajax follow. A mirror on the stairwell—a stern-faced reflected praetorian staring hard and sneering. 'See,' mutters Ajax. 'What do I say? Her sun is fuckin' setting.'

∞

A shadowed room with a lit poker table. Three seats and a screen instead of a fourth. The King of Clubs leads them silent across deep red carpet and waves them to chairs. Ajax accepts the invitation but Chilly doesn't. Leepus raises an eyebrow. 'Problem, Atalanta?' he asks her.

'I'm expecting this game is heads-up.'

'As the party whose fuck-up initiates this situation, The Major's keen to worm in on the action, maybe earn rehabilitation.'

'He comes to you then or you don't know that.'

'Everyone has an agenda. It's up to you how you read it.'

Chilly moves and takes the seat furthest away from Ajax. The mercenary clears his throat and leans in to engage her. 'Sorry if I'm intruding, ma'am, but our interests have coincided. You take the lead here, I follow.'

'Shut the fuck up,' says Chilly. And then she looks at the King. 'That's all. If we need any drinks we call you.'

'Just whistle and I come running,' the King says dry and withdraws.

The heavy wooden double-doors swing shut sweet behind him.

Leepus sits and lights a weedstick. Chilly watches him smoke it. Ajax shifts on his arsecheeks.

'Okay,' says Chilly when she's ready. 'I need to have sight of the subject.'

Leepus taps at a touchscreen panel. Some twitchy pixelation. And then a low-res image—Marcus strapped to a swivel-chair under lights in a scabby basement. Chilly grabs a shot with her fone and runs some biometrics. Leepus waits for her conclusion.

'ID's good,' says Chilly. 'Obvious you don't have him here, so now what?'

'Maybe he stashes him in his tower,' suggests Ajax. 'My lads can go and fetch him.'

Chilly refrains from comment.

Ajax takes a couple of seconds and tries again. 'So we just hurt him until he tells us.'

'He doesn't know,' says Chilly. 'Moron.'

'Can't argue with that assessment,' on-screen Marcus says suddenly loud through a speaker and chuckles. 'You're out of your depth here, Arturo.'

'First name terms now, Major?' Chilly staring stony. 'That's a new disclosure.'

'Prisoner's just a random abscon-prefix to me, ma'am,' bluffs Ajax showing a neck pulse. 'Someone's running a game here, trying to seed division.'

'The jury's out,' says Chilly but it's clear it isn't.

Leepus lights up another weedstick.

'I'll say it again,' says Chilly. 'Now what?'

Leepus shrugs. 'A live head-to-head can be arranged—as long as the subject's willing.'

'Willing?' Ajax thumps the table. 'This fucker's fuckin' property. He's a fugitive, man, we own him.'

'No you don't,' says Leepus. 'I do.'

'I want my fuckin' gold back.' Ajax sucking wind now.

'Gold?' says Chilly icy.

'Fine.' Ajax cuts his losses. 'Flesh and blood it is, then. Let's talk about logistics.'

'Your call, mate,' says Leepus to the screen. 'Happy to take it to the next level?'

'Give me a minute,' says Marcus. 'The Major's intentions are clearly prejudicial to my future, so his further involvement's vetoed.'

'Good call,' says Chilly and whistles.'

'Somethin' you need?' The King of Clubs in the doorway flanked by muscle.

'Something I don't,' elucidates Chilly with a nod toward Ajax. 'Kindly take the trash out.'

'Certainly, Commander,' the King says and pauses thoughtful. 'Just from the premises, is it—or the wider sphere of existence?'

Chilly doesn't answer. She studies Marcus on the screen as one steroid-sculpted flunky hoists Ajax in a headlock and the other snags his feet. The King gets the doors while they haul him out and then he follows.

'Just the three of us, then,' says Marcus.

'Call it a goodwill gesture,' says Chilly. 'A step towards reconciliation.'

'I'm all for civilised stuff like that,' says Marcus smiling. 'But I'm still in the dark about just what it is I've got that you want.'

'We haven't got all day, mate,' says Leepus drumming fingers. 'GhostFone times out in two minutes.'

'Ghost what?' says Marcus puzzled.

Chilly smirks. 'Leepus is paranoid. He thinks we're running traces.'

'Are you?'

'Come on, Colonel Hare. You know the protocols.'

192

'If I do once then I've forgotten.' Marcus frowns. 'Same goes for any intel, if that's the big attraction.'

'You'd be surprised what old skeletons can be resurrected with the right incantation. And you should consider me an adept.'

'Thirty seconds,' says Leepus. 'No more time for flirting. Shit or fucking get off.'

'I need to see the lady's eyes. How about a close-up?'

Marcus and Chilly leaning face-to-face through screen glass. Chilly's hands palm-down on baize—Leepus is sure they're sweating but her face is staying deadpan. Marcus' eyes dart as he speed-reads her features. Pupil flare and a nostril twitch. And then he winds his neck in—leans back in the swivel chair and contemplates his feet.

'So?' Leepus urges the tessellating image.

'Do it, bud,' replies Marcus lost behind dark glass now.

∞

Leepus and Chilly sitting thoughtful. Leepus lights another weedstick. Chilly takes it from him. 'So what the fuck is that shit about?' she says inhaling.

'Shit?'

'Ajax. And the bullshit negotiation. The deal is a lock from the outset—you're never gonna stiff me.

'Ajax is a golden goose—but also a vicious backstabbing bastard who needs to be pushed to a showdown and busted. If only because I don't like him. And maybe it's a moral flaw, but betrayal's always a lot easier if your victim is complicit.'

'Especially when he's your brother.'

Leepus stands—shifts towards departure.

'And Marcus is your brother—Virgil,' pushes Chilly.

'Irrelevant,' says Leepus. 'And also bollocks.'

'You're a weird fuckin' fish,' says Chilly with her head cocked. 'Kind of wish I have more time to get to know you.'

'Don't take it to heart,' says Leepus smiling, 'but I'm personally

193

grateful you don't.'

Leepus holds the door open. Chilly stands and moves to pass him. 'You need to relax about sharing,' she says handing back the stick. 'Research suggests secrecy causes cancer.'

∞

'Stub it!' growls the King of Clubs. 'No fokkin indoor burnin'.'

They're upstairs now in the atrium. Leepus moves to the doorway to comply with the King's instruction. Praetorians abandoning tables in a side room—assembling around Chilly. The formation's incomplete though. One of them's outside—down below on the apron by a TacTruk talking to Ajax.

Leepus frowns. 'I think Chilly expects that scrote is gone now,' he says to the King beside him.

'That's what I tell her fokkin pretties. They say he's wearing uniform and I need to be more respectful.'

'Not like you to roll over.'

'They're praetorians, griz. You can't touch 'em.'

'Right,' says Leepus thoughtful. 'I sniff disaffection. Chilly might have a problem.'

'What do I fokkin care?' says the King.

A rhythmic bustle behind them. The creak of carbon-fibre armour and tread of jackboots—Chilly's phalanx marking time. 'Move it, dirt!' barks a noncom. 'Or you're gonna get striped for obstruction.'

'Dirt?' Leepus raises an eyebrow. 'That's a bit fucking cheeky.'

'Big guns and an excess of testo,' says Chilly winking. 'What you gonna do? Feel free to file a complaint for hurt feelings if you want to.'

'I'll be in touch,' says Leepus standing aside. 'Maybe twenty-four hours.'

'What's wrong with now?' Chilly frowns. 'Let's get this thing wrapped up, huh?'

'Sorry. Other fish to fry in the short term.'

'Twelve hours fuckin' max.' Chilly's expression suggests impatience. 'Or else I start taking heads.'

And then she's a strutting flash of red surrounded by black armour. Leepus and the King of Clubs look on as the phalanx clatters down the steps—crosses the lawn to the quadrocopter and boards it. And then the thing howls airborne. Ajax salutes its departure standing by his TacTruk. 'Twat's pushing his luck,' observes Leepus. And maybe Chilly hears him. Because the copter's circling back low now—tumbling the mercenary head over heels across the gravel in its downdraft.

'Okay, I'd best get off,' says Leepus when things are quiet enough for talking. 'I suppose I've got to put up with that fucking Roosta driving me back?'

'Either that or you're walkin',' the King says winking droopy. 'Cuz there's only one fokkin seat, brer, on poor ol' Lesta's kripkart.'

∞

It's not raining when the Roosta drops Leepus back at the tower and there's a couple of hours left of daylight. Just as fucking well—Bodja's ignoring all his calls and Leepus needs to straighten him out sooner rather than later. He snags a bottle of decent grog and a bundle of top-notch weedsticks—sallies forth to patch-up bridges.

He's thinking the first round goes pretty well as he turns along the stonepath. A nice stack of loot banked from Ajax and the contractor's pitch queered with Chilly. The amount of shit the fuck swallows lately you'd almost think he likes it. Just a mild concern on Leepus' part that he overdoes the pressure. Demoralised and disabled is good—but an enraged and desperate psychopath with a paramil legion probably isn't.

Leepus treads soft approaching the oxbow so as not to spook his quarry—takes a sneaky route through Bodja's scrapyard to have a shufti from cover. All quiet. A kingfisher on the taffrail of the houseboat. It flashes down electric-blue—shatters the black mirror of the lagoon and beats back dripping to its perch to choke down a gudgeon. So Bodja's probably not aboard. Unless he's sleeping. But the skiff's moored land-side there at the wharf—so he's not out at Rat Island either. Leepus decides to stay hunkered down—try another ping to see if he gets an echo. He does and it's right behind him. 'All right, Bodja, are we?' he says starting to turn around.'

'Don't fuckin' move,' says Bodja. 'And wherever fuckin' Mike is, stand her down right fuckin' now, Chief—or you feel a sudden sharp pain in your heart.'

'Easy,' says Leepus. 'Mike's nowhere fucking near, mate. I've only come for a friendly chinwag.'

'Fukkoff.' Bodja snorts. 'Why would you think you're welcome?'

'I know.' Leepus inching round incremental. 'I get the wrong end of the stick there, jump to a bad conclusion. What can I say? I'm sorry.'

Bodja staring at him hard from the shadows of a rotten horse-box snarled in bindweed. He doesn't lower his crossbow.

'Fukksake.' Leepus shifts impatient. 'All that evasive bullshit you feed me, why wouldn't I taste guilty?'

'Because, after all those bastard years of so-called friendship, you should have the fuckin' nous to know I'm not some sick cold fuckin' cock-monster out to rape children—even if they are near full-grown and fuckin' tinkish.' Bodja twitches his weapon. 'Now step out of those bushes and onto the wharf. And take your fuckin' coat off and toss it.'

'Fair enough,' says Leepus complying. 'But I don't get the fucking coat bit.'

'I know the kind of clever shit you've got stashed in those pockets, remember? I'm not that keen on getting baffled by sub-lethal prestidigitation.'

'Fuck me,' says Leepus. 'Where does a simple scrote like you dig up that kind of fancy language?'

'You say it once,' says Bodja moving in behind his crossbow. 'Time we're both drunk and you're teaching me coin tricks. Always like the sound of it. First chance I get to use it.'

Leepus sighs—sits down on a damp mooring-bollard. 'Come on now. Lose the fucking crossbow, Bodja. You know you're not going to shoot me.'

Bodja squats on another bollard a safe distance along the wharf—props the weapon handy beside him. 'So what now then?' he says despondent.

'I bring you smokes and a bottle to take the sting off.' Leepus nods at his coat sprawled crumpled on the boards between them. 'Get stuck in if you want to.'

Bodja looks tempted but wary. 'Probably a fuckin' adder in the pocket, or it's stitched with poison fish-hooks.'

'So use a fucking stick, mate.'

'Take my word I never hurt young Peewit? Except when I run her over—and that's plain accidental.'

'Peewit?' Leepus raises an eyebrow.

'What's wrong with that?' says Bodja. 'I reckon it's a pretty name for a gurlee.'

'So it is, mate,' says Leepus gently. 'But she's still a wild fucking rover, and you know you can't fucking keep her.'

∞

They chew it over on the wharf for another twenty minutes or so before the heavens open. It's way too wet to smoke outdoors and Bodja wants to enjoy his bonus more than he wants to be arsey. They move the debate onboard the houseboat. But they don't make a lot of headway.

'No!' Bodja slams his shot glass down on the cabin table. 'I don't force her to fuckin' stay here. She just don't want to go back to being beat all the time and 'sploited, and you can't fuckin' make her.'

'Fukksake.' Leepus pours another shot from the bottle—resists the impulse to use it to bash Bodja's recalcitrant head in. 'Try and see fucking reason. She's a young girl in her prime, man. And you're just a smelly old sod with a rotten boat, a yard full of junk, and a hopeless infatuation. Hardly romantic, is it? Get your head out of your arse, mate. Ask yourself what the little vix is really fucking after.'

'There you go again. Just because you're a twisted manipulating arsehole who always looks on the black side, doesn't mean everyone's at it. Show the kid some respect—and me too, for that fuckin' matter. What me and Peewit've got going on's a good thing. It's not an infatuation, nor romantic. And it's not about shaggin', neither. I'm not a fuckin' fiddler, so why do you have to spoil it?'

'Because you're a fucking mug. It's a typical rover dodge. Send a pretty gurlee into town to look for trouble. If she gets a bite she plays it—next thing you know her clan is on hand demanding reparations. But this time it's not straightforward, so she has to adapt her playbook—clamps onto a puddled old codja, keeps her head down and jacks the price up.'

'It's not true.' Bodja glares. 'Peewit really likes me. She says I'm kind and gentle, and she "nevvuh meets nah cock before 'oo dunt evun try t' tup us." That's a sad thing, ennit? She's hardly even grown. Shit shouldn't fuckin' happen.'

'I know, mate, but it does.'

'She says I make her laugh, too. She's always got the giggles. Cheers me up, it does. You forget what it's like to have someone around when all you have to talk to is the fuckin' coots and turtles.'

'So why not come clean from the start, instead of lying to all and sundry and marooning her on Rat fucking Island? Better to take it to a meeting, mate, explain the situation, get her fucking adopted, under parish protection.'

'Don't talk like a twat. Peewit's tinkish, ain't she? No one's going to let her in, an' risk getting burned out by her savage clan an' seeing all their kids slaved.'

Fair point, mate,' says Leepus. 'Easier to have a whip round and just buy her—I'm happy to put some gold in to kick it off.'

'Maybe it's not too late,' says Bodja hopeful.

Leepus shakes his head—says, 'Yeah, it fucking is, brer.'

'Then there's nothing left to do, is there?' says obstinate Bodja standing. 'Have to push the boat out, take me and Peewit downriver.'

'You'll be wrecked and food for catfish before you're out of sight. And how does that help Shithole get out from under?'

'Shithole's not my problem, Chief. You'll have to think of something clever.'

'Right.' Leepus stands and pushes past Bodja on his way out through the wheelhouse. Silence glares while they board the skiff and Bodja poles them wharf-ward.

'How long have I got before Mike comes?' Bodja says in a strange flat voice as Leepus disembarks. 'I'll be needing to patch some leaks up, service the old girl's engine.'

'I'll try and give you a nod.' Leepus watching the skiff drift back out over the still black water—Bodja in the stern standing stoic. 'Least I can fucking do, mate. There's still a few days to think about it. Don't do anything hasty.'

'Thanks,' says Bodja sarcastic. 'Appreciate the effort.'

'Yeah.' Leepus pushes off distracted through a rank wet curtain of weeds. An afterthought detains him before the stonepath. 'Sorry—nearly forget,' he calls turning back. 'A little bit cheeky, I know, mate—but I need a loan of your quaddie.'

'Cunt.' The skiff wobbling as Bodja fishes a key from his pocket—sends it arcing over the water. 'Make sure you don't fuckin' break it.'

◊◊◊◊◊

20

Three a.m. at the World's End. It's not raining but it's foggy. A ShuvTruk thickens the miasma idling out front on the wasteground. A twitch of curtains at an upstairs window—someone nosing. 'Twenty minutes they're sat here, griz,' Mother Mellow says to a fone. 'Get a shift on, will you? I can do without a crew of pissed-off pretties putting my door in.'

'Just around the corner, mate,' lies Leepus into his headset. 'Ping the runner to be ready.'

'Done,' says Mother Mellow. 'Good luck and I'll see you for breakfast.'

Two hours overland on Bodja's quaddie and Leepus wishes he's not so hasty dismissing the Roosta. Most of the roads in NoGo are indistinguishable from collapsed buildings. At least they are to Leepus. He tries to miss the worst of the potholes and brick-slides— but his arse is still raw as pounded meat and his kidneys are fucking patty. If he doesn't stumble on the rendezvous soon he'll have to eat shit and ping Chilly to put a flare up.

But that looks like the shell of the burned-out barracks ahead in the murk now. If he swings around it to starboard and runs downhill he hits the old allotments—and The World's End's just beyond them.

But maybe he misremembers the ground. Or gets disoriented in the fog. Because it's another five minutes rodeo-riding before Leepus sees a flash of camo in his headlights. He guns across decaying tarmac—slews to a stylish stop that rattles the ShuvTruk with gravel. And then he sits and catches his breath while Chilly climbs down from its cabin saying, 'Glad you could make it, asshole.'

'Sorry,' says Leepus attempting a grin. 'Navigation skills are rusty.

Grateful to you for waiting.'

'Right,' says Chilly stepping up chic in two-tone shadoCamo—raising combat goggles and peering. 'But I'm touched you bring me flowers.'

Leepus ignores the non sequitur—attempts a confident dismount. But something fibrous tightens around his throat and stops him. 'Ah,' he says a bit sheepish catching on.

Fifty feet of tangled runner-bean vine tethering him to a quaddie is no easy thing for an exhausted griz to deal with. By the time he's free of his humiliation Leepus is hot and bothered. 'Vegetables,' he says and sniffs. 'What the fuck are they good for?'

Chilly smirks and nods at the ShuvTruk—says, 'You need a serious vehicle, Virgil, if you wanna go off-roading. All obstructions obliterated.'

∞

Two praetorian bodyguards and a driver inside the armoured vehicle with Chilly and Leepus. They're belted up and rolling five kliks out from Mother Mellow's. No lights—the runner's blinking LED leading them into mazy ruins. 'Nice ride,' says Leepus idly. They're grinding over rubble drifts and it feels like they're cruising the PayWay.

'Possible hostile contact, ma'am,' announces the helmeted driver tapping a dashboard keypad. 'Range one hundred twenty-five. Multiple individuals. Semi-aggressive posture. No identifiable weapons. Ready to deploy threat pre-emption on your order.'

'Negative,' says Chilly. 'Gratuitous. Steady as you go.'

'Right,' says Leepus supportive as the driver eyerolls behind his visor. 'Probably just skavvas out there mining trinkets.'

'Fuck's it sayin'?' one bodyguard asks the other. 'Is that shit even a fuckin' language?'

'Beats me,' replies her comrade. 'All I hear is jabba.'

'That's because you're mentally deficient cultural inbreds.' Leepus smiles inoffensive. 'And cheeky fucks into the bargain.'

'Wha?' One praetorian staring amazed. The other one's hand on her kill-knife.

'Ask your boss if you need a translation,' says Leepus helpful.

'Uh-uh.' Chilly wags a finger. 'Keep your weapon holstered. The asshole's a mission asset.'

∞

Ten more minutes through eroded urban-canyon badlands. The LED blinking stationary now—a lighthouse on a dark jagged island of disrupted concrete in the corner of a wide plaza. The ShuvTruk growls to a stop adjacent.

'No imminent threat,' says the driver rattling his keypad. 'There's a rat-hole under the slab pile, ma'am. Want me to piss a little hot-sauce down there?'

'Back off, killa,' Chilly says to the driver and turns to Leepus. 'So what? I'm guessing he's not coming to us.'

'Open a channel for local comms,' Leepus replies. 'Wait for an invitation.'

'Do it,' Chilly instructs the driver. 'Put it through on speaker.'

A bit of hiss and whistle—and then Mike's dulcet tones phasing stereophonic: 'Out of the vehicle and into the tunnel and follow the signs. Two bodyguards only permitted. Try not to fuckin' get lost.'

The driver stays to run top-cover from the vehicle. The rest of the party dismounts. The plaza wide and empty in the darkness. Scaffolds of melted high-rise frame-steel gaunt around it. Crushed-glass beach underfoot. Leepus crunches towards the blinking LED. Chilly and her two praetorians follow.

A low crevice under a wonky collapsed-slab lintel—Leepus slips on his OwlEyes and leads them in. Concrete steps descending into a derelict dripping subway.

'This situation is shit, dog' mutters the female praetorian to her buddy. 'Easy to fuckin' die here.'

'Dying's what you're born for,' snarls Chilly. 'Shut the fuck up and stay alert.'

'Second on the left,' says Leepus deciphering a ghostmark amongst ancient graffiti.

A half-mile more of discreetly signed turns and incongruous waypoints. A flooded section to paddle through past a row of smashed urinals. A skeleton chained to a grime-furred overhead conduit. A thousand old shoes in an alcove. Fifty feet of cave-painted stick figures having an orgy. And then a lift-shaft with buckled doors jammed halfway open. 'This is it,' says Leepus prompted by a last ghostmark.'

'Lead on,' says Chilly craning past him to look up a ladder. Then she taps a praetorian's armoured bicep—says, 'You set up here and get our backs. Something nasty comes out of the dark feel free to shoot it.'

Leepus comes up in another tunnel. It's blocked thirty feet in either direction by a jumble of concrete rubble and lit by an array of candles in bottles. Leepus blinks against the sudden dazzle and takes off his OwlEyes. He clocks Marcus cuffed to a rock at one end—and then Mike tucked into an alcove handy with her shotgun.'

'Here's how it works,' Mike calls as the others clear the ladder to stand behind Leepus. 'Man here's content to chat away till the cow's come home, but any attempt at forced removal means he claims an immediate right to silence—due to me blowing his fuckin' brains out. Any questions?'

'No,' says Chilly. 'You're bluffing but I'll buy it.'

'Good decision,' says Marcus. 'All things being equal.'

'Uh-uh,' says Chilly stepping forward as Leepus moves to follow. 'This conversation is classified. You get to go sit down quiet at the back of the bus and stare down a carbine.'

'So let's move it, cum-stain,' the praetorian says snarky and twitches her weapon.

∞

Chilly and Marcus a yard apart and face-to-face fifty feet away in the half-light. It's too far to read their expressions. Just body language for Leepus to go on—and the occasional random dialogue-fragment whispered into his straining ear by a teasing quirk of acoustics.

First Chilly sits for a full silent minute staring. Her head slightly cocked. Legs crossed. Hands clasped neat over knee with index

204

finger tapping. Marcus squirms a little distracted. It's not that he's antagonised by her scrutiny—maybe more embarrassed.

Something eventually said by Chilly. 'So—' Leepus hears, 'gonna pretend—know me—dick-brain brother—?' Her intonation suggests it's a question. Marcus shakes his head then—mumbles and looks a bit rueful.

Some more stuff that's unreadable—and then Chilly again saying, 'Yeah—should be—one day—bedtime story—asshole—then—gone forever.'

Marcus shakes his head kind of helpless. 'Sorry—' Leepus catches the sibilance, 'can I say? Wish—different but—up to me—in another—huh, kid?'

And then Chilly lashes an arm out. The slap reverberates around the chamber. Now she's rigid on her feet glaring down with a face like marble. And it looks like Marcus is shaking his head trying to keep from crying.

Fukksake, thinks Leepus. This isn't the play he's expecting. And then Chilly's lip is going too—she's leaning and reaching her hand out.

But now there's an insect buzzing inside the praetorian's helmet. When he turns she's saying ' 'Kay,' into her chin-mic—and her armoured gauntlet's moving. It impacts Leepus' solar-plexus like fist-shaped locomotive. He gasps—folds double and goes down puking.

'Everyone count to ten,' says the praetorian now holding dribbling Leepus erect with a hand wound in his hair. Her kill-knife's in the other proximate to his windpipe. 'And the chick with the shotgun, toss it!'

'On the ground, Commander.' The other praetorian popping up out of the throat of the shaft holding a shot on Mike.

Chilly takes half a second to run the numbers—and then complies with the instruction saying, 'Whatever you fucks think you're doing, you're fuckin' up.'

'Be quiet, ma'am. You're under arrest. Internal Security warrant,' says the praetorian vaulting up lithe—moving brisk to scoop up Mike's dropped weapon and give her a prod with a stun-gun.

Leepus and Mike are cable-tied and gagged with gaffer tape in short order. Chilly gets disarmed and cable-tied too but they let her off the gagging. Mike's still too electrified to cough up the key to Marcus' cuffs—but the pretties have a gizmo for popping locks so it isn't really a problem. And then they're moving out.

It's thirty minutes stumbling in single-file before they reach the steps up to the plaza. The praetorians' 3D-orienteering tek is acting a bit buggy—and Leepus doesn't feel like interpreting ghostmarks. They pause on the steps under cover. A praetorian peers out at the ShuvTruk. 'On your perimeter now, four live bodies owned,' she offers into her chin-mic. 'Awaiting clearance to mount up.'

'So?' says the other praetorian after ten seconds.

'Repeat, awaiting clearance.'

'Fuck muss be asleep, or diggin' his fuckin' rhymes.' The male praetorian shifts impatient. 'C'mon, man. Let's do this.'

'Protocol says no voluntary exposure without cover,' Chilly says cool and dry. 'I advise you don't contradict it.'

'Your advice don't count for shit, ma'am,' says the male praetorian moving out. 'Hold them here and wait for my sit-rep.'

'Sorry,' Leepus hears Marcus whisper to Chilly. 'You must wish you never come looking.'

'Uh-uh,' she whispers back. 'As a general rule in the intel business, it's better to know shit than not.'

'Wha?' the praetorian gasps then in response to a buzz in her helmet. 'His fuckin' throat's cut how?'

An automatic weapons' burst from ambush—shells hammering into glass shingle through the point-man's collapsing body. The surviving praetorian ducks and tries to pull back further under cover. Chilly's right behind her though and shoving.

Another burst of fire. Multiple high-velocity impacts—concrete chips and glass-grit ricocheting around them. Bloody helmet-chunks too. And a generous splatter of brain gore. 'Sorry,' says Chilly smiling but not nicely. 'That was clumsy of me.'

An amplified voice rings out metallic across the dark plaza saying,

'Show yourselves one at a time, hands in plain view, no weapons, and no one else needs to die here.' It sounds like a robot Ajax.

No one moves but Mike—she's trying to grind her cable-tie through on a jagged edge of concrete.

'No compliance within twenty seconds,' squawks Ajax, 'and we're starting with grenades.' But Mike's free and ripping off her gag-tape. Doing the same for Leepus and Marcus—then grabbing the corpse's kill-knife and slicing off ties.

'Fucking shambles, this is,' says Leepus restoring circulation while Mike loots back her shotgun and the dead praetorian's weapons. 'Sick shit old Marcus here's holding on Ajax must tilt him into amok mode. He thinks he's playing for his life here.'

'He is,' says Mike with feeling.

'And some,' growls Chilly getting a grip. 'But Arturo's got an edge in the short term, so we pull back into the tunnel and resist or the fuck fuckin' disappears us.' She pauses inviting dissent—then says, 'So give me a fuckin' weapon.'

'Help yourself to what's yours, girl,' says Mike. 'But I'm the security rep on this mess of fuckin' bollox—so everyone track back pronto to the backdoor past the lift-shaft. I stay here and work rearguard.'

'Me too,' Marcus says firm and grabs the praetorian's carbine. 'Only one ambition left now, and that's slotting Arturo Ajax.'

'But—' Chilly's momentarily stricken.

'Keep the faith, kid,' says Marcus winking. 'Who knows? Maybe next time round I do better.'

And then Mike signals and breaks out doubling right and Marcus matches her leftwards. 'Fuck,' says Chilly turning into the darkness. 'Fuck this shit and all its shitty fuckin' offspring. This is not how it's meant to go.'

'Right,' says Leepus blundering after. 'With you on that, Atalanta.'

Two seconds around the first side-turn off the subway and the shockwave flashes past them. They're still reeling and choking in the dust-cloud when a second grenade brings the slab-pile down and seals the exit behind them.

It's black as death and Leepus' ears are ringing like a cathedral. He fumbles his OwlEyes on. Even then he can barely see Chilly in the smog of pulverised concrete. Her eyes are wide and staring blind and there's a dribble of black from one flared nostril that hints at a nosebleed. Leepus reaches out sympathetic. She jumps—his touch electric on her shoulder. 'Easy,' he says. 'Bit of a cooler there, but we're not so deep in the fucking hole that we can't come back with some grit and imagination.'

It's not apparent Chilly's reassured. Or even if she hears him.

◊◊◊◊◊

21

It's near dawn before they stop moving. For Leepus there's no option—except collapsing and dying. Maybe it's different for Chilly

They've been scrambling the last two hours. First back through the subway network and out the backdoor like Mike tells them. Then into a concrete-walled cutting choked with cars crushed under rubble. The going isn't easy—but the sporadic percussion of a nearby firefight suggests Mike and Marcus are still buying them time and it seems ungrateful to waste it.

Chilly doesn't say much as they clear the cutting—move into a thicket of brambles creviced by kid-runs. Leepus puts her reticence down to shock. When it comes to life-and-death scenarios Chilly usually enjoys the front end of the equation—a rapid reversal of fortune is bound to be perturbing. If it isn't all so hectic Leepus probably gloats a little.

But they need to bunker up and regroup now and this isn't the place to do it. Tykes'll be nesting in the thorny hummocks with their dogs and weird diseases. And there are probably snares on the pathways—and pitfalls with shitstiks to spike the legs and poison the blood of nocturnal infiltrators.

The gunfire dies as they leave the briars to follow the intermittent rusty steel of a long-derelict urban light-railway. And there's a quadrocopter up now—rotor-clatter phasing through dense night air as it circles above the plaza. That could be a problem. Three dead pretties and a renegade XTRK commander on the lam is the kind of aberrant bollox the Citadel wants fixed promptly. Leepus hopes he knows which track they're on and where it's headed—that the tunnel he expects around the curve is more than wishful thinking.

A lightless void ahead—an arch of engineering bricks fringed with ferns and dripping. Pigeons applaud as Leepus and Chilly pass into darkness. They pause and catch their breath then. A stationary fluttering persists. Leepus puts on his OwlEyes. It's a pigeon snarled in a birder's mist-net. He considers wringing its neck—they might need some rations later. 'First things fucking first though,' he mutters breathless.

'What?' says Chilly frowning—flicking on a map-light.

'Citadel's got to be stalking your signal. We're screened while we're in the tunnel, but it's only a fucking short one. I've got a stealth pocket for your fone—what else can light us up?'

'Dog-tags,' says Chilly fingering her neckline.

'Give,' Leepus instructs her. 'Unless you're secretly hankering after rescue.'

'Fatalities incurred as a result of an unauthorised mission? A flogging and then Court Martial?' Chilly gripping her dog-tag and yanking. 'That's not a tolerable option.'

Leepus takes the neck-chain from her—rips off its titanium chip-tag. Then he reaches and grabs the pigeon—disentangles it from the net while Chilly watches frowning. He scans the ground. A length of heavy cable half-buried under rubble. 'There.' He gestures bird-in-hand. 'Strip the end off that and get me a strand of copper.'

Wiring the tag to the scaly foot is not entirely straightforward. But they manage it between them—and at least the pigeon's still alive when the task's completed. Leepus takes it clear of the entrance and tosses it airborne. They hear it climb and circle—and then it's beating eastwards to meet the morning. 'Okay,' says Leepus leading back into the tunnel. 'Off we fucking trot, then.'

'Where to?' says Chilly hollow—maybe sensing the best is behind her.

'No idea,' says Leepus. 'Let's just find a cosy spot to hole-up and dwell on our options.

So then it's a mile of charred timbers and hogweed.

After that a stop to bail rainwater from a rusty tank to wet their whistles and calm Chilly's rash down. Hogweed sap is a serious irritant to certain skin-types. Leepus overlooks this and Chilly suffers.

After the hogweed a cart camp—pull-dogs kicking up a ruckus and foul-smelling fire smoke. They keep their distance and go around it. Leepus might risk saying hello if he's on his own here—but then he's not wearing shadoCamo and talking loud Republic.

Another mile along the river. A gradual greying of sky and water. A mishap crossing a tributary—black mud up to their armpits. Leepus' breath rasps like a handsaw and his knees have got the wobbles.

'There,' says Chilly pointing. 'Not exactly top-end, but it's cover and it keeps the rain off.'

The outfall pipe is about a yard across and protruding over the water out of a scrub-covered embankment. Chilly gains access without undue exertion but Leepus needs assistance. The concrete tube is collapsed a body-length in and blocked by a dirt-slide. Snug enough for one—for two it's plain claustrophobic.

They've been settling down now for about ten minutes—irritably jostling to annexe space but enjoying the human comfort of unavoidable body contact. Daylight comes with a side of sleet. Chilly sits hunched and looking out—watches ring-ripples drift on the water. Leepus watches her watching.

And then black sleep enfolds him.

∞

Leepus wakes before Chilly. If he's hoping his subconscious dreams up a plan he's disappointed. He shuffles to the pipe-mouth in search of distraction. Kneels. Unlaces. Idly squirts an arc across the mud reaching for the river. He achieves a brief frothing of black water but his sense of triumph is fleeting.

'Nice,' says Chilly behind him—and then prods his arse with the sharp toe of her boot making him moisten his breeches.

'No obvious hue and cry,' says Leepus as she joins him looking out. 'Maybe they're still chasing the pigeon.'

'We need more information—an update on the rearguard.'

'I call, it's like lighting a beacon.'

'So what then? Chilly strips foil from a combat ration—breaks it in half and shares it. 'I'm just an innocent abroad here. You're the one with local knowledge.'

'I've got a few friends downriver,' says Leepus with his mouth full of blood-flavoured toffee. 'But no clean route to get there.'

Chilly spits. 'Fuckin' filthy wasteland. Why would humans even live here?'

Leepus doesn't have a useful answer. He chokes down his ration looking out across the oozing river at wet rolling dunes of rubble. There are rookeries tumbled beyond them—and then SafeCity. But the murk is too opaque today to offer a glimpse of these wonders.

A soft splashing then from upriver. A raft of mackled lumber and plastic barrels with a ragged plastic awning—a woman and child inside it huddled over a smoking fire-pot. A gaunt man at the stern—he's holding onto a steering oar and leaning against the current.

'Cool.' Chilly moves beside Leepus. She's reaching inside her battledress and pulling out a handgun.

'Fukksake—how come I don't know you've got that?'

'You need to pay more attention,' says Chilly aiming. 'So now we neutralise these fuckin' tribals and commandeer their transport.'

Chilly's trigger-finger squeezing. Leepus realising she means it—he lashes out and slaps her hand against the concrete. The gun discharges but she drops it. A plop from below as sodden mud consumes heavy metal. The helmsman flinching and losing his oar. The raft in unguided slow-motion—then a vagary of the torpid current beaches it ten yards downstream.

'Fuck you, asshole.' Chilly kidney-punches Leepus. 'Now what—wrestle them down and fuckin' drown them?'

'I'm thinking maybe just make friends and buy our passage,' says Leepus showing himself and waving. 'But then I'm not desensitised to the casual slaughter of innocents by a culture of impunity, am I?'

∞

It's almost relaxing drifting along with the current enjoying a weedstick. To start with there's a bit of suspicion—but ten-minutes

212

diplomatic banta and a timely glitter of gold-dust earns them an onboard welcome. And then they're underway. The raft-wife hands round a hospitable jar of fishgrog and the kid offers turtle jerky. Leepus sips and chews polite but Chilly turns her nose up. The helmsman volunteers that praetorians are patrolling—but mainly: "Ovuh eastly 'yond shiteponds, n'further on roun' 'fin'ry n'out on salt-mud," which is reassuring. Leepus rewards him with a weedstick. The man smiles slack for the next mile or so and their course gets a bit erratic.

An hour later and they're floating through the afternoon gloom flanked by broken buildings and scrub willow. Chilly's still mourning the loss of her gun—not acknowledging Leepus. He isn't broken-hearted. It's not entirely clear to him why he hasn't already ditched her. He makes good on his promise to put her with Marcus—it's her end that collapses and dumps her into a shitpit. He should be back at the tower by now sorting out the rovers. The woman's just a distraction—he doesn't even like her.

But yet Leepus feels a connection. 'So you must have a few regrets,' he suggests observing her stoic profile. 'Or do you get what you want from Marcus?'

'What do you think?' Chilly says bitter.

'I think I'm missing too much information to make an accurate judgement. But the old boy must cast a potent spell to suck you out of the Republic's embrace and leave you down and outlawed in wilderness Inglund.'

'It's not a permanent situation. I piss off local admins, underestimate Ajax's ability to exploit his Citadel connection—never mind his fuckin' death-wish. But I've got friends in XTRK Command who trade big in fear and power. I cash in a couple of favours and we're shipping heads in truckloads.'

'Fair enough,' says Leepus. 'You just need to stay alive, then.'

Chilly smiles wry and takes his point—says, 'I can use some help doing that in the short term.'

'So give me something in return. What's the deal with you and Marcus?'

'Someone tells me you think you're a reader, Virgil.' Chilly offers her face for inspection. 'I'm surprised you don't work it out yet.'

∞

They reach the end of the navigation an hour shy of dusk. A flotilla of rafts and houseboats jammed thwart-to-thwart in a silted basin. The river once joins a canal here—but the locks collapse several decades ago and the cut gets choked with garbage.

The rafters are gathered for a wedding—well stuck into the fishgrog already. There's a fire on a wharf with a pork on a spit and revellers jigging round it. A couple of salty pugilists penned by a chanting crowd in a corner. Kids are screeching and chasing all over—youths flirting round the grog barrels and shagging in the shadows. Leepus feels at home here but Chilly doesn't get it. He leads off grumpy through some tumbledowns and his prissy companion follows.

At the edge of the ruins the reed-beds—soft wind rustling through them wavy. Warblers flitting frond-to-frond. They skirt the marsh to the west until they reach the plank causeway. 'Asshole,' says Chilly pausing to eye the walled complex squatting dark at its end in the gloaming. 'You bring me to fuckin' jail, here?'

'Think of it more as sanctuary,' says Leepus nudging her forward, 'a chance for some quiet reflection.' And maybe he is an asshole—because he can't deny a degree of relish imagining the look on Chilly's face when she finds her potential guardians are veiled and wearing black burkas.

∞

In the event her reaction exceeds his expectation. The black robes fluttering and closing in around her trip Chilly's fight-or-flight switch. There's nowhere for her to run to so she concentrates on fighting. It takes six strong girls to restrain her. And probably she gets hurt a great deal worse if one of the sistas doesn't recognise Leepus and summon Aunty.

'Fucker,' yells Chilly spitting blood and tooth-chips as they strap her to a gurney. 'However much these sick fanatics pay you, I swear it costs you your fuckin' balls, man.'

'My advice. Stay calm and be respectful,' says Leepus waving her off. 'Trust me—I'm doing my best here.'

Chilly responds with raucous laughter and a diarrhoea of cursing—provokes a sista to apply sedation.

'Leepus again, is it? squawks Aunty rolling up on her golf cart. 'I'm thinking you should take more care selecting your consorts. This predilection for coarse women really can't be healthy, brotha.'

'Sorry,' says Leepus. 'But cut the lass a bit of slack. She gets her schooling from the Republic and doesn't know any better.'

'An oppressor? You bring evil into our stronghold without invitation or warning?' Aunty studies him over her veil. 'I like you, brotha, and we sistas are hospitable ladies—but you're definitely probing our limits.'

'I know, and I feel bad about imposing,' says Leepus trying for abashed. 'But there's a payday here for you and your girls that I don't think you want to pass on.'

'That depends, griz,' says Aunty squinting sly, 'on the steepness of the downside.'

'How about a trade then?' Leepus winks. 'A caffy for an explanation?'

◊◊◊◊◊

22

Two hours after dawn the morning after—Leepus enjoying a weedstick while he waits for transportation. He's laid up in a scrub-jungle a mile from the Sistas' stronghold. Mike point-blank refuses to rendezvous any closer. She claims she might find it too hard to resist "disembowelling a couple or three-fuckin'-dozen of those stuck-up fuckin' cultists" if they get in her face again. Leepus suspects pride may also be a significant issue but it doesn't seem wise to push it. Her tone when he calls to arrange extraction suggests Mike's not entirely happy about getting "dunked in a fuckin' shit-an'-fuckin'-bloodbath due to fuckin' half-arsed mission planning". At first Leepus is hurt by this accusation—then relieved when he understands Mike's harsh words are likely just down to her guilt at being a survivor when Marcus isn't.

Leepus experiences a few mood fluctuations in the aftermath of hearing the unfortunate news of the old boy's passing. There's anger and frustration—an urgent desire for payback. Regret features a little too. But it's the weird cold hollow sadness that disturbs him most profoundly—a sense of irretrievable loss that he'd rather not examine. It's lucky Aunty finds him an oblivion potion or his night is a lot more restless.

And now Mike's booming in on her combo through the echoing tumbledown gorges—parking up and revving impatient. Leepus stumbles from cover—nods and clambers into the sidecar. It's three hours rough-riding back to the tower. Neither of them speaks till they get there.

∞

'Turns out there's four shooters in the kill-team, with fuckin' Ajax and a driver in a TacTruk,' says Mike nursing her brew in the kitchen.

'Clear your man Marcus has pro skills in countering ambush and winning firefights—and if the killa inside him isn't degraded by age and years in a fuckin' dungeon, I reckon those paramils get reduced to zero—and Major Cunt's noggin's a trophy.'

'That's not how it goes, though.'

'He shows himself and draws their fire, moves wide and picks a useful spot for defensive engagement—then keeps those snipers busy while I shift about finding angles. I grab a couple of headshots. But then the TacTruk's moving. The live ones shovel up the dead ones, and then they all fuckin' do one. I'm thinking it must be they're spooked by inbound Citadel first-responders. So I go to collect old Marcus.'

'And find the poor bastard resting eternal?'

'Not quite. But he suffers serious perforation—high-cal through-and-through the fuckin' torso. He squirts a lot of claret. I give him a syrette of joy-juice and jam a field-dressing in his hole—then hump him clear of the hot-zone just ahead of the 'copter gettin' on station.'

'You must fucking like him, I reckon.'

'Cunt's stand-up, griz. Can't leave him to die alone there.'

'How long does he last?'

'Twenty minutes maybe—I forget to set my stopwatch.'

'Any last words?'

'It's mainly the joy-juice talking. He sings me a few old leggie songs, then tells me how he's proud of some girl, and he's sorry for smashing the greenhouse window with his slingshot and blaming it on his brother. Reckon he thinks I'm his mother. Wants me to hold his hand, griz—seems like the least I can do.'

'Right.' Leepus blinks—whiffs a sweetly incongruous trace of ancient face-powder and mince-pies. The scent is oddly affecting. He hawks and spits in the sink to clear it—says, 'You must be going soft, mate—tell me you don't start lactating.'

'Can't say either way, can I?' Mike studies him suspicious. 'Since I only speak fuckin' Inglish.'

'Never mind,' says Leepus. 'It's just the prick in me talking.'

'Yeah.' Mike nods assent. 'So the old lad's looking a bit pale by now, and I'm thinking he's gone in a couple of minutes, and what's my best route out to where I stash the fuckin' combo? And then his eyes are wide-open and staring—and it seems like he's back in the here-and-now, talking like a soldier. "Listen up, killa," he says. "I'll tell you something useful. Pass it on to your pal Leepus. He's a hopeless clown with his head up his arse, but basically he's decent—and I reckon he might just have the wit and inclination to figure how to extract max value, or at least find someone who has if he hasn't. Tell him I trust him to do the right thing. Get Atalanta off the hook first, by now he knows why that matters, and then deploy the equity to the general good of dear old Inglund." And then he mumbles some kind of half-arsed wisecrack, pukes up a gallon of gut blood and it's over.'

'Fuck me,' says Leepus with a shiver. 'So what's the poor scrote say then?'

Mike shuffles and bites her lip. 'That's the thing, mate,' she says. 'Too much shit to deal with. I kind of forget it, don't I?'

'What?'

'Sorry,' says Mike staring glum at her fone.

'Fukksake.' Leepus shakes his head. 'That's that then—you drop a right fucking bollock there, mate.'

Yeah.' Mike tapping fonescreen now—looking up and winking. 'I worry that might happen. That's why I record it.'

'Remember what the winna says—if you want to get ahead get a hatchet,' croaks Marcus thin from the fone.

Leepus on his feet now—strutting off in high dudgeon to fetch paper and pencil. He can't believe she fucking does it. 'Gotcha,' Mike's saying—beaming and slapping her thigh. 'Right between the eyes, griz, and you never see it coming.'

∞

'Arsehole,' Bodja says later by way of greeting at the oxbow. 'Where's my fuckin' quaddie?'

'Ah,' says Leepus. 'Fly in the logistical ointment.'

219

'You wreck it, you bastard, don't you?'

'Not that I remember—but I have a few other things to deal with. I'll sort it when I get a free minute.'

'It's not right,' says Bodja with arms folded sullen. 'I reckon you should pay me compo.'

'I tell you I don't fucking wreck it,' says Leepus a bit testy. 'It's parked up at Mother Mellow's. Someone'll go and fetch it.'

'Not the point, mate, is it? I lend it you as a favour so—'

'Shut your fucking yap now, Bodja,' says Leepus losing patience. 'I'm here for a chat with your gurlee.'

'Peewit.'

'No disrespect intended.'

'She's still over on the island.'

'So fuel up the outboard, mate—I'm not fucking swimming, am I?'

'All right.' Bodja sniffs. 'But I come too. I let you take the skiff on your own guaranteed you sink it.'

Leepus shrugs silent and lights up a weedstick.

∞

'Okay,' calls Captain Bodja as the skiff noses through the eddies towards a muddy beach on the downstream side of Rat Island. 'Be ready to drop the mud-weight as soon as we hit slack water.'

'Mud-weight?' Leepus scans the bilges.

'There,' says Bodja scowling and pointing. 'Look sharp, you hopeless bastard.'

Leepus follows his direction—hoists the heavy chunk of scrap that used to be Bodja's doorbell and chucks it over the gunnel. The painter spliced to it tightens—leaves the skiff riding at anchor still several yards offshore. 'Too fuckin' soon,' says Bodja. 'Now we have to paddle.'

Lucky the water's only knee-deep—but it's cold and the landing's a mud-bank. Leepus slithers out crocodilian among the tree-roots. For once he's grateful of a timely cloudburst. He stands for several minutes as the downpour sluices the slime off. Bodja pushes on through the alders to Peewit's bivvy.

∞

'Peewit, this is Leepus,' says Bodja. 'Leepus, this is—'

'Hey,' says Leepus joining them at the cooking fire in the shelter of the bivvy's open door-flaps. 'Nice to meet you, Peewit.'

'Dunt luk all that fooken chiefy t'us, Bodj mun,' says the rover girl eyeing him beady.

Leepus eyes her back. A body not quite full-fleshed—she's a couple of years shy of grown. Quick dark eyes that look a lot older. A brush of red hair that she's proud of adorned with a magpie feather. A twitch of doubt in her narrow mouth but a chin that can meet a challenge. It feels like she wants him to trust her but she'll play him if he doesn't.

'Get yow's eyeful, griz, why dunt yow?'

'What fambly you belong to, Peewit?'

'I's born'd Windhover, or thass wha' they fooken tells us,' says the rover girl flicking her hair back. 'But Ro'buks fooken nab us on a razz when I's a craydul maggit.'

'You dopted now, or slaved?'

'Pends dunnit.'

'What on?'

'If'n us duz good in us fooken testin', mun—haul nuff bastid gol' fer dowree.'

'Testin'?'

Peewit looks to Bodja. 'Go on,' he says. 'Tell him how they work you.'

'S'posed t'fish us a fooken simpul.' Peewit shrugs. 'Rope some dirty ol' nag out they shanties an givvit a gallop. Aftuh, gurlees gi'us a nice thumpin, put a foo fooken lumps on, an' then Queenie sends us back wi' a razzle o' cuzzes, t'spray a bit o' blud-dredd aroun' an' scareup some juicy compo from they frit fooken simpul shitturs.'

'Easy enough hooking mucky Foxy.'

221

'Yuss.' Peewit smirks. 'If thass wha' yow fooken call 'e. Snagglemouth cont's pox'd danglas is mine fer choppin'. Allus need t'do is claw scrote's scabby 'ide up, so's us word gets tooken true when usall comes back pointin' finger.'

'Attack of conscience, is it?' says Leepus raising an eyebrow.

'Wha'?' The girl frowns.

'He's asking how come you don't set your hook in Foxy proper.' Bodja's eager to be helpful.

Peewit shivers—says, 'Gi's us sicky wobbuls, dunnit? See'e wi' 'is breeks dyn roun' 'is 'ocks, mun, an' 'is fooken pizzul waggin'. Us thinks, thass fooken near enuff, gurl, yow dunt wan' t'get nah fection—so nevuh min' yow testin', 's'time yow fooken duz un. So off us fooken coneys.'

'And then I run her over,' says Bodja. 'And—'

'You tell me that already.' Leepus sparks a weedstick.

'He's saying my read is likely shwonki—'cause I'm a fuckin' simple,' Bodja says arsey to Peewit. 'He thinks I get leery on you, and then you fuckin' fish me to earn your dowry.'

'Duzzee?' Peewit cocks her head. ' 'E's a cheeky cont, then.'

'Coming from you?' says Leepus raising an eyebrow. 'But hey, I'm open to correction.'

Peewit hijacks the weedstick—sucks a lungful and holds it.

'In your own fucking time,' says Leepus.

Peewit exhales and passes the stick to Bodja—feeds a handful of twigs to the fire. Then she looks at Leepus saying, 'Wunt say us dunt 'madjun it fer a move, mun—bein' lump'd up rottun wiv'ee fooken quaddie already.'

'But not deliberate,' reinforces Bodja.

'An'ee trets us well foin an' gennul, duz Bodj—nah evun a littul bit cocky, evun when'ee gets us leggins off us an' rubs balm-erb on us sore bits. An'ee tellus jokes an' tales an' all, an' feeds us broff wiv meat in.'

'See,' says Bodja to Leepus.'

222

'Evun'ee sez 'e'll ride us 'ome t'campgroun' on'ee quaddie, when us is propuh perky—but us sez as us dunt wannuh, dunt us?'

'Like I say,' says Bodja nodding. 'She doesn't want to be dopted and popping out kids forever, nor gettin' beat and worked to death by savage fuckin' tinkish.'

'Steady, Bodj.' Peewit glances a warning. 'Rovers, mun, nah tinkish—an' alla they's nah bastids, nah fooken evul neethuh. Some o' they is luvlees thass juss livin' 'ow them 'as to.'

'Let's just say ignorant, then, and leave it,' says Bodja shrugging.

'Bodj shows us 'bout 'sheens an' stuff, an' 'lectrics—'ow yow can put bitsa sun in battrees, wiv soluh. An'ee tellus wha' they stars is.'

'He's a regular fountain of knowledge.' Leepus sniffs. 'Not to mention bullshit.'

'That's why she wants to stay here now, mate, ennit? She's got a brain, has Peewit. Wants to use it to learn shit—p'raps sign on at the Academy. And I want to help her do it, give her a safe place to grow up in, look after her like a—' Bodja hesitates and blushes. 'Like a father, fukkit.'

Leepus looks back and forth between them and lights a weedstick.

'Say something, then,' says Bodja.

'Sorry,' says Leepus. 'Can't do it. Nice idea and all that, but I can't risk the fucking village just 'so you can play dadda. It's gone too fucking far now. If she stays we're at war with Queenie.'

'It's not about me.'

'Nah matter, Bodj. Juss leave it. Chief's frit shiteless, an us duzznt fooken blame'ee.' Peewit takes her mentor's hand. 'Bless yow fer bein' rychus, but us tells yow 'e wunt 'avvit. I rekkun us bess get on 'ome, mun, cop fer us fooken beatin'—an mebbe Queenie settuls fer a littul bitta compo off yowsall an' nah need fer nah mad blud stuff.'

'Thanks for understanding.' Leepus hands her the weedstick. 'Wish it could be different but I really can't see it. I'll put in a word with Queenie. Maybe she'll go easy.'

'No,' says Bodja standing sudden—staring down on Peewit. 'Say the thing I tell you.'

'Nah,' says Peewit sucking smoke. 'Grov'lin' juss shames us.'

'Say it now, for fukksake,' Bodja urges. 'Don't let the sly fuck play you. You can see what he's doing, can't you? You volunteering gets him off having to do the right thing. Don't make it easy—say it.'

Peewit stares at the fire while she chews it over.

'Say what you like, girl,' says Leepus taking back the weedstick. 'But only if you want to.'

'Yow juss laffs yow spuds off, betchuh.'

'Try me.'

'Sylum,' says Peewit and sniggers embarrassed.

'What?' says Leepus feeling the trap close.

'Sylum, mun.' Peewit giggles. 'Us claims sylum in fooken Shithole.'

'Fuck.' Leepus stares at the fire. 'That's not fucking funny.'

'Yuss'tis,' says Peewit creasing again. 'Ev'ry time us sezzit us pidduls.'

'Nice one, Bodja,' says Leepus dry. 'Surprised you have the nous, mate.'

'Have a word with the Prof, mate, don't I? When I go up to sort out his voltaics. I don't say nothing about Peewit directly, so don't go giving him grief—just ask if there's stuff in the Articles about people who need protection. And he says about asylum—how Shithole can't turn no one away who claims it.' Bodja pauses triumphant and beaming beardy. 'So plug your chuff with that, mate.'

'Fair enough,' says Leepus. 'Can't go against the Articles or everything falls apart.'

'Dunt geddit, mun,' says Peewit looking pleased but puzzled. 'Articuls muss be some evvy ol' spellin', us rekkun.'

'How about we break out a bottle and grill up a catfish?' says Bodja. 'Celebrate Inglish civilisation?'

'No fucking time for that shit,' says Leepus. 'Need to work on a magic word to ward off Queenie's rampagers—or soon all that's left of our civilisation is blood and fucking ashes. So let's push the fucking boat out.'

'No hard feelings I hope, mate.' Bodja shrugs chagrined as Leepus disembarks back at the oxbow. 'I have to do it, don't I?'

'Course you do, you hopeless cunt,' says Leepus without smiling. He turns and walks away then. He's not going to say it aloud but he's quite glad to have the weight off. Chances are in a couple of days every poor scrote in Shithole is either dead with their head on a pointy stick or fucking slaved. But at least he's off the hook for Bodja's summary excommunication—and for denying a kid with an obvious spark her one slim chance of evading a grim life of harsh disappointment.

Although Mike's a lot less sentimental and probably sees it different. She's got a thing about fighting rovers. And when the jovial burgers of Shithole hear they're obliged to risk their arses giving refuge to some sly tinkish runaway the bastards probably riot. 'But fuck 'em,' growls Leepus splashing through puddles. They all signed up to the Articles—so they either live by them or they ship out.

Leepus is still half a mile from the tower when his fone rings. He checks the screen—takes a breath and lights a weedstick. 'Queenie,' he says brightly then. 'You must be fucking psychic, missus. I'm just about to call you.'

◊◊◊◊◊

23

'Sounds a bit risky to me, babe,' says Jasmine on the fone. 'What if this Queenie sniffs out your bluff and re-raises?'

'Doesn't add up,' says Leepus on the tower-roof watching evening puddle gloomy along the hedgerows and in the hollows. 'She calls it bad and the Ro'bucks are over.'

'Right.' Jasmine still sounds doubtful. 'Folding's her rational move—but rovers aren't renowned for playing by the numbers, and they don't like to be pushed around. Maybe she gets arsey and gambles.'

'Thanks for the reassurance.'

'And why not just do it on the fone instead of trekking alone over the blasted heath to slap your balls on her table?'

'Because only an idiot with a death wish does that if he's not sitting pretty,' says Leepus noting hooves in the lane below. 'And I'm not playing solo—unless Mike finally goes fucking AWOL.'

'Her loyalty still in question? I turn over plenty of stones, babe, but I don't find anything nasty.'

'I don't know. Something isn't how it should be.' Leepus pauses to light a weedstick. 'But I'm leery of fronting her on it. I get it wrong with Bodja and he's pure ABC—next to him Mike's an impenetrable cipher.'

'Everyone makes a mistake now and then,' says Jasmine sympathetic. Don't let it get you down, babe. And talking of ciphers, I should get back to chewing on this code-string your dead hostage coughs up with his lifeblood—seems likely it helps you get the best out of Chilly and scoop a nice pot.'

'Cool,' says Leepus exhaling smoke as the portcullis clangs open. 'Soon as you fucking like, gal.' He hangs up then—looks down over the parapet at Doll leading a pair of swayback nags into the shadowed compound on a rope. Leepus is not a natural equestrian—the prospect of a hack up and over the moor at night is enough to give him serious arse-ache.

∞

'I get 'em off Warty Annie. Pick of her bleedin' paddock. Wants a nundred each a day,' Doll says—and a yellow-toothed pony laughs and slobbers. 'That's supposin' you don't lose 'em. Cost's you five-'undred a piece if you do—or two if they're dead but you bring the meat back.'

'What about fucking saddles?'

'She says sixty on top for them, cheeky mare—so I tell her stick 'em, you'll go bareback.'

'Fukksake, Doll. I'm riding out to do single combat with a bloodthirsty horde of rovers—keep them from torching Shithole and eating your grandkids. At least you could fucking haggle, get the old leech to chuck some tack in.'

'I already knock her down from a nundred an' fifty to ninety each,' says Doll affronted.

Leepus frowns. 'Don't you just tell me a hundred?'

'Ten a day each is my commission, ennit?' Doll says sniffy. 'Bleedin' fair enough, I reckon.'

Leepus opens his mouth to argue but can't be bothered.

' 'Sides,' says Doll heading into the tower, 'Mike's with you riding shotgun—so you ain't that big of an 'ero.'

∞

Leepus at his medicine chest selecting herbal tonics. He feels a need to spice the broth Doll's boiling-up pungent in the kitchen with a few useful psychoactives—something to help him stay sharp and cheerful and come home a winna. He considers self-defence aids too—they're probably redundant. If he's in a spot that calls for force sub-lethal doesn't cut it. He grabs party favours instead to hand

228

round and maybe win friends with: a tin of Electric Snuff and a fistful of weedsticks. Probably safer than grog.

'An awful shame, that is griz,' says Doll in response to the news about Marcus. 'He's a nice old chap with a lot of go—I'm sorry for your loss, there. Makes you right heartsick, don't it, when kin gets reaped shockin' like that? I near cry my bleedin' innards up that time our brother Rocco gets mangled an' ate by wild porks in the forest—an' I don't even like the sod.'

'I tell you he isn't kin, Doll.'

'So you do, mate,' says Doll ladling lumpy liquid. 'But I don't believe you, do I?'

∞

Mike's late turning up at the tower. Leepus' tonics have kicked in strong long before they're even on horseback. And Mike's mood is not lighthearted—Leepus' attempts at casual chat are deflected monosyllabic. There's something eating at her—stirring uncharacteristic emotion. For a mile or so plodding up the moor road he wonders if she's menopausal. He counts back their years of acquaintance. Can she be as old as that already? Time slips by if you don't pay attention.

Three hours after midnight. They're off the road now—pushing up the valley through wooded dripping darkness. Mike reins in her pony and dismounts sudden.

'Whassup?' Leepus hisses—his neck-hairs alert to danger.

'Piss break.' Mike reaches him her bridle. 'Hold this walking dog-meat and light me a fuckin' weedstick.'

A fierce gushing from path-side shadows. Leepus tries to ignore it—shields the stick from the mizzle and sparks it. Flame-light defines foreground branch-tangles scabbed with lichen—intensifies the blackness beyond them. A fox-bark in the mid-distance. Or maybe it's a deer. Or rovers. Leepus kills the light and cups the glowing ember—listens to his ears sing and his heart beat.

'Gimme,' says Mike suddenly back beside him. He jumps and drops the weedstick. 'Fukksake,' she snarls. 'Let's get a fuckin' grip here.'

Leepus sparks up another. 'Here,' he says passing it over. 'Suck up a bit of sweetness, mate—smooth the fucking kinks out.'

'Meaning?'

'Forget it.' Leepus sniffs and hands the reins back. 'It must be two hours still to the Ro'bucks' campground and I'd like to be there for breakfast.'

Another silent half-hour through the trees and they're out on the tops at the head of the valley. The sky boiling wide about them. A grey mould of clouds rimed with moonlight. A grouse explodes from a hoof-stamped tussock—whirs clacking across the heather. Mike's pony dancing and snorting—kicking into a canter. Leepus' mount lurching after. It's a mile before they come to rest in the lee of a derelict farmstead. 'Fuck this shit,' Mike's saying as Leepus reins back alongside her. 'I think I burst a kidney.'

'Quiet, mate,' says Leepus. 'Listen.'

A skirl of canine yowling wind-borne over the dark horizon—rising and then subsiding obedient to silence.

'War dogs,' Mike says and sniffs the air. 'I smell fuckin' tinkish.'

'It's not that bad,' says Leepus. 'Maybe just wash your armpits.'

'Prick,' says Mike—and then she smiles. 'Let's have another smoke then.'

They sit at a charred kitchen-table in the three-walled roofless farmhouse. The ponies are roped to a rusty range. Leepus is relieved to sense Mike's mood's a little lighter. 'So we're close then, you think? he ventures.

'Across the valley to the ridge with the ring ditch on it. They're camped just over the top—down the scree slopes by High Tarn, if Bodja's wench gives you kosha intel.'

'Queenie calls it Ol' Mam's Pisspot—says it's "bess t'drop a bitta gol' in when yow's passin' tha' black water, save Ol' Mam bobs up all gummy an' sucks yow lights out thru' yow shite'ole." But I reckon that's probably just a folk tale.'

'Your call,' Mike says shrugging. 'It's you walking down there with your arse out. I'm staying nice and snug up on top with my fuckin' deer gun.'

'Have pinch of Electric Snuff, then.' Leepus pulls out his tin. 'Help you keep your eyes skinned.'

'Nah.' Mike sneers. 'One of us needs their fuckin' head on.'

'Right.' Leepus sighs and stows the snuff-tin. 'You think I'm playing manic again and it's giving you the hump.'

'I don't know what you're fuckin' doing, mate, and I don't think you do either. We've got Ajax begging for payback for fragging poor old Marcus, this XTRK vix banked with those fuckin' fanatics and the Citadel in uproar—and I still don't get how come you don't just push her down some badlands sinkhole and fuckin' forget her. And now here we are tryna game the fuckin' tinkish off of wiping out fuckin' Shithole because Bodja gets bamboozled by some fuckin' gurlee blud-bait.'

'Peewit. And she claims asylum.'

'Fuck asylum. She should be hogtied over the back of my nag now— ready to be dropped in Ol' Mam's fuckin' Pisspot. Fuckin' tinkish can fish her out if they want her—if not she can drown and I'm not crying.'

'Rovers, Mike, not tinkish. How many fucking more times?'

'Bollocks.'

'And asylum's in the Articles—and they're what we fucking stand for.'

'Whatever,' says Mike standing sudden—setting the ponies shifting edgy. 'It's all a bit fuckin' much, mate—doing my fuckin' nut in.'

'All?' Leepus raises an eyebrow.

Mike stares down breathing hard. Leepus knows it's a bonkers notion but it looks like she might be about to start crying. And that would be fucking scary. But then she's turning away—unhitching the ponies and leading them out. Leepus gives her a second and follows—takes a chance laying a hand on her muscled shoulder saying, 'Easy, Mike. I know it gets a bit harum scarum lately and I'm all over the place. But I've got my head round it now. Everything's coming together. As long as I know you've still got my back, mate, we're fucking laughing.'

'I've got your back, you silly cunt,' says Mike and shrugs him off then. She's fifty yards off and trotting her nag into the grey-green crack of a sickly dawn before Leepus is even mounted. He pauses for a snort of snuff—sneezes kaleidoscopic and gives his beast its head.

∞

Halfway down the scree slope and the pony's sliding on it's haunches. Leepus' fists are wound in its mane and his teeth are gritted. Mike tells him he should walk it but the snuff fucking overrules her. Gravity and luck combine to get man and mount intact to the bottom. He pauses to light a weedstick—lets his nag reward itself with a guzzle from Ol' Mam's Pisspot.

A morning breeze stirs the mist from the peat-dark water of the tarn—carries their scent across to the islet. Rover ponies whinny and stir around a dry-stone paddock. Dogs kick up a ruckus. Leepus looks back up to the ridge to check Mike's set up in position. A hand flickers momentarily above a limestone turret—a ragged flight of ravens veering and dipping below the skyline. Leepus dismounts a bit clumsy but tussocks of marsh grass break his fall so he's only winded for about thirty seconds.

The black-mud track leads around the lake to a rocky causeway. Leepus squelches along it. His roped pony plods behind. The Ro'buck camp comprises maybe forty tarpaulin benders randomly scattered around the treeless islet. Some have chariots parked beside them—and wagons made from cut-down box-vans and old horse-trailers. There's a long-house on its highpoint. It's mackled from rough-hewn bleached tree-trunks packed with turfs and decked with heraldic antlers. A turbine on a mast behind it—but not enough wind now to spin it. Peat-smoke eddies heavy in the air and prickles his nostrils acidic.

Twin cairns mark the start of the causeway. On each of these a human skull with patchy weather-tanned skin adhering. The pony shies and snorts disgust as Leepus leads it past them. He settles it— then clears his throat and fills his lungs. 'Ahoy the camp,' he bellows and listens to the echo. 'It's Leepus here coming over on his tod to have a chinwag with Queenie. So keep your fooken dogs roped and get us a nice fooken brew on.'

∞

232

'Yow dunt bring us back nah gurlee, then Chief? An' nah fooken gol' an' trinkets neethuh?' Queenie spits and wipes her chins with a brawny forearm—tattooed ponies gallop up it and under her badger-skin jerkin. She's sitting on a big leather sofa out on the porch of the long-house. There's not room for Leepus to join her even if she invites him. Queenie's a substantial woman.

'I don't,' says Leepus rolling up a stump from a firewood pile to squat on. He lights himself a weedstick before he continues. 'Turns out young Peewit's full of beans and setting up house in Shithole. So I reckon we don't need to pay you.'

'Yow's a fooken daft cont, then, t'trot up 'ere an' tellus.' Queenie lets a fart rip—wafts her leather skirts to gust it. Sequins made from old polished-coins jingle in glittery motion. The rovers gathered round them stamp and whistle agreement. A bare-arsed urchin with a stick picks up a dog-turd on it—makes to flick it at Leepus.

'Don't.' Leepus raises a warning finger. 'That'd be bad manners, boy—and bad manners makes bad stuff happen.'

'Pissoff, yow twat-face simpul.' The urchin launches the turd and giggles. 'Touch us an' us cuzzes fooken guts yow.'

Leepus stands and shakes the shit from his coat—eyes the urchin darkly from under his hatbrim. 'Don't need to touch a rude kid, do I, to make him dedded? I've got devils riding in my pockets who do that cruel shit for me.' And then he takes his hat off.

Three seconds of curious rover frowning—and then the stag-skull nailed to the apex of the long-house entrance explodes into bony shrapnel. Its antlers whirling airborne—one branch clattering down in a nearby heap of old car-axles and the other clipping Queenie. And then the belated boom of Mike's deer gun rolling around the valley. Most of the rovers duck and cover. The urchin just stands staring and dripping a snot slug.

'Cont,' says Queenie untangling the antler from her feather earrings—reaching with it to snag the urchin's tattered vest and drag him close enough for punching. Her blow lays him out stone-cold in the mud—and now his snot-slug's oozing bloody. Leepus feels a bit sorry for the lad but content the point's well made.

'Apology accepted.' Leepus replaces his hat—sits down and

233

straightens his weedstick. 'Now lets everyone be friendly and keep the devils in my pocket.'

'Brock sezzas 'ow yow's a dirty playuh an' us rekkun 'e dunt fooken lie, mun.' Queenie folds arms over swollen bosom—looks down at Leepus hard and nasty. 'Fair play yow's got sum cont up aloft thur wi' a long-gun—so us'll bartuh on if yow wannuh. But tha' gurlee's us'n ketched an' branded Ro'buck from a littul babbee. So wha' gol' yow gunna offuh?'

'No gol', missus,' says Leepus eyeing her steady. 'Nor any other fucking treasure. You put that girl in harm's way to fish a simple and squeeze some blud out. We catch you fucking at it—so now she's ours and you cut your losses.'

'Mebbe us sez yuss, then, an' sends yow 'ome all cocky,' Queenie says and cracks a knuckle. 'An' then comes dyn an' razzes yowsall up propuh come some 'evvy killin' wevvuh.'

'That'd count as cheating and hurt the Ro'bucks' reputation. Evul brings down evul. I reckon you fucking know that.'

'So mebbe us juss sez fook this cont wiv 'is chiefy fooken 'at on—gi's a wink t'us foin lads 'ere t'jump yow an' tramp yow fooken bonce flat. Likely a brace or so gets winged or dedded, fair enuff mun—but yow wunt be suckin' nah air nah more, an' ress of ussall's leff standin' tall an' looken fooken perky.'

'Don't be daft,' says Leepus mild and pulls out a fistful of weedsticks. 'Big old gal like you is an easy mark for a sniper. You're dead before fucking I am.' The urchin's back on his feet now—holding his nose and staring. 'Come here,' says Leepus to him. 'Hand these round to your cuzzes. Keep a couple for yourself and let's bury the hatchet.'

The urchin does as suggested while the matriarch dwells on her options. The atmosphere sweetens with weedsmoke. Leepus has a pinch of snuff and tosses the tin to Queenie. 'Give a taste of that to your best stallion next time you're feeling romantic. Guaranteed he gallops your tits off.'

Queenie tucks the tin away in her cleavage and the company cackles.

'And I see young Brock leering about at the back there,' says Leepus squinting shrewd then. 'So just so there's no misunderstanding going forward—if I'm not back in Shithole and chippa by nightfall,

234

missus, serious fucking bad-evil rains down hard from the unfeeling sky and evaporates you and all your people.'

''Ow's that then?' says Queenie sullen.

'The Citadel loses one of its own. There's a bit of a hue and cry on. Easy enough to put it about that Ro'bucks are holding the renegade hostage. Next thing you know there's 'copters dropping out of the night chockfull of jacked praetorians looking for an extermination party.'

'But us dunt 'ave no fooken 'ostage.' Queenie is affronted.

'My pals tell them that you do, though—and I'm betting the Citadel believes them.'

'Cont.' Queenie's face screws arse-like. 'Yow fooken fox us propuh, dunt yow? Keep tha' gurlee if yow fooken wan' 'er, then—an' us 'opes 'er gi's yow stinky knobrot.'

'That's the way.' Leepus winks. 'No shame in mucking to a pro. Maybe you even learn a lesson.'

Queenie glares and looks doubtful. Leepus stands and stretches— adds, 'So, in avoidance of any festering resentment poisoning our well of understanding, maybe I cut you in on a move that saves you Ro'bucks a bit of face and lets you rake a nice stack of chips back. How does that sound, missus?'

'Can't say, Chief, fooken can us? 'Less yow fooken tellus.'

Queenie hawks and spits dismissive—but her eyes are telling Leepus that a sniff of a chance to grab back some win has her snapping his fucking arm off. 'Rain coming,' he says, 'and it's getting a bit parky. Let's go inside and have a brew—talk through the nitty by the fire in a spirit of cooperation.'

The matriarch sighs—wafts a hand as big as a ham to conjure up assistance. Two old boys in ankle chains shuffle clanking out of the long-house. They hunch the sofa round—heave it into smoky interior darkness with Queenie sprawled regal on it. Tormented casters shriek in protest.

'Make sure my nag gets fed and a bit of a rub-down.' Leepus flips a five-chip to the urchin—steps onto the porch after Queenie.

An avalanche of black clouds above now rumbling thunderous. The other rovers doubled and running for their benders. 'It's good to be a winna,' says Leepus to himself, 'living free and on the gamble in Merrie Inglund.' Then he ducks into the long-house gloom to seal the deal with Queenie.

Leepus spends the next half-hour in relative comfort—shares a ceremonial hub-cap of congealed horse-blood intoxicated by dense peat-smoke. Not that he's keen to leave though. Outside the wind whines inconsolable as the deluge lashes the islet and sets Ol' Ma's Pisspot seething.

◊◊◊◊◊

24

Leepus at his dashboard reviewing strategic progress. It's several hours since they get back from the rover excursion but the Electric Snuff's still going strong and he feels quite energetic. Mike's a bit more feeble—says she's sitting out till the sun's up tomorrow.

If it's up to Leepus they're already on their way to the Sista's stronghold. A dose of psychoactive spices combined with fresh air and winning action puts a nice sharp lead in his pencil. He's got a read on the metagame now—and a shot at playing Chilly to a globally beneficial outcome.

It's a treasure map: says Jasmine in her message. *It takes me a while to see it. Turns out the first clause is the encrypted address to a strongbox hidden in a dark corner of the subnet—the key is in the second. Just turn letters into numbers and shuffle. A simple but effective mnemonic—this fugitive's not silly. I have to tread a bit careful—make sure there's no alarms, booby-trap auto-wipes, etc. Those old deep-storage levels are getting creaky now. It's easy to bring the roof down if you don't know what you're doing—get yourself tombed along with the glitta. Long story short, it looks like a handy haul, babe. A catalogue of historical sins and nefarious dealings by old Republic movers and shakers, and a couple of College traitors. A lot of it's probably shitty water under the bridge now—but I recognise a fair few names who still have major weight to throw about. No time to pick all the bones out, but a cursory analysis suggests detonation of a few choice revelations in structurally sensitive locations might provoke considerable political upheaval. Anyone who thinks that's a good thing likely wants to be your friend.*

Leepus pings Jasmine back—tells her to: *Clean out the cache as fast as you can, stash a couple of mirrors somewhere handy and dead-*

letterbox me some nice samples at Mother Mellow's. A few moments later he pings her again: *Thanks,* he adds diplomatic. *Top work you do there, gal. It's not true when they say you've lost it.* He breaks for a stick and a brew then—takes them up to the roof.

Two pigeons dancing formal on the parapet billing and cooing. They clatter off shy to the nearby trees—put the rooks up kiting and cawing. The afternoon cloud is high and gauzy—the breeze soft with the scent of pollen. There's definitely some weight off Leepus. He's almost having fun now. 'A game,' he says when the King of Clubs answers his call. 'I think you might want to play, brer.'

'What's the fokkin buy-in?'

'Freeroll. You're just the pig in the middle, between my end and the College. I need you to haggle paydays.'

'This XTRK commander in the package? Because I get a big bid on her from Ajax.'

'Roll them up together, throw in a library of sick intel that rattles a cadre of tainted Republic senior-admins and flushes some old College rats out. I reckon that adds significant value.'

'What's my end?'

'Fifteen percent seems fair. There's other investors need paying.'

'The Citadel don't like to get done over—they might fokkin tax me. I'll need to buy insurance, griz. I only play for fifty.'

'Twenty-five.'

'Forty.'

'Thirty-five's my absolute best. Say yes while it's still on the table.'

'Fokkin tinkish blood in you for certain,' says the King. 'Thirty-five is good enough then—but only 'cause I like you. An' if it goes bad I foreclose on Shithole, slave your fokkin peasants to jolly rogers—at least the ones with work in, the scrotes just go for KashBak.'

'Fair enough,' says Leepus happy. He gets off lighter than he's expecting. 'Very Inglish of you.'

'Fokka,' says the King ending the conversation. 'No call for needle, is there?'

Leepus smokes another weedstick. He thinks about fishing Ajax—decides it's probably better handled by proxy. And anyway—here comes Doll up the lane now to fetch back the rented ponies.

∞

'Good,' says Leepus in response to Doll's enquiry after the outcome of his mission. 'I reckon I play a blinda.'

'At least you're back with your bleedin' skin on.'

'And the Ro'bucks are my pals now.'

'Shit'ole's off the 'ook then, for that little tinkish gurlee?'

'She's a rover, Doll, and her name is Peewit. But yeah, peace with honour seems likely—as long as my ducks stay in line.'

'Don't want to piss in your happy cup, mate,' says Doll mustering weary ponies, 'but word is the kid shouts "sylum", an' people ain't thrilled about it.'

'People?'

'Bob the Butcher, mainly. 'E's 'oldin' court in the Queen's 'Ead bar with a rabble of leery piss'eads—says Foxy gets banned on account of that sly slag, but you an' Bodja's thick as thieves, so 'e gets a letoff for 'is fiddlin' about an' bringin' the bleedin' savage tinkish down to shag us.'

'Bob the Butcher farts with his mouth.'

'An' some folk like the smell, griz. There's talk of a posse marchin' down to the oxbow an' 'avin' a burn-out.'

'Fukksake,' says Leepus. 'I'm not having that fucking ignorant bollocks. Stick your head round the door, mate, on your way back down to Annie's. Tell the scrotes I say the rovers are sorted. And there's an Article against fucking lynching. And Mike's down there on the boat waiting with her shotgun. Not to mention Bodja's got his crossbow.'

'It's just a bleedin' bluff, though,' says Doll moving towards the portcullis. 'Mike's not really down there.'

'No, mate. But Bodja is—and if he thinks those morons threaten his boat he loses his shit for certain. And then there's bloodshed and

239

domestic uproar.'

'All right, griz. I do me best,' says Doll and leads the nags out. 'I send Ryda up to fetch you if they don't listen.'

'Appreciate it,' says Leepus sparking a weedstick. 'Just make sure wobbly Bob gets the message—anyone dies because of his shit, he's out on his arse in the wilderness with a nice fat bounty on his head looking for a hole to hide in. And I make sure every scalper knows it—as well as the "savage tinkish".'

∞

An hour after dark and Leepus goes up to check from the roof that there's no fire-glow over the river. He doesn't think there will be— Bob the Butcher's a shitter. But any spark of perceived injustice can be fanned into conflagration. Sometimes sly incendiarists need to run into a cooler. So far Leepus is diplomatic handling Bob but if the bastard keeps on pushing he'll be having a chat with Mike.

The sky is dark and smoke-free. Wind gentle. No rain. A glimmer of moon above the forest. An owl tooting low and seductive. Leepus is restless—he wants to get on. Maybe a night walk passes the hours and calms him?

Or better yet a poka tourney—and crack another tin of Electric Snuff.

∞

Dawn finds Leepus still at his dashboard and buzzing. His situation hasn't changed when Mike arrives an hour later—sits outside in the compound revving impatient. It takes him ten minutes to finish his hand—get kitted up and join her.

'No fuckin' rush,' Mike says sarcastic. 'It's only my life you're wasting.'

'Sorry,' says Leepus, 'but I'm on a bit of a roll there, winning steady. And an hour more in bed today probably doesn't hurt you either— you look like fucking shit, mate.'

'Coming from you?' Mike says looking him over. 'And it's days since I sniffed a bed. So shut your fuckin' yap-hole and lets get going before I punch you.'

Leepus does as he's told.

∞

An hour or so's hard riding and Mike leaves him at Mother Mellow's. She doesn't even want breakfast. 'Stop whining,' she says when he protests her overhasty departure. 'I tell you I've got commitments. You'll have to manage on Bodja's quaddie.'

'Some backup'd be reassuring.'

'Now you don't trust your freaky new girlfriends?'

'Anything can happen.'

'You're a winna on a roll, mate,' Mike says winking bloodshot. 'Just relax, keep those novelty weapons handy and I reckon you're fuckin' golden.'

'Fukksake,' says Leepus stung. 'Just because you've got the fucking arse-ache, don't get snide with me, mate.'

Just as well Mike's on her way already so she doesn't even hear him. Leepus sulks off to the World's End to pick up the keys to the quaddie—grab a brew and choke down a burga.

∞

'I'll put it on your tab then,' says Mother Mellow sketching a route on a napkin for Leepus.

'What's that, mate? Leepus replies wiping his chin clean of ketchup.

'Breakfast, mapping service, processing data. Setting up this sucka, Ajax. Sorting out the badlands bunker and ghostFone—plus the runner who guides you and the pretties to it the other night. The window Mike smashes the last time she's here—and fuel for the quaddie and a shine-up. I reckon twelve hundred for that lot.'

'Double or quits?' says Leepus fishing out a chip to flip with.

'Times are hard,' says Mother Mellow. 'I'd rather have it my hand, griz.'

'On the tab it is, then.' Leepus heads for the door.

∞

'It's nearly time for my hot-tub,' says Aunty as her eunuch wipes Leepus' coat down. 'Join me if you want to—get the rest of the slime off, smell nice for your charming young lady.'

241

'She's not my young lady, Aunty—and 'charming' doesn't fit either.'

Aunty cackles dry and says, 'My sense is ironic, brotha. A rabid cat has better manners. If it isn't you who pleads sanctuary for her I lose my patience, let the sistas trade her to HateBoyz.'

'As bad as that?' says Leepus. 'Thanks for your perseverance. I'm indebted.'

'That you are.' Aunty looks shrewd. 'So when are you going to settle?'

'Soon as I negotiate her ransom from the College. You want your end in gold or goodwill?'

Aunty thinks about it—says, 'A mixture of both is favourite—we can talk about proportions. And I want the vix gone by nightfall.'

'Understood,' says Leepus. 'So I'd better skip the hot-tub then—get on and finesse her compliance.'

'Off you run then—coward.' Aunty feigns disappointment. 'Just shout if the finessing fails and you need to resort to violence. There's a couple of hefty sistas who'll be only too happy to help—as soon as they finish digging your quaddie out of the sink mud.'

'Thanks,' says Leepus. 'I'm embarrassed.'

'No need for that, griz.' Aunty chortles. 'The width of that causeway's deceptive. Anyone could drive off it.'

∞

'Fukksake, Atalanta,' says Leepus as the cell-door clunks shut behind him. 'I don't expect you to take vows, girl.'

'Asshole,' says the black-robed woman without venom. 'Those fanatics take my fatigues, man. I'm not sitting here in chains and fuckin' naked.'

'No,' says Leepus sitting down on the polished-wood bench beside her and lighting a weedstick. 'Even as metaphor that's excessive.'

'Give me that,' says Chilly snatching for the weedstick. But her wrist-restraint snaps her hand up short and she looks foolish.

Leepus waits a beat and hands it over saying, 'So why do they take your clothes, then?'

'They get shredded, and all muddied up and blood-stained when I bust out over the wall. There's a lotta swamp and thorn-brush.'

'Don't I say you should stay calm and respectful—that the Sistas are playing on our side?'

They're fuckin' weirdo cultists. They try to make me do slave work, man—dig vegetables in their dirt-patch, clean out the head and the kitchen. I tell them I'm a prisoner of war and they can't force me. And the crazy bitches just fuckin' laugh into their face-rags. I'm a Warrior of the Republic trained in unarmed combat—it's my duty to offer resistance.'

'I'm guessing they overcome it.'

'Some giant sack of blubber gets me in a bear-hug. They hold me down and make me swallow some filthy potion. When I wake up I'm intoxicated—everything's all warm and fuzzy and the sick fucks are sitting around me in a circle stroking my hands and saying they love me. Turns my fuckin' stomach.'

Leepus can't help smiling. 'No harsh interrogation, though? No torture? No punitive amputations?'

'They put me in a room full of ugly squealing kids—shitty diapers and snotty faces. Maybe you don't call it torture, but it's abusive exploitation, contrary to the rules of war. I figure I need to escape or die trying.'

'And you end up in a dungeon.'

'Yeah—and now what? You gonna fuckin' trade me?' Chilly's chin juts defiant but her eyes are a tad doubtful.

'That depends,' says Leepus reaching to unchain her, 'on whether you've really got what it takes to fight back and win this.'

'I'm a little low on bullets.'

'I can fix that,' says Leepus. 'But I need to be sure our interests coincide before I let you get busy. So let's have another weedstick and a chinwag.'

Chilly takes the stick that Leepus offers—leans back against the rough cell-wall with her eyes closed and sucks a lungful. 'So you're still tryna join the dots up,' she says. Her voice is cool and steady—

but there's a pulse bouncing the foot of one crossed-leg suggesting interior tension. 'You're thinking: this XTRK hotshot has a nice career serving the Republic and advancing global civilisation—so why does she roll over here to shit-bucket Inglund, piss away her reputation on some fuckin' random mission?'

Leepus launches a smoke-ring lasso towards her head—studies the flare of her nostrils through it and the minute play of facial muscles.

'I ask myself the same question,' Chilly continues. 'The Republic is my life and soul. It raises me to womanhood and makes me what I am. I give it my allegiance—love it without question.'

'And then it betrays your trust? You find out a secret you can't handle?'

'No. The Republic stands by the deal with honor. It's me that's fucking deficient—fundamentally flawed. There's something missing inside me, a hole that just gets bigger. It undermines my identity, impedes the execution of my duty—sooner or later I know it destroys me if I don't find a way to fill it.'

'And you think the answer's buried in Inglund?'

'I've no idea where it is until I get busy digging. I rewind back through the archives trying to find the start—glimpse the lost little orphan-girl who the Republic adopts and renames Atalanta Honor-Trublood and analyse her inception.'

One moment Leepus is just watching her speaking—in the next he's finally understanding. 'Ah,' he says feeling sudden chagrin. 'I think there's something I neglect to tell you.'

'Huh?' Chilly opens her eyes and says distracted by his interruption. 'So what the fuck is that?'

'Your father,' says Leepus trying for gentle. 'I'm sorry but he's dead, girl.'

'Really,' says Chilly flat. 'Finally you get there.'

'I know. It should be obvious from the outset but I'm looking in the wrong direction.'

'I guess he buys it in the rearguard action.'

'Yes. Poor old Marcus. Mike says he plays like a hero—and his legacy hands us all we need to get you back in the saddle and fuck Arturo Ajax.'

'That's nice.' Chilly doesn't seem brokenhearted.

'Bit of a blow, I expect,' says Leepus. 'The shock probably gets you later.'

'Shock?' Chilly wrinkles her eyes. 'That won't be a problem. I only know the miserable prick for fifteen minutes—it's not likely that I miss him.'

'He's still your dad, though.'

'And you're my Uncle Virgil. Life is full of disappointment.'

'I'm not admitting the former,' says Leepus shaking his head. 'But the other bit's on the money.'

'Admit what you like.' Chilly sneers. 'It's all laid out in the archive.'

'We can talk about that,' says Leepus lighting a weedstick to cover confusion. 'But I think you're being too tough on Marcus. It's hard to be a proper father when you're tombed in a Republic black site.'

'It's better if they crucify him—the fuckin' backstabbin' Inglish rat-bastard. My mom's a loyal Daughter of the Homeland. She deserves better than that traitor. Turns out I'm only three years-old when he tells her sorry but he makes a mistake and walks out of her fuckin' life—right after he gets his citizenship.'

'A lot of people get confused then—after the Reduction. Nobody knows what they're doing.'

'Speak for your-fuckin'-self, man. That's not how it reads in the record I uncover. Marcus has an agenda for certain—he's a corrupt fuckin' double-dealer working to sabotage the Republic. Mom's just his ticket to the action. I don't even fuckin' matter.'

'One state's traitor is another's loyal agent. He's just working for his birthright.'

'Fukkoff.' Chilly laughs harsh. 'Inglund's not a state, you prick—it's a basket-case fuckin' dominion begging for protection.'

'I suppose you have to see it that way,' says Leepus shrugging. 'So what happens to your mum, then?'

'Her heart breaks. She has a meltdown—crawls into a bottle. Human Resources picks up the pieces—takes me in and schools me in warrior values. The Republic's too big to bear grudges against innocent children. Five years after that, Marcus gets snatched up and interrogated—though I don't know that till I see his file. Turns out he's up to his bloody armpits in a foreign conspiracy to disrupt the succession. XTRK has to investigate Mom—she's so ashamed of her poor life-choices she drinks poison as an act of contrition.'

'I'm sorry for your loss, Atalanta.'

'Yeah.' A weird little snort from Chilly. She blinks—says, 'On the upside I get a cool new name to live up to. Sally's what my mom decides to call her baby—pretty fuckin' sappy.'

'Sally Hare?' Leepus shrugs. 'You think your life is different if you live it under that label?'

'What do you think, Virgil?' says Chilly. 'Besides, I don't want my life to be different. I get satisfaction in the Service. I've got talents and I get to use them in defence of the Republic's interest. The world is a mess of adversaries trying to destroy our lifestyle—constant vigilance is essential to subvert evil. I'm proud of all the work I do with XTRK—identifying those filthy diseases, determining their weaknesses and targeting effective suppression. Not everyone has the stomach.'

'Right,' says Leepus. 'When it comes to governing empires compassion translates as weakness.'

'Kill your enemy before he kills you.'

'So, I'm guessing you're not looking to quit, then—start a humble new life of charity amongst the downtrodden wretches of Inglund? Your ancestral curiosity's sated? If there's chance for you to flee your degenerate fatherland, get back to fulfilling your potential for wrangling blood and intel, you want to bet it, do you?'

A gleam of hope behind the hard slate of Chilly's eyes now. 'Yes,' she says. 'Show me some cards, I'll play 'em.'

'Maybe you're too proud to be bankrolled by Daddy? What if you find out Marcus is deeper than you read him and that rocks your comforting worldview? Maybe you lose your perspective, fuck your play up and get busted—and then your inheritance is squandered.'

'I'm not going to fuck my play up. What does the bastard give me to work with?'

'Power,' Leepus says and sparks a weedstick. 'A treasure chest of inside information—and the freedom to use it for good or evil.'

'Everything's relative, Virgil.'

'Leepus.'

'Time to give that shit up, man. The truth's in your genes and you can't deny it.'

'Here's the thing.' Leepus blows another smoke ring. 'Power comes with preconditions.'

'Go on,' says Chilly wary. 'Always room for negotiation.'

'Condition one,' says Leepus. 'All residual traces of the pre-Reduction entity identified as Virgil Hare get permanently excised from the global record. No literary footprints persisting—no genealogical listings or associated metadata. This ghost gets fucking laid, right?'

'You're admitting that it's you?'

Leepus taps the ash from his smoke in silence.

'Okay.' Chilly shrugs. 'But I still don't get why it's so important.'

'Some things defy explanation, Sally. Think why you wanted to track down your father—how you felt when you finally found him. The empty hurt and confusion. Maybe it's kind of like that, but twisted around and flipped over.'

'It's hard for me to imagine how the world is before it changes—all those mad billions of people living easy, thinking history is over and this is how it is forever.'

'A slightly distorted perception,' says Leepus smiling wry. 'It's true most of the happy idiots don't have a clue what the writing on the wall says—but a few sick individuals get off dreaming of disaster, anticipating catastrophic adventures. Maybe they even make their living relishing bleak outcomes, when they should energised by terror—spurred into desperate revolutionary last-ditch action, manning barricades of hope to preserve a future for their children.'

'They must feel bad if their kids die but they're survivors.'

'Some of them probably go a bit crazy living on *ad infinitum*.'

'Consign the past to the garbage? Write a new story to live in?'

'It's a theory, I suppose,' Leepus says and shivers. 'There might be others equally valid.'

'Okay, Leepus.' Chilly commandeers the weedstick. 'Condition one is accepted. What else is on your agenda?'

∞

'Great beverage,' says Chilly sat with Leepus on the floor beneath Aunty's cushioned dais. The old lady cranes her head back and gargles drain-like.

'The best,' Leepus agrees. He holds his tiny caffy-cup up for the eunuch to refill. Aunty pouts her wizened lips—spurts her own precious mouthful across the floor tiles.

'Good. I'm tickled pink,' says Aunty arch, 'to finally find something that meets with your approval.'

'Pink?' says Chilly baffled watching the eunuch mopping up.

'Figure of speech.' Leepus kicks her ankle. 'Don't we just talk about how taking things at face value leads to destructive cultural misunderstandings?'

'We do?'

'Yes—and you tell me your institutional indoctrination makes it hard for you to appreciate the kindness of strangers. So maybe you give Aunty the wrong impression?'

'Yeah, right.' Chilly swallows hard. 'Like acting up and kicking off instead of showing my gratitude for the hospitality and protection of my - uh - caring sistas.'

Aunty cocks her head birdlike.

'So I apologise - uh - Aunty,' Chilly says tight-lipped. 'And ask you to pardon my crude behaviour.'

'Granted,' says Aunty with a wink to Leepus. 'Always happy to give a second chance to a misguided but humble oppressor. And I'm sure you'll find a way to ensure the Sistas are suitably rewarded for our indulgence in your negotiations with the College.'

'Huh?' Chilly turns to Leepus. 'The fuck's she talking about now, man?'

'You need cover from the Citadel, and some help to analyse the mess of intel Marcus gives us—select appropriate targets. The College provides covert logistical support and protection—in return for a few favours upfront and a degree of influence going forward.'

'Fucker.' Chilly's on her feet now. 'Now my ass gets rendered to some crappy native intel-fiefdom's asset-evaluation dungeon and they try to rinse me and turn me? And I'm just thinking maybe you're stand-up.'

'Easy,' says Leepus as Aunty stifles a snigger. 'I think you're over-reacting. At worst it's a week or two in protective custody and debriefing—with minimum duress guaranteed in return for cooperation. And I put The Numbers' beheading on Ajax, in case guilt over that makes you anxious. Plus I advance you enough nuggets from your inheritance to convince them you're a serious player—the final balance payable when the conditions we agree are honoured.'

'It's true what they say about the fuckin' Inglish.' Chilly glowers. 'They stink and they play dirty poka.'

'Must be in our genes, girl,' says Leepus and Aunty cackles. 'And in a handful of yours too, I reckon.'

'Fuck you,' says Chilly sullen.

A veiled sista coming in then—leaning to whisper to Aunty. 'Your transport awaits at the gate, child,' the old lady announces to Chilly. 'Another caffy perhaps, before you go—in honour of this historic advancement of cross-cultural respect and understanding?'

∞

'Don't be a stranger,' says Aunty from her tricked-out golf cart as Leepus fires up the quaddie at the stronghold gate. 'You sure you don't want one of my girls to drive that out for you over the causeway?'

'Thanks for the thought,' says Leepus eyeing the prospect. 'But it looks a good bit wider now, and my old eyes aren't so dim in

249

daylight.'

It's ten minutes since the College handlers bag Chilly and load her into a snatch-bus camouflaged as a KashBak collection wagon. They offer her sedation to ease the discomfort of the journey but Chilly doesn't want it. She says she doesn't trust them not to mix her up with the corpses—drop her off at 'some fly-blown fuckin' chopshop'.

Aunty finds that thought amusing—says, 'Any parasitic priv who gets their refurbed bits and pieces from a poison-vix like you wakes up feeling sicker than they are to start with—all bitter and twisted and wanting a refund.'

Chilly doesn't share the company's amusement. Leepus has to remind her she's playing a long game and it's best to be compliant. It seems as though she listens—but a second before the bag's zipped closed she spits in his eye like a cobra.

Leepus circles the quaddie now to demonstrate his mastery of it. He pulls up alongside Aunty—doffs his hat and says 'Nice playing with you, sweetheart. Here's to future fun and paydays.'

'Bless you, griz,' Aunty says coy—lifts her veil and offers a cracked-leather cheek for kissing. 'Foolish man,' she whispers then as he accepts her invitation. 'I'm you I run away now, before I lose my self-control and opt to keep you for my own wicked pleasure.'

Leepus fancies he can still hear the old lady cackling ribald above the quaddie's motor long after he clears the causeway.

◊◊◊◊◊

25

'I 'spect I can manage that, griz,' Big Bethan tells Leepus when he drops in to see her in the Queen's Head on a Spike. 'As long as the price is right, mind.'

'Spend that first,' says Leepus sliding an eighth-bar over. 'If it runs to more we can haggle later.'

'Gol', is it?' Bethan raises an eyebrow. 'Ain't you the fuckin' flash 'un?'

Leepus winks. 'A thing turns out better than it might do. Sharing good fortune is lucky.'

'Nice. It's a while since Shithole 'as a proper shindig. Last fat night is the one where poor ol' Arfa the Larfa guzzles too much toadstool tea—comes to grief trying to shag that ol' godly statue. Must be you remember that, griz—puts a right damper on the merries.'

'Only till we pry the berk out from under and swab the blood off the dance floor.'

'I'm thinkin', do it at the Party Palace this time too.' Bethan glances around. 'What with the scaffolds still 'oldin' the walls up 'ere? Things is likely to get lively, griz—an' we don't want the fuckin' roof down, do we? An' the crippled an' bereaved all whittling after compo?'

'We don't,' Leepus agrees. 'But talking about compo, I'm sorting out a payday from the arsehole who holds you hostage and provokes the shit to kick off in the first place, if you'll pardon the expression—so you can let me have the masons' tariff.'

'Sweet,' says Bethan. 'I'll 'ave the scrote's fucking bollocks for earrings too, mate, while you're at it.'

'Next full moon's three nights off, according to the Prof. I'm thinking that's a good time for a shindig.'

'Fair enough,' says Bethan. 'Leave it to me an' I'll put the word out.'

∞

'Daffs,' says Leepus triumphant. The brilliant yellow flowers are nodding at him from the bankside all the way up the lane. Until now their name escapes him. He grabs a fistful for Doll on impulse— stuffs them into his coat-pocket as his fone rings.

'All's well, I hope babe,' says Jasmine.

'I'm not one for counting chickens, gal.' Leepus fishes out a stick— sits down on a stump to light it. 'But everything's coming up roses.'

'Roses,' Jasmine says wistful. 'I'm thinking you buy them for me once—before your romantic inclination withers and drops off.'

'Crazy days,' says Leepus. 'But I can't imagine buying flowers—most likely I find them in a graveyard.'

'Another illusion shattered.'

'Sorry,' says Leepus watching ladybirds fuck on a twig. 'So how's your gigolo doing?'

'Nearly there.' Jasmine giggles. 'If he can hold his breath for a couple more minutes.'

'Sticky buds.'

'I'm not sure I follow.'

'Never mind.' Leepus looks up at tiny fresh-green tongues unfurling against pale-grey sky. 'Just having a seasonal rush to the head. You remember frog-spawn, catkins, nature tables?'

Maybe, if I try,' Jasmine says quiet after a moment. 'But it probably makes me weepy.'

'Pigtails? Playtime? Plimsolls?'

'Bastard,' says Jasmine. 'Stop it.'

'Yeah.' Leepus blinks and fast-forwards. 'So—picking up any whispers from the College?'

'A couple of seats newly empty at the refectory top-table. A whiff of blood in the corridors. Prefects taking names.'

'Good. Must be Chilly's getting busy.'

'Can't be long before the Citadel gets a whiff of something wicked rolling towards them. I hope the lady understands she needs to shove before they do.'

'She knows her play is all or nothing. You deal her enough good cards to do the right sort of damage?'

'I doubt she needs to bluff much to crush them—and I hold back a couple of aces like you say, stash 'em in the war chest for a rainy day.'

'It's a safe bet there'll be one of those soon enough,' says Leepus—and it seems as if the sky darkens. He totters to his feet and stretches. 'Anything on the whereabouts of Ajax?'

'Currently off-radar. Is that a problem?'

'Not likely—but if I read him wrong it could be. A loose cannon spoils the party.'

'Party.'

'Shithole's throwing a full-moon shindig. All welcome. Bring your gigolo if you want to.'

'Tempted,' says Jasmine, 'but my wild days are over, babe—and the countryside makes me nervous.'

'Shame.' Leepus turns—mooches on towards the tower. 'Maybe next time we throw one at your place.'

'That's right.' Jasmine sighs. 'There's always a next time.'

'I'll save you a slice of our Doll's magic cake then.'

'Sweet of you,' says Jasmine sounding far-off. 'Try to bring it before it's stale, babe.'

∞

Leepus up on the tower roof and skulking restless. The money's in the middle now—it's all over bar the shouting. But there's too much time till the shouting starts and he doesn't know how to kill it.

He watches a yellow butterfly wing-flexing on parapet lichen. But it doesn't hold his attention. He lights up a weedstick—takes one drag and stubs it.

He thinks about making a brew for a couple of minutes. But Doll should be here any time now—why should he bother when she can do it?

He pulls out his fone and yells Bodja. It takes him a lifetime to answer.

'All right, mate?' says Leepus. 'I'm thinking about rolling over—bringing back the quaddie and having a bit of a chinwag.'

'Up to you.' Bodja sounds less than enthusiastic. 'But me an' Peewit are sweatin' blood here, trying to clear some crap from the yard and build her a pole house.'

'Pole house?'

'Yeah. A nice little cabin on stilts. So she don't drown in her bed when the floods come up. She don't need to be out on the island no more—an' it's a bit too snug on the fuckin' boat to be proper decent, ennit?'

'She's staying, then?' says Leepus.

'I reckon she fuckin' ought to—after all the aggro we go through. I have a word with the Prof, an' he's happy to learn the girl her letters, an' I'm going to train her to fix stuff. She's right handy with the old tools, man.'

'Fair enough,' says Leepus. 'I'll see you at the shindig.'

'Right.' Bodja sounds a bit doubtful. 'Thing is, mate—I'm not sure if we make it.'

'Fukkoff, Bodja.' Leepus snorts. 'You never miss a shindig. Besides, I need you to rig the soundscape.'

'Peewit's a bit fuckin' shy though. Not too sure of her welcome—what with some of them scrotes up the village talking snide about how she's a dirty tinkish that don't deserve asylum. I worry some of 'em get leery, maybe try an' razz her. And then I have to kill some cunt to defend her.'

'No, mate,' says Leepus reassuring. 'That's not going to happen. Tell Peewit if she's not there dancing away in her best beads and feathers I'm mortally fucking offended. And if anyone demonstrates ill manners, Mike teaches them a lesson. And then slaps their fuckin' ignorant heads off. And the rest of them is pork-feed.'

'I'll see what she says, mate.' Bodja still sounds wary. 'She can be bit fuckin' stubborn.'

'Just be there, will you, for fukksake? It's a point of principle now.'

Leepus hangs up then. He takes a half-dozen calming breaths and then taps out Mike's number. He listens to the ringtone while a rook flaps by with a twig—adds it to one of the scraggly clumps in the nearby raucous treetops. It flies off and comes back with another. But Mike doesn't fucking answer. Lucky Doll is coming up the lane now or he probably starts to get grumpy.

∞

'I s'pose I might fit in.' Doll sniffs as she mashes his brew. 'In between me other numberless tasks, like.'

'Everyone says your cake is the bollocks.'

'I'll need chips to get the 'gredients off the erbwitch an' Dredd Gary— and paid for all the bakin'.'

'Sounds fair enough,' says Leepus. 'Whatever it costs it's worth it.'

Doll delivers his tea to the kitchen table and eyes him suspicious. 'You ain't feeling poorly, griz?'

'I'm top,' says Leepus. 'Why?'

' 'Cause you're being all nice an' that's not normal.'

'Must be the weather.' Leepus shrugs. 'Think I see signs of spring for the first time in years this morning. You remember seasons, do you?'

'What—you mean like warm-wet an' cold-wet?'

Leepus thinks about explaining but can't be bothered. 'I saw these and thought of you,' he says pulling the daffs from his pocket. Their stems are bruised and limp now and their trumpets battered and tattered.'

Doll takes the posy from him and studies it down her nose. 'Saying I'm puddled, are you?'

'I just think they look pretty and I'll make a spontaneous gesture. What are you talking about—puddled?'

'Them blobs they 'ave underground, what you don't bother bringing—s'posed to be med'cine if you mash 'em up. For olduns with the bleedin' brain-worm.'

'You live and learn,' says Leepus as she drops them in the rubbish.

'So I hear.' Doll sniffs and turns to scrubbing pots.

'How's your Ryda going on?' says Leepus off the cuff. 'Good work the lad does for Mike the other day. Tell him I say so, will you?'

' 'E's all right, I s'pose—when he ain't moonin' about all bleedin' day an' gettin' under my feet, or ramblin' on about 'is bonkers dream-shit. Majinashun, the Prof calls it when 'e goes to the 'Cademy back when 'e's little. There oughta be a potion to fix it.'

'He still looking at his books, then?'

'Book. 'Es only got the one. It's all ragged an' wore out now. Anyhow, it's mainly juss pictures, ennit? An' Ryda says 'e likes how words spell better.'

'Right,' says Leepus as a draught drifts in from the tank room—stands the hairs on the back of his hands up. He lights himself a weedstick—wanders off to his dashboard and leaves Doll to it.

A message from Chilly headed *SitRep* waiting for him. 'About fucking time,' he mutters and keys it open.

Surprise, asshole! I'm still alive and kicking butt—but only fucking just, man. Negotiating with these sly Inglish fucks is like pushing water up a mountain. Lucky Marcus' legacy is super-rich pay-dirt, or I'm quarantined and playing head-games in this fucking madhouse forever. You don't need to know the detail but I finally wrangle a mutually agreeable outcome. Upshot—a whole bunch of ugly chickens are coming home to deliver overdue justice to Admin bad-hats. I'll be flapping along right behind them back to the Homeland to help instigate regime change—supervise interrogations and executions. Between you and me I can't fucking wait to get started. There'll be some house-cleaning too at your end. The Citadel incumbents who ass-fuck me can expect to experience serious payback. A hard wind's gonna blow, man, and those dicks'll be twisting in it.

Meantime, the College hauls its own trash out and buries it in a shit-pit. (Those OurFuture prefect-kids sure have a mean streak, don't they?

I'm you I worry about their ambitions going forward.)

And that brings me to matters outstanding—namely Arturo fucking Ajax. This prick is square in the frame for historical harm to the College and they're eager to make him an example. They already dismantle his organisation but they don't retrieve a body. You need to come up with him fast—else my deal doesn't get signed off on. And that means you suffer major blowback—no settlement for Aunty and her fucking sick-fanatic chick farm. And the King of Clubs doesn't get paid either—so your domestic reputation gets catastrophically degraded. Not to mention I make sure everyone remembers to call you 'Virgil'. Plus you get branded with a global 'hostile adversary' designation.

For a tribal outlaw peasant you play a pretty slick game, man—and while I never share your fucked-up worldview I almost grow to respect you. So I'd rather that bad stuff doesn't happen.

That's all. Just yell when Ajax is in the bag and the College sends reps to collect him. They bring those random riders you insist on with them, and you and me are quits then, free to pursue our individual agendas.

Yours in the enduring glory of the Shining Republic—

Atalanta Honor-Trublood: Warrior & Cohort Commander INTL-XTRK (promotion pending)

Leepus sits back and relights his weedstick. He thinks about offering reassurance—decides to let the evil vix sweat for a day or two longer. Doll comes in to say goodbye an hour later—finds him happily engaged in the virtual cut-and-thrust of high-stakes poka.

Leepus is not quite winning yet but expects he will be before it's over.

◊◊◊◊◊

26

For a moment there's a full moon peering around the steeple of the Peasants' Party Palace. Then someone draws the curtains—leaves the ancient structure silhouetted against a soft-grey glowing cloudscape.

Leepus ducks through the lych gate. Lanterns perched on gravestones illuminate the path—reveal the interior mysteries of overhanging yew trees. A complex heartbeat reverberates from the huge stone chest of the Palace as he approaches. Its pulse spreads through the path slabs—electrifies his soles. The buried dead around him tap their bony feet.

The dancing eyes of firebrands flanking deep porch-shadow. A gust whips spark-tears from them. Leepus ducks into the maw—steps up to the studded timber door and heaves it open.

A bright galaxy of candles. A smoky firmament—a hundred coloured oil-lamp suns hung from a web of sooty rafters.

Megalithic speakers dominate the altar. A universal booming—the shuffling congregation melded in the rhythm.

Leepus breathes in deep—inhales the satisfying incense of multiple smouldering weedsticks. He snags a slab of magic cake when Doll drops by this morning so he's already well-primed for shindig. He pushes through the tight-packed friction of hot bodies—reflects the grins of enraptured faces. Stone steps dished by generations of godly liars leading up to the canopied pulpit—the arcane bestiary conjured by superstitious chisels writhing eerie on its black-wood panels. He takes his place on the rickety high-stool—leans on the carved-eagle lectern and looks down benign on his people.

Bodja there in the chancel at his dashboard sculpting sound-shapes—Peewit cross-legged beside him on a woofa riding the bass.

Big Bethan and her crew behind the east-aisle colonnade managing a long row of barrels. Doll's cake and other trippish fancies spread on trestles down the west side.

The general level of ecstasy rising. Some of the youth with their tops off—lads dervish with buxom lasses bouncing free on their shoulders. A few riderless bucks at rut in front of the altar saving face in a melee of headbutts. Bare arses pale in transept shadows—humping against pillars with plump legs wrapped around them. Even the Prof there in the corner holding onto an ale-jug and puffing away like a goodun.

Leepus leans back in the pulpit. Rests his head against cool stone. Stargazes contented. The bleary heavens shift and swirl—a stellar gleaming above the smoke-clouds. He casts the chains of gravity off—spirals into the infinite glitter as the shindig evolves below him.

∞

An aeon passed astral-travelling before Leepus is suddenly earthbound—Doll grinding his ribs with an urgent knuckle. 'Bleedin' wake yourself up, griz,' she's saying. 'Summut shwonki's occurin'.'

'Fukkoff,' says Leepus discombobulated. 'Just get Mike to sort it.'

'Can't find 'er, can I? So it's up to you, mate, ennit?' Doll slaps him. 'An' mind your fuckin' manners.'

Leepus gets up from the pulpit floor and shakes his head. Calm-down music oozing from the speakers now and the air is cooler. No one left on the dance floor. At least not standing upright. A few spent revellers sprawled here and there on the flagstones—easy to imagine there's been a bomb blast. A tangle of clasping bodies reminiscent of mating frogs by the font in a slick of vomit. Ferrety Phil hanging bat-like upside-down from the rood screen. Big Bethan asleep on the altar beneath him in her undies.

'So what's the fucking problem?' Leepus frowns confused. 'Looks like a regular shindig come-down.'

'An' that's just how it is, mate—up till a moment ago,' Doll says steering him down from the pulpit. 'The walkers are all floatin' off 'ome feelin' fine with their 'eads expanded, an' them as is too ruined to move is kippin' quiet where they fizzles. Ol' Bodja's sortin' out some lullabies to leave loopin'. I hear him tell that kid Peewit it's time they're gettin' off now. She says: "Fair enough, Bodj—juss nippin' owt fer a piddul." Next thing I look up an' see Bob the Butcher shifting out of the bell-tower door, with a couple of them wild boggies 'e hires in when there's porks plumped an' needin' killin'. An' there's John Fox slopin' after.'

'John Fox is fucking banned from Shithole.'

'That's what I tell 'im, griz—get a gob in the eye for me trouble an' then pushed over in puke.'

'Sorry, Doll. I tell Mike to make sure the scrote remembers that when she does him.'

'No 'arm done to me, mate. It's that gurlee that's in trouble.'

'How's that, then?' says Leepus. 'And where's Bodja when this happens? Don't tell me the prick shits it again.'

'No, griz. Bodja tries 'is bleedin' best, mate—rares up good an' proper. But one o' the boggies 'its 'im with a cudgel. An' the other one stamps 'is bollocks. " 'Ere's the thing then, you sly fuck," Bob says to 'im right nasty. "Your dirty little tinkish does Foxy a bad fuckin' wrongness. And then you give her shelter, an' worm round that cunt Leepus so Foxy gets his arse banned—an' you get to keep the rancid savage for your own fuckin' private shagbag."

'Fucking Bob the Butcher. He can't say I don't give him chances.' Leepus takes a couple of breaths—settles his blood pressure. 'Where's the fat fuck now, then?'

'I'm tryna tell you, aren't I? Doll says huffy. 'Bob's tellin' Bodja he reckons, "It's only right old Foxy here gets his fair go at that slag, and then maybe another if 'e can manage—and then I'm doing her after, bent over one of them gravestones." Old Bodja just starts up growlin' like a bear then. Almost gets 'is paws on Bob, 'e does—you can see in the scrote's face how it frits 'im. But then the boggies are all over poor ol' Bodja with their cudgels. An' Peewit's in the doorway. She has a shufti an' does one, an' Foxy's trottin' after. "Take 'im to the crypt and hold him," Bob tells the boggies, an' then wobbles off after Foxy like a sow about ripe to farrow.'

'Fukksake,' says Leepus handing Doll his fone and starting for the door. 'Make sure those fucks can't get out of the crypt—then call Mike and get her arse here.'

∞

Outside the path-side lamps are all burned out now. And it looks like someone snags the firebrands to stagger home with. There's pallid moonshine through slow-broiling clouds—everything earthly tinted black or tarnished-silver. A shower's dampened the grass in the graveyard. A dark trail of footprints through dewy glimmer. Leepus sets out to follow wishing he packs a few self-defence aids.

The trail leads round the corner of the Palace. A breath of wind in the yews—otherwise it's silent. Disorderly ranks of crooked gravestones and listing godly-monuments standing by impassive. Leepus blinks—tries to up the contrast. There—a tomb chest jutting from the shadow of a buttress. Disturbed weeds ranged tall around it. A leg trailing oddly twisted. 'Fukkit,' murmurs Leepus moving closer reluctant.

It takes him a couple of seconds staring down to understand that the limb's not Peewit's. A weird musculature eerily exposed by dead moonlight—knotted and contorted under peeling scabs of bark and lichen. Leepus resumes respiration. Kicks the branch off the eroded sandstone slab. Sits down for a celebratory weedstick.

And then the horrible wailing starts up somewhere out under the boundary elms along the haha.

It's hard to imagine such a raw shrill scream comes out of the throat of a human. It sounds like a pork getting slaughtered—runs a live-wire down through Leepus from nape to perineum. And he doesn't want to be but he's moving. Tripping. Sprawling in the rank wet grass—lumbering up and stumbling onward.

He pulls up at the rim of the haha—teeters over the ditch. The terrible screeching has stopped. But there's shouting now from somewhere not too far-off. Leepus tries not to picture the action—casts around for some kind of weapon. Fucking Mike should be here.

Movement below in the gloom. A twitch of black clumped-nettles. Leepus jumps down and feels his knee pop—hobbles over dreadful.

It's not the rover girl curled foetal with both arms rigid. Hands clamped tight between thighs. Last-gasp gurgling out through gap-tooth gape. Leepus grabs John Fox's bony shoulder—rolls him over and straightens him out. A dagger-handle juts from his groin clasped in a fist like a stubby hard-on. Black blood welling from the root. Midriff and breeches glistening sodden.

Maybe its just nervous relief but Leepus almost chuckles.

But there's still shouting somewhere back up in the graveyard. He limps over to the haha—fails to scramble up its crumbly drystone embankment. Every footfall hammers his kneecap as he lurches off around the ditch in search of easier access and the origin of the shouting. Fifty yards of pained exclamation at every footfall—then Leepus can finally make the words out.

'Now your fucked then, encha?' It's Bob the Butcher snarling breathless. 'You're cornered now, you tinkish fuckin' rat-bitch, an' you en't got another shank. I'm gunna kick your rotten mush in an' do you in every 'ole.'

'Try it then if yow wannuh, yow fooken pizzul-waggin' gut-sack.'

Leepus gets a toehold in the haha stones with his good leg—lifts his eyeballs above graveyard ground-level. The moon brightens—peeps down prurient through cloud curtains. Bob with his back to him twenty yards off and lumbering forward elephantine. Peewit with a nosebleed. Her torn jerkin flapping open. A dark wriggle of blood down her breastbone. She's backed hard against the wrought-iron gate of a semi-collapsed faux-classical mausoleum—hemmed in by a stack of reclaimed stone and a heap of rotten timbers. She crouches and rabbits forward aiming to duck past him. But Bob is fast for a bucket of lard and his hands are big as shovels. He swoops one down and snags the collar of her jerkin—yanks her from her feet and whirls her out of the garment. Her body crunches into the stone-stack. She lays there winded on the ground while Bob grabs up a hefty log and Leepus scrabbles croaking, 'I'm watching you, you sick fucking scrote—so don't you fucking do it.'

Bob swivels in search of the source of the warning. He frowns into the shadows but doesn't see Leepus—turns back about his ugly business. But Peewit's already up and at him—talons raking face-flab.

Bob bellowing—flailing blind. Peewit running up the stone-stack. Peewit airborne—her feet coming down hard on her enemy's

263

shoulders. A sound like a shot in a pillow. Bob cursing—circling with limp-wing trailing. Peewit dancing round him then. Dipping past the wood-pile. Coming up with a naily timber.

Leepus' foot finds purchase on the drystone. He heaves up—slithers over the top.

Bob smearing blood from his eyes and roaring—trying to locate Peewit. He needs to look behind him. She's ducking in low and swinging the timber like a cudgel—planting its nails deep in the meat at the back of his knee.

Bob down on his haunches and howling—the cudgel torn from Peewit's grip trapped spiky and likely painful in the fold of his collapsed leg.

Leepus on his feet now and moving forward. Peewit back up on the stack of stones and crouching—getting a two-handed grip on a slab. And then she's braced statuesque in the moonlight with it raised above her head—a pale half-naked angel of destruction.

'Shit, girl,' Leepus hears himself saying. 'Are you sure you want to do that?'

'Wha?' says Peewit swaying under the poised weight of her burden.

'Can't deny you've got the right,' says Leepus stepping closer. 'But the aftermath gets messy.'

Peewit looks down—thinks about it. Bob on all-fours below her retching and dripping face-blood. ''E's a rottun cont an' 'e fooken 'urts us. So us sez 'is fooken 'ead needs fooken squashin' us duz.'

'Staying alive is probably worse for him in the long run.'

'Ow yow fooken reckun tha', then?'

'There's Articles on rapers. And on spoiling shindigs with violence.'

'Leepus?' Bob blinking bloody and peering. 'Help me—I'm bastard crippled here, man.'

'So you are,' says Leepus without compassion. 'Maybe it's time you start begging for mercy.'

'Fuckin' scab—I ain't done for yet,' snarls Bob bundling forward brutish. 'I'm 'avin' that tink savage.'

'Yow cont, yow's fooken not tho',' says Peewit hurling the slab down.

∞

The sun is an hour above the horizon but the smother of cloud means it's barely light yet. Leepus sits on a pew in the porch of the Party Palace—enjoys a thoughtful weedstick shivering in his shirtsleeves. He loans his coat to Peewit. Her jerkin ends up ruined by Bob the Butcher's gore and shock gives her the shivers. It's all a right fucking carve-up.

But Bodja and Peewit are both breathing at least and winnas by a fair margin. And the boggie scrotes who help Bob kick it off are down in the crypt in shackles and well-battered. Lucky there's a couple of brace of firemen still with their heads on to go down and do the business. But it should be fucking Mike's job.

Bodja's got some nasty lumps and a bit of a stagger on him when the firemen liberate him. But Doll goes and fetches the erbwitch to patch him up and slap some balm on. Leepus isn't too sure what happens next though. There'll need to be a council and a judging when Shithole's awake and its breakfast digested. There'll be plenty not happy with Peewit—saying kindness shown to vicious tink-spawn always gets repaid with double blud-and-trouble. Likely Leepus has to filibuster—drone the scrotes round to his way of thinking.

But they pay a lot more attention if Mike's standing up behind him.

Fucker picks her time to go AWOL. Leepus isn't happy. It's an unforgivable dereliction. He feels like his right arm is missing. He's just fishing out his fone to ping her again when young Ryda hurls through the lych gate with a deer-hound loping beside him. 'Trouble, lad?' Leepus asks redundant as the breathless youth hammers up to the porch.

'Fuh—fuh—fuckin'—fuckin' 'elp!' Ryda pants exhausted. 'Need t'get int' tower, griz. Need t'ring fuckin' firebells—get some fighters out.'

'Easy, mate,' says Leepus. 'Let's hear first what it is that spooks you.'

'It's fuckin' tinkish, ennit? I'm out on the commons runnin' me dog there after coney, an' I sees 'em all fuckin' comin'.'

'All?'

'Ten pony-boys at least, griz, all done up in feathers—an' another 'alf

265

as fuckin' many battle chariots. I run me fuckin' arse off but they're already up top o' High Street.'

'Right,' says Leepus thinking fast. 'Way too late for firebells, lad. Get inside and bar the doors while I go out and parley.'

'Whu-what if they cuts your 'ead off?'

'It's likely I'll be dead, mate.' Leepus winks and heads for the gate. 'And not fondly remembered, either.'

∞

Leepus waits in the derelict old bus-shelter on Red Barn corner. He has time to finish his weedstick before the rover war-band turns off High Street in his direction. He tries to keep his hand steady as the pony-boys trot up and fan out around him. Anyone else who's watching keeps their head down.

A tongue-click and a low whistle. The riders sidle—a chariot nudging through. Leepus lifts an arm in greeting. 'Is that young Brock there with the pretty mare, looking chippa in his fine doe-skin and feathers?'

' 'Tis,' Brock says nodding. 'Rare day as us comes 'mong yow fooken simpuls. Us loiks t'make a preshun.'

'Queenie doesn't fancy an outing?'

' 'Er duz but 'er feels poorly.'

'Sorry for that,' says Leepus. 'Here's hoping the old gal recovers.'

' 'Er's shot thru 'er dugs in the battul. Wiseun stops 'er 'oles with mossy an' keps 'er juice in, but yow cud'n call 'er zackly jolly.'

'This battle then,' says Leepus. 'Tell me you fucking win it.'

'Wipeout.' Brock flashes pearlies—snaps chariot reins and spins the rig in a tight circle. And then he's back in position—Ajax spilled from the back hunched hogtied on the pocked tarmac.

'So it happens as predicted?'

'Us tekks a duzzn bonces, an' daft Runtee's onee Ro'buck cuzz gets dedded. Killas all comes 'cross fooken causeway inta campgroun' juss 'fore fooken sunnup. Onee we'sall outside lurkin'. Thissun dyn in dirt thur's 'ollerin' bold f'rus t'bring out 'ostage an' then 'e spares

266

us—so us slips fooken war-dags to chomp they bastids fooken innards—then us gallops up an' fooken chops they. Boss thur loses a foo fooken bitsa meat, loik—but us keps 'im lively 'ow yow tellus.'

'Nice,' says Leepus. 'And their weapons and vehicle and bits and bobs are good enough compo, are they?'

'Us rekkun some bunce's fittin'—since yow's fooken axin.'

'Do you now, Brock lad?' says Leepus frowning. 'Normally I tell you to piss up your own cheeky arsehole.' He pauses. Faces darken—ponies jostle restive.'

Brock has a shufti around them. 'Us rekkun ol' killagurl muss be lookin' onnus wiv 'er fooken long-gun, or yow's nevvuh s'fooken cocky.'

Leepus ignores the interruption. 'Occasionally I might haggle,' he says strolling over and toe-jabbing Ajax. The mercenary moans and snots bloody bubbles. 'But, seeing as how you deliver this hopeless turd in the nick of time and just about fit to face College justice, I'm minded to give my generous streak an unaccustomed outing—reward you with a nice fat bonus.'

'Fair play to yow, Chief.' Brock grins wide and pulls a fone out of his fringed breeches. 'Us tells rest o' they bad bucks out up yond on 'eath, then. So's themall can trot on 'ome, loik, an' nah bothuh t'blayzup all yow's fooken 'ouses an' get t'razzin' yow's squealin' gurlees.'

∞

It's a couple of hours after the firemen stow Ajax in the crypt and bring up the shackled boggies that the prefects roll up in a ShuvTruk. The mercenary still doesn't quite get how it is that Leepus sucks him in—sets him up for the Ro'bucks with the shwonki tip on Chilly's whereabouts delivered via Mother Mellow. But then he is a bit under the weather.

The Rovers roll homeward happy with their bonus. The boggies are bit knocked about but generally hale and hearty. Plenty of valuable life in the bastards. The Ro'bucks do well if they chop them in for KashBak—but probably even better if they slave them to jolly rogers.

Leepus feels more chippa with Ajax in the bank—has second

267

thoughts about holding a council. He earns credit now for getting Shithole out from under the rovers. Maybe he can push a bluff through—get things all done and dusted before too many hungover citizens mooch up asking awkward questions.

He sends Ryda to put the word round that the trouble isn't over—they should stay in their beds and keep the doors shut.

He tips the firemen a long-stack apiece to lose Foxy's body in some sink mud and keep fucking mum about it. Naturally word leaks in time—but by then it's just another shady Shithole legend and people can believe it or not.

He packs Bodja off to hobble home to the oxbow with Peewit to nurse him. She says she's 'Sorry ferall t'fooken 'assle, griz—but us wishus tha' rock duzznt juss tek tha' fat cont's fooken lug off.' And then she gives Leepus his coat back. He turns his head as she shucks it off but her modesty's preserved now by an old baggy woollen Doll lends her.

Leepus meets the ShuvTruk at the lych gate. 'Two to go,' he says to the black-armoured noncom in charge of the cohort.

'Two?' The prefect checks his handheld. 'I'm only tasked with one, griz.'

'Late addition to the roster—dispatcher must be slow with the update.' Leepus whistles and waves to the firemen.

A nod from the noncom to one of his 'fects stood by with a couple of packets. The stud steps up brisk and presents them to Leepus. One's rectangular—a heft to it as expected. The other small and flat. Leepus sets both aside on the wall as the firemen come out with the captives. Two of them carry Ajax slung between them. The other two lead shambling Bob the Butcher on a neck rope. The erbwitch puts a bandage over his amputated ear and binds his knee up. His face is scabbed and his eyes sunk deep in black-bruised swelling. He droops to the left where Peewit cracks his shoulder bone—fat arm supported by a sling improvised from his grimy vest. He looks a bit apprehensive.

'The one in the shoddy uniform's your special guest of honour,' says Leepus to the noncom as studs chuck Ajax into the load space. 'He goes all the way home to the College.'

'And this fucking slab of flab?' The noncom sneers at Bob the Butcher. 'Barely looks fit for KashBak.'

'Transportation,' says Leepus.

'Transportation where?'

'Anywhere you like, mate.' Leepus winks at Bob. 'Pick a nice a spot an hour or so into NoGo and just drop the arsehole off there.'

'What?' says Bob the Butcher catching on. 'Fukksake, Leepus. You can't fuckin' ship me out without an 'earing. Look at me. I'm all mashed up by that tinkish skank—an' I ain't got even a shave of glitta to buy a kip with'. An' what about my business?'

'Anyone can chop up porks and overcharge for manky meat, Bob. I'm you I'm counting my fucking blessings. If young Peewit doesn't wobble when she lets that slab go, your head's a squashed paper-cup with mushy brains in. Be grateful it just grinds your ear off.'

'But how am I the one who gets transported—when the fuckin' vix shanks old Foxy dead in the bollocks an' gets away without a mark on her? There's supposed to be fuckin' rules, man.'

'Foxy?' Leepus raises an eyebrow. 'Foxy's banned from Shithole, Bob, so the Articles don't give him shelter. Besides, no one finds a body—so maybe you only dream you see him.'

Bob looks from fireman to fireman. A couple of them shake their heads. None of them meets his eye. 'Cunts.' Bob spits. 'It's a rotten fuckin' stitchup. And anyway, I don't even poke 'er, do I?'

'That's taken into consideration—plus the fact she duffs you over good and proper. You're still down for violent bigotry, though. And for spoiling my fucking shindig.' Leepus pulls a handful of chips from his pocket. 'Here's fifty to buy you some time to heal and learn your lesson. Maybe, if you manage to stay alive and wobble your way back to Shithole, I let you address a meeting—make your case for asylum. But I wouldn't be in too much of a hurry.'

'Come on, Leepus—you don't 'ave to do this,' Bob says with a bit of a whimper. 'Give us a letoff, eh mate?'

'Sorry,' says Leepus nodding to the noncom. 'The answer is no. You're not my mate, you're a prick, Bob. And I don't fucking like you.'

It takes four fit young studs considerable effort to heave Bob aboard the ShuvTruk. Leepus lights a weedstick—watches the vehicle grind off in a gust of diesel. And then he thanks the firemen one last time—shakes hands with each of them in turn and then wanders off to the tower to grab a nap.

∞

Leepus is playing cards—cheating at poka against Marcus. Marcus is dead but he's still winning and the bastard thinks it's funny.

It's the rumble of the lift that shakes Leepus from the dream. His first assumption is that it's Mike rolling up with an explanation. He scrambles from the sofa and stumbles across the tank room—finds it's Doll there in the lift-car tugging the concertina-gate open one-handed. 'Fuck,' he says disappointed.

'Fuck yourself.' Doll sniffs. 'An' don't just stand there gazin' gormless. You can see I'm bleedin' laden.'

Leepus opens the gate. Doll bustles past like a loaded forklift. He follows her bleary into the kitchen saying, 'So what do you want, Doll? I'm resting.'

'That Big Alun Stoat the fireman stops by, don't he?—on 'is way up the Queen's for a guzzle. Says you leave these on the wall outside the Palace. So I think I'll do you a kindness an' drop up 'em here. Now I'm wishing I don't bleedin' bother.'

'Ah,' says Leepus as she dumps his packages on the table. 'I forget them. Lucky some scrote doesn't tax them.'

'Valuable are they?' Doll at the sink now filling the kettle.

'The big one sets you back a full bar or more if you have to buy it. No clue what's in the other.'

'There'll be a reward then, I reckon—for me to divvy with Alun?'

'Fair enough.' Leepus turns the flat package over curious in his hands—peers at a handwritten message on the wrapping: *For Uncle Virgil—couldn't resist it. Sally.*

'Couple of bottles of Yellow Scorpion, then?'

'Why not?' says Leepus tearing paper.

'An' throw in a jar of best buds?' Doll pushes sensing weakness.

'Second best,' says Leepus frowning at Chilly's gift. 'Greed is unbecoming.'

'So it is,' Doll says contented. 'You ready for a brew, then?'

And then Leepus' fone is buzzing. 'Mike?' he answers it without looking. 'What the fuck's happening with you, mate?'

'Some fokkin rich fish who think they know how to play poka,' booms the King of Clubs. 'Couple of seats left to the fill at the table. Can't help you with fokkin Mike, though.'

'When?' says Leepus wandering distracted through to the tank room.

'This time tomorrow. Say 'yes', griz—way you're rollin' lately, guaranteed we come out fokkin golden.'

'I take it the College appreciates your assistance in delivering a satisfactory outcome.'

'I'm their most favoured son, now.'

'Enjoy it while it lasts, brer.'

'So say you'll fokkin play, then.'

Leepus thinks about it riffling pages. 'Okay,' he says after a couple of moments. 'I'm in—but there's one condition.'

∞

Doll brings Leepus' brew to him on the sofa. He doesn't look up as he takes the hot mug from her. 'What's your prezzy then, griz?' she asks nosing over his shoulder.

'Nothing. Just a daft kids' book some old fool once wastes his time with.' Leepus snaps the book shut. An illustration on the cover—a boy poling a raft through a flooded city with seabirds wheeling around their nests on misty high-rise ledges.

'What's that spelling on it say, then?'

'Huh?' Leepus looks up at her from somewhere faraway.

A beach with white gulls sailing. A young woman in a breeze-fluttered sun dress. A little naked blond girl crawling on a spread blanket—her brother sat propped against the picnic rucksack beside her. He's looking up from his library book saying, 'It's okay, I s'pose, but it ought to be better—when are you going to write one for me?'

'The scribble on the front, mate,' Doll presses. 'The title or whatever you call it?'

'It says: *SUNK— a Finn of the Islands adventure. By "Jack Rabbit"*.'

'Jack Rabbit's the one as makes it? You know 'im do you, griz?'

'Not that I recall,' says Leepus vague. 'Likely it's a pen-name.'

Doll sniffs. 'I never get a wrapped-up gift. I'm you, I'm more excited. Who's it bleedin' from, then?'

'Just an arsehole with cruel streak who thinks they're fucking funny,' says Leepus picking up the poker—unlatching the door of the stove.

Doll frowns. 'So now you're gunna burn it?'

Something in her tone makes Leepus hesitate. He stares into the glowing firebox—imagines paper crisping black and then flowering bright and hot. 'No,' he says standing then and handing the slim volume over. 'Take it home with you if you want, Doll. Maybe young Ryda likes it.'

'Thanks, griz,' Doll says beaming. 'The lad thinks he finds treasure, I reckon.'

'I'm worried about Mike,' says Leepus.

'Yeah?' Doll raises an eyebrow. 'That's not much like you, mate.'

'I know,' says Leepus. 'And I don't know what to do. It's a bit of a fucking problem.'

'P'raps the old girl's laid up poorly out at 'er 'ome-place. Why don't you go an' check her?'

'Home?' Leepus is disconcerted. 'If Mike's got a fucking home, mate, I don't know where it is.'

'Donchuh?' Doll relishes small triumph. 'Fetch us summat to scratch on then, griz, an' a marker. I bleedin' draw you a road-picture, ennit?'

◊◊◊◊◊

27

It takes Leepus half a day to get there on Bodja's quaddie.

A dozen abandoned villages along the sodden bottom of the valley.

An hour haggling a toll with highwaymen to get up on the Top Way.

And then a detour round a caravan of fervent godly pilgrims pitched up by a fogbound shrine. The makings of a bonfire. A wagon with a cage on the back with a praying heretic inside it.

Turn west at the burned-out hotel.

Through a gloomy conifer plantation. He stops at a desolate roadside viewpoint overlooking a crow-flocked crag—guzzles a jug of Doll's broth. A sound like wolves howling in the distance.

'Foller track down rill to humpy bridge,' says a snotty playing in a car-shell outside a row of smoky hovels. 'Up tuthuh side to broke-down gate—tenundred steps puts y'innit.'

'Obliged,' Leepus says to the skinny kid—flicks her his half-smoked weedstick.

'Best make sure y'yellout shrill, griz,' the child calls as he putters off. 'Them up thur un't all that frenny. An' thur's bin some bovvuh 'appuns. Like as not they put takdags on yuh if y'unt well-knowed un' 'spected.'

∞

A stockaded farmstead beneath a dark wood tumbling off the moor down a narrow valley. A double berm of half-buried knackered farm-machines blocking the rutted drive to heavy vehicles. Leepus tacks the muddy jitty through them on the quaddie—follows narrow tyre-ruts to the steel and heavy-timber gate that's hanging open. He turns off the motor—dismounts stiff. A buzzard keening above him as he eases the gate wider and noses. Loose chickens cluck and scatter across a weed-cracked concrete farmyard. Penned dogs growling and yapping. A stack of rotting hay-bales. Rolls of rusty fence-wire. Rotten-veg juice seeping from a trailer with flat tyres. Mike's combo parked up in a barn. No smoke from the chimney of the house—it's kitchen door standing open. 'Alright.' calls Leepus stepping towards it. 'Alright the house. It's just a friend of Mike's in your pound—not any kind of trouble.'

Leepus ducks under a grey-stone lintel splotched with yellow lichens—crosses the foot-worn threshold onto mucky floor-tiles. A black-iron bootscraper outside by the door but it doesn't appear to be used much. 'Anybody home? Fukksake, Mike—it's Leepus.'

A knocker on the open door cast in the form of a hanging bat. Leepus chaps it three times. It reports like a hammer driving a nail—but the air inside is dead and dense and the sound doesn't penetrate deeply. Leepus has a shufti.

Big square sink with dirty crocks in.

An ancient table full of clutter.

A blackened range with pots on—cold. Grey wood-ash spilled from firebox heaped on hearthstone.

A dresser of fancy china and bright little animals made out of glass.

Cleavers hung on 'S' hooks above a time-carved chopping block. One hook with nothing on it.

A rabbit gun propped in the corner.

Stone steps and a higgledy passage. Leepus stoops and moves along it. Rough plaster scrapes his shoulders.

A gloomy parlour with dark furniture. Saggy chair by chilly fireplace. Photographs of history—a congregation of ancestors trapped in frames on a dusty mantel. A low cot in the corner—pisspot tucked beneath it. Yellowed quilt turned back. Grey hairs on a musty pillow. The impression of a slight body.

The room next door is brighter. Threadbare-carpet island in a sea of draughty floorboards. Overused toys and a ruined township of faded coloured-plastic bricks spilling from a playpen. A fireplace with guard around it. Vigorous portraits of family-members chalked on a board by a manic infant. Bunk-beds with blankets trailing. A handprint smeared on a ladder-tread. Maybe shit—or blood.

A scullery. Some cubby-holes and claustrophobic domestic cupboards. A dank khazi with a stained shitta. Nothing much more to see down here—Leepus moves to the foot of the crooked staircase. 'Mike?' His foot creaks the bottom tread. 'Anybody up there?'

A low humming audible now—a vibration. He tries to imagine its origin as he climbs. Or maybe he tries not to.

Dull light from a tiny window in a cobwebbed recess at the kink in the top of the stair. Closed doors along the landing. Some watercolours on the walls. Prize-fight in a ring of jeering. A gun-dog with dead partridge. A pair of goldfinch on a thistle. The humming getting louder as Leepus nears a corner. Now you'd have to call it buzzing.

A splintered door in an alcove smashed inward and hanging from hinges. There's a bed inside with tumbled furniture and strewn clothing—a loud dizziness of flies. And way too much rank gore splashed about the floor and the walls and the ceiling for Leepus to contemplate anymore detail. The smell's a bit nasty too. He holds it in all the way back downstairs and along the passage. And then he spatters the kitchen.

Leepus sits on a mossy bale in the farmyard and smokes a weedstick. The penned dogs pick up the fresh blood-taint clinging to him—tremble and yip and whimper. 'Fukksake,' says Leepus to them low and soothing. 'Mike's combo in the barn. A deserted house and a riot of blood. What horrible thing happens here, then? And where are the fucking bodies?'

Leepus takes a few deep breaths—fetches the rabbit gun from the kitchen and then carries on exploring.

It takes him an hour to find the orchard hidden behind a thick hedge of hawthorn beyond the trees at the back of the farmhouse. Tall grass trampled flat leads him through the rows of gnarled fruit-trees to a far corner. Mike there with her back to him and sitting on a handcart.

Leepus relaxes a little—clears his throat and steps up closer. 'Wait,' says Mike a bit gruff. And she isn't turning round. Leepus follows her suggestion. He has time to count the fresh grave-mounds as Mike tugs a grubby rag from her waistband—wipes her face and eyes with it and blows her nose like a bugle.

' 'Kay, mate?' says Leepus and steps forward.

'Why the fuck are you here? Mike still keeping her back turned. 'How do you fuckin' find me?'

'Doll draws me a map,' says Leepus.

'Right.' Mike spits. 'Bitch should mind her own business.'

Leepus doesn't feel the time's quite right to challenge Mike's unfairness. 'So what's all this, mate?' he says looking down at the graves. One's newish but with nettles sprouting on it. The other four are damp and raw. Two of them are adult-sized. Two of them are tiny.

'Family graveyard,' grunts Mike standing—combing her hair back with muddy fingers.

'You never say you have family, mate.' Leepus might almost be offended.

'Yeah.' Mike stoops and scoops up pick and shovel—clatters them onto the handcart. 'Well I fuckin' haven't now, have I?'

Leepus says, 'So tell me.'

Mike just looks at him deadpan—shoves the cart into motion and marches off.

Leepus catches up with her in the farmyard rolling the combo out of the barn. She leaves it by the gate—goes over to the dog pen and lets the pack out. They circle her for a moment—then she whistles and they're off and running. Mike moves on to a shed in the corner—shoots the bolts and swings the door wide. Leepus follows—peers after her from the threshold. A big copper vat—valves and looping coils of tubing. The sweet tang of fermentation. Mike wrestles a fifty-gallon drum over to the doorway. 'Biodiesel still,' she says in answer to Leepus' silent question. 'Frank grows beets in the back field.'

'Frank?'

'Brother.'

'Younger?'

'Yeah. Lot. Takes the Ma by surprise. But at least he's still fit to work the place when the Da's fuckin' days are over. The drum on its side now—Mike rolling it like thunder across the yard to the house. 'Gets himself a sound woman too.'

'And a couple of children?'

'Michael's the first.' Mike swallows. 'Liza's only just showing with Mistry when Frank goes out on a spree one night and gets himself fuckin' press-ganged. She's gone two when he gets his compassionate discharge—comes home short of a foot and an eyeball, with a couple of chunks of a fragged sniper-round jagging around in his brainbox.'

'The lad's equilibrium a bit unsettled, I imagine.'

Mike grunts—uncaps the drum and heaves it over in the kitchen doorway. Wipes her hands on her jacket. Watches it glug towards empty. 'Most days he's just a bit simple—now and then he's a vicious sick fuckin' arsehole, putting lumps on Liza an' giving his kids the horrors. Usually the Ma can calm him down, though. And when she can't I do it.'

'He goes bang a bit more often though, just lately?'

'Headaches.' Mike heading to the combo—rooting about in the back of the sidecar. 'He says it's like some cunt's scraping all his thoughts out with a red-hot fuckin' spoon, man.'

'No effective analgesic?'

'Treble joy-juice doesn't even touch it.' Mike walking back to the building—weighing a grenade in her palm. 'An' then the Ma fuckin' shuffles off.'

'Lot of stress on you, mate. Makes me feel a bit of a prick for being so demanding. Why don't you include me?'

'You've got your own fuckin' secrets,' Mike says patting down her pockets.

'Yeah.' Leepus can't deny it. 'But fukkit, Mike, we're partners and—'

'I need a smoke and I'm empty.' Mike holds out her free hand. 'Shut up and fuckin' load me.'

Leepus lights her a weedstick and passes it over. And then one for himself.

'Long story short.' Mike sucks hard—burns off an inch. 'Liza shouts me Frank's on a major rampage while we're out fuckin' up the rovers. Time I get my arse up here he's fuckin' done them all. I find them in the bedroom. There's been a lot of chopping.'

'And Frank does himself then, does he?'

'Nah, mate.' Mike spits. 'He seems to think that's my job.'

Leepus thinks about that but he doesn't comment.

Mike finishes her weedstick and discards the butt with a wrist-flick—hooks the grenade-pin with a finger—says,' You might want to back off now, mate—else you likely get your fringe singed.'

'I s'pose torching the place is cathartic,' says Leepus walking backwards.

'Whatever fuckin' that is.' Mike smiles grim and ring-pulls.

A flat bang and then a boom as fire belches lurid from the doorway. The empty drum launched skyward—coming down with a clang on the corrugated barn-roof. Black smoke boiling out through shattered windows—rolling over treetops. Mike standing there in the scabby yard staring fierce at the inferno.

Leepus waits outside the gate until she joins him. 'Done now, mate,' he says quiet as she trundles the combo alongside the quaddie.

'Yeah,' says Mike getting mounted. 'I'm birthed in that fuckin' bedroom—spend the next dozen years getting my fuckin' arse kicked around the house. Life here is shit from day fuckin' one. That's how come I end up a fuckin' mental killa leggie.'

'Right.' Leepus winks. 'Every cloud has a silver lining.'

'Cunt,' says Mike donning goggles. 'Give us another fuckin' weedstick.'

A few pensive smoky minutes—then Leepus says, 'Best head back to

Shithole then, before it gets too dark, mate.'

Mike looks at the sky and pulls on her gauntlets. 'It all works out with the fuckin' rovers?'

'After a bit of a scramble. Bodja and Peewit do a lot better than Bob the Butcher.'

'The shwonki shit with Marcus and fuckin' Chilly?'

'I think I finesse a long-term advantage.'

'So it's all fuckin' squared away, then?'

'Couple of itches still need scratching—just to leave things nice and tidy. Tomorrow should see it over.'

'See—it all turns out fine in the end. You only think you fuckin' need me.'

'Don't say that,' says Leepus—his hand on Mike's leathern shoulder. 'It's never the same without you.'

'Reckon I take some time, mate,' Mike says kicking up the combo motor as Leepus takes his hand back. 'Fancy a bit of a wander. Need to hunt up somewhere to let the wolf out—have a bit of a fuckin' monsta in a place no cunt who I like gets damaged.' And then she revs up and does one without further comment.

Leepus sits on the quaddie as the combo blurts off down the track. It's safe to say his emotions are mixed. He pulls out a weedstick and lights it—listens to the roar of fire and farmhouse walls collapsing. 'So mind how you fucking go, mate,' he says with a gust of smoke.

∞

The King of Clubs experiences a near-fatal attack of hilarity when Leepus chugs up to his palace at dusk on the quaddie. 'You only have to fokkin ask, brer,' he says when he gets his breath back, 'and I send the Roosta to fetch you.'

'That's what I'm afraid of,' says Leepus lighting a stick. 'But speaking of the Roosta—how's Lesta?'

'Still missing his knee, I'm guessing,' says the King leading them up the wide steps to the entrance. 'Why not give the old boy a wave? He's likely watching you now, griz—over a fokkin gun-sight.'

279

'Right.' Leepus settles the package that he's carrying more comfortably under his arm. 'Can't really blame him for being mardy.'

'So what's in the box?' the King says. He's paused by an atrium mirror adjusting the hang of his ermine. 'An' stub that fokkin weedstick.'

'Peace offering, brer.' Leepus hands the package off to a liveried flunky—fishes a bottle of Yellow Scorpion out of his pocket and passes that over too. 'Something to give Lesta his bounce back.'

They walk together to the stairs that lead down to the King's private card-room. Leepus waits for the King to ask but he doesn't so he has to tell him. 'Republic military-grade prosthetic lower-leg and knee-joint—with self-matching skin-tone. Lifetime guarantee. And a voucher for a top fucking sawbones to fit it.'

'Nice.' The King whistles low and approving. 'Kit like that doesn't come in a cracker. Must be worth at least ten-times Lesta's fokkin KashBak. Wanna bet me the mope tries to hock it—trades up to a motorised kripkart an' blows the profit on fokkin krakkle?'

'Either he does or he doesn't,' says Leepus peering through a door-window into the card room. 'At least I give him options.'

'You're all fokkin heart,' says the King.'

Leepus looks back deadpan over his shoulder—says, 'Yeah—sometimes. And sometimes I'm pure arsehole. Versatility's the key to surviving in modern Inglund.'

'Fair enough, griz.' The King grins wolfish—punches Leepus hard on the shoulder. 'Time for some versatile fokkin poka.'

∞

Five players already at the table waiting for the King and Leepus.

Big Bobby back hopeful in seat two with his lucky Greenfield lapel-pin.

Seat three is a sallow kid sporting an OurFuture armband.

A chubby old gal with dead eyes and a dazzle of glitta about her is settled in the fourth trap. Leepus makes her for a slaver.

Five is a griz in a funny hat with a cape draped over his stooped

280

shoulders. He looks disconcertingly godly.

The King smiles a toothy greeting to his guests and takes seat six.

The Leech is in seventh position. He swallows hard and looks suddenly poorly as Leepus sits down across the table.

'So this is a nice surprise,' says Leepus stacking chips and licking lips. 'Moving up a couple of pond-sizes from Sick Dick's damp-patch, are we? Fancying a swim with the sharks?'

The Leech shrugs uneasy and doesn't answer—fumbles to pick up his grog glass.

Leepus smiles reassuring. 'That's right, mate—you have a couple of swallows of backbone. Probably no one spikes it.' He riffles chips for a moment or two—then inserts the needle deeper. 'So here's how it likely happens. We play until I bust you. And then you re-buy. I bust you again. You re-buy again—and so on until you're bled white and crying for your mummy. Then you waddle off home alone in the rain while I drop in for a brew and a chuckle with Tattooed Sally. Tomorrow she pops into KashBak with her eldest and sorts out a juicy new kidney.'

The Leech is blinking rapid and his mushroom head is clammy. He struggles to find some banta—eventually offers, 'Brag like that takes some living up to. Far as I know we're playing poka, griz—so anything can happen.'

'That's the spirit, killa. There's always fucking hope.' Leepus' smile is warm at first—then suddenly its not. 'And even idiots sometimes get lucky.'

And then the King of Clubs is rapping the table—booming, 'That's enough fokkin gabba. Shuffle up and deal!'

◊◊◊◊◊

The End

Jamie Delano also writes comics.

He admits responsibility for contributing to the development, among others, of such titles as:

CAPTAIN BRITAIN - *Marvel Comics*

NIGHT RAVEN - *Marvel Comics*

HELLBLAZER - *DC Comics*

ANIMAL MAN - *DC Comics*

CROSSED - *Avatar Press*

His original comics work includes:

WORLD WITHOUT END - *DC Comics*

2020 VISIONS - *DC Comics Vertigo*

THE TERRITORY - *Dark Horse Comics*

GHOSTDANCING - *DC Comics Vertigo*

CRUEL AND UNUSUAL (co-written with Tom Peyer) – *DC Comics Vertigo*

OUTLAW NATION - *DC Comics Vertigo*

In 2012 he published his first prose novel, **BOOK THIRTEEN**, under the name **A. William James**

It's likely that there will be another **Leepus** novel underway when he gets his breath back.

Cover & title logo: ©2014 Richard James | richardjames-art.co.uk